When Duty Calls

John beckoned into the dark. "Come out, come out, my grubbers. Don't you want to see your uncle at work?" Two wide-eyed, emaciated children shuffled out of the dark, dressed in naught but rags and grime, towards Pennyedge, giving the groaning prisoner a wide berth.

"Tell me," said John to the prisoner. "He was one of the three?"

"One of them fell from the tower. The other was taken by the Boiler Men."

John's eyebrows squirmed. "The Boiler Men? Foul news. He'll have to be retrieved." He locked iron rings around the prisoner's legs and another around his neck.

Pennyedge's unfaltering stare began to grate on Bergen's nerves. It was a constant reminder that he was an outsider, an employee, rather than family.

John loosened the drawstring of the bag over the prisoner's head. He gestured to the children. "Step up, little pups. Don't be afraid."

They cautiously moved around to stand in front of Pennyedge. With a flourish, John whipped the bag off. The children screamed and fled back into their corner.

"My hunchback is quite a craftsman, isn't he?" John caressed the iron bands that encircled the prisoner's head, held there by thick nails punched into his skull.

"Marvelous work. Don't you think so, grubbers?"

"How dare you do this to children?" Bergen growled. His hand twitched towards his gun. Duty was all that kept him from putting a bullet through the man's forehead. . . .

WHITECHAPEL GODS

S. M. Peters

A ROC BOOK

ROC

Published by New American Library, a division of
Penguin Group (USA) Inc., 375 Hudson Street,
New York, New York 10014, USA
Penguin Group (Canada), 90 Eglinton Avenue East, Suite 700, Toronto,
Ontario M4P 2Y3, Canada (a division of Pearson Penguin Canada Inc.)
Penguin Books Ltd., 80 Strand, London WC2R 0RL, England
Penguin Ireland, 25 St. Stephen's Green, Dublin 2,
Ireland (a division of Penguin Books Ltd.)
Penguin Group (Australia), 250 Camberwell Road, Camberwell, Victoria 3124,
Australia (a division of Pearson Australia Group Pty. Ltd.)
Penguin Books India Pvt. Ltd., 11 Community Centre, Panchsheel Park,
New Delhi - 110 017, India
Penguin Group (NZ), 67 Apollo Drive, Rosedale, North Shore 0632,
New Zealand (a division of Pearson New Zealand Ltd.)
Penguin Books (South Africa) (Pty.) Ltd., 24 Sturdee Avenue,
Rosebank, Johannesburg 2196, South Africa

Penguin Books Ltd., Registered Offices:
80 Strand, London WC2R 0RL, England

First published by Roc, an imprint of New American Library,
a division of Penguin Group (USA) Inc.

First printing, February 2008
10 9 8 7 6 5 4 3 2 1

PUBLISHER'S NOTE
This is a work of fiction. Names, characters, places, and incidents either are
the product of the author's imagination or are used fictitiously, and any resem-
blance to actual persons, living or dead, business establishments, events, or
locales is entirely coincidental.

The publisher does not have any control over and does not assume any
responsibility for author or third-party Web sites or their content.

If you purchased this book without a cover you should be aware that this
book is stolen property. It was reported as "unsold and destroyed" to the
publisher and neither the author nor the publisher has received any payment
for this "stripped book."

The scanning, uploading, and distribution of this book via the Internet or via
any other means without the permission of the publisher is illegal and punish-
able by law. Please purchase only authorized electronic editions, and do not
participate in or encourage electronic piracy of copyrighted materials. Your
support of the author's rights is appreciated.

For my wife

Acknowledgments

To the incomparable Alan Moore, who provided the inspiration for this work; to Don Maass and Don McQuinn for their down-to-earth advice; to Liz for giving me a shot; to Joel, Fraser, James, and the rest for years of good times and great ideas; to my brother for his help in revision and for his friendship; to my parents for their support and love; to Mike for sorting out that shillings/pence confusion; to Jessi for everything; to all—thanks.

Acknowledgments

Prologue

Ancient, let your colours fly, but have a great care of the butcher's hooks at Whitechapel; they have been the death of many a fair ancient.

—From Beaumont and Fletcher's
Knight of the Burning Pestle

With a hiss of steam, mechanisms inside the walls shot a steel beam across the door as Aaron slammed it and leapt away. Something struck the door from the other side with a deafening impact, and the surface of the steel door bent into an impression of knuckles twice the size of a man's.

Searching his coat pockets for a weapon, Aaron stumbled back into Joseph, who grabbed him by the shoulder and shook him.

"Lad," Joseph cried. "There's no way out!"

Aaron threw off the older man's hand and shoved past him onto the walkway. "There's always a way."

But there wasn't. Barely visible through the currents of smog and falling ash, the walkway took a sharp downward twist, ending in a tangle of rent braces. It was a gap of almost thirty feet to the other tower; in between, only hot, stinking wind and a hundred-storey drop to the street below.

Joseph moved up beside him and wrapped his white-knuckled ham fists around the bent rail. "Tell me ye've got some flying machine in them pockets of yours, lad," he said between clenched teeth.

Another impact cut the air as Aaron frantically dug through the many pockets of his greatcoat. His fingers closed over lenses, tools, dynamite, compasses, devices for measuring pressure and voltage, and a dozen other objects whose function he could not remember just then. Nothing that could provide a crossing. With a shock of realisation, he willed his hands still.

"It was here," he said. "I checked on it just an hour ago."

"Bugger all." Joseph slammed one fist down on the rail and looked up into the muddy sky. "A damn dog deserves better," he said. Then he bent forward and began to quietly pray.

Aaron struggled to control his suddenly rapid breath. "There's a way, Joseph. I just need to think."

"Not every problem falls to thinkin' " was the reply.

On the next impact, one of the bolt's fittings popped loose from the wall and the door fell open an entire inch.

"If it had been any other walkway . . ." Aaron looked to both sides, where similar walkways stretched between the two hulking buildings.

"Aye, but it isn't," Joseph said, drawing a heavy army revolver from his jacket pocket. "I think it's time ye made yer peace, lad. Let's make a fight of it."

"One cannot fight the Boiler Men," said Aaron, suppressing the chill in his stomach and wishing he hadn't sounded so certain.

"We'll see" was Joseph's reply.

Trembling, Aaron withdrew a tin box from one of his pockets. He unscrewed the lid and looked at the thin coiled strip of paper inside. Coded letters ran its length in small type.

Think . . .

A boot sheathed in iron slammed into the bottom corner of the door, folding it up like tin. Unblinking electric light spilled from the hole onto the walkway, mingling with the hazy glare from the towers above.

Aaron quickly screwed the lid back onto the box and wished he'd had the time to decode it. He withdrew a stick of dynamite and a pack of matches, conscious that the walkway was too small to escape the explosion when it came.

How many times had he been told that he must be ready to die for England?

How many times had he told others the same thing?

He readied a match and waited.

There must be a way . . .

The air shuddered as a blast of steam exploded through the hole in the door. It struck Joseph first and the Irishman's scream cut the night. As the white cloud crashed over him, Aaron threw his arms in front of his face. Too late: the steam swept over his hands and head, scorching every inch of exposed skin. The pain drove him to his knees. He crawled blindly towards the walk's edge, where he pitched his head over the end and took a laboured breath of the foul Whitechapel air, collapsing into a fit as the ashes and grit sanded his raw lungs.

He heard the door pop loose from its hinges with one final strike and felt it clatter to the walkway, and he realised they would never escape.

There's a way . . .

Aaron's eyes quivered open. He spotted Joseph's twitching form through the dissipating steam and dragged himself towards his friend. His raw fingers tore on the walk, a sting even more painful than the fire all over his skin.

Aaron grasped Joseph's sleeve. "There's a way!"

Joseph's eyes streamed tears as he cried and screamed. Aaron shoved the tin box into Joseph's hands and forcibly closed the old man's fingers around it.

"Aaron!" Joseph said. "I can't get up! I can't . . ."

Aaron shoved the tin closer to the man's chest.

"You can take it back," he choked out. "Find someone who can read it."

Without waiting for an answer, he planted his foot on Joseph's chest and shoved. The other man let out a yelp before rolling backwards off the walk and into space. In seconds, the grey of Whitechapel's smog swallowed him, though his muted scream echoed from the towers for some moments longer.

The pounding of iron-shod feet shook the air. Aaron stared down after his falling friend, crying freely.

You'd probably want me to die on my feet.

Aaron slung one arm over the bent railing and hauled himself up. He turned to the monstrous shapes silhouetted in the doorway's glow. The gaze of those cold glass eyes made him feel shriveled and small, and he found he could not stop shaking.

He wished he'd chosen a different walkway. He wished he hadn't lost the matches. He wished he'd done a thousand things differently.

The Boiler Men reached for him with iron hands and he wished most of all that he wasn't about to die.

The First Day

A horrible black labyrinth, think many people, reeking from end to end with the vilest exhalations; its streets, mere kennels of horrent putrefaction; its every wall, its every object, slimy with the indigenous ooze of the place; swarming with human vermin, whose trade is robbery and whose recreation is murder; the catacombs of London darker, more tortuous and more dangerous than those of Rome, and saturated with foul life.

—Arthur G. Morrison, 1889

Chapter 1

They first came to me before I was old enough to speak. She was a red heat from beneath my crib; He, a scratching from the shadow beneath my windowsill. They spoke to me not in words, but in intentions and desires that my terrified infant mind could not comprehend. I cried out and hid from Them beneath my blankets. My mother rocked me and soothed me and told me They were imaginary. How could she have known, I wonder, when I was not old enough to tell her what I saw?

—I. xi

Bailey was not surprised when the doctor's first incision drew up something darker than blood.

The patient writhed and struggled in the bed, fighting a pain that distorted his features into something less than human. He was a comrade named Tor Kyrre, though Bailey could barely recognise him. Spikes of iron had sprouted from his bald pate and his bare chest was riddled with gears and bulbs of all types of metals, the tips of much larger growths festering beneath the skin. As the doctor made his second cut, lateral and shallow, across the base of the rib cage, black oil welled up, slipping down Tor's flanks and staining the sheets and blankets.

The doctors called the disease the *morbus imperceptus incrementum.* Other folk called it the "clacks."

Tor spasmed and groaned, the pain of whatever was eating him inside proving too much for even the powerful whiskey the doctor had fed him.

Bailey sucked on his cigar, inhaling the smoke right down to the base of his lungs, where it burned in tiny bursts of heat. It was wrong that a man should die this way, that he should be so robbed of his dignity in his final hours.

Bailey bit back an impulse to ask Dr. Chestle to cease the surgery and let his patient pass on.

No more! Not one more life will I surrender to this horrid city. Chestle, though he looked frail and of weak nerves, was as skilled as any two of his peers, and Tor had the fortitude of a bear. If this blasted machine-disease insisted on taking him it would have a fight on its hands.

He was about to slip away into the hall when Chestle cried out. The doctor jumped back from his patient, wildly flailing his left hand. Something black toppled to the floor, flinging oil and bits of foulness all across the floorboards.

Chestle backed into the corner, holding his scalpel in front of him like a weapon.

The object twisted and gyrated, slashing at the floor with shapeless, pointed appendages. Bailey took three steps towards it, swept up a stool, and crushed the object under the stool's foot, bearing down on it with the weight of his knee. A screech and a crunch followed, and the thing went still.

Bailey lifted the stool to reveal a twisted mass of metal gears and articulated fingers.

"Was this the source?"

Paler than his patient, the doctor nodded.

"Then you're finished. Sew him up."

The look of blank terror lingered on Chestle's face as he again bent over Tor and went to work. Fifteen minutes later, with Tor's chest sealed and covered in gauze and bandages, Chestle nodded at the door. Bailey opened it, admitting Tor's wife, who went directly to her husband's side and conferred with the doctor in her broken English. Bailey extinguished his cigar now that a lady was present.

Chestle mopped the oil off his hands with a towel and tried without success to look encouraging. "Please keep the bandages fresh, Mrs. Kyrre. He should be given only thin soup for now. I shall call tomorrow to see how he is doing."

"Thank, thank," she said.

Bailey took out his handkerchief and gathered the remains of the foul object on the floor before Mrs. Kyrre had a chance to see it.

The housekeeper brought in a bowl of heated water and soap. The doctor washed the gore and oil from his hands and surgical instruments, the sweat from his thin moustache, and packed his tools into a leather handbag. Bailey snatched up a candlestick and led him out into the hall.

Bailey shut the door quietly behind them. He unwrapped the crushed object and laid it in the palm of his open hand, bringing the candle close to examine it.

"What is it?"

Chestle shook his head slowly, facing away from it, as if unwilling to even speculate. His voice shook with repressed fright as he spoke. "I'm afraid I don't have an answer, Winfred."

"But you have seen it before."

The doctor smoothed his small moustache and faltered over a few words before speaking further. His slim figure looked skeletal in the candlelight, his close-cut hair thin and loose. "This is the fourth such case I have treated since Sunday. I had one young woman die of it." He straightened with obvious effort. "The growths have always been common, particularly in the poorer towers, but up until now they have not been . . . harmful."

Bailey pocketed the object and they headed towards the stair at the hall's far end. Seeing the hesitation on Chestle's face, Bailey motioned for him to continue.

"The people I have seen with this condition . . . ," the doctor said, "they were, the prior week, free from any trouble. The onset is sudden, the damage at once rapid and extensive. If this were to happen to all those who were infected . . . My God, Winfred, the loss of life . . ."

Bailey nodded that he understood, to save the man the expression of his horror. Chestle's fingers absently rubbed the brass bulbs on the back of his own hand.

"What is the cause of it?" Bailey asked.

"Something in the air? Something in the food?" The doctor swallowed hard. "If it were any but you, my friend, I would not even speculate, but . . . since the gods . . . since the changes that . . ."

"Out with it, George."

"I think that it is Whitechapel," Chestle said. "Not the air or the food or the conditions, but the city itself."

They descended the stairs, passing into a foyer and to the front door of the dwelling before Chestle spoke again, and when he did it was with great care.

"And it is not my opinion that it can be cured."

"It can be."

"Winfred, with all honesty, I—"

"It *will* be," said Bailey. "Once we cast down Grandfather Clock and Mama Engine—once the baron and all the rest of their servants lie burning in hell and Whitechapel belongs to England once more—*then* you will have your cure."

Chestle nodded and donned his felt bowler hat.

He moved to leave, and Bailey stopped him with a polite hand on the arm.

"Be ready. The battle may begin anytime now."

"You need merely call on me. I . . . believe I will pray tonight."

They shook hands firmly, and the doctor departed.

Bailey stood a long minute with the door open, staring out. His gaze was drawn upwards, past the rotting rooftops of the neighbourhood, past the gleaming Cathedral Tower, where those most loyal to the baron lived with the luxuries of health and security. He felt his jaw tighten as his eyes came to rest on the top of the looming iron mountain barely visible through the blackened air: the Stack, home to the gods and to the man who had betrayed his country and his kin to serve them.

Yes, things would happen quickly, one way or the other. If all went well, the means to reclaim Whitechapel might be in Bailey's hands by dawn. If all did not go well, he and all the agents of the crown might soon be lying in oily graves.

Aaron had gone tonight to steal a weapon.

He was two hours overdue.

"You know what the real problem is, Ollie?"

Fighting his irritation, Oliver pulled his eyes off the street and glanced over his shoulder. Tommy crouched behind him in the filthy alley, a madcap grin flowering on his rectangular face.

Then Tommy stabbed himself in the heart with a knife. "People don't properly die in this town," he said with a smirk. Oil welled up around the blade, staining his shirt.

Oliver scowled. "We're on mission, Tom."

"I never tire of the look on your face, Chief," Tom said, and yanked the knife out with a flourish. He licked it clean. "Tastes like honey and brown sugar."

"Vile," Oliver said, turning back to the street. "Absolutely vile."

"I swear it isn't so. You want a taste?"

"I need your attention on the mission, Tom," Oliver said, eyes darting about the street.

"Always the responsible leader, eh?" said Tommy. "A regular John Bull, if you're a cove."

Oliver couldn't help but smirk. "And yet I still thump you at Heckler's card game."

"Ah, but you do it so *seriously* . . ."

"Quiet."

A crowd poured out of the pub three buildings down towards Aldgate Common: a group of middle-aged men fancied up in bowler hats and suits, carrying canes they couldn't possibly need and all of them three sheets to the wind. Traitors. Collaborators. The baron's business partners and secular employees, selling out their fellows for a few shillings and the privileges of good food and running water.

Oliver's eyes jumped from face to face, until they settled on a handlebar moustache to rival the worst American aristocrat.

Oliver stiffened. "That's him. Get ready."

With a grunt and no small manner of squealing from his joints, Tommy lifted himself to his full height. He always seemed to be fighting his weight; he lurched like a rhinoceros trying to stand on its hind legs.

Tom took a few clanking steps forward. Oliver glanced back, teeth clenched and a grimace on his face.

"I doubt anyone will notice the difference," said Tommy. He gestured vaguely upward at the ceiling, where, beyond the steel crossbeams and braces that supported the next floor, some unseen factory or mechanism chunked and chugged away. The noise echoed everywhere through the concourse.

Oliver grunted, but couldn't argue.

Tommy noisily hunkered down behind him, peering over Oliver's shoulder at their comrade across the street.

An instant before, Missy had been another invisible passerby, clad in drab grey and camouflaged against the soot-stained streets and thick air, but her pale skin popped to life as she stepped into the lamplight. With one subtle manipulation of her arms, her short coat fell open at the shoulders, revealing a blouse slightly too large for her frame. It hung just low enough to reveal a scintillating hint of neck, while looking for all the world like an innocent mistake of the wardrobe; a fault of the shirt, somehow.

Tommy whistled behind him. "Good Lord, she is a peach."

Her lips came together, pursed in a perfect, pinched look of utter disdain, a shock of red in a world of greys and gaslight.

She's a professional.

Missy cast one glance towards their hiding place, her lips cracking into the barest hint of a smile. She adjusted the silk ribbons on her hat and smoothed her skirt, fingered her sandy hair where wisps of it crept down over her ears. Then the distant look returned and she whirled pointedly towards her quarry.

She's even working us, Oliver marveled.

"Get ready," he whispered over his shoulder.

Tommy shifted uncomfortably. "But I want to watch."

"Do your moving before they get here," Oliver snapped.

"Fine." Tommy creaked as he rose, then clanked with every step as he retreated to a doorjamb that barely contained his shoulders.

Oliver's eyes followed Missy's approach to the crowd. She walked as if she had somewhere very important to be. The men all halted and doffed their hats to her as she passed. She gave them each the barest nod of acknowledgement, fixing each, Oliver knew, though he couldn't see it, with her lingering gaze, punctuated by a twitch of the eyebrow, an ever-subtle quickening of the breath. Some stepped forward to introduce themselves even as she dismissed them with a blink and shifted to the next. This left a gaggle of befuddled men in her wake, all looking terribly unmanned.

Oliver held his breath.

Missy slowed as she passed the man with the handlebar moustache, a falter in her step, then a pause, the same interested look.

The target stepped up like a dog to a strip of bacon.

The noise of the factory above prevented any eavesdropping from this distance, but Oliver knew how it went. The man was extending his hand, offering to walk her home because it was frightfully improper for a lovely lady like herself to be wandering these streets without a gentleman escort; not the kind of place a lady would be safe, no sir. And yes, she would quite fancy an escort. Oh! Did she use the word fancy? Quite improper. A slip of the tongue.

Inside a minute she had the gentleman hanging on her arm. The rest strode off, engaging in excited conversation over the grand fortune of their comrade and puffing themselves all around as if they'd had some hand in it.

"Next time, I want to be the lookout," Tommy said. Oliver could almost picture him stamping his foot like a boy of five.

Oliver glanced back. "When you put some grease on those joints of yours, I may consider it."

Tommy's face contorted in a deep frown. "A right miser, you are. A hoarder."

"The lion's share, Tommy. Perks of being a regular John Bull." He turned back to the street.

To find it empty.

He cast his eyes back and forth. The street was entirely vacant but for the remainder of the pub goers vanishing into the smog, and the wanderings of one stray dog.

"Something up, mate?" Tommy asked.

The fizzling of the gaslight and the constant smog obscured most of the street. Oliver stuck his head around the corner, risking detection, and peered into those shadows along the near side of the street, where Missy was supposed to bring the fox. Nothing. Her white neck, at least, should be visible.

"We've lost her, then?" Tommy said.

"She's run off." He squinted hard to see into the alleys she would have passed walking that way.

"Maybe she wants a quick peck before we do our thing," Tommy suggested.

Oliver felt himself flash angry. "Not when we're on business, surely."

"She might do it just to get your goat, Chief," said Tommy.

"At the least, she would signal us before getting out of sight," Oliver said.

"One would think."

Oliver scanned the buildings lining the street, apartments stretching the entire five storeys to the roof of the concourse. Some even went higher, tangling themselves in the braces of the next level: five storeys of twinkling lights and their attendant residents, any one of which could bring the cloaks crashing down on them.

There was nowhere to hide once they left the alley.

The lampposts shed dim and inconsistent light, but such was their frequency and the genius of their placement that there was no route down the sidewalk that would not risk detection. They could not pass for locals anyway, with Oliver's shabby clothes and Tommy's angular bulk sure to arouse suspicion.

"She may have ducked off too early," Oliver thought aloud. "Do you see a way around to the next alley?"

"Didn't notice one," said Tommy. "Unless you're game to see where this door goes."

Oliver retreated from the street into the alley's darkness. He found Tommy leaning easily on the door frame, arms crossed. The man's shoulders stuck out like knifepoints under his coat. His iron hand glinted in the half-light as he tapped his fingers on the door.

Oliver looked past him. The alley ended at the rear wall of another apartment, which provided no entrance but a blackened window. The manhole they'd come up through led to such a maze that he balked at the time required to navigate it, especially if Missy was in trouble.

"Can you do it *quietly*?" Oliver asked.

Tommy grinned toothily and put a finger to his lips. Oliver gave him a nod.

The big man placed his iron hand flat against the door at the approximate height where a locking bolt would sit, then leaned in with his shoulder and hip. One sharp push later, the bolt clattered to the floor on the inside and the door swung open on squealing hinges.

Oliver grimaced. Tommy just shrugged.

From the slip of light bleeding into the room, Oliver surmised it to be a storage room or pantry, of sufficient size to service the whole building. He set a cautious foot upon the floor within and tested it with increasing weight. The boards did not squeak. He entered and pattered swiftly across. Tommy followed, placing each step with great deliberation to avoid clanking, with moderate success.

Oliver felt his way to a door, then scuffed his foot to guide Tommy over to him. In absolute silence Oliver tried the latch, only to find it locked.

In the dark, no less. He knelt, drew a set of lock picks from his vest pocket and set to work. *Probably did duck for a peck, damnable woman.*

In thirty heartbeats the lock ticked. Oliver replaced his lock picks and tried the latch. This time it opened smoothly.

Oliver pulled the door open an inch and peeked through. Beyond stood a spiral staircase with a thick oak banister that circled up to the higher floors. A candle flashed upon the stairs: a watchman.

Oliver slid back from the door. He heard the watchman take a few hesitant steps down to the main floor.

Oliver shrank back against a shelf, wrapping himself in shadow and the scent of cabbage. A few more steps sounded from beyond. Oliver heard the door handle jiggle.

The door shrieked again as it swung open. A candle poked into the room, followed by an extended hand holding a billy. Oliver realised with horror that he could clearly see the shine of his own boots in the candlelight.

A pointy nose appeared, followed by a set of shrewd eyes flicking their gaze about the edges of the candlelight. Oliver balled his fists and tensed for a quick leap.

The eyes turned his way. Just as they began to widen, and the billy to rise, a monstrous shadow a full head taller than the watchman materialised behind him.

Tommy popped the man sharply across the back of his head. Oliver darted forth and caught the man as he collapsed. Burning wax splattered across his hand as he wrested the candle away. The billy clattered to the floor.

They set him down comfortably, then wasted no time crossing into the hall beyond. They found a series of dormant pumps and machines in the room across the hall. Oliver led Tommy through to a door on the far wall. The bolt slid clear easily and the door opened in silence.

They found themselves on a narrow side street devoid of residents and streetlights. Directly across, a lamplight flickered in the window of a countinghouse. Through the diagonal crosshatch of the glass, Oliver could see a familiar statuesque figure.

He dashed across the street and silently pulled the door open. He stepped through and Missy nearly put a knife through his eye.

Oliver clamped his fingers on Missy's wrist before she could finish her thrust. "For Jesus' sake! Michelle, it's us!"

She wrenched her hand away. "Well, had you announced yourselves like gentlemen, I might have been more accommodating, but that is a fair amount to expect from you."

Tommy followed through the doorway, chuckling. "No claim to be gentlemen, miss."

Missy's petite upturned nose wrinkled. "You did at one time claim to be part of a *team,* did you not?" She shook the knife at them. "Was it your intention to leave me to my frail, feminine self or were you simply dawdling?"

"We were in the *next* alley, Michelle," Oliver said, hands still raised in defence, "where you were *supposed* to bring in the fox."

She folded up the knife and shoved it into her handbag. "And I suppose it would have been far too much trouble to cover two alleys."

"There should have been no need," Oliver said. He noted ominous blots of colour around Missy's fingernails. "Are you all right?"

Missy wiped her hands off on her skirt, leaving dark smears behind. "All right? There's a plumb joke."

Oliver's chest tightened as he spotted a clock hanging on the wall behind her.

"*You* wanted his documents," Missy continued, "and he was lecherous enough to divulge their location. Do not begrudge a girl a little initiative."

Oliver saw something dark pass over Missy's eyes, saw her jaw tighten. Tommy let out a low, buzzing whistle that knotted up Oliver's insides.

Dare I? "What is it, Tom?"

"A stinking pile of shit trouble, Chief."

With clenched teeth, Oliver turned his head. The little office held two desks of black mahogany and a tidy bookshelf of ledgers and records below the wall clock.

Their target lay sprawled in a sea of scattered papers against the far wall. Dark stains peppered his coat across the chest and stomach, and he was perfectly still.

Oliver shut his eyes and rubbed them, trying to erase what he'd just seen.

"Thoroughly done" was Tommy's comment. Oliver opened his eyes again to see Missy fold her arms tight against her abdomen and stick her nose in the air.

"He overstepped the bounds of propriety," she said.

Oliver stood aghast, looking back and forth between Missy and the dead man. Missy stared coolly at the corpse, eyes sunken and dark.

Oliver shook his finger at her. "I've gone five years without *this,* Michelle. This was all you could think to—" He stopped himself, swallowing his reprimand for a more appropriate time.

"We'll have words," he warned.

Missy scowled at him. "I hardly think words are our most pressing concern, Mr. Sumner."

"Right." Oliver snatched the dead man's hat and hung it over the face of the wall clock. If Grandfather Clock had been looking through it, his gold cloaks would already be on the way. He shared an earnest look with Tom, then spoke to Missy.

"Where are his documents?"

Missy gestured stiffly at a small steel safe in the corner. "Tom."

The big man raised a quizzical eyebrow.

Oliver pointed to the safe. "We can't make less of a spectacle than we have, I think."

Tom shrugged, then bent down and hammered the safe door in with a quick blow of his iron knuckles. He pried it out and tossed it on a desk.

Oliver reached in and retrieved a sheaf of papers bound with string. He flipped through it.

"This is it," he said. "Back we go."

They slipped across the street and back through the machine room in the apartment, Oliver in the lead and Tommy in the rear. The hall and stair beyond were vacant. Oliver led the way across, feeling ahead of him in what was almost complete darkness. Through vague touches, the pantry door revealed itself. Oliver grasped the handle and lifted the door slightly before opening it, which served to dull the noise to a whimper. He waved the others forward and entered the room.

He saw a flash of movement in the shadows and ducked low. Boxes and tins from the shelf behind rained down on him as the watchman's next blow swept high. A warm body came in close against him, and he tilted his shoulder and ploughed into it. He caught his foot on a tin and stumbled, but not before propelling his assailant away. He lost track of the other man in the crash of more falling tins.

Oliver scrambled back to his feet and tried to raise his hand in front of his face. Something moved in front of him, hidden by the darkness. He heard a few clanks, then a few wet crunches.

Tommy's voice drifted out of the dark. "Let's get on."

Suddenly thankful for the dark, Oliver led the way to the door and out into the alley. Missy was next out the door, stepping down from the stoop, the picture of poise and ladyship. Tommy shambled after, wiping his iron hand with a white handkerchief. Oliver picked up a pry bar from where he'd hidden it and levered the sewer hole open. Instead of escaping, Missy produced a cloth sack from beneath her skirt and handed it to Tommy, who accepted it without comment.

Oliver stepped onto the first rung of the ladder within the manhole. The stench of sewage and grease floated up to greet him.

Missy peeled off her tweed short coat and stuffed it in the bag.

Oliver waited a moment to be acknowledged, but Missy remained oblivious. She added her hat to the bag, then began on her skirt.

"Surely you can do that once we get to safety."

"I will not," said Missy, jaw and neck tight as cords, "allow my good clothing to traverse your vile sewer exit unprotected."

"Aldgate has *telephones*," Oliver stressed. "If anyone in the building heard us, they'll be bringing the cloaks right down on us."

Missy made no reply. She stepped out of the grey tweed skirt and added it to the sack. Beneath she wore a smaller skirt of worn and stained wool, a match in quality to the poorer attire Oliver and Tommy wore.

"Be a dear and carry that for me, would you?" she asked. Tommy shrugged and nodded.

Still not gracing Oliver with a look, Missy proceeded to the manhole, shouldered him aside, and swiftly lowered herself in.

Tommy stepped up. "You're in for it now, mate," he said, shooting Oliver a wink. He tucked the bag under his arm and slipped down into the underground.

"You've no idea."

These papers are probably the only thing that will keep Bailey from shooting me.

Instead of capturing their fox, they'd left him stiff and cold, and been spotted on top of it. Oliver had not presided over so botched an operation since the Uprising. He clutched the papers tight in his hands and forced that particular set of memories into the dark.

He placed his feet on the ladder and started his descent. As he pulled the manhole cover back into place, he heard the clear report of approaching feet running in perfect time.

He dropped the cover down, and his world became dark and silence and stink.

Chapter 2

*The whole of Her garden will grow from a single
iron nail, which I will plant between the cobbles
in a back alley of Pelham Street. There, a man
lies dying of consumption. His will be but the first
of the souls She will need, for Her fires grow
hungrier by the day. To make great things, much
heat is needed; and for much heat, much coal.*

—II. ix

The prisoner struggled. Bergen yanked on the chains
and the man toppled to his face.

"That was unpleasant," Bergen said. "Do not make
me do it again."

Muffled curses escaped from the canvas bag covering
the prisoner's head. Bergen delivered a kick to the man's
ribs. The prisoner groaned and rolled onto his side.

"Behave yourself," Bergen said. "Now, on your feet."

The prisoner fought to get onto his knees and wobbled
to his feet. The man's arms had been tied together behind his back with piano wire, which had sliced his skin
in a few places. Five chains led up under the canvas
hood, attaching in some unseen way to the prisoner's
head. Bergen gave them a light tug.

"Walk."

The prisoner obeyed.

Bergen led the man through corridors of warped wooden floorboards and ragged plaster walls. At uneven intervals, oil lamps hung from hooks in the ceiling, yellowing everything with their sickly light. They passed through dozens of intersections of identical corridors and through several wooden doors, some hanging off their hinges and splattered with castoff plaster.

Bergen frowned at the sloppy workmanship. *Probably done by some urchins, hired for a pittance and then cast off the tower to die in the streets.*

Only by long habit did he know which corridors to follow and which doors to open. A wrong turn would place him in the path of a trip wire–triggered rifle or a door that opened onto a wall of protruding poisoned needles. It was a place to rattle a dead man's bones.

Was it duty that kept him coming back to this tomb? Or was he so callous now that he could no longer find fault with its madness?

He found the door he sought. Rather than reaching for the knob, he probed the topmost hinge with a single finger until he found the trigger buried in the oak door frame. With a click, the latch sounded, and the door swung open from the hinged side. A complex series of pulleys and gears, all fabricated of wood, slid the door aside just enough for a man to step through.

The room beyond was as black as night, lit only by a few candles in the far corner. A quaking voice floated out. "Tick, tick, tick, tick . . ."

"I know you heard me," Bergen said. "I have the thief."

"Ah, by all means, bring him in."

Bergen roughly shoved the prisoner ahead. Bergen stepped in after him, turning to the corner farthest from the candles.

"Bringing your barking iron in here?" said the voice.

Bergen laid a casual hand on the heavy Gasser revolver hanging at his hip. "This is my fist and my voice," he said. "Would I ask you to set aside such things?"

The corner cackled like a nervous schoolboy.

"Cautious. Heh. A good sign, that. Take note, my little grubbers. Take note."

The corner shuffled, and John Scared slunk silently into the candles' light. The sixteen-year-old mute that John called "Pennyedge" emerged as well, stepping into the light from a different corner. The boy stood loose, long-limbed, and long-fingered, waiting as always to execute Scared's merest whim.

In his customary black long coat and top hat of beaver fur, John Scared seemed little more than a pock-scarred face and two knobbly hands. Grinning toothily, John grasped the small table that held the candles and moved it closer to the room's centre.

John beckoned into the dark. "Come out, come out, my grubbers. Don't you want to see your uncle at work?"

Two wide-eyed, emaciated children shuffled out of the dark, dressed in naught but rags and grime. Their eyes flittered fearfully over Bergen's person, and they shuffled away towards Pennyedge, giving the groaning prisoner a wide berth. They settled themselves behind Penny's legs, peering around. The mute kept his arms crossed, the fingers of his right hand fiddling with his sleeve. His eyes never left Bergen's.

Do you think I cannot see that knife, boy? Do you think you can get to me before I can draw? Bergen deliberately broke eye contact.

"Let's get him comfortable," John prompted.

Bergen hauled the prisoner to his feet by the collar of his vest and shoved him roughly into the oak chair.

"Tell me," said John, placing the table to the right of the chair. The candlelight lit his chalky skin in dancing colours. "He was one of three?"

"One of them fell from the tower. The other was taken by the Boiler Men. Hobbyhorse found this one wandering lost in the bottom of Aldgate. He is one of them; I am certain."

John's eyebrows squirmed. "The Boiler Men? Tick, tick. Foul news. He'll have to be retrieved." He locked iron rings around the prisoner's legs and another around his neck. "I'll get Boxer to handle it. Close the door, if you would."

Bergen reached back and tugged a small cord that hung from the door's pulley system. A catch released and the door slid back into place with a quiet sound. Pennyedge's unfaltering stare began to grate on his nerves. It was a constant reminder that he was an outsider, an employee, rather than a member of the family. If any of John's wretches could shoot half as well as he could, Pennyedge would have slit his throat long ago.

The room seemed to grow hotter the instant the door closed. There was a smell as well, an organic rot that Bergen was wary of trying to identify.

John loosened the drawstring of the bag covering the prisoner's head. He gestured to the two small children, flashing his yellowed and blackened teeth. "Step up, little pups. Don't be afraid."

They cautiously moved around to stand in front of Pennyedge, but went no closer.

Satisfied, John turned back and with a grand flourish whipped the bag off the prisoner's head.

"*Gott in Himmel!*" Bergen swore. The two children screamed and fled back into the darkened corner. Pennyedge did not react.

"My hunchback is quite a craftsman, isn't he?" John said. He reached up with his gnarled hands and caressed the iron bands that encircled the prisoner's head, held there by thick nails punched into his skull. The chains dangled from rivets in his jaw and cheeks.

"Not even much blood, considering," John said. "Marvelous work. Don't you think so, grubbers?"

The two children gasped unseen in the corner. Pennyedge simply nodded and returned his gaze to Bergen.

"How dare you do this to children?" Bergen growled.

John's eyes twinkled. "You'd prefer I left them to starve or be hauled off by the Chimney gangs, then? Besides, I've done much, much worse. And so have you, I might add."

Bergen's hand twitched towards his gun. Duty was all

that kept him from putting a bullet through the man's forehead.

He spat on the floorboards. "I do only what is necessary, Scared. You are an abomination."

"Quite. And I wouldn't trust your sanity, *mein freund*, if you held any other opinion." John reached up and unscrewed the lock holding the man's jaw shut tight. "Now let's hear what this one has to say, eh?"

The man spat up blood and bile as soon as he could open his mouth. He said nothing. John examined him for some long moments, looking for a weakness.

Bergen had seen this before. John was exceptional at reading a man's faults. Bergen, on the other hand, was exceptional at hiding such faults. Perhaps that was why John hadn't killed him yet—he hadn't *solved* him as he might a chess problem or a mathematical equation.

John leaned back on his heels. "Penny, my boy, cut a piece of the fellow's ear off, would you? The gauze is under the chair."

Bergen crossed his arms. "Must I witness this?"

John perked up. "The great hunter squeamish? The German Terror of Africa unmanned?"

"I was not the one burgled today," Bergen said levelly.

John's eyes narrowed. "Shrewd. Heh. I like that too."

Pennyedge had retrieved the roll of gauze. He tore off a small slip of it, then held the prisoner's head still with one hand and drew his knife with the other. John shuffled over to Bergen. Bergen's nose wrinkled at the onion stench of the man.

"Our little secret is in the hands of the man who fell," John said.

"Or in the hands of the Boiler Men."

John shook a finger. "No, no. If that was the case, we'd already be dead, don't you think?"

"It is your secret, Scared."

"Ah, but I would, of course, with much hesitation and under great duress, tell them it was your idea."

Bergen shrugged. The prisoner screamed through clenched teeth as Penny did his work.

"So it needs to be retrieved."

"Smart. Heh."

Bergen rubbed his fingers through his chin stubble and tried to ignore the prisoner's moaning. "I want Mulls and Hobbyhorse."

"Mulls is a brute. He's yours." John turned briefly and assessed the prisoner. The man's face was awash with blood and sweat, eyes clenched and teeth locked together. Pennyedge stood behind the man, pressing the bloodstained gauze against the man's ear.

"Another bit, if you would, my boy," John said. "He's not quite ready."

He turned back to Bergen as Penny bent to his task. John waved one yellow-nailed finger in Bergen's face. "Hobby will go with Boxer. You get Penny."

Bergen glanced over at the boy's face. It hung slack and expressionless even as he sawed away with his knife. Bergen was about to protest that the boy was too young, but thought better of it. *He may have already killed more men than I have.*

"I cannot use him," Bergen said. "He cannot be made a scout on account of his silence, and he's not nearly a good enough shot."

John knitted his fingers together. "You'll find his talents more than make up for his little deficiency, I think."

John's smile grew wider and wider.

Bergen nodded slowly, realising. *Penny is along to murder me if I try to go to the baron.*

John smiled, his message understood. "Lots of beasties to hunt in the downstreets, too. Like your old grounds, eh?"

"Africa is a land of beauty," Bergen said. "Your Whitechapel is a *Hölle auf Welt.*"

"It's not *my* Whitechapel," John said, then added with a twinkle, "Yet."

It's the queen's Whitechapel, you traitor. Bergen buried the thought, hoping John hadn't read it on his face.

He indicated Penny, who stood impassive, holding fresh gauze over the ruins of the prisoner's ear. "The child will need arms. Have him meet me in the warehouse when you are done with him."

"It won't be long" was the reply. John returned his attention to the two children still huddled down in the shadows of a far corner.

"Come forth, come forth, my beautiful, innocent little sons," he said, beckoning with his skeletal hands. "This will be your trade someday. Best learn."

Bergen's stomach turned. He yanked the cord that rolled the door to the side and strode out.

Bergen walked into the workshop to find Mulls shouting and bashing his fist on a table.

"What do you mean it's not done, you rotter?"

The shop master, Ferdinand von Herder, leaned comfortably back on his stool and sighed deeply, as one might when dealing with an unruly child.

"Good sir," he began, his voice ancient and tired, "the weapon is not ready. Nor will it become ready until our mutual patron furnishes me with more nickel and copper."

"Is there a problem?" Bergen asked.

Mulls whirled about, coming up straight when he saw who had just spoken. He was one of Scared's children, raised in the filth of the streets and badly ravaged by the clacks, but loyal and capable, if not amiable. His already primitive features had become a mess of stray wires and misshapen bits of iron, and his thick limbs bulged in some places into unnatural angles.

Von Herder cocked his ear and turned his sightless eyes in the direction of the door.

"Herr Keuper, is it? Welcome. Mr. Mulligan seems to think he should be the bearer of our only functional steam rifle."

"Wouldn't be a problem if he'd bloody made two of them like he s'posed to," Mulls complained.

"You will carry a flasher," Bergen ordered. "And an air rifle loaded with steel rounds."

"Fine." Mulls snatched an air rifle and a belt of ammunition from the weapon racks lining the wall and headed for the stairs leading back to the maze. He mumbled under his breath, as if the others couldn't hear him, "Stupid hun, hogging all the good stuff to yourself."

Bergen and von Herder waited for his muttering to fade with distance. Two teenage assistants in the back of the room disturbed the silence, having hardly slowed their pace at all during the argument. When von Herder spoke, he did so in German.

"Unpleasant men are not hard to find in this country, don't you think, Herr Keuper?"

Bergen shrugged, though he knew von Herder couldn't see it. "Herr Scared attracts only the worst. The *Englisch* are mostly a jovial people."

The old mechanic blinked his milk-white eyes and scuffed his fist over the scraggly whiskers on his cheeks. "Strange for you to be praising the *Englisch*, I think. Your partnership with Nicholas Ellingsly was legend in the penny magazines—always rivals for the bigger game."

"The *Englisch* consider such contests the height of sportsmanship, Herr von Herder."

"A silly people, to confuse friends with opponents."

Bergen scanned the tables and racks in the rear of the workshop. "Is it ready?"

"Of course! How unprofessional of me to waste time on blather." Von Herder swiveled slightly on his stool and called for his two assistants to bring up the steam rifle. As one they dipped behind the far table and rose again straining and grunting. They carried the weapon up and set it on von Herder's table with tremendous strain.

"Thank you, my lads," von Herder said. He ran his hands over the length of the rifle with an almost loving touch. His eyes slowly fell closed.

Bergen surveyed the weapon from barrel to boiler: fully five feet in length, with a barrel the breadth of a man's fist, a coal furnace and boiler in the place of a breech, and a padded stock that allowed the butt end of the weapon to rest atop the shoulder. It had been polished precisely, and shimmered like a mirror in some places.

"It is a different colour," Bergen said.

"Yes, I replaced most of it with a new alloy. Much stronger so less can be used, which should lighten it a bit. I've also installed a new boiler." He indicated each section as he spoke, dancing his fingers over the components, checking fit and sturdiness. Then he gestured for Bergen to pick it up. "Test it. Test it."

Bergen bent and hefted the monstrous weapon from the table. The stock fit perfectly to his shoulder. He gripped its two handles, one perpendicular to the barrel on the inside, the other parallel on the outside. He experimentally thumbed the trigger on the outside handle.

"It is much lighter. My compliments, Herr von Herder."

"It will still be a heavy load to carry through the downstreets."

Bergen smiled. "Africa has touched me, sir. It will be as nothing."

Von Herder grinned back, displaying gums shrivelled by age. "I am told the sunsets are magnificent there."

"There are few greater pleasures, sir." Bergen placed the rifle back on the table. He retrieved its special holster and a band of ammunition and tossed them in a canvas shoulder sack. Bergen surveyed the rack of breech-loading rifles and air rifles and considered whether Pennyedge should be armed.

The boy would be useless against the creatures of the downstreets with just his knife, and yet Bergen felt some hesitancy at arming a boy who was under orders to kill him. The essential question was, did giving the boy a firearm make him more dangerous than he already was?

"You were from Stuttgart, weren't you?" von Herder asked.

"Hm?" Bergen murmured, breaking out of his thoughts.

"If I recall, you are from Stuttgart."

"That is correct."

Von Herder tapped two fingers absently on the table. "It is puzzling me, because you do not sound like you are from Stuttgart."

Bergen paused, wondering just how much the blind man's ears could reveal. He chose his words carefully. "I have not been back to the fatherland for years, Herr von Herder. Perhaps you are hearing some tribal variation I have acquired."

"Of course," said von Herder. "I'd forgotten."

Bergen selected one air rifle and a bandolier for the boy. "Do you have any paper, Herr von Herder?"

"I haven't much use for it," von Herder said with a chuckle. "But Andrew is learning his letters." He called back for the boy to bring up some paper and a pen.

The assistant appeared, carrying a slip of paper dark around one edge with spilled ink, and a small bit of charcoal.

"Beg pardon, sir, but me pen's been leakin' terrible of late."

"Well then, fix it," von Herder snapped. "How can I let you lay your hands on firearms if you cannot even fix a lousy pen?"

The poor lad froze up for a moment. Bergen held out his hand. "Whatever makes a mark," he said.

Relieved, the boy crammed the paper and charcoal onto Bergen's palm and fled.

"Lad's a dullard," von Herder said in German, "though he's competent enough on the furnace."

"Hmm," Bergen said. He laid the paper on the table and scribbled a few words.

One caught by Ironboys. One caught by Scared. They can't hold. Third fell from tower, has ticker-paper. Leading expedition to retrieve. Cannot delay; under watch.

He blew the excess charcoal off the paper and folded it in quarters.

"What were you writing, I wonder?" von Herder mused.

"My obituary."

Bergen wrapped the steam rifle in its holster and swung the monstrous mechanism onto his back. It really was lighter, perhaps sixty pounds. He slung the various bandoliers over his shoulder, gathered a few more packs prepacked with food, water, and supplies, and hefted Pennyedge's air rifle in his hand.

"Auf Wiedersehen," said Bergen, and left.

He dropped the paper in a sewer grate on the way to the warehouse.

Chapter 3

My professors at the college told me that my buildings would not stand up. They pointed endlessly to leaning walls and angled beams that could support no roof short of a canvas sheet. I nodded and vocally agreed, and so they tolerated me, but I always knew my buildings were exactly as they should be.

No, they would not stand as I had designed them, but they would grow, and one day they would stand on their own.

—I. xxv

Grandfather Clock was watching.

Oliver tilted his hat back enough to see the massive white marble and wrought-iron clock hanging above the entrance to the boarding platform. Its regular ticking rang like a hammer and anvil through the space above. Suspended on chains from the steel ceiling supports, it almost seemed to be leaning forward, surveying the people below.

Oliver ducked his head and pulled his hat brim down. An old chill crept up his spine, the wearing, gnawing awareness of scrutiny, and then a sharp dread at the

possibility of being recognised from last night's operation. He hurried his pace through the crowds at Shadwell
Station, a sea of men and women in grey tweed and ash
hats, stinking of coal smoke and grease and human
sweat.

The operation *could* have gone well, if he'd only been
given time to research and plan.

"It must be tonight," Bailey had said, overpowering
all objection. "England needs you. It is your duty to
the crown."

Oliver shouldered his way around a tin cart and the
man pulling it, and wondered what Bailey thought he
owed to the crown. Oliver was Whitechapel-born and
-raised, and but for blurry glances through the smoke
and ash, had never even seen this great nation he was
fighting for.

Did that sour man not think Oliver had enough of his
own reasons to want Baron Hume and his two gods to
be cast down?

*He simply doesn't trust me. He wouldn't trust anyone
born outside his God-blessed kingdom.*

Perhaps the correct question was: why was he following Sir Bailey's revolution, instead of running his own?

Because I tried that before, and look at what came of it.

A series of rhythmic clacks and a screech echoed out
of the boarding platform ahead, the sounds of brakes
upon the cable, stopping the car's descent from Stepneyside Tower. A gaunt-faced ferryman withdrew the gates
from the platform's entrance, and the crowd began to
shuffle forward.

A short, round man wearing pale blue coattails and a
matching silk top hat shuffled in close to him on his
right side.

"Eyes ahead, lad," the man said. "There's trouble."

"There's always trouble with you, Hews."

"Hmph. You're one to talk of other folk making
trouble."

The pressure of the crowd eventually pushed them
through the arch and onto the boarding platform, where
a cable car sat ready. Pulleys and machinery chugged
away on every wall. Oliver noted that the crew rushing

about pulling switches and turning valves all wore the black cloaks of Mama Engine's servants; they had some grand name in the rags, but Oliver and most folk just called them "the crows." They were rarely seen outside the Stack, preferring, Oliver assumed, to be near their goddess, working in her furnaces deep inside that mountain of iron. The red glow of their own heart-furnaces leaked through burns and holes in their heavy clothes; some even had mechanical limbs, which held to no human shape. Last time Oliver had taken this car, the crew had been ordinary men of the working classes.

"Keep your eyes straight, lad," Hews hissed. "They're in a mood today."

Oliver made to turn his head forward again, but his eyes lingered. Something on the catwalk above, half seen amongst the enormous gears and wheels that ran the car, tickled at his attention. Slowly, his eyes made out the gleam of round black armor and the long, precise line of an Atlas repeating rifle. A bolt of panic shot through him.

"What are the Boiler Men doing here?" he whispered.

"I don't know. Now walk straight and don't draw attention to yourself."

Oliver felt a chill creeping through him. The Boiler Men: the baron's personal army. Silent, unhesitating, they acted and killed with the detached ease of things wholly mechanical. Unlike the cloaks, not a one of them had ever been human. If Baron Hume had deployed them outside of the Stack, something must have happened to cause him no small worry.

A stern-faced gold cloak held the door at the entrance to the cable car, scrutinising people as they passed. Brass plates covered half his face, and his right eye had been replaced by an oversized orb of porcelain. Like most of his order, he wore not an actual cloak but a short cape over finely tailored clothes: waistcoat, jacket, slacks. Oliver had no sympathy for the cloaks. Their mechanical growths were not the painful fruits of any disease, but rather gifts from the baron and his gods, given when a once–human being walked into the Stack and took communion with Grandfather Clock or Mama Engine.

Their mechanisms were their thirty pieces of silver, the price of their souls.

Oliver was glaring hard at the doorman when Hews tapped him on the shoulder to bring him out of it.

"Anonymity is your friend right now, lad," he said. As they entered, he placed himself directly between Oliver and the gold-cloaked doorman and gave the fellow a friendly tip of the hat. The doorman's gaze lingered on Hews long enough for Oliver to slip into the car. He came close enough to hear the man ticking.

Hews joined him a moment later.

"They're looking for someone," Oliver said.

"I had better not find out it's you. Let's retreat to the back."

They pushed through the crowd to the end of the car, farthest from the door and farthest from the tin clock set into the ceiling at the front. They found a place in a corner, where they were pressed against the walls as the car slowly filled. Oliver turned to stare out through the wire mesh that served as a window, hiding his face from the clock. Hews did likewise.

"They came out of the Stack in force this morning." Hews said. "I received a telegram from one of my old partners about it. Apparently there have been frequent arrests."

Oliver felt himself flush. "And how does that differ from a normal day?"

Hews shushed him with a gesture, tilting his head back towards the car's occupants. Oliver bit his tongue until the anger passed.

They fell silent a few minutes as the last of the passengers filed on and the gold cloak shut and locked the door. Hews slipped his fingers into the pockets of his waistcoat and rocked back on his heels.

"On a different topic," he said, congenial once again, "how was last night's work?"

When Oliver didn't answer right away, Hews grimaced and rubbed his muttonchops.

"It went badly, then?"

Oliver exhaled deeply and rested his forehead on the window. "You might say that."

"Did anyone spot you?"

"Likely."

Hews cursed under his breath.

"Well," he said, "nothing to be done now. This seems a lot of attention for just you, in any case. We'll talk when we get to Stepneyside."

The car jolted and began to move. Wheels and gears screeched away, and hidden engines erupted into deafening noise. The passengers braced themselves against the walls and against one another as the car picked up speed. In a few seconds, it cleared the boarding platform and flew out into London's yellow-grey smog.

Oliver laced his fingers in the wire mesh as the car began to wobble side to side. Ahead, Stepneyside Tower slowly faded into life from within the clouds and the swirling ash. Its thick steel beams arched gracefully together, crossing and tangling, and at the top spilled back down in all directions, giving the tower the appearance of a huge black flower. The scattered lights of human habitation blinked between them like orphaned stars.

"Look there," Hews said, pointing out the car's right side. "On a clear day you can see the gun emplacements at Wapping, and sometimes the Thames."

Oliver turned to look but saw only more grey sky, with the twisted shades of other towers lurking in that direction. Somewhere beyond stood the impassable wall separating Whitechapel from the rest of London, topped with electric defences and guarded by untiring Boiler Men. Just beyond it, human soldiers of the British army stood ever ready, standing fast against any expansion of the baron's city.

"You're from Wapping, Hewey?" Oliver asked.

Hews shook his head, as if ridding himself of a clinging memory. "Chelsea, actually. Someday, I'll show it to you, lad."

A blast of hot, oily wind battered the car. Oliver held on to the mesh and closed his mouth and eyes against the stinging ash that swirled past. A violent bounce caused screeching and twanging sounds to echo through the car's roof.

"Haven't I always said it?" Hews grumbled from behind his kerchief. "It's the lifts and the cables that will be the death of us. The Boiler Men needn't lift a bloody finger."

A flash of red light illuminated them from the right. A half mile in that direction, Oliver made out the square and orderly Cathedral Tower, gleaming and clean despite all the grit and dirt of the air, and looming behind it, the black mountain of the Stack.

That was where Mama Engine's inhuman children laboured without pause on her Great Work, and where, day after day, good coves worked themselves to death at her machines. Red flame blasted through the clouds around its uppermost tip. Smoke blacker than coal shot upwards, fanning out to cover the city like a shroud.

Oliver nudged Hews in the arm.

"Seems that's been happening more often of late."

Hews squinted at the spectacle. "Aye. Pity we can't get a man inside. I'd love to know what they're building down there."

"Could always join up with the crows, Hewey," Oliver said with a grin.

Hews' expression laid plain what he was going to say, but after a quick glance at the men and women pressed in on them at all sides, he simply replied, "I may at that, lad."

The Stack burst once more, then guttered and went out. Smoke continued to seep into the sky.

A few more jolts brought them into the Stepneyside station. This station was much larger than the one in Shadwell, and featured cable car passage to Montague Tower and a raised rail heading to Cathedral Tower and the Stack. Oliver and Hews stepped into the crowd and let themselves be carried along in the human current as it spilled out onto the boarding platform. Hews used the same trick to get Oliver past the gold-cloak watchman.

"Peculiar," said Oliver. "All this for some fop bookkeeper."

Hews snorted. "He isn't just some bookkeeper, lad. Didn't Bailey tell you?"

"Bailey wouldn't tell me the bloody sky was grey,"

Oliver said. Then his stomach clenched a little tighter.
"Er . . . what was he then, if not a fop bookkeeper?"

"*Was* he?" Hews echoed, with a searching glance of
Oliver's face.

Oliver shook his head, an indication not to discuss it
in the midst of a crowd. They shuffled along in silence
towards the exit. Above the entryway to the station hung
a montage of small clocks, all ticking out of time with
one another and orbiting around a central, larger clock
by the action of some mechanism hidden from the eye.
To the left of the entrance stood a half squad of six
Boiler Men, five holding Atlas rifles against their shoulders and one a steam hose connected to a copper boiler
strapped to his back. Oliver and Hews tipped their hat
brims down, flipped their collars up, and walked by without a glance or a word. Oliver felt the heat from the
steam hose from a full five yards away. He wondered
with a shudder if it had been fired today and tried not
to remember what he'd seen it do to the human body.

They did not speak again until they had escaped the
station and found a side street hidden from the view of
the station's massive exterior clock. The alley led between two tilting tenements connected by a slanting support beam that emerged from the second floor wall of
one building and entered the third floor of the other.

They found a recessed doorway and took a moment
to remove their hats and coats and shake the ash from
them.

"I think perhaps you had better explain yourself,"
Hews said.

Hews expected a direct and honest answer, Oliver
saw. Oliver thought of Missy and knew immediately he
wasn't going to give one.

"I had my knife on him to keep him quiet," Oliver
said. "He just dove onto it. I think he may have been
trying to strangle me."

Hews' face drooped. He swallowed hard several times
before speaking. "So he skewered himself?"

Oliver nodded, fighting the guilt welling in his abdomen. "Without any warning at all. I made an honest

attempt to pull my knife aside, but it was all very sudden."

Hews rubbed his muttonchops and stared at the ground. Oliver felt a weight of sadness coming off the other man, feeding the gnawing sensation in Oliver's gut.

"Sad way to meet one's end," Hews said. "Damned shame."

"We got off fine with his documents," Oliver offered. "Heckler seems to think they're a key for translating some sort of cypher."

"You told him who you worked for?" Hews asked.

"He can't exactly turncoat on us now."

Hews flapped his hat angrily. "Damn it, lad. Did you tell him who you were?"

"Hewey, that isn't something my crew normally discusses while on mission."

Hews flushed red. His jowls vibrated as he spoke. "Bailey's using you on my good word, lad, and when he hears this he'll have us both hauled off. Do you understand that?"

Oliver threw a finger into Hews' face. "Well, if our muck-a-muck had told me anything more than a name and a time I'd have brought that fox in spit polished like a brass kettle."

"You should have bloody told him who you were."

"And if Bailey had trusted me, I'd have known to do it. Just because I wasn't born in the—"

"He was one of *ours,* Ollie."

Oliver froze. His finger wavered. "What?"

"Your fox was one of ours." Hewey jammed his hat back onto his head and shouldered back into his coat. "He was a bloody inside man."

Oliver's arms dropped limply to his side. His hat slipped from his fingers and settled quietly on the pavement. "I . . . didn't know."

"Of course not. Bailey thought—correctly, I might add—that you would make a mess of it and might get caught. Aaron Bolden was running a separate operation tonight which might have thrown suspicion on your fox, so he had to be retrieved."

Oliver moved his lips for a minute, running in his

mind every conceivable apology, from humbly admitting his mistake and resigning from Her Majesty's service to prostrating himself on the ground and wailing piteously for forgiveness.

"Christ" was all he said.

Hews' face cracked and he choked out a sad laugh, which Oliver couldn't help but echo. His gut sank another few inches towards his toes.

"So what shall we do now?" he asked.

Hews took a deep breath. "Now we get all our ducks in a row. Was he drunk?"

Oliver nodded.

"Good. Bailey will buy that. Lawrence was always a lush."

An image of the dead man flashed in Oliver's imagination. His stomach churned.

"Jesus, Hewey. I didn't need to know his name."

"You'll get past it, lad. It isn't as if this is the first man you've killed."

In the heat of armed rebellion, yes. But not like that: unarmed and unawares, and without offence so far as I know. Missy had not elaborated on her justifications. In fact, she'd barely spoken at all.

"Though," Hews continued, eyes hopping this way and that without looking at anything in particular, "let's have Thomas do the actual deed. He's careless as a bull on his best days."

"But that isn't how it happened."

Hews gave a chuckle that could have been a sob. "Well, I doubt a one of us is generally truthful, eh? Though Bailey may check on it, so it would be prudent to review it with your crew."

"He knows that Tommy never uses a knife."

"But he carries one."

Oliver nodded. "Good a tale as any, I suppose. We'll look like fools no matter the details, I think."

Hews smiled and stepped down from the doorway. "I've looked worse on many occasions, lad. All in the name of queen and country, eh?"

Hews slumped off, his shoulders dropping under some unseen weight.

"Queen and country, aye." Oliver pulled out a shilling, and for a moment gazed down at the stern female face on the back side.

But not my queen. Not my country.

He plopped it back in and followed after.

"I don't like the look of it," Hews said.

Oliver bit into the ha'penny biscuit he'd bought, and spoke around the dry crumbs. "Not a coincidence, today of all days."

Hews faked a jovial smile for the benefit of the two gold cloaks prowling the opposite side of the street and took an altogether too-large bite of the sausage roll he'd bought. The canaries were in what they must have considered disguise, having traded their gold livery for identical suits of brown and fur hats. They still moved in short jolts of motion like all of their ilk and their coats showed the conspicuous bulges of weaponry.

The gold cloaks didn't seem interested in Hews or Oliver. Rather, they scrutinised the people passing close to the building across the way, which was also Oliver and Hews' destination: a warehouse with a condemned store in its front, which narrowed like a pyramid towards its top floor.

Oliver turned to stare down the length of the concourse, so as not to draw the cloaks' attention. "Do you think we've been discovered?"

Hews licked a bit of grease from his lips. "Possibly, though Bailey's always careful. Would be a tough bit of deduction, that."

But what else could it be? The warehouse was one of Bailey's safe houses, a hideout for him and the agents loyal to Queen Victoria. Bailey's safety measures were extreme: he enforced anonymity and held all his information in his head. He kept no documents, no records, spoke to no one outside his organisation. In fact, other than Bailey and Sims and a few others, Oliver didn't even know who the other crown agents *were*, or what they looked like. The cloaks knew of Bailey's crew and had been hunting them for more than a decade, but had always, always come up empty. The thought that the cloaks had found Bailey out was unthinkable. Yet . . . there they were.

Oliver turned back to Hews. He faked a smile and their talk took on the outward cast of a friendly conversation between gentlemen.

"Well, they don't seem likely to be off anytime soon. Is there a back entrance? Or a subterranean one?"

Hews tipped his hat to a passing lady, who glanced at him fearfully and hurried her pace. Hews sighed, and picked some ash off his roll.

"Now that isn't proper," he said. "Out in London we'd have shared a smile and a few kind words."

"You've told me."

"All this," Hews went on. "Baron and Ironboys and cloaks and clocks and all—it has everyone fearful beyond their wits. If there's any reason you need to be doing this, lad—that's it."

"I've always had reasons, Hewey."

"Aye. I suppose you have."

Oliver watched the lady stride away, her skirt stirring up dust and fallen ash from the sidewalk.

He'd never believed Hews' tales of London. In Whitechapel, anyone a man spoke to could be an informer to the baron and thus to his divine masters. Granted, that wouldn't be the case outside the walls, but even then, what guaranteed that the hawker one was speaking to one moment wouldn't turn villain and rob him the next?

He failed to mention this to Hews, who pulled himself out of his melancholy in due time. Then Oliver asked again:

"Are there any other entrances, Hewey?"

Hews nodded, then stepped closer to Oliver and dropped his voice. "There is a way in from below, though I don't care for it owing to the fact that it's little more than a few thin beams."

Oliver gulped down a sudden burst of fright. "Do you think we have any other option?"

Hews sighed. "I suppose not. Just let's finish our breakfast first."

A few minutes later, they started off towards the far

end of the concourse. The street rolled up and down in this section of the tower, tilting and curving to take best advantage of the support of the beams beneath it. Electric lights blazed down from above, accompanied by the occasional fuzzy hint of sunlight bleeding though the incomplete ceiling.

After two or three buildings, Hews turned between two shops. He led them down the alley, kicking a path through skittering clickrats, to where the pavement ended and the street fell away.

Oliver leaned over the edge as Hews paused to catch his breath. He saw a small tangle of beams just beneath, then a drop into the murk of the downstreets dozens of storeys below. He clamped his hat on against the gusting wind and clutched the wall for support.

A curse escaped him.

"You were never afraid of long drops as a child," Hews snorted. "Made a habit of trundling along the ledges as I recall. There's a fine stair on the left."

By "fine stair," Hewey must have meant a set of beams crossing in a kind of thatch pattern. They descended it carefully, Hews huffing the whole way and Oliver clamping white-knuckled fingers onto any hold he could find. When they had gone twenty or so feet, they came to a horizontal beam wide enough to walk abreast.

"Mind the wind," Hews said.

Stepneyside Tower did not have an underbelly. Over the side was nothing but a drop to the invisible streets and buildings of old Whitechapel far below. Oliver paused at one point to look over the edge, instantly regretting it.

The braced concrete floor of the concourse blocked all the light from above. They worked their way by feel along the beam to its opposite end, where a wooden ladder stood, tied to a crossbeam by lengths of weathered and stained twine. Hews climbed the first few rungs and felt around on the underside of the concrete above.

"Always bloody hard to find . . ."

Oliver crouched down at the foot of the ladder, trying not to acknowledge the queasiness of his stomach.

"You may want to check before we go up," Oliver suggested, "what with the gold cloaks out front and all."

Hews snorted. "I was just doing that."

Oliver hunkered down and waited.

After a few minutes, Hews descended the ladder and squatted beside him.

"I'm hearing unfamiliar voices," he reported. "Bailey is still up there, playing the role, trying to blather his way out."

Oliver shook his head. "And after he's done that he can convince the sun to take a loaf for the day."

"Bailey's pigheaded enough to try it anyhow. This door opens quietly enough, and comes up through a cabinet on the back wall. We'll have a plain view of the warehouse."

Already beating quickly from their precarious walk across the beams, Oliver's heart jumped into a yet faster rhythm. "You expect to just rush them?"

"By the saints, no." Hews reached beneath his coat and withdrew a .45-calibre revolver from inside his vest: a Webley British Bulldog. "But this may lend some perk to Bailey's lack of eloquence, eh?"

"Just the one? And how many canaries do you think?"

"One?" Hewey said. "Aren't you armed, lad?"

Oliver swallowed hard, then reached into his pocket and produced a four inch wood-handled flick blade. Next to a firearm, the weapon looked more fit for sticking sausages than fighting. Hews' face constricted in a pained expression for a moment. Oliver stared dumbly down.

"I haven't carried an iron since the Uprising," he said.

Hews sighed and shook his head. "Just stay behind me and look like a mean-spirited Scot, or something."

Hews mounted the ladder again. Shortly, two clicks sounded and a faint square of light materialised above Hewey's head.

"Quickly, now."

After some few seconds of manoeuvring his belly through the tight trapdoor, Hews slid up and disappeared. Oliver clenched his miniature weapon tight in his right fist and steeled himself against the quivering fear in his gut. *Just up the ladder and to it.*

He ascended.

The cabinet turned out to be not quite large enough for the two of them. Oliver had to bend his knees and neck at an unnatural angle to fit entirely inside. Hews had a similar problem, being quite unable to bend forward to the small crack between the cabinet's two swinging doors on account of his belly. Hews gestured at the trapdoor, and Oliver closed it silently by lowering it with his foot.

Bailey's wine-rich baritone rumbled from beyond the doors.

"Well, I *do* take it as an affront, sir. You and your ilk have no respect for the sanctity of a man's property."

Another voice answered, punctuated by a springlike clicking sound on every glottal syllable.

"I've shown more respect than you rightly deserve, being traitors and spies."

Bailey harrumphed. "How dare you, sir, after damaging my door and assaulting my comrades?"

As the crack between doors was out of Hews' reach, Oliver bent his neck farther and lined up his eye with the soft orange light filtering through. Already his neck had begun to ache.

Just beyond the door sat wooden boxes half the height of a man. The room seemed to extend perhaps thirty yards to the other end. A jowled, sour-faced man stood perhaps halfway across, dressed in a grey suit and bowler hat. He wore no cloak to signify his position but had enough gold on his person in terms of hat ribbon, cuffs, chains, gloves, and tie to make up for it. He brandished a revolverlike weapon the length of Oliver's forearm.

When the man spoke, his facial muscles moved in tiny stops and starts like the hands of a clock, eventually resting in a configuration resembling a tense grin. "I'll savour dashing that out of you before we hand you over to our brothers in armour."

"You have made a threat on my person, sir," Bailey said. Oliver heard something that might have been Bailey spitting. "And that I will not tolerate. Let's settle this without delay, hand to hand, as God intended."

The gold cloak squinted suspiciously. "I'll not have you starting a ruckus and warning your coconspirators."

Oliver felt a poke in his ribs and turned to Hews, who spoke in a whisper that was little more than an exhalation shaped by the lips.

"A view of the room."

Oliver moved his head left to right, swinging his small slit of vision to encompass as much of the room as possible. In order to do this without sound, he and Hews squashed and bent themselves into poses that became downright painful. It was also getting uncomfortably hot. Oliver bent low, further craning his neck, to whisper into Hews' ear.

"Bailey and Sims on the left, possibly another—I saw a hand. The chief canary's just out front, beyond a set of boxes. Two more at the door with Enfields. Can't see right or left wall."

Hews nodded. "I can't believe you don't have a gun, lad," he whispered.

"I've had enough of them," Oliver shot back. "What now?"

"Sit tight. Ready when I say."

Oliver nodded.

Outside the cabinet, tempers were flaring.

"I call you coward!" Bailey roared. "Pass me a pistol. I challenge you, sir."

The gold cloak emitted a noise like a sputtering engine. "You'd like that, wouldn't you, you filthy renegade? You'd play me for a simpleton."

"You doubt my honour, sir, only because you have none of your own. Tell me, when they cut out your heart, did they relieve you of your manhood as well?"

Hews held up one finger and gestured at the door. Oliver readied his knife.

"You fucking rotter," the gold cloak bellowed. "I'll kill you right here, Ironmen or no."

"Praise England!" Bailey cried. "Long live the queen!"

Hews jabbed his finger forward. Oliver's heart leapt

into his throat as they crashed pell-mell out of the cabinet. Hews fired two shots the instant the doors swung clear, then hurled himself down hard behind the two crates. Oliver stood dumbly for a moment, watching the chief canary topple backwards, then plopped down flat to the floor as the gold cloak on the right brought his rifle to bear. The cabinet door splintered an instant later.

Sims dove in next to Hews. Bailey followed, rolling on his shoulder and coming to one knee suddenly armed with a derringer in his right hand. The third man—Kerry—produced a .38 from his coat and fired several times as he moved to join them. Then his back exploded and he dropped to the floor like an abandoned marionette.

Things became quiet for an instant.

Groans and noises like the breaking of violin strings sounded from beyond the boxes. To Oliver's left, Bailey rose to an apelike crouch, muscles and tendons rigid under his sun-worn skin. The expression in his eyes denied the age that showed in the spots at his hairline, the grey in his moustache. Silently, he tossed Oliver the derringer and reached to the back of the second crate. He jammed his fingernail between two slats and levered it open, revealing a set of pistols. He passed one to Sims and clasped the other in both hands.

Bailey and Hews shared a silent look. Oliver scrambled to right the derringer and fit his long fingers around the handle. Muttered curses accompanied sounds of movement over the crates.

Bailey counted down on his fingers. Oliver turned himself over into a squat and got ready. Three. Two. One.

They all leapt up at once, and the room filled with light and noise. Oliver's first shot went into the ceiling. Then he took aim on the gold cloak who'd shot at him and let fly with the second. The cloak went down, tumbling backwards. The chief cloak, his fine coat a mess of blood, brown grease, and black oil, staggered to the door despite the bullets slamming home in his broad back. The cloak on the left spun and fell, his rifle tumbling from his hands.

Suddenly all firing ceased. Oliver brandished his

empty derringer as fiercely as the others now held aim on their last quarry.

"Buggers, all of you," the man said. He grasped the door frame to stay upright, and shot a snarl over his shoulder at them. Streams of oil streaked his face. "The noble Grandfather will bring me back, and I'll execute you all."

The two cloaks from outside appeared in the doorway, eyes wide in alarm. Bailey and Hews, who, Oliver realised, had been saving their last rounds, shot the two men through their foreheads.

"You don't even die like a man," Bailey scoffed, lowering his now-empty weapon.

The gold cloak's sneer dissolved into a slack, vacant expression, and he slumped to the floor with a sloshing sound that chilled Oliver's bones.

Hews relaxed his arms. "Perhaps he does."

Bailey turned to Kerry's sprawled body. Only a small black-rimmed hole marred Kerry's chest, but beneath him lay a slowly spreading pool of blood.

Not a bad way for it to end, Oliver thought. *Better than the Chimney or the steam guns or any of the other horrors of this city.*

The other three faced their fallen comrade and bowed their heads. Hews removed his hat.

"A great honour to die in the service of queen and country," Bailey said, voice hard. "We salute this man who gave his life for the cause."

"Flights of angels," Hews muttered. "We shall see you at the gates, my friend."

Bailey turned to face the rest of them, dismissing Kerry's body like so much scenery. He gestured towards the cabinet.

"Everyone down."

One by one they fled through the trapdoor. Hews came last, sealing it behind and fastening the unseen catch. They knelt and huddled close against the stinking, grime-heavy wind that greeted them below. Everyone took a moment to hide their weapons away and draw handkerchiefs to cover their mouths against the sickening air.

"How did they find you?" Hews asked, pressing his hat down to keep it from flying off.

Oliver almost reeled back at the anger that flashed in Bailey's eyes. Bailey made a fist with his free hand. "Aaron has been captured."

Oliver knew the name, having heard it passed in casual conversation between other revolutionaries. As usual, they hadn't trusted him with the details of Aaron's role. Oliver had assumed he was another agent like himself, but Hews' startled gasp indicated otherwise.

"Lord in heaven," Hews muttered.

"Contact your people and order them into hiding," Bailey ordered. "Reconvene at the den in Dunbridge Tower." He and Sims backed up, dropped off the edge of the beam, and disappeared.

Oliver turned to Hews. "Hiding? What did he mean?"

Hews ground his teeth, staring inwardly. "If Aaron gave up this hide, he'll give up the rest of them, lad. Not a one of us is safe now."

Oliver's heart leapt back to a racehorse pace. "This man didn't know my crew, Hews."

"We can't take any chances. Let's get up and find a telegraph."

Hews touched Oliver on the shoulder and pointed back the way they'd come.

"How're we to get all the way to Dunbridge?" Oliver asked. "They're certain to be watching the cars."

Hews broke out of an internal reverie. "They didn't seem to know *our* faces. It's Bailey and Sims who have to be careful."

They crawled in silence for a moment, walking on three limbs to counter the wind. Oliver glanced over several times at Hews, whose brow grew more and more wrinkled, and his manner drew more withdrawn.

"Hewey, who was this Aaron?"

Hews loosed a long, frustrated sigh.

"Our hope, lad. Our best bloody hope."

Chapter 4

The first principle of the machine is Purpose. The machine designs itself to this chosen end, aligning all functionality to a single outcome. The machine, by its nature, cannot fathom or choose its purpose. It must be handed down, as revelation or as doctrine, from a being of higher stature. In this way could it be considered divine.

—IV. ii

Ticking: a thousand clocks echoing into endless dark, the motion of a million gears grinding and churning, a morass of straining forces clashing against shaped metal, a finely tuned symphony of coordinated motion, culminating in a single tick—repetitive, deafening, implacable.

The mind of Grandfather Clock.

Aaron had imagined himself shrieking and writhing, struggling against the bonds that held him. He imagined a line of Boiler Men at the entrance to his prison, standing ready with rifles, rods, and steam guns to block his eventual escape. He'd imagined a door locked with steam-powered bolts, to seal in this man who was such a danger.

It wasn't so. He hung now in a chair, arms and legs

supported by thin scraps of brass, six copper tines penetrating his neck. He spasmed randomly. He drooled. He bled dark oil from his eyes and ears. To his left and right, above and below, thousands more trapped souls shuffled mindlessly, their bodies jerking in the indecipherable rhythm of the Great Machine.

He'd fought when they dragged him here, to the Chimney. He'd despaired to see the endless column of quivering humanity vanishing upwards into the core of the Stack, and to know the fate of those there interred. He'd soiled himself from terror, and begged for death instead.

But the baron, in his passionless monotone, had directed the Boiler Men to string him up and keep him conscious while the tines did their work. The baron had stood and watched with immobile copper eyes as the encroaching cacophony of Grandfather Clock's thoughts had hammered their way into Aaron's mind. Aaron's last visual memory was of that man's featureless face: not even a smile of triumph, nor a vicious grin to condemn Aaron as a man. Aaron was a mere faulty part in the Great Work, now tempered and put to better use.

Aaron threw imaginary arms over an imaginary head. He ran on imaginary legs, desperately searching for a spot to hide, but in the Chimney all was Grandfather Clock. Every turn took him between grinding gears or into the path of uncoiling springs.

He ran this way for ages, in an agony beyond measure, swallowed, like all the others, worn down until he was but a dead man who hadn't properly died. The tines tore into his neck as the gears and the noise tore into his mind, and he gave up every secret he had ever held. He gave up his friends, his plans, his secret hideaways, his many paltry indiscretions against propriety and against God—anything to make the pain stop. But Grandfather Clock cared nothing for pain, as long as the gears turned.

After countless long hours, something changed. The million ticks did not come together in one. For a single instant, they cascaded like a short but powerful wave as Grandfather Clock hesitated.

Aaron came alive again. He stole the smallest and

quietest of breaths, and as he did so he felt his body do the same. What was it he felt drawing the attention of the vast being all around him?

He reached out, felt the gears and springs around him clacking in their altered pattern. The rhythm came to him, clearer now that it was not so loud. His subconscious did its work, and impressions formed in his imagination: thickened, greyed images of Grandfather Clock's purposes and directives. Huge, unfathomable, yet with character, with flavour.

Apprehension: that the Great Work may not be finished.

And then a command: to seek, to capture, to preserve.

Joseph, Aaron realised. *Joseph escaped.*

He laughed.

And suddenly the ticks came together again. A crashing slap of sound battered him. A hundred thousand bells exploded into chaotic song—church bells and electric buzzers, alarm clocks and hammers striking anvils.

Grandfather Clock had seen and heard Aaron's thought. All the sharply ordered energies of the machine tumbled onto Aaron's head. He felt bones breaking in his real body.

Stop laughing! was the command.

So Aaron laughed more, even as he screamed.

Grandfather Clock crunched him down like a mechanic scraping rust off a stubborn bolt. Aaron flaked apart and drifted away. What remained tightened securely, then began to spin at its designated frequency. It became part of a work greater than itself, part of an infallible string of physical logic inside the perfect machine.

It was the chin, Missy decided. The broad chest, the muscled arms, the swept-back short blond hair were certainly no drawback, but it was the square, almost Roman chin that really caught her attention.

The man had taken position on the edge of the road, head down, back to the closest wall. He and Missy and all the other grubbers of the Shadwell Underbelly stood squashed to the edges of the street as the Boiler Men passed through. The cloaks, one could have fun with: a shoe in the wrong place when passing was always good, seeing as they were too proud to sully their dignity with childish finger pointing; a little flash of ankle at the right moment was amusing as well, for the canaries at least— eyes like hawks, them, but feet like an elephant on a frozen lake when their blood rose up. With Boiler Men, one just kind of got out of their way.

If she was like most people, Missy would have dropped her eyes and tipped her ash hat down and tried to have no more presence than a pig in a butcher's shop. She would have held her curiosity down with fear and shuddered in her shoes until the Ironboys passed, then gone on about her business as if all was fine and the sun was due to come out any minute. But Missy was not like most people, and neither was the man with the chin.

He watched the Boiler Men with narrowed eyes. Missy noticed his hand had twitched towards the large leather-wrapped object he carried on his back the instant the Ironboys had appeared. He'd restrained himself, evidently, and had retreated to the steps of a storefront flanked by his two companions, a brown-clad ogre and a slim urchin boy. The vantage allowed him an unobstructed view of the grim procession, and Missy an unobstructed view of him.

Now what is this lovely specimen up to? she mused. He was far too fixated on the Boiler Men to notice her, and so she was free to study him at leisure. He stood with muscles taught, legs comfortably wide as if he expected to dodge aside at any moment. His thick moustache and mop of hair seemed to bristle like tiger's fur. He stood alert, tense, exuding an aura of control.

You must not judge a client by his looks, nor his manner. To you, all men are Adonis and Casanova.

Missy frowned at the thought, and wondered if it was wrong to wish that they had all been like this one.

Even though you flee me, the lusts are still on you. You were born to this work, child.

The Boiler Men moved off, though their heavy, synchronised footsteps would echo in the Underbelly for some time yet. The crowd began to swell out into the street again, silent at first, gradually building to hushed conversation.

The object of Missy's observation conferred with the ogre at his side a moment, then gestured with his head for the lad to follow. He shot a glance sideways, directly into Missy's eyes. Her heart jumped at first; then her face flushed with sudden anger. *He was playing me!* She responded automatically with a coquettish smile and a wave.

The man quickly looked away and down, shifting his focus to the street ahead and the crowds swarming about.

Ready for anything but the tempting touch of womanhood, Missy realised. *Refreshing, after a fashion.*

The three hurried ahead at a good clip, purposeful and terribly out of place in the Underbelly. Missy walked more naturally, mimicking the shifting wanderings of the tower's occupants. Though her quarries moved faster, their directness clashed with the aimless dance of the crowd, and Missy kept pace without difficulty.

The floor of the Underbelly was like a giant bowl of concrete, warped and misshapen to conform to the vagaries of the tower's steel supports. She tracked the three strangers between two- and three-storey tenements, inexpertly constructed of whatever spare wood and plaster could be scrounged from the city above. The place had a ruined graveyard quality about it, enhanced by the few ghostly street lanterns that Missy had always detested. When this silliness with the queen's agents had run its course, Missy intended to make Oliver buy her an apartment in Aldgate. *Oh, why compromise on fantasy? . . . in Cathedral Tower!*

She trailed her foxes into a nest of rum dives and two-step alleys called, for reasons unknown, the "Blink." *They must know the area,* she decided, *to stride so confidently into that labyrinth.* Why, then, had she not seen them before? The other two, though odd in stance and motion, would pass for locals with a little effort. The man with the chiseled chin, however, she would surely have remembered him. She slipped into the alley some minutes after them, to ensure they'd passed the first of

the alley's many pointless corners. The hem of her skirt
brushed the narrow walls, and she gathered it together
in front of her to keep it from staining on the piss and
puke all over. Why was it the drunks never managed to
quite make it to the street?

She stopped at the first corner. Cursing sounded from
ahead, echoing off the stained walls above: possibly the
ogre having trouble manoeuvring through, and the chin
man's backpack as well. She peeked around the edge
and saw, just as she thought, the ogre's wide shoulders
stuck between loose window trim and a pipe. The chin
man must have been in the lead, for she saw only the
teenaged lad. He cocked his head, and began to turn.

She darted back into cover with a stifled yelp. Something in the lad's posture, head lowered between raised
shoulder blades, suggested a cat about to pounce, or a
dog about to growl and charge.

A sudden fear blinked in her mind like an electrical
spark: why was she following these men?

*Because Oliver will ask you what they were up to, and
if you don't have an answer he is sure to chastise you
like a little girl and sulk the rest of the evening.* There. It
was on his head now.

*It is preposterous to maintain belief in the innocence
of your motives, child. You sully the very idea of goodness in people by your association.*

Heedless of the noise, Missy slapped herself hard on
her cheek.

I'm done with you, old woman. Leave me be!

Gradually the cursing ahead subsided, and after a few
minutes in silence, Missy plucked up her courage and
followed.

After a few more turns, she emerged into one of the
little plazas that were referred to by a term she wouldn't
repeat, even to herself. Lit by a single oil lantern hanging
off a second-storey windowsill, the plaza gleamed with
moisture and stank of filth of every kind. A descending
stair on the left led to a rum house entrance, a boarded
door on the right to a condemned shop with broken
windows.

Three more alleys led off. All three took their first

turns too early to see very far along, and the only sound audible, despite the constant muted thrum of the factories from above, was some murmuring and a badly played tin whistle from the rum house. She could find no trace of her little foxes.

Well, that's that. Perfectly acceptable, me losing them in here. And Oliver can't rightly argue with me not wanting to take my lone, feminine self into a grog house, can he? She dusted her hands together in symbolic dismissal of the whole affair and turned to leave.

A man stepped from the dark of the rightmost alley. Missy's hand flew to her chest as her heart began to thunder. Words came automatically to her, rehearsed and practiced so many times before: "Goodness, you do give a lady a fright, sir."

The man with the exquisite chin gestured for her to step towards him, and backed into the alley.

"If you would, miss," he said. His voice was rich with a husky Germanic accent, though it was also scratchy, as if he had spent a lot of time yelling.

Missy fixed him with her most disarming flutter of the eyelashes. "Now that would hardly be proper, would it? Me following a strange man into a dark place."

"You have been following this strange man for some time, miss."

The bastard prick knew. She smiled shyly. "Sharp eyes on you, I see."

He made no response to that, though his eyes flicked for an instant a little lower than her face. Revulsion surged in her gut for an instant.

Remember that your client has come to you to be toyed with. It is his wish to be led by your wiles and have that responsibility lifted from him for a time.

Something useful from you for once, old bat.

As an experiment, Missy took one direct and intentional step inside the range of his arms. He responded by backing away, wary, hands by his sides but open and turned out slightly to be ready to reach up at any moment. She fancied she saw his skin pale and chuckled inwardly. Why was it the big strapping ones were always the easiest to unman?

"Now, what's a fellow handsome as yourself doing in the Underbelly, I wonder." She gauged his pained squint to mean she could safely proceed further. "Nothing that can't wait, if the company's right, I hope."

His neck flushed red. Missy folded her hands sweet-as-you-please in front of her, the back one slipping her switchblade partly out of her sleeve. Befuddled though he was, the man carried a sidearm just out of sight in the shadow of his right hip, and she wondered if the slight lump beneath his shirt just above the waistband might be a belt of ammunition, like Heckler carried. The man's right hand held steady just above the sidearm's grip.

"I am not interested, miss," he said.

Her fingers wrapped around the knife's grip. *Oh, but you must be, for I'm ready for you.*

"Well, not yet, love. But the day is young, and you'll find I know a mite of pleasurable conversation, among other things, if you'd give a doe a chance."

The flush and jitteriness vanished, to be replaced with a cold, discerning stare. The man's entire posture grew fierce, and Missy suddenly realised just how large he actually was.

Stupid. Too forward. Now he's . . .

"Why were you following me, miss?" he asked, voice flat as cold slate.

She retreated one step from the force in the man's eyes and managed to sound cross.

"I've told you already, sir. Well, I can see you're not interested. Good day to you and I'll be on my way."

She stuck her nose up and spun away. What on earth had possessed her to trail this man into the Blink of all places? *Dignified, now. Slow down. Dismiss him. He's nothing at all.*

His hand engulfed her shoulder and spun her back around like a top. She found herself staring into startling blue eyes, as hard as steel. She tugged the flick-blade loose. A quick poke and he would drop like a domino, just as before.

From some unexplored part of her, a primal rage welled up, a screaming order to thrust the knife through his heart. He deserved it. They all did. All these cruel and lecherous swine that thought they had so much power.

She pressed the catch and the blade leapt into place. Was it the eyes that made her hesitate? Was he just that much faster?

He never broke their gaze. His other hand snatched her wrist the instant she began to thrust. Shoots of pain darted up and down Missy's arm and out into her fingers. She cried out and the knife clattered to the street.

She couldn't move her arms. She couldn't run. He leaned in closer, filling her nose with his scent.

"Listen!" he hissed. "Do not continue following us. My associates are heartless villains and they will murder you. Do you understand?"

She nodded meekly. He shoved her away.

"Play your *Versuchung* games elsewhere."

She nodded again, swallowed to quell the shaking of her insides, and retreated. She kept him in sight, watching his eyes and his firing hand until she reached the little plaza, then spun and bolted down the nearest alley. She ran through the twists and turns, bashing her elbows on the downspouts and scuffing her dress on the walls, and did not halt until the vast lamp-lit cavern of the Underbelly opened around her.

She found a rotting crate behind a bakery where no one could see her from the streets, and sat down. Tears poured out of her eyes, soaking her cheeks and chin, dribbling onto her jacket.

"No, no, no," she muttered. She crammed her fists into her eye sockets.

Do you require further demonstration of how powerless you are, child? Surrender these unladylike ideas of independence and return to me.

Her entire body shivered. Her insides rolled and squirmed. A sharp pain began throbbing between her legs. From inside her mind, Matron Gisella fixed her with a tight-lipped scowl.

The world abounds in examples of your weaknesses. You are as frightened a little girl now as you were when you were dumped upon my doorstep.

No, no, no, no . . .

She pulled her slick fists away from her face and clamped them down on her legs and then her arms, until they went stone still. Then she hugged her midsection so tightly she thought she might break it.

She held herself in that death's grip until her insides stilled and Gisella's voice fell silent. Then she inhaled with great deliberation, rose, straightened her clothing, wiped her face.

She would get another knife. She would get a gun. Then she would teach that Kraut bastard not to make her feel like that. She would teach anyone who crossed her that she was powerless no longer.

She headed for the hideout.

Chapter 5

*I see a great city behind my closed eyes. It is the
vision of all my failures of architecture, standing
together against all possibility. I see humanity living on these creations, driven far from the mud
of which they are made. I see our homes and
churches broken; I see our God snubbed and ignored; I see our books rendered unreadable by
smoke and by ashes.*

—IX. ii

A passing wash of smoke hid the platform even as the
cable car settled into its berth. Oliver had tied his kerchief over his mouth and nose before disembarking, but
that did little to stop the sudden burst of fire in his
lungs at the first taste of the air. This close to the Stack,
breathing and not breathing were of equal detriment to
one's health.

The Dunbridge Concourse was constructed on a
sharply slanting hill with the station at its base. By virtue
of the way the steel girders had grown up, the black
cloaks had elected to build only on the west side of the
tower; the east stood open to the air and the rain. The
dwellings of Dunbridge rested one atop the other, with

all the order of a stack of rubbish, and for the most part were devoid of light.

Every station and street they'd passed through in Stepneyside and Cambridge-Heath had been crawling with gold cloaks. Even the women and children members of that bizarre order worked the crowds, eyeing up the midday commuters as they passed. The burlier and better-armed canaries randomly hauled people from the crowd to perform searches of their pockets. This had happened to Oliver only once, and he was able to palm his knife and derringer while the man roughed him over. The cloak had contemptuously shoved him aside to make space for the next victim, whom his lackeys were already dragging up.

"This is an affront to basic human dignity," Hews had said. "What do they honestly expect to find with all this? In the whole of Whitechapel, we can't number more than a few dozen."

"Spreading fear, perhaps," Oliver had suggested, "to scare the average cove away from helping us."

Hews had perked up at that, and a little of that prideful red glow came back into his cheeks. "Ha. British men don't scare that easily."

Oliver had thought of Missy. "Neither do the women."

After that, they'd both lapsed into silence. The constant proximity of Grandfather Clock's followers and occasionally the Boiler Men limited the instances of their conversation.

Oliver was dying to know more about this Aaron. He wanted to know how a man who knew so much could be allowed to fall into enemy hands. When asked, Hews snapped that it was not the time to discuss it and fell back to his silent worrying.

Hews' first breath as they stepped out of the car sent him into a fit of coughing. Oliver hooked his arm and gently drew him out of the way of the rest of the passengers as the coughs evolved into wet hacks. It was several minutes before Hews regained his composure. He righted himself and wiped the spittle away from beneath his kerchief. A sudden sheen of sweat mixed with the soot on his face. The man seemed drained of all vitality and every seeming of health.

"That entertaining, am I?" Hews croaked.

Oliver swallowed. "Is it . . . ?"

"Cancer of the lungs, aye," Hews said. "The same as took my Barbara."

"You might have told me."

"You knew it," Hews scolded. "As a lad, you were never less than observant. She always told me so."

"There's a difference, knowing it and hearing it," Oliver said.

"You needn't tell me that, lad."

They stood in silence a moment, while Hews stowed his handkerchief and tied on a fresh one from his vest pocket.

"She was kind to me," Oliver said to fill the silence.

"Aye, she was. And her only price was the enduring of her constant sermons, bless her Anglican, Anglican soul."

Hews cleared his throat and straightened his coat and hat. "Well," he said. "Now that I'm done making a spectacle of myself, let's get on, shall we?"

"But . . . are you all right?" Oliver asked.

"Chipper as the day I shot out of my mum, lad. I'll have none of your pity." He began a brisk walk. Oliver scrambled to keep pace.

The station exited onto the lowest point of the concourse: a half bowl of concrete that sported benches, unconvincing false trees, and dormant wrought-iron lampposts of angular design. It was almost deserted, owing, Oliver figured, to the choking air. A black cloak scuttled by, moving on all fours like a spider, emitting an audible mechanical grinding as she moved.

Oliver shied away.

"Sold their souls," Hews said once she had gone. "Nothing in their hearts now but a few lumps of burning coal and Mama Engine's excrement."

And they'd do it to all of us, if we let them, Oliver thought. The metal grew in a human being as easily as in a tower or a factory; a man would not know he had it until black iron started poking through his skin. Thomas was already half a machine, and he had never joined any order.

In a few steps they lost themselves in the fog.

"I hope you know the way, Hewey."

Hews waved him on. "I know it better than my own wrinkles, lad. Just follow me, and make sure there's something under your foot before you commit to the step."

Oliver halted in midstride, foot hanging above the concrete ahead. The air was so thick, holes in the concourse would not be readily apparent. He shot Hews a venomous look.

"Did I not look preoccupied enough for you?"

"Not at all, lad. Just wanted to warn you to watch your step, that's all. One never knows, in a place like this."

"You're a fiend, Hewey," Oliver said. For emphasis, he stomped his front foot down hard. The satisfying smack of rubber on concrete echoed back up.

Hews smiled weakly. "Mr. Savvy today, eh? Well, if you take such pride in your own wit, try to tell me where we are twenty minutes from now."

Frowning, Oliver followed Hews' ghostly shadow through the smog to the start of a rickety staircase. They ascended several storeys before coming to a landing, then found another stair, another landing, another stair, and so on for what seemed an eternity. Never could Oliver see more than five paces in front of him. Soot-stained walls and greasy windows passed by on both sides. The heavy air suppressed all ambient sound, until all Oliver could hear was his own breathing and footsteps.

Hews paused on a landing to catch his breath. Oliver stumbled up beside him.

"Does it worry you that we haven't seen another living soul this whole time?" he asked.

Hews panted, and spoke with a scratch in his voice. "All staying inside, slothful buggers. Some buildings here are connected by tunnels, where the air isn't so bad."

"Then why are we out here?"

"So no one can bloody see us. This is a *secret* meeting, in case you'd missed that."

The aforementioned twenty minutes passed and Oliver had to admit that he was hopelessly lost. After a few more landings, Hews led them to a pitted oak door and into a lit parlour.

The air within was almost as smoky as that without. Heat pushed its way past Oliver as he entered, filling his nostrils with the smells of opium and human sweat.

"Even in Whitechapel you can't escape these damnable places," Hews muttered.

A single oil lamp with an Oriental paper shade hung from a hook in the ceiling. Its wan light illuminated a dozen or more men lying about the room on couches and carpets, twitching in their rumpled clothes. No one moved. No one spoke. Only a moaning from an area on the left, cordoned off by hanging curtains, dared break the silence.

Stepping carefully over the still forms on the floor, Oliver followed Hews to the back. Hews rapped on the door there, to the rhythm of "Bonnie Banks of Loch Lomond." It opened, revealing a squat, hair-lipped Chinese woman of considerable age.

Hews doffed his hat. "Mrs. Flower, a pleasure, as always."

She greeted him with a wrinkled smile and some words in a singsong dialect, and ushered them both inside. She led them through a tiny back room equipped with several short tables and stools and a potbellied stove. A skeletal Chinese girl laboured over the stove, grating cake opium into a sieve that sat over a pot of boiling water. Mrs. Flower led them to a stained curtain against the back wall and drew it aside.

"Here's one more." It was Bailey's rough voice. "Is anyone with you, Lewis?"

"Only Mr. Sumner," Hews replied. "Where are the others?"

The Chinese woman gestured for Oliver to follow.

Oliver turned his attention to the room, to find it lit only by a half-dozen thick candles in the centre of the room's circular table. Spots of smoke and grease blackened the plaster walls. Bailey, Sims, and two gentlemen Oliver had never seen before occupied the table.

One of the unknown men, a red-faced gentleman with precisely cut moustache and sideburns, replied, "We can only hope for them."

"Just hurry and seat yourselves," Bailey barked. "We haven't a lot of time."

Hews settled into the last empty chair. Oliver stood at a loss for a moment, feeling more and more the impatience of those assembled, and finally elected to fetch a stool from the previous room. He seated himself on it and tried not to look as ridiculous as he felt, a head shorter than all the rest with his knees pulled up to his chest.

"Thank you," Bailey said to Oliver, with edged sarcasm. He sucked a moment on his cigar and then addressed the table. "I see four missing."

One of the two unknowns, a bald man in an expensive suit and pince-nez spectacles replied, "We got the word through. Perhaps they are simply tardy."

"A fanciful hope," Bailey said. "The canaries have been assaulting our hides since dawn, even my own. Until they knock at the door, we will assume the others have met their fate, so it falls to us to tackle the task at hand."

"The task at hand is escape," said the unknown moustachioed man. "Grandfather Clock and Baron Hume won't soon forget about us, and with everything Aaron knew we'd best vacate the city and get the Crown to send someone else."

Bailey's heavy brows dropped low. His cheeks creased around the edges of his moustache in a scowl. "Our *task* is to retrieve the ticker tape that was Aaron's objective. According to our source in Scared's organisation, one of Aaron's crew fell from Aldgate with it in his possession. John Scared is certainly already looking for it, and perhaps the baron, too. We must move with all possible haste if we are to discover it first."

"Why is it important?" Oliver asked, and immediately wished he hadn't. Bailey glared at him as he might a child who had spoken out of turn. Only the bald, bespectacled man spoke up.

"Yes, out with it," the man said. "You've kept us all too far in the dark on this. Since Grandfather Clock and his pet baron almost certainly know by now, your compatriots aught to."

Sims and the other unknown nodded their heads.

Bailey's glare lingered on Oliver for a moment, cigar smoke curling up his cheeks.

"Then I will start at the beginning." He addressed the table again. "Our conundrum has been this, gentlemen. With careful planning, we could probably assassinate the baron, and with enough men, we could probably defeat the cloaks, but such acts do us no service as long as the Lord and Lady survive. Ultimately, we require a method to slay them in order to ensure their influence is gone from England, but bodiless as they are, we've encountered no lack of difficulty with this. Aaron has been, for some years, working on a way to kill Grandfather Clock and Mama Engine."

"And he found such a method?" the bald man asked, leaning forward.

"No. He told me from the start that the task was beyond him. It was John Scared who found a way."

Low muttering passed across the table. Oliver reeled a bit on his tiny stool. John Scared was the baron's lapdog, his eyes and ears on the Whitechapel streets. Could this be dissention in the enemy ranks?

Bailey continued. "Scared placed the calculations for this method on a coded ticker tape. Aaron insisted on leading a team to steal it."

It was the bald man's turn to reel back. "And you let him? God, with how much he knew . . ."

"He argued that John Scared would have set out traps too devious to deal with without his . . . special talents. From what our source has told me of Scared's lair, I had no reason to doubt this."

"But the risks, man!"

"The rewards more than outweighed them, sir," Bailey said, overpowering the smaller man. "At last a way to free Whitechapel from these God-cursed machines!

What risk isn't worth that? And the opportunity is still there. Our task, gentlemen, is to retrieve that tape, implement whatever strategy it contains, and get it into the Stack to do its work."

Hews rubbed his muttonchops. "No small order."

"I don't anticipate any one of us keeping his freedom very much longer," Bailey replied. "So we must abandon the dark lantern shenanigans we've been playing at, anonymity included, since it is likely the baron already knows our identities. Joyce, get your engineering crew ready for anything that tape may contain." The moustachioed man nodded. "Lewis, you and Lawrence will need to pull in your connections in the Stack. We may need access to the Chimney or the Work Chamber."

Oliver visibly cringed at the mention of the dead man's name. He inhaled and mentally plucked up his courage. Now it would come out that Lawrence had met his end at the hands of a comrade, and Bailey would sack him. Well, then, Oliver would simply run a rebellion on his own again, nervous as that made him feel.

Hews just nodded. "We'll get it done," he said.

"Good," said Bailey. He turned to give orders to Sims and the other man.

Hews had lied straight to Bailey's face. A lie of omission. Oliver was aghast. It wasn't just for his sake, surely? But why else would Hews do such a thing?

"Sumner."

Oliver snapped to attention to find Bailey glaring at him from behind his thick moustache.

"Do you have Lawrence's manual?"

"Yes, sir."

"Good. With luck, it will contain a key to decode Scared's tape."

Oliver raised his eyebrows.

Hews leaned over and muttered an explanation: "Lawrence was in contact with Scared through intermediaries. He'd been compiling this for some time."

"We will be using the Shadwell Underbelly to gain access to the downstreets," said Bailey. "I want your people to loiter in the lift station and on the main street and to monitor the activity of cloaks and Boiler Men.

Distract them or assault them as necessary, but keep them away from our point of egress so we can be certain of a clear path back. When we have obtained the tape, we will pass it into your hands, and you must see it safely to Joyce's workshop since we are unable to move freely on the streets now that our faces are known. If the Boiler Men arrive at Shadwell in force, you are to give us fair warning and perhaps a distraction while we escape to the Docks Tower."

Oliver spoke before he'd thought it through: "Watchmen? Is that all, sir? My crew is capable of handling much more."

Bailey bristled. He gestured sharply with his cigar. "Oh? I was remiss, then, in not clearing our plans with you first. You and your crew—I am placing you where I need you. If you have some problem being *necessary,* we can review that at your leisure at a later date. This afternoon you will be watchmen and nothing more."

Uncomfortable foot shuffling and the quiet clearing of throats followed. Oliver felt heat creeping up his neck. His hands had at some point balled themselves and now shook with barely contained energy. Oliver was seized with the sudden urge to leap across the table and throttle the man. *Damn the consequences, damn your rebellion, and damn that old, fat queen of yours.*

He caught Hews glancing sidelong at him. Oliver unrolled his fingers, forced a calm, slow exhalation.

"Yes, sir."

Bailey nodded.

The next twenty minutes covered logistics and timing. Bailey's crew were to leave for the downstreets within the hour by the "rusted stair" below Shadwell. The crew of the bespectacled man were to set explosives in Cathedral Tower with the intention of drawing cloaks and Boiler Men out of the Stack if necessary. Oliver clarified the location of Joyce's workshop, which turned out to be in Montague Tower, the tiny ten-dwelling stem growing from the Stack's base. Talking in specific details about the assignment settled his nerves a bit.

"Never forget Scared," Bailey said to the table. "He's likely to have sent a team already, and will be watching

Shadwell. The man employs children, and if our source is accurate, has pull and clout with both the golds and the blacks. He's likely to discover our presence no matter our level of caution."

The table murmured acknowledgement.

"Bow your heads."

The men complied, most with genuine reverence, Oliver as a matter of course.

"Lord, you have set these trials before us and we are grateful for the opportunity to do your work," Bailey said. "We thank you for all the assistance you have rendered us in the years past and ask that you aid us today in our battles. With your blessing, we will soon wipe these devils from the face of your good Earth. In Jesus' name, *amen*."

The table murmured assent. Bailey then looked at them each in turn, as if appraising them, their worth perhaps, their dedication. At length, Bailey nodded, apparently satisfied.

"Praise to England," he said. "God save the queen."

The sentiment was echoed all around, and the men dispersed. The others left one by one, spacing their exits to intervals of five minutes, as measured by an odd, water-powered clock that hung in the small kitchen of Mrs. Flower's establishment. Oliver loathed clocks. The thought of Grandfather Clock staring out at one's family or one's personal affairs kept the majority of homes timeless places, and the majority of pockets empty of watches. He mentioned as much to Hews, but Hews only shrugged.

"That clock was built in the East somewhere. Grandfather Clock has no influence on it, or so Aaron seemed to think."

Another few minutes' wait brought them their turn at the door, and they tied their kerchiefs over their faces and braved the exterior once again. Impossibly, the air had grown thicker since they'd last breathed it. The only things now visible were a two-yard stretch of warped wooden platform all around them and the dull glow of the Stack, huge and omnipresent, in the sky to the south, and even these were little more than phantoms in the smog.

When they'd gone some distance and Oliver determined that they were thoroughly lost, he decided a few words had to be said.

"Thank you," he began, "for your silence in there. I thought I was going to be sacked for certain."

"No thanks is necessary, lad," Hews replied. "It's a rare opportunity nowadays that I have a chance to do you a good turn. And in any case, Bailey didn't need the headache right then and neither did we."

"But won't Bailey discover it when Lawrence doesn't report?"

"Lawrence was a member of *my* crew. Bailey doesn't know him by face, and so won't really miss him, assuming I can hold up my end."

Hews' crew. Oliver suddenly felt ten inches tall as the realisation rushed into his consciousness. They'd killed a man, a good man with friends like Hews and possibly family.

"Er . . . was he a married man, Hews?"

Hews nodded.

Oliver could only close his eyes and halt. He steadied himself on the railing. Images played in his mind, of a mother at home, pacing, fretting, images of children sitting silently at a breakfast table, casting nervous glances at their mother, porridge untouched.

"You coming, lad?"

Oliver swallowed hard past the lump in his throat.

"Hews . . . God forgive me. I'm so sorry."

"I know, lad" was the reply. "You can say as much to his widow when there's time."

Oliver longed to see Hews' face, but the smog rendered him ghostly and insubstantial.

"Let's get on," he said. "The cloaks are already moving against us, and we're a long way from Shadwell."

They called it Sherwood Forest.

The tenement took that name from the branchlike protrusions of steel that poked out of the walls at odd angles. The building had been constructed around a central set of two spiraling beams that roughly resembled a trunk, the floors having been constructed at uneven intervals conducive to the use of the trunk's branches. Missy agreed that it did look rather more like a tree house than a proper dwelling for human beings. Parts of it even hung over the edge of the Underbelly, perched with a preposterous slant above a twenty-storey fall. Oliver had purchased it some years ago, with money gathered through the ill-conceived thefts of his earlier years.

Oliver Sumner, respectable landowner. One half of her giggled at such silliness. The other half tallied this as a point in his favour. She had always fancied tall men. And if that tall man had wealth, youth, other men in his employ, and connections . . . well, that made him attractive indeed.

Now if only it weren't for this distracting rebellion, and I could work on him a little harder . . .

She pursed her lips and chafed inwardly at that sentiment.

Yes, my dear, you are a heartless, calculating shrew, as I made you.

She hiked her skirts just up to the ankles and held them to the right as she climbed the grime-coated concrete steps to the door. An endless battle raged between organic and mechanical spiders in the brick door frame, sometimes spilling out of its many holes to harass unwary solicitors. She gently pushed away some fresh webs and twisted the door handle first left, then right, then left three turns. The lock clicked. The door opened.

Heckler's traps lay dormant on the left and right sides of the inner arch. She did not care to muse on how they worked or their intended result, and brushed past them into the foyer, where the stair twisted around the steel trunk, and an uneven mezzanine ringed the room on the second floor.

Sherwood Forest had a kitchen, a dining hall, a lounge, a smoking parlour and eight apartments. Oliver had offered her one of them once and she'd nearly slapped him for it. An unmarried woman living under a roof with four unmarried men? She knew exactly what people would say about that.

Rumours are vicious little things. What does a lady have if not her reputation? One of Matron Gisella's lectures.

In honesty, she had simply been terrified of the thought of men having uncontrolled access to her bedroom. Missy had taken her own one-room flat down the street, one with sturdy locks and a fat, scatterbrained landlady.

She sat for a moment on one of the foyer's worn benches and fished her cigarette case from her handbag.

Unladylike, those accursed things, the matron had always complained.

Funny how all the girls smoked them anyway, behind your back, you old shrew.

Now, now. Some respect is due. After all, did I not feed you and clothe you and instruct you in all the fineries of etiquette?

You sold us for two guineas a night, you black-hearted villainess!

The match lit on the first strike and she drew. The acrid smoke that stung its way down her lungs was really no worse than the air outside; nor was it any more pleasurable. *Why smoke them at all, then?* She left the question unanswered.

She found the occupants upstairs, gathered at a small table in the parlour. Thomas, Phineas, and Heckler lounged in moth-bitten high-backed chairs, drinks in their hands, cigars in a tray on a small side table made of battered tin. Moderate sums of money were spread on the table, as were several piles of cards from Heckler's star-backed fifty-two-piece deck. Portraits of stern-looking, haggard people of both sexes hung around the perimeter of the room; they had been there at the time of purchase and were now silent companions to the dwelling's new occupants.

Thomas wore a beige wool shirt a tad tight on his large frame, revealing the irregularities of his structure, particularly his metal arm. Missy had never seen him clean shaven, and yet never with a beard; he seemed to have perpetual stubble. Thomas stared at Heckler with squinted eyes and sweat beading on his brow.

Heckler was dressed in a crisp and clean white cotton shirt with tweed slacks and suspenders, looking dapper as always. Missy secretly suspected he made a point of dressing well to hide his sunken chest and bony shoulders. His face drooped in that lifeless way he referred to as his "poker face." Phineas sat slumped, nestled down in the same filthy black ulster he always wore, with an oversized, crushed top hat sitting low on his head—like a leprechaun down on his luck. He also wore a thick blindfold across his eyes.

Slowly, and with no hint of a smile, Heckler laid his cards solemnly on the tabletop.

"Codswallop!" Tom said. He slapped his cards down as Heckler smugly swept the central pile of coins to his edge of the table. "Some Yankee trick, that was. I'll bet those bloody cards are marked."

Heckler stroked back the corners of his handsome moustache and smiled serenely.

"Bad luck's the heritage of mankind," he said, his American accent drawn and smooth like stretched linen. "You know Ah might have up and shot you, you gone accusin' me of cheatin' back home."

"Cards ain't marked," Phin said through teeth clenched on the stub of his cigar. "Bastard's just better'n we are."

Tom downed the remainder of his whiskey. "And how would you know that, you hunchbacked codger? Not peeking, I hope."

Phineas spat the cigar onto the silver tray along with a sizable trail of saliva, where it all landed exactly in one corner. "I inspected the deck during the first shuffle. You think I trust this Yankee—or you, you pile of rust?"

Tommy smiled, warming to the moment. "So you were looking at the deck after all, you limp waddler. Why would one who stinks like a gull-eaten trout think he can one-up me dressed like a Shoreditch beggar?"

"Ah, you're one to talk, you chamber-pot reject. Probably spit rust out yer pecker. By the bye, there's a lady present."

Missy smiled innocently as Thomas and Heckler shot out of their seats, faces reddening. They struggled to hide drinks and extinguish cigars.

"Why, *thank you,* Phineas," Missy said, swaying her hips as she stepped into the room. "I was beginning to wonder if these men had *any* manners at *all.*"

Phineas grunted, and lit another cigar.

"Beggin' pardon, miss," Heckler said. He smoothed out his felt vest and tugged his shirtsleeves back level with his wrists. "Was quite improper of us."

"Smoking and drinking *and* gambling?" Missy said. She sucked daintily on her own cigarette and waltzed to the table, where she lifted Phineas' drink right from his hand. "Positively vile activities, the lot. You gentlemen should be ashamed of yourselves."

Heckler blanched, then shifted his feet in place like a boy of seventeen. Thomas held a serious expression on his face for all of two seconds, then exploded into laughter.

Phineas just shook his head and stole Tom's drink.

Heckler strutted around the table. "Mademoiselle Plantaget," he said, gracefully sweeping up Missy's hand. Missy held his gaze as he lifted her hand to give it a kiss.

His nose came within an inch of the cigarette before he noticed. He coughed and withdrew, retrieving his handkerchief and stuffing it against his nose as if he could wipe the smoke out. This time both Thomas and Phineas laughed.

"Poor dear. Lost in my eyes, I suppose."

Heckler faked a chuckle through his obvious shock.

"Ah, lass," said Phineas, "stop punishing the pup for being a gentleman. You'll ruin him for other English-women."

"He will develop a taste for it," Missy said. "I'm certain he left those Colonial homestead girls behind for a reason." She raised the glass to her lips and drew the whiskey across her tongue. It slid down her throat like melted chocolate.

Heckler looked as if he was about to say something, then sat down and began to total his winnings as if that had been his intention the entire time.

Tom gave him a friendly and devastating slap on the

shoulder that nearly threw him into the table. "You'll get used to it, chum."

Heckler gasped in his lost breath, his neck turning red above the starched collar. "Certain Ah will, suh."

"He's a duck, isn't he?" Missy said. She settled into the table's fourth chair, an oak and velvet masterpiece of comfort that had seen better days. Heckler jumped as if he'd been seized around the neck.

"Beggin' pardon, m'lady, but that there's Mr. Sumner's chair."

"Oh?" She fixed him with a slow blink and a stare, as an elder matriarch might use to silence her disrespectful grandchildren.

Heckler flushed fully up to his hairline and squeaked out a response: "He's real particular about it."

"God Almighty, let up on him, lass," Phineas said, refilling his glass from the bottle.

Her eyes never left Heckler's. "But he is such a charming young man. Shouldn't I get him under my thumb as quickly as possible?" *Shouldn't you claim him as one more ribbon in your hat? One more loaf of bread in your carry basket?*

"Ah, Michelle, but you are a cold bitch," Phineas said.

A stinging in her abdomen. Missy's composure broke, and she flinched visibly.

Truth is a difficult thing to accept in any guise, said Gisella's voice. *If I recall, you have used such atrocious language to refer to myself on many occasions.*

Her guts clenched and twisted and a horrid, potent loss and sadness gushed up. She pushed it down with a careful, slow, ladylike inhalation, and painted a smile back onto her features.

"Oh, but I'm very warm as well."

They chuckled, and the moment of tension passed.

She moulded her face into a scowl for a moment. "And you, sir, are not to call me by my proper name."

Phineas' eyebrow snaked out from beneath the blindfold.

A sigh, and Missy elaborated. "The use of such is reserved only for very particular individuals with whom

I share a relationship of a type not to be discussed in impolite company."

"Ah."

Silence fell for a moment as Thomas gathered the cards and the other men scooped their winnings or remaining capital back into pockets and purses. It was a pity: Missy had always wanted to see how this American game was played, but the presence of a woman always seemed to bring it to an irretrievable end.

Missy settled back into Oliver's chair, doubtless referred to as a "throne" when its king was abroad.

You've designs on him. It was no accident you sat in this chair.

Or perhaps it was because it was the only one unoccupied, witch. The rest of the whiskey she tossed into her mouth without ceremony.

You're much cleverer than that, my dear. You wanted to announce your intentions to these three. Romantics that they are, they'll nudge him in the right direction. You think that and your whorehouse charms will be enough to land him? It is an insult to both of you.

Gisella's voice quieted as the alcohol fire bloomed in her stomach. She passed her glass to Thomas with an if-you'd-be-so-kind. He refilled it to half its previous volume and passed it back to her.

"How were the rounds today?" Thomas said.

And you forgot to do the rounds. Stupid little girl.

Oliver insisted at least one of his crew go 'round the Underbelly every day, chatting, eavesdropping, mingling. Then the roundsman had to give a report, a long, silly report in exhausting detail about the state of things, the places people wandered, the things they talked about, the things they needed done. And with that dutifully categorised and compiled in Oliver's mind, he would set the crew about helping those in need and so forth.

Why does the man bother to toss away his earnings on building repairs and doctor's bills and food baskets? He must have an angle, a sinister purpose in all of this, mustn't he?

Missy knew men too well to think otherwise, and yet

that assessment fell flat every time she tried to assert it regarding Oliver.

The others were waiting. She cleared her throat and began with the one piece of information certain to distract them.

"The Ironboys are in town," she said.

The three of them fell instantly still. She continued.

"I saw them marching up the Parade, a full dozen, without cloaks to clear their way. I made some inquiries. Apparently they entered the Blink from the south and descended into the downstreets." Actually, she had overheard it by pure chance on the walk back to Sherwood, but there was no need to disclose that.

Thomas scraped his iron knuckles over his stubble. "Did they say why they were here?"

"No," Missy said, sipping daintily at her new drink. "Not that they are the most talkative of gentlemen."

Phineas, still blindfolded, looked to Heckler. "Lad?"

Heckler nodded. "Ah'll take a look." A little smugness showed as he hefted the velvet bag into which he'd slipped his winnings. "Just a quick trip to mah room first, Ah think." He strutted from the room.

"The precociousness of youth," Tommy commented wistfully. "Those were the grand days, don't you think, barnacle-bugger?"

"You're half my bloody age, grease-breath. You go talkin' like that again, I'll crush out your bile and use it to polish my shoes."

Missy sighed. "Charming, Phineas. It has always amazed me that you never married."

Phineas untied his blindfold and tossed it into the corner. "Ah, I'd have an impossible time slinging the seed at my age, so what's the point? Unless I had some o' that seal-testicle tea they make in Bangkok."

Missy pointedly dismissed him and turned her full attention to Thomas, who stopped whatever pending insult was about to escape his lips.

Missy swirled the liquor in her glass. "Is Oliver due back?"

"Yes, ma'am. Should be anytime, I'd say."

"You'll give us fair warning, won't you Phineas?" Missy asked sweetly.

"I'll hear him before he rounds the block," Phineas muttered, then paused, regarding Missy from the dark beneath his hat's brim. "The lady here's about to ask us 'bout the chief, brass-balls."

Thomas fiddled unskillfully with the cards, trying to align them in a single direction. "Well, salt-spit, shall we wait and see if this is an inquiry that deserves answering?"

Missy leaned forward.

"I want to know about the Uprising."

Thomas' hands fell still. Silence. Cold. Suddenly Missy's breathing was too loud for the room. She swallowed and pushed on anyway.

"Oliver led it, didn't he?"

Phineas opened his eyes fully, eyes that might have been blue beneath frosty cataracts. He and Thomas shared a long look, exchanging an unreadable communication.

Phineas slid his eyes back into a tight squint.

"Aye, he led it," he said. "Started with a little girl. Chimney gang hauled her right out o' her mother's arms and cut 'em both with a knife when they protested. Ollie was working some angle for Hewey at the time. Can't recall, now . . ."

"Tracking opium," Tommy said.

"Right-oh."

They fell still. Missy shifted in Oliver's chair. At length, Phineas continued.

"Ollie never talks about this, y'see, but the way some o' the blokes tell it, he just went off. The gang had a cloak leading it and Ollie went manic and beat his head inside out with a milk jug."

Missy gasped. The image of it assailed her—the violence of the act.

He wouldn't. Would he? Is he capable of it?

The man is a criminal and a spy. Of course he's capable of it.

Thomas took up the thread, staring dully at the unmoving cards. "That might have been the curtain for him, but when he took his first swing at that canary, all the regular coves and sweaters and coal backers on the street just charged in. Forty or fifty to hear ol' Hosselton tell it."

Phin chuckled. "Wish you could hear Hoss tell this. Now, there was a man with a gift."

Thomas continued as if Phin had not interrupted. "Ollie did what every red-blooded man in Whitechapel had always wanted to do. He stood up to the damn cloaks. Those forty or fifty on the street that time, they were Ollie's first crew. A week later, they went and blew up a canary chapel in Cathedral Tower."

"Woulda taken some stones, let me tell you," Phin put in.

"After that," said Tom, "word got around. I heard about it through the gossip when I was backing at the air docks. A heroic young man leading a rebellion, killing cloaks—so many of us had just been waiting for it."

Missy sipped her drink, finding the fire unwelcome. "I remember the rags," she said. "It went on for weeks."

Phin drained his glass with sudden exuberance. "I remember thinking 'What's this, a bloody kid's in charge here?' "

Thomas swirled his own liquor. "I believe your exact words were, 'Sod it, I'm going.' "

"But there were so many by then, see," Phin said. "More than a hundred, and they were all reg'lar coves— family men, and youngsters and the like. And old, useless codgers like me. Ollie had us planting bombs, ambushing cloaks, cutting trams lines. Everything that happened, he had a plan. Those were the glory days, eh, clunker?"

Tom nodded. "And Ollie took care of us, split us into crews, showed us the best places to hide. Hell, he had these tunnels built under Shadwell so's we could move 'round. Never got caught, ain't that a lark? Not once'd they get us."

"Not even the Boiler Men," Thomas said, finally reviving his smile. "You can't rightwise kill 'em, but they're damned slow."

They smiled together, and Missy smiled with them.

But this was not what she had asked for, and they knew it. No light anecdotes, but the meat of the matter.

The laughter died away into the same grim silence.

Phin refilled his drink. "The lady, here, knows how it ended."

Missy nodded. "I read it."

"Ollie saw it coming," Phin said. "Wasn't but a handful that listened to him."

"All the men and firearms and gumption on the whole of the Earth are not enough," Thomas said, raising his glass. "One cannot fight the Boiler Men. They cornered us down here, blocked up the elevator so we couldn't get out, and shot every man they could find."

Phineas finished for him: "And when they couldn't find the men, they shot the women."

They sat for some long minutes in silence. Thomas wiped his eyes with a handkerchief. It came away stained brown.

Phineas set his glass carefully upon the table and slid his chair back. "If the lady would excuse me," he said.

"Of course. Thank you, Phineas."

The old sailor slunk from the room without another word.

Thomas began to work on the cards again.

"So why only three men, now," Missy asked, "if he could rally hundreds before?"

"Three's a lot fewer as can be killed, Miss Plantaget—oh, sod these things." Thomas made a snort of disgust and scattered the cards over the table. "The Ironboys came down on us with those awful Atlas guns and steam cannons. You know they're strong enough to push over a building with their bare hands?"

Missy shook her head.

Thomas continued. "Was all we could manage to keep ordinary folk alive. A few of the crews helped out with evacuating people to the tunnels, but most of 'em were just too angry and . . . Those sorry buggers. Makes no damn sense to charge down an Atlas rifle. No damn sense."

He flicked at the cards with his metal fingers. "We lost a lot of people that day, fighting men and ordinary folk both. Me and Phin stayed with Ollie, saved whoever we could. Tried to save the women and the children, at least. We didn't fight, 'cause what was the use of it?" He sighed. "Ollie's a clever cove, but I don't think he ever realised that no one put the blame on him for what happened. Hell, half the Underbelly's just waiting for him to raise the banner again."

A long pause. The portraits stared down from the walls.

Tom spoke again into the quiet.

"We're just waiting on him to come back to himself. He's not been right since that day."

They sat in silence a long time, lost in their respective contemplations. Missy let her mental rendering of Oliver stack up against these new images. It was no wonder he did things quietly now.

Except when inept little girls go on murdering his foxes, eh?

She ignored that.

"Why didn't the cloaks come for him?"

Thomas shrugged. "My guess is that they only cared about stopping the rebellion. Once that was done . . . and done thoroughly . . ."

Thomas' mounting sorrow filled the room. Missy had what she wanted, but . . . *I can't simply leave him in such a state.*

"I have one more question, Thomas."

"Happy to answer it."

Missy blessed him with a smile. "Why will you drink and smoke and swear in my presence, but never gamble?"

Tommy fidgeted, but his face had already relaxed some with the change of subject. "Well, it isn't right to gamble with a lady present. One has to draw a line somewhere."

"But you two are atrocious. Why bother at all?"

Thomas worked his tongue inside his cheeks for a moment. "Well, there has to be a line. Wouldn't be proper otherwise."

"Would you like to know what I think, Thomas?" Missy said with a twinkle.

"Certain as sunrise I would, miss."

"I think that you don't want me playing this game of yours because you know I would beat you."

Thomas' eyebrow crept up. "That's a mite presumptuous of you, miss."

Missy placed her drink on the table, then gathered the cards and tapped them into a neat pile. She passed the deck into Thomas' meaty palm. "Teach me the game and we'll see, won't we?"

Phineas chose that moment to reenter the lounge. He carried in his right hand a velvet bag that looked suspiciously like Heckler's, and which jingled suspiciously as if filled with Heckler's money.

Thomas sipped his brandy. "What did you swap him for it?"

"An ill-tempered rat," Phin said.

Missy was aghast. "You villain!"

Phin grinned his gruesome gap-toothed smile. "'S what he gets for fleecin' us. If he screams like a girl we might even give him his winnings back, eh, pewter-pecker?"

Thomas waved the cards in Missy's direction.

"Still want to learn, m'lady?"

Missy rapped sharply on the table, and Thomas began to deal.

Chapter 6

Though I call them prophecies, they are not the visions of John and Daniel. What the Lady and her Consort consent to show me of the future is derived of exacting calculation and long-practiced methodology. He is a masterful observer with a capacity of extrapolation that parallels the omniscient. She is a force of will stronger than the very tectonic plates of the Earth.

This future that I have been shown is more true than any premonition, for it is a future they will build themselves. If these visions were prophecies only, I may still have hope.

IX. i

Bergen's neck tingled. Like a dull knife run up and down over the hairs, the sensation saturated his muscles with tension. It was a familiar feeling, one honed in the jungles of the dark continent over half a lifetime of travel there—a feeling Bergen linked with the savage heritage of man, a relic of primordial times when danger lurked all around.

He was being watched.

"Ready yourselves," he ordered.

Mulls and Pennyedge unslung their air rifles.

Bergen unbuckled the straps of the steam rifle's holster and lowered it carefully to the ground. He scanned the shifting smog around them.

For the tenth time he cursed the air that clung to the downstreets. It was a suffocating blanket of oily yellow blackness, staining everything it touched. Just to breathe it required a cloth tied tight across the mouth and nose that had to be kept wet at all times and regularly scraped to remove the buildup of grime. The eyes, too, needed protection, for the air would sting and water them. Von Herder had given them fish-bowl spectacles: half spheres of glass ringed in rubber and held tight over the eyes by a leather strap. Their curvature distorted Bergen's peripheral vision, and he cursed them, too.

"Nothin' out there, Gov," Mulls grumbled, sweeping his lantern side to side.

"Quiet." Bergen braced his legs and hauled the heavy weapon from its holster. He set the butt end over his shoulder, nestling it in the slight dip between his deltoid and his neck. The heat from the gun pressed in on his face as he raised it. The boiler was heated electrically, and rapidly came to full pressure.

"Not like we's can see anyway," Mulls grumbled.

"Quiet!" Bergen snapped. "I want a circle, torches facing out."

Mulls muttered something under his breath and complied. Penny obeyed without question. The boy's eyes darted from shadow to shadow, and he held himself in a ready half crouch. The boy held the air rifle like it might be a spear, and shuffled his feet side to side. In contrast, Mulls and Bergen stood tall, straight, relaxed, weapons slightly lowered so the eyes could scan wide, but high enough to snap the guns into aiming position when necessary. Bergen nodded to himself at Mulls' form. The man must have listened to his instructions after all.

Something metallic scraped in the dark as it moved. Mulls started badly. Pennyedge merely angled himself towards the sound, remaining ready. The American-made electric torches tied to their belts illuminated more of the falling ash than the surrounding terrain; beneath the Shadwell Underbelly, no other light existed. The shifting air hid whatever other motion might be visible.

Bergen knew what it must be: he felt the rhythm of an animal prowl. *Like Africa,* he thought. *Like the Dark Continent watching me through the eyes of her supplicants.*

He mentally dropped the analogy. These were not tigers, nor lions, nor even wolves. These creatures would not halt to consider whether their prey was worth the trouble. These creatures merely considered the best way to close for the kill.

"They are coming. Both of you be prepared to drop low. Hit them in the face or shoulders to delay them. The killing shots will be mine."

Seven heartbeats passed.

A scrape and growl exploded from the ashfall near Mulls. Mulls locked his rifle into position and planted two solid shots into the charging creature's head. The air rifle puffed soundlessly as it discharged, stirring Bergen's hair with wind. Bergen did not turn for that creature yet.

Another leapt from Penny's side, at the far right of Bergen's field of fire. Penny threw two haphazard shots into it. The beast whirled and skidded to its right, directly into the path of the steam rifle. Still Bergen did not fire.

Another charged from behind. Bergen let Penny take that one as well, knowing Mulls could hold it back if Penny could not. Mulls fired twice more at his own quarry.

Bergen leveled the steam rifle and sighted along the length of it. Between the weapon's bulges and lengths of crinkled metal tubing, he watched the creature right itself to all fours, then spin on him. The torchlight bounced back off brass-knob eyes, cast-iron skin, and teeth of tarnished steel. The beast roared, a sound like a great machine collapsing, and leapt for Bergen's throat.

He put a round between its jaws.

The steel bullet vanished into the creature's body trailing a blast of steam that burst into a dance of lightning an instant later. The force of the discharge torqued Bergen's body to the right. He let the momentum carry him in a spin, dissipating it in motion rather than in tearing his shoulder apart. His target vanished, sparking, into the smog.

The sweep of the weapon carried Bergen's field of fire to the area behind him. He found Penny crouching, still holding the air rifle like a spear, hurling his last few rounds into the swerving mechanical horror beyond. Bergen hauled back on the rifle's handles, pushing it into his shoulder to stop the spin. His next shot was sloppy, splattering steam across Penny's back. It took the target through the shoulder, splintering a portion of its torso and casting its gears over the ground.

He'd been unprepared for the recoil. The rifle kicked into his shoulder like a horse, and he felt muscles twitch and spasm in his chest and back as he strained to keep hold of it. Penny dropped to the ground as the steam cloud's electric discharge jolted him. The beast fled into the dark with a yowl like glass scraping on glass.

Mulls cracked off two more rounds and Bergen knew without keeping track that they were his last. A grunt or growl escaped Bergen's lips as he tried to pull the steam rifle around and sight on the third beast.

Mulls dropped to one knee, scrambling to pull cartridges out of his belt. His target, knocked flat by his last shots, pulled itself effortlessly to its feet. In a heartbeat, the creature had dug in its heels and leapt at him, stretching wide its beaklike maw.

Bergen bit down against the pain in his shoulder as he steadied the steam rifle.

Mulls brought up his weapon and jammed it horizontally into the creature's mouth. The steel teeth crushed the barrel and splintered the stock and casing. Mulls screamed as one of the creature's forepaws landed on his chest and began to tear into his coat.

Bergen took an extra second to steady himself, bending his knees and bracing for the discharge. The creature tossed the shredded remains of Mulls' rifle aside and plunged its jaws towards his face.

Bergen put the shot into the base of its neck, parallel

to the spine. The rush of steam blocked all vision, but Bergen knew it was a hit.

Silence descended quickly after that. Bergen let his arms drop and settled the steam rifle bore-first to the ground.

Freed to move again, his shoulder burst into a storm of pain. Muscles spasmed up along his back. He couldn't help but drop to a collapsed squat, wondering if anything were sprained.

"Unspeakable rotter!" Mulls cried.

He was alive, then. Good. Bergen reached a shaking hand up to wipe the condensation off his spectacles.

"Help me, you sots," Mulls said. "The rotter's bloody heavy."

Bergen laid the steam rifle on its side and staggered to help. Penny joined him, still walking light and tense like a cat, and together they wrestled the metal carcass of the third creature off Mulls' chest. The big man gave the thing a kick, then sat up.

"Stupid beast. What in God's name was it?"

"They are called Ticker Hounds."

"Blimey. Didn't think they's real. Just stories, you know." Mulls accepted Bergen's hand and stood. The action, so unconscious a reflex, strained Bergen's throbbing shoulder.

"Are you wounded?" Bergen asked.

Mulls' eyebrows twitched up; a metallic growth in his cheek swivelled a bit. He patted down his chest. "Nothing but me coat, Gov." He stretched the coat away from his body to show the three tattered slashes across the front. "Bit o' the vest beneath. Bit o' the shirt beneath that, I wager. Christ, but it had nails."

Bergen glanced at Penny, who, besides breathing harder, maintained his disinterest as he examined the hound's body.

Mulls crossed himself. "That thing is downright unholy."

The carcass of the hound lay on its side. Its back from the base of its neck to its hips gaped wide, streaming black oil and a colourless ooze onto the flagstones beneath. Its guts had laid a cone-shaped mark behind it, some ten feet long. Twisted bits of metal had been scattered across the area, with some wet lumps that might have looked like flesh in better light.

The thought came to Bergen that there might be more.

"Boy, give Mulls your weapon," Bergen ordered.

Penny spun on him with narrowed eyes. Bergen stared coldly back.

"The weapon goes to the man who will make the best use of it, boy."

Bergen could feel the lad's suspicion. Still Penny hesitated.

Bergen placed his right hand on the hilt of his sidearm. Tendon and bone grated together inside his shoulder and he winced. He tried to disguise it as a sneer.

"I have not the time for this *Bockmist* right now."

An empty threat, and the boy knew it.

"Easy, mate," Mulls cut in, addressing the youth. "You can have the flasher. You're better in close than me anyway."

Not breaking eye contact with Bergen, Penny reached out one hand with the rifle. Mulls fully wrapped his fingers around it before attempting to haul it away, and passed over the flasher. Penny snatched it and let it hang from his fist by the leather shoulder strap. He made no move to put it on.

"Do you know how to use that?" Bergen asked.

Penny did not answer.

Had John *wanted* this sojourn sabotaged, sending along such a disobedient child?

"Answer, boy."

Bergen's frustration mounted. The boy clearly considered himself Bergen's equal, and would take every opportunity to challenge him from then on out. Allowing that balderdash was no way to run an expedition.

"Come and kill me, then, boy," Bergen rumbled. "See how far the two of you make it. What will you do when there are five or six hounds? What will you do when the clickrats in their hundreds become hungry for your bones, or the nesses drag you down into their holes? How is your sense of direction, boy? How is your sense of time?"

Penny's lip twitched at the corners. *Angry? Good. As long as you're listening.*

Bergen beat a fist against his chest. "I have crossed the Sahara and the Alps, boy. I have been in and out of the Congo a half dozen times. You are here because John Scared assigned you to me, and for no other reason. I will have your concentration and your obedience or I am done with you. And when you think of murdering me, think first of this: I am quite capable of returning to the city under my own direction and with the help of no one else. Therefore: I can kill you, but you cannot kill me, lest you doom yourself. Is that clear?"

Though Bergen saw no change in Penny's outward expression, he felt the boy's presence diminishing, until he seemed less an adder than a toothless dog trying to affect ferocity.

"Put on the flasher. I will waste no more time on these childish games." Bergen turned his back and bent to wrap the steam rifle in its holster.

He is not a toothless dog, said a thought in Bergen's mind. *Right this instant he is contemplating how best to dispatch you. He knows he is faster than you.*

Bergen ignored the thought. He'd left the boy little choice but to fall into step, and so the boy would fall into step.

Bergen detached and switched the handles on the steam rifle. Von Herder, in one of his characteristic fits of brilliance, had designed the weapon with the ability to be configured for left- or right-hand firing. The right shoulder would not heal sufficiently for some hours. Fortunately, Bergen was left-handed.

Mulls stood nervously to the side, shifting weight from one foot to another. Bergen might have chastised him for it, but that he didn't want to give Penny any reprieve from the embarrassment of his censure. He calmly reloaded the steam rifle's empty chambers, then hefted the mechanism onto his back. The right shoulder strap bit sharply into the skin, a sure sign of a developing bruise.

"Come," he ordered. "We are barely past Lenman Tower."

He marched into the gloom without looking back.

Oliver idly watched a clickrat gnawing on Tommy's boot. The little creature looked more like a truncated snake than a rat, sporting a pointed silver head and a stump of a tail, and getting around on six spiderlike tin legs. It did have prodigious teeth, though, which it put to use with some vigour on its chosen prey. Tom fluffed his newspaper and didn't seem to notice.

"Always seem to come to Shadwell the instant anything goes awry, don't they?" he said, turning the paper over.

Oliver looked up to see a group of four gentlemen gold cloaks striding purposefully down the street towards the lifts at the far east end. Their gold capes gleamed against the background of grey- and black-clad humanity that wandered antlike along the street towards their homes and families after a long day at the factories. The street was officially named Marlowe Street, and ran the length of the Underbelly, from the lifts at the one end to the sheer drop at the other. The natives had named it, as well as the people who walked it, the Beggar's Parade.

"They came from Phin's area. Think he marked them?" Oliver asked.

"He probably tried to engage them in dither." Tommy folded the newspaper neatly in two and passed it to Oliver. "Ah. There he goes."

Oliver scanned out into the crowd, picking out a crooked hat bobbing on the river of humanity as certain as a leaf on a true stream. It floated after the cloaks as they turned up a side street called Disraeli's Amble. Phineas had them well in hand.

Oliver wondered briefly what a real river looked like.

"Queer bit," Tom said, "and a waste of personnel, getting one whole crew to watch the Underbelly. Only one way in, after all."

"Sir Bailey is keeping us out of his way," Oliver said with undisguised bitterness. "Thinks we're all rabble. A lesser class." The newspaper turned out to be the mid-

day edition of the *Whitechapel Guardian,* a rag put out
by Baron Hume's personal publishing house in Cathedral. "Why are you reading this tripe, Tom?"

Tom shrugged, cocked his head, and watched the
clickrat nibble his boot. "We're all a lesser class, Chief.
We were born here, weren't we?"

"Mmm . . ." Oliver scanned the yellowed paper. The
topmost story read "Engineers Confirm the near completion of the Great Work." It went on at some length
about the heroic strides of the crows in bringing Mama
Engine's mysterious goal to fruition. They had been saying the same thing for years, so Oliver passed on. The
next story detailed the capture of several groups of rebels in league with the British Crown, and dwelt at
length on their various evils and the degree to which the
streets would be safer now that they were gone. Oliver
almost tore the paper in two right then.

The rest read like an advertisement for the grand benefits of joining up with the canaries. *Yes, please cut my
heart out with a dull pick and replace it with a bunch of
gears and springs. That would be smashing.*

"Why are you reading that tripe, Ollie?"

"Shut your trap." He folded the paper over and
tucked it under his arm, with the intention of throwing
it down the next hole he came to. "Did you notice if
the cloaks were still performing searches?"

"Mainly up towards the lift," Tom said. As he regarded the relentless assault of the little clickrat, a dull
smile crept onto his face, as of a stern parent finally
relenting at his child's cries for candy. "I think I'll
keep him."

Oliver frowned. "Keep him? That creature would eat
the nose from your face."

"Got some energy, eh?" Tom pulled a length of wire
from the pocket of his oversized long coat. Oliver
watched with fascination as Tommy bent down,
squeezed the rat's cheeks with his mechanical hand to
make it release his boot, and held it fast while tying its
jaws shut with the wire. That done, he lay the clickrat
on its back in the palm of his hand, where it squirmed
and clicked furiously. He removed another length of

wire and bound all six legs together against its body with an ingenious multiple-layered loop.

Thomas held his prise high.

"I shall call him Jeremy Longshore the Third, and I dub him King of the Clickrats. May his reign be long and fruitful, free from tribulation, and rife with bountiful harvests and competent public works ministers."

He dumped the struggling creature into a coat pocket and returned his attention to the Beggar's Parade as if nothing had occurred.

Oliver shook his head in amazement. "Just don't bring it in the hideout."

"Aye, Captain."

The hiss of steam echoed across the Underbelly, drawing both their eyes to the lift. It ascended the shaft on clacking chains, vanishing behind the massive clock that hung halfway up. Canaries would be stationed at the top of it as well as the bottom.

"We'll have a bit of difficulty getting Sir Bailey's prise out of this place, what with all this company," said Tom.

"Not if Missy takes it."

Tommy cracked a toothy grin. "Good call, that, mate. You've had this planned out for a while, then?"

"You know I'd have planned a deal more if Bailey deigned to render me as much information as we render him."

Tommy made a sympathetic face.

"Yes, you'd surely be running all the crews by now. Poor Ollie: your greatness languishes unrealised."

Yes, that's it. Like a kick in the shins the morning after a good gaff. He'd thought many times about breaking with Bailey and fighting their silent war independently. He'd worked it out to the last ha'penny: financing, recruiting, placement, encoding and packaging information—even a method to smuggle any gathered intelligence out of Whitechapel via the German airships. He was still working on a way in and out of the Stack, but Hews could help with that. It was his perpetual daydream: to personally contrive the fall of Baron Hume and his puppet master godlings.

But then his mind always came back to the Uprising,

and the magnificent plan fell to ashes and scrap. He knew that no one blamed him for it. Many of the Shadwell locals still looked on him with awe, even gratitude, that he had dared to pick up a gun and do what he did. But the fact was that when the Boiler Men had marched down in their hundreds and shot half the men and a third of the women, he hadn't been prepared. That was the truth of it.

As if to break their silence, Tom patted his pocket where the clickrat still fought furiously for his freedom. Tommy squeaked in mock outrage: "'Give me liberty or give me death!'"

"He's a Yankee, then?"

"He quotes freely from rebels and state heroes alike."

Tommy stuck his mechanical hand into the pocket and made cooing sounds.

"Perhaps I'll leave you two," Oliver said. He straightened his vest and coat, then dragged one finger around the brim of his ash hat. It came back nearly clean. It was the one positive trait of the Underbelly: almost none of the grey snow got past the Concourse above. "I'll be back around in twenty."

He stepped off the sidewalk, tipped his hat to a passing madam he knew, and fell in step with the Parade, natural as donning an old slipper.

He moved along, shuffling and loping with the gait of the tired but vocal backers and sweaters, greeting those he knew, smiling politely at those he didn't, until he was able to angle into the Amble. Disraeli's Amble struck such a contrast to the busy and noisy Beggar's Parade that for a moment Oliver's ears rang with imagined shouts. The Amble never seemed to have carts, hawkers, or even much foot traffic. Everyone in the Underbelly agreed that it was named for Disraeli's ghost who, having lost his famed "blank page" between the Old and New Testaments, had gone there to mope about it, and no one likes a mope.

He found Phineas in wide-eyed contemplation of a streetlamp. "Where are they?"

It was several seconds before the old sailor answered.

"In their impossibly subtle way, they're askin' Bart Cagey about the state of the Underbelly."

"Jolly good. He'll be as helpful as a spokeless wheel," Oliver thought aloud. "You'll keep a watch on them?"

"I'll keep an ear on 'em if it's all the same. I can hear a lot farther than I can see."

"Whatever suits."

Phin cocked his head. His crushed top hat slid down over one ear. "Bart's shaking hands now, tellin' 'em how honoured he is to have 'em in his shop."

"How far *can* you hear, Phin?" Oliver asked.

"A few blocks, now that I'm out of that blasted crowd. There's a cloak coming up the Parade, by the bye."

Oliver peered down to the sea of hats, looking for the signs: stiff-legged walk, rhythmic steps, straight spine. In seconds he'd picked out the cloak, a tall middle-aged man in a vest and beret, a stock of books balanced on a tray he held in front of him. A hawker not hawking, despite being shoulder-deep in potential customers. Why did these people even bother attempting stealth?

"I'll dog him," said Oliver. "At least until he gets onto Missy's block. Keep that sharp ear open."

Phineas nodded, already turning his attention back to the lamp. Oliver jogged down the Amble and took his place in the Parade.

Oliver had never been a good hound. He was far too tall, standing on average a full head above the stunted forms around him. His trick was to seem unimportant, so that when he inevitably drew a target's eye he would render the appearance of a mere sweater, haggard and worn down by work and smoke and dark, and not worthy of more than a glance.

The cloak appeared oblivious to pursuit, a blind fox in a field of dogs. He walked purposefully ahead, maintaining the exact pace of the crowd, looking neither left nor right, not up at the dim ceiling many storeys above, nor down at the uneven and ever-shifting roadway.

Oliver had decided years ago that he hated crowds. People moved on the streets like herds of animals, barely daring to whisper to one another, lest they be overheard

by some spy. They spoke to one another only in the
safety of their own homes, and then in low voices, for
their neighbour might own a clock, or their son or
daughter might have been induced to betray them. Such
was life beneath the thousand faces of Grandfather
Clock and the omnipresent breath of Mama Engine.

Hews had once mentioned the congeniality of London,
where people would speak easily on the streets, comment on weather and current events, shake hands, tip
hats, and go off merrier than before. Oliver suspected
more than a little romanticising on Hews' part, for such
was his habit, and Oliver had declared the whole story
poppycock. Were there not policemen in London? Were
there not ministers and noblemen and landowners?
What was the difference if one's overseers were flesh
and blood instead of iron and brass?

Hews had told him to wait until he saw it.

The crowd slowed as it reached the "domino hole," a
gap in the Parade spanned by numerous wooden bridges
of varying quality. The hole split the Underbelly from
east to west, and on each side thin ledges ran along the
sides of the closest buildings, called, respectively, Alley-
on-the-Left and Alley-on-the-Right.

The disguised cloak huffed across the large central
bridge with the flow of the crowd. Oliver was about to
follow when he noticed a small child watching from
Alley-on-the-Left. Oliver squinted at him over the heads
of the crowd. *Do I know that one?*

No, he realised. That one wasn't a native of the Underbelly, or was perhaps a new arrival, but Oliver
thought not. He would be one of Scared's children.

Oliver caught back up to the cloak rather quickly. The
man seemed to have slowed the instant he touched the
south ledge. Still, he walked with focus, staring ahead.

A little bell began ringing in Oliver's head. On the
pretence of stretching a sore neck, he glanced behind
him. Two more gold cloaks, hard-eyed young gentlemen
who had chosen gold vests instead of cloaks, hustled
over the bridge in his wake. A third followed unhur-
riedly behind, a wide-beamed gentleman dressed in an

impeccable grey suit and hat with a gold Albert chain and gloves.

"Christ on his bloody cross!" escaped Oliver's lips. He barely noticed the offended looks from the people closest to him.

Oliver recognised the man. He was the one Oliver had seen shot dead just that morning in a warehouse in Stepneyside. They'd left him an inert and bloody mass staining the warehouse floor, and now he walked steady and stiff, in the manner of the gold cloaks, and had nothing to show for his injuries but a bruise on his cheek and a few isolated spots of oil showing through his vest.

He thought of Tommy stabbing himself in the heart, and a sourceless rage flushed into his face and neck. Men should *die* when they're shot or stabbed. Men should greet women on the street. Children shouldn't be hauled off by Chimney gangs or recruited to work for lizards like Scared!

His long fingers slipped around the grip of the derringer in his pocket. He gritted his teeth, fighting the instinct to whirl around and place a shot between the man's eyes. He knew he could do it—he was tall enough to fire over the crowd, and his earlier shooting mishap, well, that had been because he wasn't ready. He hadn't the will, then.

His fingers uncurled. And he didn't have it now. These poor sweaters and charwomen marching all around him didn't deserve such a random end as a battle here would give them. It wasn't their fight.

But it *was* their fight, damn it. Every able-bodied man should have taken up arms at the first opportunity. How could they go to the Baron's factories and give their lives to Mama Engine's Great Work? How could they drink the baron's oily sludge and breathe his air and let their children do the same and do *nothing*?

He forced the anger down. His feet had carried him automatically in pursuit of his quarry, who was leading him expertly towards the thin, dead-end alley between a slanting bookshop and a yellow-windowed public house. He cursed himself. *You stupid bugger. You're being led like a locomotive on a rail.* It occurred to him that the man might be a local, to have passed several other alleys all equally crooked and misanthropic and angled to the only one that ended without escape.

They were trying to trap him, of course. Oliver and company had done the same thing to their foxes many times. Luckily, then and now, the trick worked only on the unobservant and the inexperienced, and Oliver Sumner was neither.

He obediently followed his fox nearly to the mouth of the alley, passing between two vendors and their wagons, built of tin strips and rivets and loaded respectively with tiny flags and cotton breathing masks. As he stepped beyond the range of the streetlamps' muddy light, he ducked suddenly and deftly to the left, stealing up the stairs and into the bookshop, sliding through the door without fully opening it.

A little bell dinged overhead.

He spun and peered through the window, squinting to see past the condensation on the outside of the glass. The cloth of gold his pursuers wore shimmered as they entered the range of the closest lamp. The two younger ones clearly wanted to charge directly into the alley mouth, but the grey-suit called to them and they stopped. The grey-suit gestured to the left and right, and the two subordinates took off along the walk at a trot. The man who should have been dead then reached behind his back, beneath his coattails, and drew forth the same large weapon he'd held that morning. He advanced with exaggerated caution towards the alley mouth.

Still feeling the sting from before, eh?

The subordinate dispatched in Oliver's direction ran past the bookshop with nary a glance. Now would be an ideal time to escape, but Oliver hesitated, wondering if the subordinates had been ordered to circle back to the alley mouth after a block or two. It seemed a prudent order, and the canaries weren't entirely fools. Better not to go out quite yet, then. Perhaps the shop would furnish another exit.

Oliver came about, and nearly jumped out of his skin.

"May I help you?" the proprietor grumbled. His face

resembled a beaten scrap of unsculpted leather, lopsided and caved in around the eyes. The piercing yellow light of the store's single electric lamp deepened all the crevices of his face and rumpled clothing. The man smelled of cinders and smoke.

Oliver cleared his throat. "Yes, of course. May I browse?"

"Suit yourself." The shadowed eyes flicked to the paper Oliver still held beneath his arm. "Glad to see the younger folk keeping current."

He swivelled without sound and vanished back into the rows of bookshelves. How had he not heard that ghastly gentleman approaching? He mentally reprimanded himself for such a lapse and retreated into the stacks.

The building from the outside appeared to lean some thirty degrees to its right, hanging over the alley and perhaps ultimately resting on its neighbour on the second or third storey. The inside conformed so perfectly to that configuration that Oliver wondered if perhaps the building had been built standing straight and had fallen over. The ceiling and walls were skewed at a disorienting angle; the rafters were steel beams thick enough to be of natural growth. The shelves were an eclectic collection of makes, styles, and states of disrepair, filled with cobweb-sheathed books arranged in no discernible order.

Oliver idly inspected the bookends and let his thoughts run. Was the crew in danger? *Likely not. The grey-suit just recognised me from this morning.* And the men captured yesterday had never seen the faces of Oliver's crew. Bailey had made sure of that by keeping contact exclusively between the crew captains and himself. Hews had mentioned something about the vast knowledge of the man called Aaron, but . . . no, he had to assume the crew was safe for now, and even if they were spotted and unmasked, they could escape through the terrain of the Underbelly, which they all knew well. Old hats at criminal enterprise, they were, one and all.

No, not criminals. Rebels. Soldiers. They hadn't even commented on their missing stipend.

The bell dinged again. Oliver ducked behind the shelf closest to the inward-slanting wall, squishing into a triangular space half his height. In the process he coated his hat and much of his left sleeve with abandoned cobwebs.

The crisp footfalls of well-tailored shoes sounded against the faint buzz of the electric light. The bell dinged again as the door swung closed.

"Fickin!" the new arrival shouted, much louder than necessary in the closed space. Oliver recognised it as the clicking voice of the grey-suited cloak. "Fickin, where've you got to?"

Oliver heard the proprietor answer: "Who is it? I've had quite enough interruptions for one . . . Oh. It's you."

"Hardly a proper greeting for one of my stature, Fickin. Have you no manners at all?"

"I hand mine out sparingly, Westerton. Now state your business or move on. I am in prayer right now."

Westerton sounded a derisive grunt. "The Lady will forgive you. Did a man enter your shop?"

"Plenty of men enter my shop."

"Just a few minutes past."

"Sticky fellow. Tall like a willow."

"That's him. Where did he go?"

"What's he done?"

"He is a rebel and a murderer. For your sake, I hope you are not concealing him."

"Your accusations are unwarranted, and frankly, insulting, Westerton. He's in the back. Browsing, he said."

Oliver drew the derringer. Two shots, and small ones at that. What good would those do against a man who could be shot to death and be taking a sprightly stroll a few hours later?

The proprietor raised his voice again. "If he must be shot, please do it on the front steps."

"Quiet!"

Conversation ceased. Only the faint taps of the cloak's shoes remained. Oliver was sure he had that oversized weapon of his out. He fished in his pockets for his flick knife, and found it missing: he'd left it on the floor of the warehouse. He snatched a heavy book off the shelf instead, almost laughing at himself. *A book and a gun shorter than my index finger. Always prepared, eh?*

A pile of books blocked the other end of his hiding spot, so he positioned himself to face the aisle he'd come from. His motion, though careful, stirred up the dust and the scent of paper and old leather.

The footsteps reached the aisle just beyond. Oliver raised the derringer, wishing it were a rifle. With only two shots, he would have to take his enemy through the eye or forehead. Any shot to the torso would probably end up lodged in springs and gears.

A gold glove appeared, followed by a grey trouser leg. Oliver's hands tightened on the derringer.

The barrel of the man's weapon poked into the space, followed by his face. The dull whirr of the man's inner workings spread into the hole, buzzing icily in Oliver's ears.

Go on, in the face.

Oliver sat frozen.

And then? Rush a man who can't be killed wielding nothing but a book?

The cloak scanned the interior of the hole briefly, flicked his gun's barrel at the floating dust particles, and then withdrew.

"He isn't here."

"You're disturbing me again, Westerton."

"Where is he?"

"He must have left. Probably robbed me as well. I was in *prayer*, Westerton. I didn't hear."

Oliver dared to breathe. How on earth had the man not seen him?

"Well, my boys will catch him if he's taken to the street. The Brothers of Time thank you kindly for your service."

"The Brothers of Creation thank you kindly for leaving me in peace."

"You are a cantankerous fool, Fickin."

"Then it seems *your* manners are also in limited supply. Now, will you be going or shall we continue this transgression against common etiquette?"

The little bell dinged. The muted noise of the street filtered in. The cloak spoke once more, with a dangerous edge in his tone.

"You have no clock, Fickin. It isn't proper not to have a clock. People will talk, you know."

The door closed. Silence descended. Oliver waited for the shop owner to retreat back into whatever room he took prayer in, but heard only the buzz of the electric lamp and the scritching of rats inside the walls.

He should get back on the street, he knew. Find the crew, locate Westerton and somehow detain or eliminate him. Otherwise, Oliver could not move safely in the open street. But how long to wait before attempting an exit? He couldn't very well stay too long in the abode of a crow, but he had to give Westerton and his cronies time to move off a few blocks.

Eventually his cramping muscles decided for him, and he shuffled out of his place of concealment. Instantly, the proprietor was there, poking his gnarled head from behind a bookcase. Oliver's fingers clenched on the derringer.

The old man smiled without guile. Perhaps he hadn't noticed the gun.

"I wondered if you had left or not," he said. He shuffled silently up to Oliver and offered a hand. Oliver did nothing for a moment, waffling between a feeling of knotted suspicion and an inbred impulse to politeness. As the silence stretched, etiquette won the field. Oliver dropped his weapon casually in his pocket as he accepted the man's hand.

His shake was frail, the skin seeming to swim on top of the bones without the intervening benefits of flesh and sinew.

"Grimsby Fickin, at your service."

"John Bull, at yours, sir."

The man winked. "Risqué to be using such a name, don't you think? I don't mind, though. I understand the old patriotism dies hard, just like the old religion. You'll be taking that, then?"

Oliver blinked. *The book.*

"Ah . . . certainly," he replied congenially. "What are you asking for it?"

He reached out a hand to the book, which Oliver passed over to him. The man let the book fall open and flicked through several gold-coloured pages marked with angular symbols in thick black ink.

"This is a fine edition," he said. "There's real brass in the pages, you know. I can't part with it for less than a crown."

Oliver coughed up the requisite coins, mentally despairing at how light his pocket had become.

Mr. Fickin vanished the money into his clothing somewhere. Oliver noticed then that the man, as well as dressing all in black, wore no trousers. Instead, a canvas skirtlike garment hid his lower extremities. Smoke trickled idly from the man's nose and ears, and he emitted an unpleasant, lingering heat.

"Good to see the younger generation taking an interest in scripture," Fickin said. "You'll be taught to read it only after you've taken your vows, but there is much to be learned through simply becoming familiar with the symbols."

Oliver nodded as if he understood. He glanced down to find himself holding a copy of Atlas Hume's *Summa Machina,* the sacred book of the golds and blacks.

Treat carefully with this one, a little voice warned him, but the man seemed nice enough and a few minutes' further delay seemed prudent, so Oliver embellished a tad.

"Yes," he said. "I've been wondering what it's about, you see. The *Guardian* rarely gets into specifics."

"Of course," said Fickin. He turned and led Oliver back through the stacks. "The bloody canaries print it. Bunch of self-important bureaucrats. I don't know why the Lady keeps them around."

Oliver's interest piqued. *Yet more dissention? A lovely day this is, indeed.* "Beg pardon, sir, but isn't that a bit blasphemous?"

The man snorted, shooting smoke out like the puff of a cigar. "Says who? Those fops are like their namesake:

pretty to look at but fragile. Now, black! That's the colour of *iron,* my lad, a sturdy and enterprising material
worthy of emulation. That's something a man can build
a dynasty on."

Oliver suffered a sudden chill. *Dynasty?* "Then, you
have children, sir?"

The man halted his soundless floating and winked over
his shoulder. "It's not really mine."

As they navigated to the rear of the shop, Oliver noticed increasing layers of dust on the floors, shelves, and
rafters, undisturbed by the tread of man or rodent. The
air also became increasingly thick and hot, and heavy
winds meandered through the aisles, reminiscent of the
skies around the Stack. Mr. Fickin led him to a mahogany door on the rear wall. It must have at one time been
quite lavish, but now sported the first pits of rot on its
panels, and dark burn marks around its edge.

The old man reached for the door handle, hesitated.
"Aren't you going to ask me why I'm aiding an ac-
cused murderer?"

I wasn't going to bring it up, in fact. "I'm no murderer, sir."

He waved off the comment. "Likely you murdered
Westerton himself. This would be his sixth time, I believe, and I wish him a dozen more. And you, lad: a
young man who reads the *Guardian* and the scriptures
and murders canaries in his spare time? A fine postulant,
I say. Mighty fine."

Oliver alternated between marveling that the rebellion's great enemy could be so divided and marveling at
his own near-mystical ability to draw paternal responses
from aged men.

Fickin's hand clenched and unclenched on the doorknob. "You wanted specifics, Mr. Bull. Well, what you
are about to see is my own humble part of the Great
Work."

Choking back his excitement, Oliver answered, "I'm
honoured, sir."

He waved that away as well. "It seems the Good Lady
favours you, my boy. You'll find, once you have one,
that the furnace"—he tapped his chest—"guides your

decisions sometimes. You'll learn to trust it. The Mother is quiet, true. She doesn't demand things of you like her consort, but she still tells you what to do, if you listen."

He turned the knob.

"And she's telling me, furnace or no, that you're ready."

The door swung wide. Oliver staggered back, his hand shooting into his pocket and snaring his gun. Beyond the door loomed a monster, a grotesque giant of cast iron, reaching two storeys in height. In its centre hung a black globe twice the width of a man, studded everywhere with brass rivets and covered in bulbous glass eyes. From this central point issued a mangled array of limbs, ranging in form from humanoid to tentacular, tipped with claws and blades and spikes of steel. Lengths of chain tethered the creature to the ceiling, while the glow of open furnaces on all sides cast it in a hellish red light.

Fickin glided into the room, across a floor littered with tools and bits of scrap metal.

"Isn't it beautiful?" he asked.

Oliver could not find an answer. Fickin did not seem to expect one.

"It's finished," he said. "For near a fortnight now, finished."

"What is it?" Oliver choked out.

"A child of the Great Lady," Fickin said. "Incubated in the hands of her adopted son. These are her seeds, and when they are sufficient in number, they will roll out over the world and grow gardens for the Mother to dwell in. All the Earth will be made a paradise in the image of her great city."

Oliver took a step back. The words escaped his mouth of their own accord. "A dynasty."

Mr. Fickin looked up at the beast with tears in his eyes. "Now kneel with me, Mr. Bull. Pray to the Great Mother."

Not waiting for a response, Fickin lowered himself closer to the ground. The skirt he wore flared out in a wide circle, revealing ominous bumps and edges.

"Blessed and holy Mother," he began, "who loveth boundlessly . . ."

Oliver jumped as the furnaces in the room's four corners flared, blasting him with heat.

"Praise to your sacred womb," Fickin continued. "Praise to your Great Work."

The furnaces flickered and their light changed from dull red to scorching orange and Oliver decided it was time to leave. He spun to find the door shut behind him.

He leapt for the knob. As his fingers closed over it a horrid electric heat shot up his arm, searing him through skin and bone. He screamed in pain and terror, plucking his hand away.

Fickin cried out suddenly: "Mother! You're here! You've come to me."

A sound like the tolling of a bell smothered the howl of the bell, fading away into a watery thrumming.

Fickin's voice echoed as if heard from the end of a long pipe.

"We, your children, who love you to the coming of winter . . ."

Rigid with fright, Oliver watched as the shadows on the wall before him retreated before an intensifying light.

Reach for the door, he urged himself. *Escape.*

He extended one shaking hand, balking at the cracking skin of its palm. The ferocious heat bit at him, reddening the back of his hand, blackening the knuckles. Oliver dared not breathe.

"Forgive us our faults," Fickin cried. "Forgive us our imperfections. We wish only to be humble . . ."

Inches from the knob, Oliver's fingers froze. The heat dribbled like a thick stew into his mind, erasing thoughts as it progressed.

Move! Oliver screamed inwardly, but the fingers would not budge. With mechanical precision, the heat slipped into every chink in his mental armour, exploiting every fear and doubt to gain entrance.

And then Mama Engine was in his head. The horrid infernal vastness of her tore apart all comprehension and blasted away his sense of the space around him. Oliver beheld a savage universe of pulsating desires given form in random and hideous shapes of iron, linked across distant leagues by strings of luminous, fiery coal. Through these tumbled the charred bodies of so many souls, worried at by shapeless creatures of molten glass.

The closest corpse turned to him and grinned.

"She fancies you, Mr. Bull."

Oliver squeezed his eyes shut against the sight, but it would not leave him.

The blistering heat on his neck woke him just enough to see the door shimmering through the shifting air before him.

The doorknob! He lunged forward. His hand exploded in a flaming ruin, but the door opened, and he toppled out into the shelves. Books fell on him. The floor struck him in the face. The floorboards scratched at his knees and palms.

He shouldered aside a bookcase that toppled into his path, kicked at another that reached for him from the side, struck a third with his fist. The lamp leapt from above in an effort to strike him, but he dodged aside and bolted for the door. It, too, defied him at first. Then he wrapped his charred fingers around the handle, planted one smouldering boot on the frame, and tore it open.

The little bell dinged. He was free.

Chapter 7

The first principle of the forge is Intention. It is this impulse, whimsical or practical, that has fevered Man for all his long ages. Man would temper this impulse oftentimes with the ethics and rationality of his own nature, but the impulse itself is slave only to its own needs. In this it is found that the words of scholar and madman have equal weight, for all creation is Holy, and the realm of the Divine.

Curse God for giving his power to creatures such as She.

—V. ii

Far away, a ticking.

As of a single watch passing its time in a vast space. It was peaceful. He lay in the warm void and enjoyed the sound, let it slide into him, let it overwhelm him, until he was nothing more than the watch's echo.

He felt a welling of sadness, as if his crushed body were weeping for him, and ignored it. All that was past him now. He'd gone beyond the fragile identities of a cruel and vulgar world. He had the void, this endless gap just beyond life, just before whatever came after.

He revelled in the stillness, inviting it into his broken mind and willing the few remaining pieces of himself to vanish into it. Lost in nothingness, every vibration ended, all momentum expended.

And he was happy for a time.

Then something else found him.

He could not tell what it was, for perception was different here, but it moved through the nothingness like a drop of dye spreading in clear water. It reached a limb for him, one too small to straddle the void.

He found no need to turn to face it, finding no existent directions to speak of. And that was beautiful in itself.

Who are you? he asked.

Its answer floated slowly to him, buoyed on an invisible ether. He caught the answer in outstretched limbs, hugged it, explored it. It was the frigid, shifting chill-warmth of the human body in sickness, and oozed a clammy toffeelike liquid into the void. The answer did not speak to him, and he was grateful, for the thought of human speech repelled and terrified him.

The answer dissolved into bubbles of oil and slipped from his grasp.

Who are you? he repeated.

His companion shifted closer, slithering through the spaces with the sinewy motions of an octopus. He could not see it, nor hear it; rather he felt it, like a piece of coarse wool dragged across the arm, or a trickle of sand running down the face. Its movements revealed themselves as might ripples in the wake of an invisible swimmer.

When it reached for him again, he stretched out to greet it.

A vision came to him.

No!

Pain. Fever. Sweat. Suddenly bone and flesh ensnared him, bound him, and he was screaming, *screaming*, as growths of metal broke his skin. He trembled and spasmed, scraping hot nerves against fibrous blankets on top and beneath. He shrieked again as hundreds of growths inside his body shifted with his shudders, tearing flesh and muscle, scraping and sawing at bones.

Light ripped into his eyes as he flung them open; noxious air seared his lungs. An unbearable cold slapped onto his forehead. Over him, a woman cried and prayed. Behind her, two pale-faced children wept and shivered.

Please end this. Please, I want to go back.

His stomach clenched and he vomited on himself. A rib cracked as he convulsed, and he clawed at his own throat with hands gnarled from age.

And suddenly he toppled back into the void, leaving the world of pain and light far above.

It was not the stillness that greeted him, but a seething boil of madness. It seized him and drew him into a fire of screeching monstrosities. Tiny metal monsters crawled all over him, biting and scratching, growling and gnashing their teeth. He withdrew as far as he could, shrinking into himself, but they closed on him, writhing.

Help us, they shouted.

Go away!

They howled in despair. They ran amok, driven by a ceaseless agony conjured with every movement and every breath. Their pain bled into anger and they fell upon one another in a cannibalistic frenzy.

At length, the creatures withdrew, leaving him in a pool of his own substance. Much of him had been broken and consumed. What little remained lay shuddering in that lightless place.

Gradually, the tick returned, and warm viscous fluid lifted him up. His companion settled into the dark beside him.

Are you the pain? he asked.

Words did not exist in the void. His companion encircled him with sticky arms.

I understand. You are the source of the machine-disease. The Mother's heat and the Father's noise hurt you, and you hurt them back, and that causes only more pain.

The thing wept tears of pus.

I will help you, he said. *I will help you to end it.*

Gratitude. His companion swept one long limb out into the void, and from immeasurable distance retrieved something that it laid before them both.

A tiny metal monster: a clickrat. This one lay on its back, jaws wired shut, legs bundled against its stomach. It did not thrash about. The bindings had prevented it from lashing out against its pain, and that pain had consumed it. It lay now empty and inviting.

A gift.

Aaron floated up and took it.

John Scared knew he was immune to the clacks, and he did not know why. The question bothered him, as all unanswered questions did. If he did not know the reason, he could not be sure of the result.

Perhaps that was why these poor, diseased wretches made him uncomfortable.

He leaned heavily on his cane. Below, dockworkers struggled to unload the goods descending by crane from two zeppelins tethered to the Aldgate spire. No single class seemed as afflicted with the mechanical growths as the dockworkers. They shambled around like parodies of men, covered in gleaming iron pustules, hobbling on malformed brass legs, and picking at ropes and crates with hooked hands and fingerless steel stubs.

Why don't you tell me what they are? he asked of the hot tingling in the back of his mind. *Are they the result of inhaling your breath, my dear? Little spores cast off by the belching of your long throat, nestling in places warm and wet and springing to vibrant life?*

"Tick, tick, tick," he muttered. A bad habit. He did it for no good reason, but that it might annoy *her*.

He lifted his gaze to the Stack beyond and watched it flare to crimson life. A cloud of black foulness like the tenth plague gushed up into the air.

Ah, my lovely, my dear, my sweet mistress. I do not understand you. Any one of your beloved children would be faithful to you until the oily grave took him, and yet you place your trust in me. You are a stupid, stupid creature.

John Scared was not averse to stupidity, as long as it was practiced by others.

He turned from the electric glare of the dock lights, hobbling like a cripple to the opposite end of the rooftop of the Pilot's Club, where Boxer hung suspended by his feet from a hook.

Astride the trapdoor leading to the Club's highest floor, where men gambled their livelihood away on fixed games, stood a broad-shouldered man in rigid military pose. Two shifting-eyed boys huddled together just forward of his reach. Scared waved at the two children.

"Come forward, my grubbers. Time for a lesson."

Scared read them as they advanced. Each piece of them became a variable: the motion of the eyes, the dip of the shoulders, the speed of the breath, the weight of the footfall. These he categorised mentally and applied against a mathematical function long ago devised, and the boys' personalities became plain to his understanding. The one on the left, called Shoe, was good for nothing more than spying and fodder. The one on the right, called Tuppence—that one could be moulded. Another Penny, perhaps, if there was time enough for more lessons.

"Did you know, children," Scared said, "that this hook was originally added to allow a piano to be hauled to the second storey? The piano fell and crushed the club's original owner." He turned to Boxer. "An accident. And a fortunate one it was for me, as it put the club on the market. Don't you agree?"

The man called Boxer hung mute and shirtless, facing the blackness of Bishop's Gate tower, and beyond that, the muted lights of London. His arms had been excellently bound behind his back by bands of iron—pounded into shape while still hot.

"Gather here, grubbers. You must see. Come, now, don't be shy or there may be no food at all."

Like hungry dogs they padded up, unconsciously rubbing their little tummies. Scared swept his arms wide, gathering them together in front of him. He settled his fingers on their shoulders, one hand on each boy, and thrilled at the warmth and the shivers he felt. He knelt behind, leaning over them so that the folds of his cloak encircled them like the wings of a mother bird.

"This man has done a bad thing," Scared explained.

"He has lied to me, you see. One may lie as much as one likes, so long as one tells only the truth to me."

He fetched his cane and poked Boxer's shoulder. The man slowly rotated around to face them. His chest had been opened, the skin peeled back and pinned to the edges of the torso. An iron plate had been riveted across his mouth. The children gasped and drew back against the rough wool of Scared's coat. He held them steady as they tried to hide their faces.

"Yes, it *is* horrible, my dears. Your reaction is nothing to be ashamed of. After more lessons—and there will be many more—I will teach you to appreciate the artistry of what our good hunchback has done here."

The military man behind them shifted the position of his feet.

Scared pointed forward with his cane, indicating the red glow that issued from between Boxer's exposed ribs.

"You see this, grubbers? Mr. Boxer's heart is not like yours and mine. His has been replaced with a coal-burning furnace, as have his arteries and vessels been replaced with pipes. Do you know what this means, grubbers?"

They did not respond. Through shudders and twitches, he watched bits of both of them curl up and die then and there. *Innocence crushed beneath the red meat of reality. A thing of beauty, is the growth of a child. Would you not agree, my love?*

"It means," he said, "that Mr. Boxer is a black cloak. He doesn't *wear* a cloak, of course. Being a deceitful man, he has endeavoured to hide his nature from me since he came into my employ."

Scared deftly flicked the latch holding Boxer's furnace closed. Boxer growled something unintelligible.

"That was his first lie to me. But he is a bad liar, and thus I have known about his treachery for some time now."

Scared passed his cane to Tuppence. "Go on, now. Give him a poke."

Tuppence reached up a shaking hand and wrapped his little stubby fingers around the cane's silver head. The polished mahogany gleamed red in the Stack's omnipresent glow. Tuppence stood still, eyes fixed on Boxer's gaping chest, as if unsure what to do next. John placed two fingers under the boy's arm and urged it up. With but a few hesitations, Tuppence reached out with the cane and tapped it against Boxer's side. He then quickly withdrew, shrinking close to himself. Boxer made no sound.

"Good, good," Scared said. "Did you feel the way the flesh bounces back? Elasticity, it's called: the pressure of moisture and fluid inside the body pushes the cane away."

The two boys nodded slowly.

"Give the head a turn, my child. Come, I'll show you."

Scared placed one hand over the boy's, gripping the cane's length with the other. Gently, he guided the little fingers in a slow swivelling of the cane's head. The boy jumped as a four-inch spring-loaded blade shot out the far end.

"Now give him another. In the same spot."

He let his fingertips linger on the back of the boy's hand as he withdrew. That was the softest part, between the rough knuckles and the bony wrist. *And very soft, indeed, on this one.*

This time Tuppence needed no coaching. He reached out with the blade and stabbed a quick hole in Boxer's flank, close to the kidney. Black oil-blood spurted out. Both children jumped back and John caught them with one hand against each small back. The blood splattered against the wall one storey down.

Scared gently retrieved his cane from Tuppence's shaking hand.

Using the cane's blade, he tapped on several of Boxer's mechanical parts as he spoke. "You will notice," he said, "that these parts of his shed no blood or oil, while these"—he ground the blade through a muscle—"shed plenty."

Boxer grunted but did not speak. John wedged the blade to a secure position between the ribs and left the cane hanging from Boxer's body.

"This man cannot be killed by the shedding of blood, grubbers. He has rejected the precious flesh given him by Our Lord, and embraced the fallacy of the machine. Now pay attention. I will show you how to kill such a man."

Scared seesawed the cane from its resting place and deftly flicked open the slotted door covering Boxer's furnace, releasing a pulse of red light and a wash of heat. He then carefully scraped out a thimbleful of embers, which fluttered down towards the glow of Aldgate Tower and vanished.

"Mr. Boxer's body is not heated by blood, but coal. Deprived of this substance, he will cool and freeze, and then he will rot like meat left too long untended. Whether he will actually die . . ." Scared shrugged. "That is up to Mama Engine."

And you do have a hard time letting go, don't you, my sweet?

He scraped the rest of the coals from Boxer's chest, leaving only a smattering of tiny embers coating the edges of the chamber. That done, he pressed the cane's blade into the rooftop and forced it to retract once more.

"I have one more task for you, my grubbers, and this lesson will be over." Scared dug out of one pocket two lumps of coal. He passed one to each of the boys. "Both of you will stand or sit, as you please, at the edge of the roof and offer him your coal. Hold your coal out to him as far as you can reach, and ask him if he would like it." He made earnest eye contact with each lad as he spoke. "Now, you are not to give him any, no matter his answer. Simply ask him over and over. Do this until I come back to retrieve you; then there will be as much food as you can eat."

The boys nodded, Tuppence more confidently than Shoe. John Scared guided them to the edge of the roof, his fingers gracing their delicate shoulders. He listened for a moment as their quiet voices made the offers, and Boxer replied with weak, muffled squeals. Then he left them to their work and hobbled over to the trapdoor.

"Something troubling you, Sebastian?" he asked.

Sebastian Moran rubbed his round chin before answering. "Not that I would doubt your methods, sir, but your treatment of Mr. Boxer is . . . unsporting."

Scared chuckled. "I do enjoy your outdated sentiments, my friend. I might have had him shot or tossed from the tower, but he presented an invaluable instructional opportunity for the children."

Scared shuffled to the dockside edge of the roof. Moran clasped his hands behind his back and kept with Scared's halting pace.

"Children are indeed a blessing, are they not, Sebastian?" Scared said.

Moran coughed. "I wouldn't know, sir. They don't make terribly sporting targets."

"I regret never having any of my own, you know," said John. "Though perhaps that was unavoidable, as no woman I have ever met seemed fit to bear them. Have you any children, Sebastian?"

"I wouldn't know, sir."

Beyond the docks, another zeppelin angled towards the dock's spire, cables already descending to be fastened on. It pitched and slid to its port as a gust of hot air from the Stack jostled it. The red, white, and black of the German empire came into sharp relief as the vessel floated into the powerful electric lights of the dock. The silence dragged for some moments.

Scared sighed. "No reminiscing tonight, eh, my friend? Very well. You have a report to make, I'm certain."

Moran nodded again, stiffly, and began in crisp military tones. "The Crown agent captured by the Boiler Men was named Aaron Bolden. My contacts in the gold cloaks report he was hooked to the Chimney soon after he arrived."

"I assumed as much. Even if he hadn't been, I don't expect any ordinary man to long keep his secrets in such hands." He rubbed a dull ache out of one elbow. "Bolden, though. I wondered who could have penetrated my defences. The man's knack with machinery is legendary."

"He's still alive, sir. Boxer's team failed to remove him."

"That was immaterial, Sebastian. I merely had to get

Boxer out of the hideout while I moved my operations
to locations unknown to him. He was a spy for the
crows, and though I am unlikely to be arrested on account of my high allegiances, I do not want the bother
of some ambitious young cloak causing trouble."

"I see."

"Von Herder will have a rifle for you by tomorrow
evening. Are you certain everything is in place?"

Moran snorted, incensed. "My men are not to be
doubted, Scared."

Scared laughed. "A mere prick in the flank to rile
you to superb performance, my friend. No disrespect was
meant." John squinted against a gust of wind kicked up
by the landing zeppelin's propellers. "Our dear baron
has far too much loyalty to his patron deities. It is a pity
his fate must be a messy one. It will be a stain on an
otherwise artful enterprise."

"Yes, sir."

John read the man's sudden uncertainty without having to look at him. "Ask your question, Sebastian."

Moran cleared his throat. "Again, sir, not that I doubt
your methods, but Grandfather Clock is only half the
problem. What will we do about the Lady and the
black cloaks?"

Scared looked out at the Stack's glowing apex. *What
indeed, my sweet? What shall we do with you?*

"Grandfather Clock is a creature of logic and precision," John said. "He allows neither change nor error
and can be handled in no way other than destruction.
Mama Engine, however, is a creature of sentiment, a
mother in truth. Leave her to me."

"Yes, sir."

"Our conference is at an end. Return to your men
and prepare."

"Yes, sir."

Moran quit the roof by the trapdoor, leaving Scared
alone with the distant clamour of the dock and the quiet
voices of the two children.

The children would run away tonight, shortly after
their meal. Repulsed by horror at him and at themselves,
they would hide in those holes they knew best. And in

a few days or weeks, when they got hungry again, they would return. They would endure more lessons to quiet their hunger. They would grow. Eventually they would see no need to leave.

Ah, I am ever accepting, my sweet. Ever patient.

The Stack threw its hellish glare into the sky. The heat in John's brain stem quivered, like a lover shuddering in a tight embrace.

But though we each love dearly our adopted sons and daughters, they will never be enough, will they?

Just think of what wonderful children we will make, once I have tamed you.

He turned from the docks to see if Boxer was dead yet.

Chapter 8

This is the crux of my self-made oblivion: I am not Job, who can endure endless quantities of earthly hardship, but a weak man and a slave to drink and opium. The hand that now pens these alien letters would have been my destroyer, but that They promised me an emptiness without emotion or memory, a release so much more profound than the restless slumber of death. How could I refuse?

And to my shame: even knowing what is to come, I do not regret.

II. iii

Oliver awoke to the cold.

It was not cold as he knew it. In the perpetual heat of the city, he knew cold to be merely a temperature at which one did not constantly sweat. He did not know it as the shriveling chill that now assailed him.

It was as if all the strength had been sucked from his muscles, all the sturdiness from his bones. He quaked uncontrollably, clutching feebly at his collar to draw it tighter. His heart lay still, his blood stagnant. His lungs scraped a minimum of air through chattering teeth, when he breathed at all. His body felt like a great hollow cavity, its sides ancient and flaking away.

He knew himself to be dying, and so did she. The subtle heat of her furnace miles distant played on the back of his neck. It beckoned to him with the promise of its warmth.

Oliver buried his creaking, shaking fingers in his armpits and waited for the darkness to take him.

Someone shook him.

"Ollie? Still with us?"

Oliver pried his eyes open. The world swished in front of him like soapy water.

The hand shook him again. It was warm and large. Oliver drew in a lungful of scalding hot air, which spread rapidly into his body, reviving him enough to speak.

"T-Tom?"

"He lives! Our own John Bull—knew we could count on you, chap. Looks like they gave you a grand thumping, though."

Two powerful hands slid under his armpits and scooped him up. Tommy's greasy stench enveloped him. Once released, Oliver staggered back into an uneven, moist wall. He drew in a second, deeper breath, realizing from the taste of it that his mouth was full of blood. He rubbed his eyes until they came back into focus.

He found himself in the courtyardlike end of a back alley that he recognised as being just off Petticoat Lane. Tommy's bureau-wide shoulders plugged most of the alley's width, but Oliver made out two smaller shapes behind him.

Tom looked like an aged sow happy her piglet had come home.

"Haven't seen you for almost an hour, mate. Feared they'd picked you off."

Oliver nodded but said nothing. Each breath brought him further back to wakefulness and gave his body more life. The muscles in his arms quivered and could move again. The cold fled, burying itself in the pits of his gut.

Someone had bandaged his burnt hand—recently, as the wraps were still free of blood and grime. The skin he could see between the wraps and his cuff was red from exposure. In his left hand, he still clutched a folded newspaper and his newly acquired copy of the *Summa Machina*.

His heart beat, and the sudden pressure of blood blinded him.

"Careful, old chap," Tommy said, propping Oliver upright with a meaty palm to his right arm. "Better get your head on. We've a slight change of plan."

One of the smaller men squeezed past and tossed Oliver a rifle. He snatched at it and dropped it, then bent to retrieve it and managed on the second try.

The shadows resolved themselves into Winfred Bailey Howe's broad moustache and humourless eyes. "Everything well in hand, I see," he said.

That roused enough ire to bring Oliver fully back to life. "You were to be here some time ago, if I recall."

Bailey's jaw muscles flexed before he spoke. "The murder of most of my men at our hideout necessitated an alteration in the plan," he said. "How did you come to be found in such an undignified position?"

Oliver started as he discovered that he wasn't entirely sure. He remembered the escape, then running into the street, crowds of people he recognised, then charred bones, then people again, then a blur. He tried to keep his indecision from his face as he concocted a plausible story.

It occurred to him that Bailey didn't really want an answer: he had already concluded that some pack of canaries had taken Oliver unawares, and that Oliver was a careless amateur. *Fine by me. I'm through trying to change your opinion, old man.*

"They got the drop on me," Oliver said.

Bailey loosed a guttural noise of frustration. "And the hand?"

Assaulted briefly by the memory, Oliver was tempted to actually tell the truth. *Fine idea, man: tell him you were visited and invaded by our mortal enemy—a sure way to earn the man's trust.*

"I burned it on a stove during the tussle."

"And I suppose they bandaged it for you?"

"No, sir. I escaped, then bandaged it. They found me again shortly thereafter."

Bailey nodded satisfaction, though his eyes still searched Oliver's face. "Walk it off," he said. "Mr. Moore, here, Mr. Macrae, and yourself are to accompany us to the downstreets. I've left Heckler in charge of the Underbelly."

Oliver's hackles rose. "You've given orders to my crew."

"Had you been among your men and conscious, I wouldn't have had to do it." Bailey spun on his heel and marched away, brushing Tommy aside with the sheer force of his presence. "We must leave immediately. Scared's group has several hours on us already."

Bailey and the man accompanying him strode away towards the flickering lights of Petticoat Lane.

Tom dropped his voice.

" 'Mr. Moore,' " he scoffed. "Like I'm a gentleman or some foolishness. So what happened, really?"

Oliver felt some tension ease away in the presence of Tommy's toothy grin. "I'll tell you when I sort it out."

"That's fair." He indicated the book. "Never fancied you for a reading man."

Oliver turned the book cover up. The title and author's name glittered on the front cover—inlaid gold?

"I was talked into buying it, I'm afraid." Oliver stowed it back under his arm. "We'll pass it to Michelle on our way through the square."

Oliver gestured to get moving, and Tommy began his clunking walk out of the alley.

" 'Michelle'?" he asked.

Oliver shrugged. "She tells me that's what she prefers."

Tommy grinned over his shoulder. "Does she now?"

Oliver did not have the energy to scry the meaning in that statement. Echoes of the flaming hell he'd glimpsed reverberated in his mind. It must have distracted him visibly, for when he next looked up, Tommy loomed down at him with a quirk of concern in his perpetual smile.

"Sure you're all right, Chief?"

Oliver nodded. "Fine enough to move my feet, Tom. I just . . . I never realised exactly what we were up against before. The Lord and Lady—they're not *natural,* Tommy."

Tommy nodded, jaw set, face grim.

Oliver sighed. "We're in deep-shit trouble."

"Wait until you see the Ticker Hounds" was Tom's answer.

It was a thrill to have a gun.

Just to hold it gave Missy tingles. The cold of it, the heaviness, the etched scrollwork on the cylinder—these things were alluring in a way, titillating almost. Her stomach burst with butterflies, and she turned it over and over.

"It's just a bitty one," said Heckler, who flinched every time she waved the barrel in his direction. "Think it might do for you, though, being not too bad on the wrists."

"It's marvelous," Missy said. "No wonder men so fancy the things." Her gloves whispered against the wooden grip as she wrapped her fingers around it.

Heckler held his hands slightly forward, as if Missy held something fragile. " 'S just a .38 and not much good beyond, say, fifty yards."

"Oh, I very much doubt I would be able to hit anything at that distance," said Missy. She took aim at an unfortunate sconce over a nearby doorway. "It is a fine specimen, as guns go?"

"Prettier'n most, if that's what you mean."

Missy sighted on a scuttling clickrat at the far end of the alley. "Forgive my ignorance, but I did not think guns were judged on their appearance."

"Oh . . . er . . ." Heckler shuffled a bit. " 'S all right in terms of power."

"How many shots would it take to kill someone?"

The American flushed. "Now, ma'am, that ain't no proper talk . . ."

"Oh, hush. You're beginning to sound like Tom and Phineas. Why lend it to me at all if you're just going to become squeamish and womanly?"

Missy smiled as the young man seesawed visibly between masculine pride telling him not to be womanly and masculine pride telling him not to be talked to in such a way by a woman. Eventually, he steadied himself, straightened his suspenders, and replied, "Depends on where you hit 'em, ma'am."

"Where would you suggest?"

"Uh . . . chest is good. Head's better but a harder shot. Stomach's good too, but real slow." Heckler swallowed. "Bad way to go."

"Is it."

The alley had one guttering oil lantern that had not been cleaned in some time. That and the light flooding in from Coll's Bystreet combined to give the metal a multitoned fire.

"Look, ma'am, you be careful with it," Heckler said. "It ain't no toy."

"I'm quite aware of what it is, Heckler."

"Well . . . just, I've seen a lot of folk shoot off their own fingers, or their brother's toes and such."

She shook her finger playfully. "Mothering me again, little man. That will not do." She dropped the gun into her small leather handbag, where it landed with an energetic thump. She hefted her handbag a little to feel the weight.

Heckler looked at her curiously.

"For protection, you say, miss?"

Missy smiled broadly. "Surely you cannot object to it in such times as these."

"Best protection's not to get shot at."

Missy swept past him towards the street. "Advice I'm certain you have ignored at every opportunity. Shall we?"

After a moment, Heckler followed her into the street.

Coll's Bystreet murmured under the meek blaze of four oil-fed streetlamps and one eye-stinging electric. People moved about it like shadows, spilling from the Beggar's Parade into Marlowe Square and washing about like leaves in a river. Hawkers, musicians, and beggars stolidly held their places, while pickpockets floated around the crowds like hungry ghosts. In the centre of the square stood a smashed, dry fountain. It had been a figure once, of what Missy did not know.

"There," said Heckler.

She looked up in time to spot three canaries crossing the square. Two were toughs, the kind of men she'd known too much of back in Shoreditch, in her previous life. The other seemed a gentleman of some stature, sporting an immaculate grey suit and silk hat. The electric light cut severe lines across their flowing cloaks.

"Now, where are you three off to in such a hurry?" she thought aloud, then to Heckler: "I'll take them."

Heckler nodded and moved off up the Parade towards the lift.

Missy took a vantage point on the front steps of a tenement on the square's corner, where she watched the cloaks jostle their way through the uncooperative crowd, who showed them only the barest of respects: a tip of the hat (causing the elbow to block the cloaks' path), a slight bow (therefore remaining in the cloaks' way a few seconds longer than necessary), a sales pitch (louder and more insistent than with anyone else). The tension of the crowd grew second by second.

They've not forgotten the Uprising, Missy realised. *Not a safe place to be a cloak, I'll wager.*

They were heading directly for St. Margaret Street. Missy slipped into the crowd to pursue. She had chosen today a large-brimmed, backwards-slanting ash hat, an oversized wool coat, and a tweed skirt. She had also neglected any makeup, and so blended in seamlessly with the Underbelly unfortunates in the square. Hiding from view was a new activity for her, unknown before joining Oliver's crew.

She'd always been a feast for the eyes. In her younger years she had fancied herself a succubus, like in the old fairy tales, stripping men of all qualities but lechery and stupidity. *And it was such fun—wasn't it, bird—to watch them drool over you?* And then things had changed, and the kindly old woman had turned out not to be so kindly, the men cruel and lustful and endless.

She brought down a wall on the memories. *It's over, love. Another life. A bad dream. You have Oliver now.*

And she had a gun.

And she'd killed. That knowledge shivered in her stomach with excitement and revulsion. It had been horrible, the feel of the act so base and vicious, and yet . . . the lecherous sot had gotten exactly what he deserved.

She felt a flush creeping into her face and dropped the sentiment behind the mental wall, returning her attention to her task.

Oliver's lessons in pursuit came back to her. *Stay behind crowds, greet people you know, look at shop windows, linger sometimes. Do not watch your fox too closely. It's your attention on them that they will notice first, even if they don't know you're there.*

So she greeted passing ladies, who gave her a polite smile, and passing gents, who gave her a lingering taste with their eyes and tipped their hats. She bought an ugly tin brooch from a vendor for a penny. She hurried when the cloaks vanished momentarily over a rise in the road or behind a group of locals, so as not to lose them.

You'd stick out like a brass boil if anyone was watching you, she said to herself. She checked around and found a few sets of eyes idly looking her way. Avoiding notice was not her strength.

She crested a rise in the road, where the lateral slant was so pronounced the buildings on the left were a storey higher than those on the right. From that vantage she could see the Blink, shimmering in the lamplight like a city of smoke—from which all the streets had been excised. The Blink's various roofs and balconies sported an improbable assortment of weather vanes and chimneys, lending the whole an appearance of an oversized pincushion. The cloaks hurried towards it.

The sight of the Blink stirred up memories of the German fellow she'd followed that morning. Raw stupidity, that was. She'd been lucky to escape with her life and person intact, and yet a part of her sat with crossed arms and pouted at the memory. *Why did he have to be such a gentleman? I could see it in his face, that sick, sinful desire, and yet he held back and didn't give me the chance to stick him.*

She gasped at that thought. One hand flew to her lips.

Oh, poor bird. What has happened to you? Suddenly her handbag felt a much heavier burden.

Well, she couldn't very well dispose of it *here,* and quite besides: it might be needed in the crooks and corners of the Blink. One never knew, in such a place.

She loitered out front of an apartment building—as if waiting impatiently for someone to meet her there—until the cloaks had slipped out of sight into one of the Blink's alleys. She counted ten heartbeats, then stole in after them.

She dogged them through the Blink's random turns, following with ease the tick-tock regularity of their footfalls. After a dozen twists, they stopped, and Missy crept to the next corner to listen.

"Where are we, you dullards?" one of them boomed.

"Dunno," said another.

"What?"

"Er . . . dunno, sir?"

"Harmony is built upon obedience, whatever-your-name-is. The spring turns the gear, and the more the gear protests, the less the efficiency of the whole." Missy heard something that could only have been a sharp blow. "So *be respectful!*"

"Er . . . yessir."

Their footsteps began again, and retreated off. Missy stepped around the corner and pursued them into a section of alley particularly twisted and misshapen.

A hand darted from a close nook and clasped onto her shoulder.

"That's right! Come on!" she screamed, whirling with one rapid step and plunging her hand into her bag. Heat and rage flared up in her so rapidly that she did not recognise the wide eyes until her fingers were at the trigger with her arm tensed to draw.

Two long-fingered hands waved surrender. "My fault. I ought to have learned from the last time I snuck up on you."

Missy gasped. "Oliver? You ass! Have you any idea what you almost made me do?"

Oliver grabbed her wrist and pulled her down a side alley. "Oh, I can imagine it."

She flushed. "I don't think you can. What are you doing here? What is all that?" She gestured to the pack Oliver wore, and the long rifle strapped to its side.

Oliver ground his teeth a moment before replying. "Bailey's called us in. We're going down, Michelle."

"Down?"

"Into the downstreets."

Missy stood stunned a moment, as the statement sank in.

I told you it would not last, bird, this fantasy of yours.

She crossed her arms to keep them from shaking. "And I suppose you're going to tell me you're coming back?"

Oliver's smile looked forced. "That's my plan, even if Bailey doesn't share it."

"You are a poor liar, Mr. Sumner."

Oliver adjusted his pack's straps and regarded her with a furrowed brow.

"I should catch up. I stayed behind only to ensure they didn't follow us."

"I suppose you should," said Missy hotly. "Duty to England and all that rubbish."

"Michelle . . ."

"I don't want to hear it, Oliver." *I don't want to hear you tell me you are not going to die, that I'm not going to have to go back to . . . to . . .* "If you must follow that madman to an early grave, who am I to get in your way?"

"I'll be back inside a day," he protested.

"I *don't* want to hear it! Your fool's crusade is your own."

"My fool's crusade is—"

"You won't come back. You know it; it's written all over your face."

"Oh, for the love of Pete—here."

He jammed a hand at her, holding a leather-bound book. Missy looked from his eyes to the golden letters on the cover and back.

"What kind of absurd gesture is this?" she said.

"I'm leaving this with you," he said. "I intend to read

it when I get back. I'm told"—his face relaxed a bit—
"that it's a ripping good read."

"Oh, now *there's* a reason for returning," she replied,
snatching the book.

Missy knew he was staring at her, but did not raise
her eyes from the golden script. As the silence dragged,
she felt an unwelcome heat creeping up her neck.

"Try not to give up on me," he said at last. "If all goes
well, we'll be eating gruel in Sherwood by morning."

Missy jammed the book in her handbag.

"Hadn't you better be off?" she said.

Oliver swallowed hard before replying. "I suppose I
should."

They shared a long look, filled with unspoken words.

Oliver turned and vanished into the alleys. Missy
stood alone for a while.

*Shall you make your way back to me now, little one,
or will you await the news?*

Be quiet.

He would have had faith in *her,* and so she would wait
until morning.

Chapter 9

An hour ago I severed my left hand with a hatchet. A new one has grown in its place. I now have fingers of brass and iron, fingers strong enough to accomplish my next task, which is the removal of my eyes.

II. vi

Oliver was afraid of heights.

"I'm not bloody afraid of heights."

Tommy snorted politely. "Come now, Ollie. You're white as a ghost."

"You clam up, Tom, or so help me I'll be riding you down like a sled," Oliver snapped.

Defiant pride managed to rise up and choke his fear for a few seconds. Oliver stepped up to the rim of the tiny ledge and raised his lantern high. The light, focused by a curved mirror of polished silver behind the flame, shot out into the dark, returning visions of smoke and the occasional gleam, indicating the presence of a sapling steel beam. Already the glass goggles Bailey had given him had begun to blur from greasy deposits that seemed carried on the very air.

He glanced downwards as long as he dared, charting

the treacherous hand-over-foot route down into Old Whitechapel. The "rusted stair" was a path over, under, and along the maze of beams that held up the Shadwell Underbelly and went on to support the Concourse above. The path, such as it was, had been marked by smears of yellow paint, the legacy of some long-forgotten explorer with more gumption than sense.

People in this city have a strange definition of the word "stair."

Bailey had led his team down first.

"How long, Phin?"

Phineas, reclining against the ladder leading to the public house above, had Tommy's captured clickrat, now eerily still, out in his palm. After a few seconds, he mumbled, "Eight minutes," and returned to his examination.

"Let's prepare, then," Oliver ordered. Bailey had directed them to wait ten minutes, and then start their descent.

Oliver adjusted the bandages on his right hand and the kerchief over his mouth, then buckled the clumsy express rifle over his shoulders, tightening the dual straps to keep it from swinging too much. He also wore a belt of ammunition about his waist, a two-quart canteen of water at his hip, and a pack on his shoulder into which had been stuffed dried jerky, kerosene, an extra face mask, a compass, a few more bandages, a matchbox, and one stick of dynamite.

"Why the dynamite, sir?" Oliver had asked.

"All men in my company carry a single stick of dynamite" was Bailey's answer.

His load secured, Oliver slipped one foot cautiously over the edge. "I feel like a packhorse."

"And look like a Swiss mountain hermit," Tommy contributed.

"More an Edinburgh vagrant," Phineas said, passing the rat back to Tom. "They can't climb either."

Oliver found purchase on the first dull smudge of paint, set his weight on it, and slowly lowered himself from the sane, flat, sturdy ledge into total structural madness. A gust of wind shoved him sideways like a soft but insistent pillow and he had to scramble for some minutes to find spaces for his other foot and his two hands.

"Bugger you both," Oliver spat through clenched teeth, that being the most scathing comment that visited him. He craned his neck around, spotted the next yellow marker, and began shuffling his way along the beam, thankful for once for the constant grit and ash that gave his fingers and soles purchase. Four agonising eternities later, he discovered two beams running parallel and almost level. Tommy trotted up behind him an instant later.

"Not so bad a climb, really," Tommy said, grinning.

"I always knew you were an ape, Tom."

"Apes walk on the ground, Ollie. *Monkeys* swing in the trees."

"*Lions* injure things when they are pestered."

Tommy guffawed merrily, having no apparent need for mask or goggles. "Our regular John Bull fancies himself a lion, then. Knighthood in the future, I'll wager."

"If it turns one into an arrogant sot like Sir Bailey, Her Majesty can keep it." Oliver fished a foot down for a suitable beam. The next marker lay some twenty feet below. Three steps later, with his nose pressed almost flat against an upshooting beam, Oliver beheld a clickrat skitter down and stop right before his face.

It's going to bite me, he realised. Slowly, he peeled his left hand from its roost, leaving his injured one bearing most of the weight, and reached for his derringer, then reconsidered and reached for the water canteen instead. One quick swat would do the job.

"Jeremy Longshore the Third hereby names you as his first knight. Arise, Sir Lion-upon-the-Cliffs."

The clickrat swivelled and scuttled up the beam, leaping to Tom's arm when it got close enough, then clambering down his jacket into his pocket. Oliver shook his head and clamped his hand back onto the beam.

"Good God, Tom, have you *tamed* that thing?"

"Jeremy Longshore cannot be tamed," Tommy pronounced. "That is the essence of him: solid will and indomitable spirit. He is the very symbol of perseverance."

Phin appeared behind him, panting. "Bugger that,

bolts-for-brains. He don't have muscles to ache or bones to pop about. Jesus, but I'm old."

"And cantankerous as well," said Tom. "Curmudgeonly, even. Perhaps churlish, if you prefer."

"Right, laugh. Enjoy that young body while you can. The clacks is like to eat you up by your thirty-fifth year."

Oliver gaped. "Phineas!"

Phineas frowned down at him. "Oh, don't be such a woman. I expect to wake up dead every morning with my nerves given out. Can't be easy on them, all this seein' and hearin' I do."

"But how could you say . . ."

Tom waved him silent. "It's all right, Ollie. That kind of talk doesn't bother me."

"You know what bothers *me*," Phin said. "Your new toy, there, is what. It isn't really a clickrat."

"Quite right," Tom said, warming back to his new acquisition. "He is such a picture of majesty as no clickrat could equal."

"I mean it in earnest, tin-teeth. It has a different seeming to it. Something different inside."

Oliver interrupted: "May we get moving? I would not lay odds on Bailey waiting for us."

He calculated the contortions necessary for the next step, and stretched out for it.

"In a sour mood, is our chief," Tommy said. His voice grew faint with distance and the intervening thickness of the air. "He needs the company of a certain good woman."

Nothing more was heard, not that Oliver would have spared the attention to listen to it.

Four marks and a thousand drops of sweat later, the faded light of the Underbelly above had vanished, and Oliver could not see the next mark. He unhooked the lamp from his belt and swung it in all directions, finding nothing but serpents of dust and ash coiling and uncoiling at random. The air moved, rolling past him like a great ocean wave. A rumbling sound passed with it, shaking the beams, like the breath of the Mother herself.

He leapt recklessly to his next perch, skidding a bit as he landed on a moist stretch of steel. Oliver scrambled to fight the platform's extreme slope, his hands flying out in all directions. His nails found rivets in the platform and dug under them. Pain pricked up his fingers; annoying, but better than the alternative. His injured hand skittered uselessly across the surface, unable to grip to anything.

I'm ill suited to this, Oliver concluded. He slid one foot carefully towards the more level beams running up the right side of the platform. Before him, the platform's slope ended in grey nothingness. Some of the toxic air slipped around his mask and down his windpipe. He coughed it out, violently, shaking as his chest caved inward. A burning sensation flared at the back of his skull.

The smoke turned and looked at him. Or maybe it was something within the smoke. Something, in any case, with eyes and a face resembling human. It blinked and was gone.

Oliver froze and tried not to breathe.

Memories of Mama Engine flickered across his mind and vision, playing on the currents of ash. Had that been something real, or the product of a violated imagination?

Oliver felt unmistakably like he was not alone. Quiet, indecipherable whispers reached out to him from a burgeoning fire at the back of his head. Eyes searching the smoke, he reached for his derringer.

When it appeared again, he swung at it—*through it*—as if it had never been there. The sudden movement twisted his left hand. Two nails tore out of place and gravity claimed him.

The face watched him slip into the dark.

Scared awoke to find the heavy curtains around his bed frayed and singed.

He sat up, wiping the drool from his chin onto his nightshirt.

You were angry tonight, my sweet. You were aggressive, savage. Quite out of character for you.

Mama Engine was not in the habit of keeping secrets from their embrace, and Scared found it irksome. Details and schematics had always been withheld—Scared cared little for those—but not her emotions, not her urges.

Those things that were *her* were his to peruse, his to catch and hold, and then release at his fancy.

Playing a game, my love? I am very good at games.

He roused himself and shoved aside the curtains. The room was cool and dark, the fireplace empty, the night table vacant. He dragged a knobby finger through the charcoal dust there and lamented the need to order servants to keep out of his room, lest his lover annihilate them: the wood paneling had been cracked and curled by heat, the floors stained with ash. The wan light of faraway electrics filtered into the room through its single, frosted pane.

He hobbled to a low-backed plush chair in the corner and dragged the leather cover from it. Beneath this, the fine velvet upholstery lay undamaged by heat, with a small bottle of yellowish liquid nestled against the left arm. Scared lowered himself into the chair's welcoming grip.

A strange night it had been. Towards the end, the nightmares had begun to creep in from the edges. They had come through the singed curtains; he was sure of it. The burns inflicted on those curtains by the night's lovemaking had weakened them somehow, and they had begun to admit all those outcast thoughts Scared had long ago banished to the far reaches of his mind.

He banished them now, clearing his head for the relentless chill of calculation. He retrieved and uncorked the small bottle, allowing the faintest scent of the liquid within to twist into his nostrils. Scared replaced the cork and settled back to let it do its work.

It is the chief folly of modern mathematics to confine calculation to the written page, Scared said to himself, almost as a mantra in the fashion of the Indians ascetics. *The scope of logical reasoning is too vast to be expressed in human symbolism. All objects in the universe are data, all forces equations. All events are the result of fast and fixed processes, algebraically perfect.*

His nose began tingling, followed by the rest of his body. His hands began to shake, but he paid that no mind now. The drug filtered into his mind, pushing the paltry needs of flesh aside, thumbing down the trappings of morality and emotion until only the endless order of everything remained. He breathed deeply, and dropped away from that chill, hidden room, into the spaces between molecules.

And now, my sweet, we will see what you have been up to.

He mentally pulled together the memories of her quivering essence as she had shuddered in his grasp. These he crystallised until every detail stood out like a diamond among stones, and then delivered them to the universe's equations.

He held his thoughts back and let the calculations run themselves. The touch of man could only sully such perfection.

Some long minutes he stayed in such a state. There was utter timelessness here, though mere seconds, perhaps, passed in the vulgar world.

The calculations delivered their answer. Mysteries became knowledge, variables became constants.

Scared leapt upwards and arrived slouched in his chair, the bottle of precious fluid rolling to a stop three yards distant—recorked, thank the Lord. He pressed his hands hard onto his thighs to keep them from shaking. Mama Engine had indeed been hiding a secret from him.

You filthy harlot, he thought. *You've found another.*

Her eye was on another man. A sudden, unbecoming tickle of jealousy nagged him. More calculation would be required to discover this rival's identity, but that would have to wait. Time and hot tea were required now to banish the remnants of the drug from his blood. He had taken too much this morning, enough to impair the flexing of fingers and bending of knees.

He reached out to the wall and pulled on the hanging cord. A wall panel, mounted on ceramic tracks and wooden wheels, slid aside to reveal a rack of bottles and tubes. At the base of the shelves sat a panoply of scientific equipment and a full washbasin. Still too tired to rise, Scared slumped back in the chair and took deep breaths to steady his heart.

The question now was what to do about his lover's new fancy. Death would be easiest, though the fickle

Lady might take that harshly. For the meantime, information would need to be gathered, control exerted. He might have delegated it to one of his boys, but—if she *was* courting another lover, if she *was* intending to betray him, the matter was Scared's alone to confront.

He let his body recover over the next few minutes, allowing automatic mental processes to wheel in the background of his consciousness. He had trained his mind so well over the long years that deduction no longer required any conscious effort. As soon as it was able, his mind would deliver to him the answers he sought. The potion was rarely needed.

Except when the deduction concerned Mama Engine—not her plans or her children; no, those were plain to the ordinary, mortal eye. It was the Lady herself that required the superhuman mental space brought on by the potion, which the Chinese called *mei kuan*. To fathom her, in her entirety, to know all the nuances of her psyche better even than he knew his own . . . that was a feat extraordinary in any set of lovers.

How many have you had, my sweet? How many have you burned to dust because they could not understand you?

He forced himself up, fighting the shuddering after-effects of the potion, and waddled to the washbasin. He splashed the warm water across his face, letting it chase away the sweat and ashes. A yellow-skinned *ghast* of the worst children's tales scrutinised him from the mirror.

If anyone were to see me like this . . .

What did it mean, her thoughts of this other man? Could she be plotting to betray him?

Do you think, my sweet, that you can use me and cast me aside? It is far too late, pet, for second thoughts.

And yet . . . she dared to spurn him.

Jealousy again, unwelcome and unbalancing. The calculations took space to function, and it would not do to have his mind so crowded with petty worries and grievances.

But . . . he had to know.

The bottle hissed as he opened it again, its previous agitation having pressurised the gas within. The blast of

scent speared up his nostrils into the sensitive flesh behind his eyes. Gasping, he squeezed the cork back into
place with hands already trembling.

I've taken too much.

The bottle clattered to the floor. No tickle came this
time, but a scraping fire under his skin. Scared grappled
at the arms of his chair. His knees cracked like dry tin-
der, and the floor rushed to meet him. A swift strike
against the boards, and he was away into that eternal,
infinite space.

He had never dared consume so much before, but as
the reaches of heaven glinted and soared all about him,
he never felt more regret for that decision. Even the
transcendent mathematics of the clear mind were inade-
quate to describe the sights he saw. More information
could be packed into a single mote of time than in all
the depths of human history.

Lover, I will tear you apart.

The memories of the Lady came in full relief as he
summoned them, playing before his eyes as if he were
witnessing them again from another body. The calculations whirled, visible now, spinning about him like a
flock of shining swallows, picking infinitesimal bits of
data from the memories to link together and compile.

His name, Scared demanded.

The image of Mama Engine flew apart in a ball of
fire, pursued to the ends of the universe by the relentless
churning of mathematics.

His heart wavered, fluctuated, collapsed. He felt an
omnipresent sting haul him back towards his lonely,
burned room. He fought it, letting that painful gravity
rake through him as he awaited the answer.

His name! Scared bellowed.

Mama Engine's flayed desires came back to him, piling
one on the other in his vision, each stark and plain.
He waited for the answer to come, burning more for
each moment he remained. Seconds passed, and his
mind began to shy from the vastness of the spaces
about him. Fear and uncertainty crept on his skin like
living things, and his nightmares frayed the edges of
his consciousness, sniffing for an entrance. There were

thousands of them—the twisted wretches of long-suppressed thoughts and memories. They scraped with yellowed nails against his soft mind.

Unable to bear it any longer. Scared fled upwards, pursued in his ascent by screaming legions of his own mental horrors. He swam up as fast as his wit would carry him, sinking his fingers into his own solid flesh even as the teeth of a forgotten memory clamped on to his ankle.

He crashed back into the burned room in a spray of imagined monsters, sparkling equations, and all-too-real vomit.

Lying on the floor, the spent remnants of the drug searing in his veins and organs, Scared began to snicker, then to chuckle, and after a few seconds he burst into wild, cackling laughter. The calculations had come together at the last second, and delivered him an answer even as he escaped to the uncomfortable refuge of his body. As waves of vertigo and nausea took him, he spat the name through crooked teeth.

"Oliver Sumner."

Aaron was happy for a time, sleeping in his new body in the pocket of this mechanical man who called him by another name. He dreamed of a dog, a little spotted terrier mutt of his youth that had chewed his toes to wake him every morning, then of a sunset witnessed from atop the chimney of his childhood home in Manchester—a moment of relaxation confounded by the dousing of the fire below.

Other dreams came to him as well, dreams of scurrying amongst garbage and dodging enormous feet, of the odd pleasantries of scratching and gnawing, and of the luscious feeling discovered once by licking up a sticky liquid spilled from a glass bottle.

He awoke wondering whether he had been a man or a rat, in the days before the void.

He uncurled himself and clambered out of the pocket. The world suddenly lit up with ambient vibration.

Aaron hooked his tail and his back legs into the fabric and leaned far out of the pocket to look down, seeing

only the fuzzy reflection of the streets, now not so far
below, and the ghosts that haunted them.

So very many ghosts.

He looked into them, using not his body's senses but
those strange knowings he'd had as a man. These souls
had a seeming of his companion from the void, as if they
were part of him, or he of them. Victims of the disease?
Wanderers lost to Purgatory?

He is the rot eating at the roots of the flower.

He clicked away the thought. What a very strange
notion. A human one, perhaps.

The mechanical man dug his iron fingers into a beam
and swung to the platform below with the grace of an
orang-utan.

The impact sent a vibration up the man's legs and
through his torso. The noise flashed like fireworks in the
strange eyes of Aaron's new body. He spun his rounded
snout to face his bearer's chest and drank in the vibrations there. Each manifested as a pulse of white across
the screen of his mind, outlining skin, bones, pumps,
gears, pistons, and the other features of the man's anat-
omy. There, too, Aaron perceived the taint of the void
dweller.

The void dweller had showed him this infection, had
showed him how it ended.

Or perhaps showed me its purpose.

A human thought again. Stuffy. Complicated. The rat
wanted to run and climb.

He scuttled out of the pocket, hooking on to the long
coat, and looked about.

"Up and about are we, Jeremy?"

The mechanical man stroked him on the snout with
his fleshy hand. The skidding of the hand's rough cal-
luses played a music of lights across Aaron's vision.
When the mechanical man spoke, his voice appeared as
a boxed and rough image not unlike the man's face.

"He's got quite the lead on us. Probably your comment about the vagrant, eh?"

"Pride is the folly of all men," said the old man, with
an audible grinding of teeth. "Particularly the young."
With a grunt, he swung himself over the same beam

and dropped gingerly to the platform. Aaron scuttled all around the rough wool of the coat, snapping at the lapels and nibbling the buttons.

"Right-oh, Mr. Philosopher," the mechanical man said. "Still, he shouldn't be *so* far ahead of us. You . . . well, you don't suppose he took a plunge, do you?"

"Unlikely, though he might have fell."

"Now you're playing with me, you codger."

"No, I'm proving my superior wit. Move that two-ton cauldron you call an arse out of my way."

The mechanical man chuckled, though it was a forced sound, betraying worry. His face creased perceptibly and he cast a halfhearted search around him.

Suddenly eager to help, Aaron opened his jaws and emitted a click. The sound bounced back and the area jumped to life as if lit with an electric torch. In a nest of twisting pipes some six or seven leaps distant crouched the third of their party, struggling to right himself and moving with obvious pain. Ghosts had gathered all around him, and floated in a rough sphere. The man pointed his rifle at one.

He should not be afraid of them, Aaron thought. He leapt from the coat to a nearby beam, clipping on to one edge with his six limbs.

Follow me, Aaron cried, surprised to find nothing more than a click and a whirr escape his throat.

"Your pet's escaping again," the old man called.

"His Majesty is merely flexing his legs. Exercise serves even the greatest of men," said the mechanical man, "and rats."

Aaron found himself clinging upside down as he approached the nest and the ring of ghosts. He had never realised before that they were solid—after a fashion. Air currents shaped through them, defining their features in layers of continually shifting ash and smoke.

He clicked at them. Two turned to look.

The sudden movement startled the besieged man, who swung his rifle about and let fly. Aaron's senses exploded for an instant, as if the atmosphere had turned solid. For a moment he stumbled, swaying above the drop.

"You unsporting bastards," the mechanical man bellowed, "hiding out there like foxes on the moor! Have the decency to shoot me to my face."

Another blast rang out, followed by three more. Each obliterated Aaron's senses, until he teetered on three limbs, tail flailing and jaws gnashing for purchase.

The beam glittered into being.

"Christ—Tommy, it's me!"

Another shot. Another blinding field of white.

The body shuddered and gave out. Aaron dropped from his perch.

The air splayed rivers of light across his vision, rippling and gorgeous, flowing from nose to tail.

Will I die when I land? he wondered. *Will the rat live? Will the man?*

The rat screamed with rat terror and went limp at the behest of its instincts. The man turned his eyes downward and despaired.

I do not want to die. There is still so much left undone.

Memories came to him, then: images of other men like himself who were his friends; of a vast city of wasted human life; and overshadowing all, two towering creatures—one of brass, one of iron; one a hammer to crush the soul, the other a mouth to devour it.

He remembered his own name. He remembered his mission.

Joseph! Help is coming!

His buzzing rang from the beams as he fell.

Bullets sparked off the beams all around.

Oliver squashed himself farther into the tangle of piping and clamped his hand down over his hat.

The last ricochet bounced into oblivion and the pipes hummed with dissipating vibration. It would be a minute before Tommy's clumsy hands could reload.

"Are you quite finished?" Oliver yelled.

The answer came back meek and wavering. "Ollie?"

"Yes, it's me, you sot. Didn't you hear me the first two times?"

"Well . . . there was a good deal of noise."

"What, were you itching to mount me on the parlour wall?"

"You shot me first."

"I didn't know you were there. I was shooting at . . ."
Ghosts? He slumped back against an irregular bend in
the pipes, wondering if he really was losing his sanity.
Maybe it was the height, and the thought of all those
seconds of empty air before impact with a beam or a
quick end on the streets below.

Something Tommy had said tingled his mental bell.

"Did you say that I shot you?"

"Clean through the chest," Tommy called back. "I
will, of course, be charging you for the clothing."

"Are you all right?"

"Aside from the hole? The picture of health. I might
mention, as well, that these express rifles were a fine
choice—hit like rhinoceroses."

Oliver shook his head in disbelief. "Can you see any
way across, Tom?"

"Can't say I see much at all. Only way's a thin couple
of pipes that a monkey would balk at."

Oliver squinted, but could make out little against the
grey air. The dull glow of Tom and Phin's lanterns
bobbed in the distance like a two-headed will-o'-the-
wisp. He retrieved the matchbox from his sack and lit
his own lantern, which had blown out during the fall.
The light revealed only the immediate nest of pipes and
the two Tommy had mentioned, which zigged and
twisted and looked thin and frail besides.

"Looks as if there's no way across, gents," Oliver
called. "I'll descend from here and try to meet up."

"Aye, Captain. Last one to the ground buys the
round!"

Oliver felt certain Tom was saluting.

The will-o'-the-wisp moved on downward. Oliver
leaned the express rifle against two close pipes and
began to reload. He might have told them about his
twisted ankle, he supposed, but that would have only
worried them enough to attempt a foolhardy rescue.
What sort of leader required a rescue? And he'd been
embarrassed quite enough today, thank you very much.

In fact, it seemed all he could manage lately was to
make a mess of things.

Well, I have two uninjured limbs, at least. That's enough to affect a climb.

He made to rise, then retreated back to his uncomfortable nook as the pain flared in his ankle. He clipped the lantern to his belt and began to massage his throbbing muscles.

After a few minutes' rest, he tried the ankle again, finding it sturdy enough to bear weight. He rose, buckled his sack and rifle to his back once more, and fished around for a possible route of descent.

Eventually he settled for an angular assortment of pipes and wires that resembled a ladder as one may have looked in an opium dream. The descent proved no more or less troublesome than previous ones had, and before long he had set foot on wide, solid beams.

He stopped to rest, sipped at his canteen, and polished his goggles to clear his vision. The human-seeming wisps of smoke had gone, but the burning in his mind remained, dulled, as if fallen into a light slumber.

Dark and heat and height had begun to take their toll: he felt exhausted. He downed another sip of grainy water and thought of Missy—Michelle. She never let anyone else call her that. Why hadn't he noticed before?

Because it was just another of the woman's damnable mysteries, that's why. She liked her secrets, that one. She had a look, he reflected, a queer expression that crept onto her face in certain instances of Oliver's kindness, which she hid behind a quickly crafted smile. Perhaps it was to keep him guessing, perhaps for other reasons—he might never know.

His train of thought breached the point at which it became more uncomfortable than continuing the descent, so Oliver stowed his water, checked his straps, and shuffled to the platform's edge.

No more yellow paint. Nothing below but a mass of near-vertical pipes slick with condensation; nothing to the sides but silent ashfall; the only way onward, a treacherous slide down the pipes with no peripheral means to reduce speed. His injured hand stung just looking at it; his guts clenched and squeezed like kneaded bread. He spoke just to get away from his own thoughts.

"For our great and noble queen," he said to himself, then shook his head. "We'll do the strangest things for a lady."

He flung his feet off the edge and dropped himself over.

"Peculiar, that," Mulls whispered.

Bergen did not bother to look. Mulls had been repeating those same words over and over for the past hour. It was a jungle fear—the fear of silence. Those few rich men and journalists he'd taken through Africa in earlier days had shown similar reactions, talking gaily and commenting on every damn thing as if noise alone would keep the snakes at bay. When he told them to keep quiet, they curled up like chastised little boys.

But he needed Mulls sharp, and so tolerated the outbursts.

By now they were well below Aldgate Tower, and it was past two in the morning. Another hound attack had left Bergen's shoulder burned by the heat and chafed by the steam rifle's straps. Penny had come through, doing much better with his flasher than with a rifle. He now held the flasher's copper-tipped striking rod in front of him like a knife at all times, and his other hand effected a constant slow rotation of the charging wheel at his belt.

The boy didn't seem to tire. He stood watch during their rest stops, took lead on climbs through rubble and old buildings, and even ranged a bit when Bergen stopped to get their bearings. His stance never wavered from its catlike grace, and he did not relax for even an instant.

He is an animal, that boy, Bergen thought. *A predator born by accident in a human womb.*

Aldgate had an underbelly, though its residents preferred to call it a "subconcourse." In an effort, perhaps, to raise their status, they had installed a dazzling array of electric lights all across their ceiling and in their streets, and it leaked through the haze into the downstreets with enough power to illuminate their route as by moonlight.

That light allowed Bergen to keep better tabs on Pennyedge. Bergen's senses had been alert for some time to the boy's attempts to circle and approach him from behind.

Bergen led them beneath Aldgate to the side closest to Commercial Street Tower, where their quarry was reputed to have fallen. The two towers were so close as to be nearly leaning on each other, with the outward-sloping base of the Stack mingling into their support beams.

The stench was vile. Aldgate residents, with their rich variety of imported foods, produced some of the most pungent shit Bergen had ever had to endure. Its odour cut through even the omnipresent stench of ash and smoke. They had passed earlier one of many vast septic pools, centred seven storeys below the primary sewer drains, and they had all nearly choked on the air.

"Peculiar," Mulls muttered.

Bergen forgot himself and snapped: "Can you make any *other* comment?"

"But that's someone moving, that is."

Mulls nudged his rifle to the left. Bergen's eyes shot to the location indicated.

Someone moving. Not a hound, or a clickrat, but a man, crawling.

"Penny, flank."

The boy vanished to the right without a second glance.

"Mulls, cover him."

Mulls nodded, then ran off to a suitably high out-cropping of rubble, where he nestled his bulk between two rotten beams and set his rifle's barrel atop the remains of a plaster wall.

Bergen carefully set the steam rifle down, then reached for his Gasser. His right hand shook under its weight as he lifted it, so he decided to leave it holstered. He was a fast enough draw with his left.

He approached from an oblique angle, through ruined buildings rather than along the old street. If his quarry noticed any of them, he gave no sign.

Bergen examined the man through the rotted holes of his hiding place: definitely human, crippled, struggling to pull himself along on his forearms, dragging unmoving legs behind like a grotesque train. Bergen spotted a flat, circular case wedged in the crook of his left arm.

And there's our prise.

He stood. The quarry noticed him immediately, staring dumbstruck for a long moment as Bergen approached. Then the man erupted with laughter.

"You find something funny?" Bergen growled.

The man gagged, coughed up brown oil, then resumed laughing.

Bergen squatted down. The man's fit choked itself out, and between ragged breaths he tilted his face upwards. Only one red eye blinked up at Bergen, the other having been destroyed by the fall along with the entire right side of the man's face.

"Yer not one of Bailey's men, are yeh?"

Bergen shook his head.

"I should have known better than to hope. For a moment I thought the lad might have devised some flying machine after all. Yeh here for the tape?"

Bergen nodded, and held out his hand.

"Bugger all." The man hung his head for a moment. "Not much to be done about it, looks like: won't be no running, nor fighting. Just answer one question of a dying man and answer true."

"Fine."

"Are ye gonna use it?"

"Yes."

"Well, there's a due turn o' luck." The man grabbed at the case with his left hand. The broken fingers scraped over its surface, unable to close together. "Mind?"

Bergen retrieved it for him. He wiped some of the slime and blood from it on his trouser leg. The broken man, relieved of his burden, collapsed to the concrete.

"Now," he said, his voice muffled by the wet ground, "will it be a mite of conversation, or should we get on with the shooting?"

Bergen slipped the sidearm out of its holster with his left hand. "I am curious how you managed to survive the fall," he said. "I expected to find a corpse."

"Oddest thing," the man said. "I've no heart, apparently. Rest o' me broke like twigs, but this thing in me chest kept pumping away. The lad knew, somehow. He pushed me over, murdering, brilliant, young man. He knew I'd survive." He chuckled. Oil burbled up from his mouth.

Aaron Bolden. He was an extraordinary man, my friend.

Bergen felt a powerful yearning to comfort the dying man, to tell him that his sacrifice would make the difference in the rebellion. Bergen made a quick check of the surrounding street: empty, with twenty feet to the nearest obstacle. If he was there, Penny would hear, and so Bergen said nothing.

"I have a daughter," the man said. "Beautiful girl, big-boned like her mother. She was going to move to Edinburrough with a tramp of an Englishman—a coal-backer, of all people! Loves the chap, though."

Bergen nodded, already agreeing to the next request.

"Ellie McWhyte," he said, "though she might be Ellie Pearson by now. Just give her me love."

"I will."

"Yer awfully polite for a German fellow. You have a name, so's I can put in a good word with St. Peter?"

He should shoot the man now—end this conversation, this dying attempt at camaraderie, before sentiment put him in danger, but Bergen had been living amongst thieves and villains so long that a few words of an honest man glittered like honey in his ears. It was stupid, but the man deserved to know he was dying beside a friend.

Bergen leaned close to the man's ear, so that his lips almost touched it as he spoke. He dropped the German accent and let his native Dartmoor shine through.

"Nicholas Ellingsly," he whispered. "Rest in peace, friend."

Bergen stood and shot the man through the forehead.

The sight of the twitching body sewed shut any hint of sentiment. When Penny appeared out of the dark at his side, Bergen's expression had become as cold as before.

And now you know I shoot left-handed. Well, who are you going to tell?

"Five minutes for food and rest. Then we head back."

He walked back to the steam rifle. Penny's eyes narrowed to razor slits and followed him step for step. Bergen stripped aside his mask and took a pull of water from his canteen, trying to quell the nagging fear creeping up through his stomach.

For the first time, Penny had come right up behind him, and Bergen hadn't noticed.

Chapter 10

The second principle of the forge is Method, or perhaps Technique. The artisan must be skilful in all aspects of Her craft. Such perfection comes only from long practice, which inevitably litters the floor with the misshapen remains of Her failures.

—V. iii

Missy had not been truly introduced to drink until she met Thomas Moore. Matron Gisella had laid down strict rules concerning imbibing by her girls: they were not to have any at all, except if the client bid it. Even then, they were to touch scant a tenth of what the client consumed. Missy had rarely had occasion to even smell brandy or scotch, as the majority of the customers were upstanding, proper gentlemen who came into the Matron Gisella's house to vent their carnal lusts and then flee into the night like robbers.

Sit up straight; fold your hands across your lap. Hold your head upright, your knees together. You are a shy, naive gentlewoman.

Missy drained her glass and poured another. The brandy seared its way down her throat.

No, she had been introduced to drink truly on the

third night that she had been invited to Sherwood Forest. She'd walked in on them unannounced, unobtrusive as she had been trained. Thomas had been caught mid-swallow, choked on his mouthful, and then scrambled to hide the glass by slipping it half full into his pocket. Thinking back, perhaps she'd wanted to spare him the embarrassment.

She'd stepped over to him, relieved him of his drink, and tossed the whole of it down her throat without so much as a sip to gauge it.

Your sleeves shall be crimped and even. Your hem shall be free of stray threads. Every hint of lace shall be sparkling white.

That vile liquid had been the strongest of Tom's collection. It had taken all Missy's aplomb to remain upright and charming as the fire surged into all her limbs, then her brain and her lips, and then lit her cheeks like twin suns rising on a winter morning.

But she'd held her composure and had reigned in her laughter at their gapes. And for one glorious, memorable evening, the matron's voice had been silent.

You shall move to reveal not ankle nor wrist nor neck lest the client bid you or take the initiative himself. Should your client wish you to surrender to his advances, then do so. Should he wish you to resist, do so.

The glass was full again. She started in on it without delay.

Sherwood stood empty. Heckler had taken watch at the lift with a pair of street urchins Oliver held sometimes in his employ. The rest of the crew were likely rotting in the downstreets by now, and Oliver with them.

She swallowed, and examined the amber liquid as it caught and mutated the light of the single oil lamp.

Always remember that your client has paid for you. I expect that he should come away satisfied and that he should return to my house when the mood next strikes him. I expect to be spoken of highly in the circles. A lady has only her reputation, after all.

More brandy scalded her throat. Since that third night at Sherwood, she had made alcohol her daily tonic, to keep the Matron Gisella silent.

She poured the brandy onto the floor, for tonight it had lost its power.

A good lady doesn't cry. Only if the client wants you to cry shall you permit yourself. Oh, don't worry yourselves; he will make it amply clear.

Gisella was lecturing from some long-ago memory. Missy had heard the speech dozens of times and remembered it perfectly: always the same wording, the same sharp gestures, and the same piercing glare.

She stomped one foot into the puddle of liquor. Droplets splattered her dress and shoes.

You wouldn't approve of this at all, would you, Witch?

My, my, isn't someone testy? Have you a reason for throwing a tantrum like a child of six?

Missy refilled the glass. She sipped it, realising suddenly how light-headed she was.

What if they didn't come back? What if Bailey's mad crusade left them all corpses and Sherwood stayed this empty forever?

Then you will come back to me, my little one. When you were brought to me, you were coated in dirt and crawled on your hands and knees. You were born a dog, little girl, by God's hand. That kind of filth never truly comes clean.

She felt oily inside and out with perspiration. It was too cruel to contemplate, that her new life should be wrested from her after three short months. Oliver had not even asked where she came from or what she had done before. Nor would he, or any of them. Here she had found men who did not judge her, and a place to rest her feet.

Her throat cringed as the brandy scorched it again and she refused to think on such things any further.

A rap sounded at the door.

Oliver had told her never to answer that door. One of the men should always do it and even they should always be armed. The caller was to be checked by peeking from the second-storey windows, and the door traps released only if it proved to be one of the neighbourhood folk.

Well, Oliver wasn't there, and she had a gun. Even if

things became dangerous, she could defend herself. It wasn't as if she hadn't done so before.

Gisella had been silent that night as well.

She drained her glass and tottered to her feet. The world spun. She snatched the lamp from the card table and her handbag from the chair. She politely forced the doorjamb aside and staggered into the hall.

The rap came again.

"Hold on," she cried, though it may not have emerged so eloquently.

Each stair smacked heavily against her feet as she descended. The railing pressed inappropriately into her side.

The rap sounded again, suddenly pounding against her ears like thunder.

"You, sir," she said accusingly to the door, "have no manner of patience at all."

Her fingers found the right switches, pulled the right chords. The deafening clicks told her Heckler's traps had been withdrawn. She grasped the handle and yanked the door wide.

A face stepped out of her nightmares and into the foyer.

"Oh, mother of mercy!" The handbag fell from her fingers. The lamp tipped and burned her hand with its hot glass.

"Heh. I see you remember me."

Her knees buckled like so much wet cloth and she crashed to the ground on her tailbone. The lamp bounced on the floor and rolled away. *It can't be real,* she screamed. *He can't be here.*

The intruder righted the lamp with a deft flick of his cane.

"Gisella was distraught when you left, Michelle. Even my considerable powers of persuasion were barely enough to keep her from murdering you."

The man closed the door.

"Imagine my surprise to find you here, of all places, in the lair of my recent rival. The Lord does indeed move in mysterious ways. Don't you agree?"

A hobgoblin face beneath a fur top hat. Gnarled

bone-white clawed fingers reaching from a black coat as large as the night sky. All the girls knew him, all had felt his nails tearing at them, heard his voice commanding them. Gisella rendered them helpless with her potions and then *he* came in fevered dreams, a visage of terror half remembered upon waking.

Sweat slicked her hands. The floor tilted and rolled as she scrambled for the bag, and for the cool, comforting lump of steel inside. Suddenly he was in front of her, squatting. He jammed a handkerchief over her face and a jolting ozone stench blasted up her nose.

"The yellow man calls this *beng lie,* my dear. It is Gisella's favourite, as I recall."

Her nails raked over the handbag's edges, spinning it towards her. Her legs and fingers began to twitch, then to numb.

"Gisella needed my help to train her little whores, you see," said the man. "You were one of my earlier attempts, as I recall. Probably, there is no one to blame but myself for your present waywardness, but I was new to this then. One learns, doesn't one, child?"

The clasp of the handbag fell apart beneath her fingernails and the bag yawned wide. Her fingers snaked inside, the motion in them dying one by one. The muscles in her back jerked and she collapsed, knocking her head on the floor.

You didn't think he would find you, you stupid girl? You came into the world dirty and vile and pretend at decency. It is God's will that you be found.

The edges of her vision swam with tears. The room swung like a pendulum. The man crouched like a gargoyle next to her, reaching skeleton hands for her face.

"Gisella will give me a tongue-lashing, it's true, but I'm afraid I shan't be returning you to her just yet."

His fingers pressed into the skin of her forehead and scalp. The contact burned and sent shoots of pain deep into her head and neck.

"I had to look to the East for this process, you know," he said. "It requires a certain exercise of the mind and the energies, but it makes Mesmer and Braid into simpletons by comparison."

His words blurred, one into the other, until they hissed and crackled together. Missy slipped deep down into a warm pool of thick liquid. His voice came to her in flickers of dream thought, as flashes of hot and cold and terror.

"Listen, now, little one. Follow carefully my every instruction. You will not remember any of this until I command you. When I do so, you will answer all of my questions truthfully and without evasion. You are to remain with Oliver Sumner. Do as he asks, and act as you always have. Remember all you see and hear."

A pause. Mind distant across expanse. No movement. Scared cleared his throat.

"My dear, I want you to discover why the Great Mother finds Oliver Sumner so attractive."

Missy vomited on herself. She choked, spat, sat up.

The foyer was empty. A single lamp lit the dark from its place on the floor some three feet away.

Oh, goodness. The mess! My lord, the smell!

She scrambled to her feet, gasping in horror at the hideous stain on her blouse. She snatched the lamp and fled to the bathroom. She filled the washbasin with water from the room's iron bathtub, then stripped off her shirt and submerged it.

If you put your coat on and run straight home, they'll never know. Just bundle the shirt and take it in a basket—surely they keep a basket somewhere.

Filth follows you like a hungry dog, dirty girl.

Shut up, you shrew.

Missy held the lamp up and surveyed herself in the mirror. Her hair had fallen out of its tight bun; her lipstain had run down the length of her chin.

"Not right at all," she murmured.

She screamed and jumped back, nearly dropping the lamp. She'd seen . . . No, it couldn't have . . . But it had been there . . . an ogre's face grinning at her from the mirror.

It wasn't him. He wasn't here.

His voice whispered to her, from far away or from inside her own ears, she could not tell.

"Tick, tick, tick."

*   *   *

At the first sound Oliver unhitched the express rifle and lugged it into his arms. At the second he had it butt to shoulder ready to fire.

Damn it, this was not just a product of his imagination. Something had been stalking him for the past hour.

He didn't even know where he was. He thought he was heading northeast, though after the long, confusing slide down to street level, he might have gone any which way. His hip-mounted lantern provided only enough illumination to see three strides around him. He probably stood out like a lighthouse down here, though he'd rather that than be in complete dark.

The sound came again: a heavy crunch, a shifting of debris out in the ruined buildings of Old Whitechapel. His bandaged hand twitched on the stock and the single unwrapped finger on the trigger.

When the streak of white blasted into the light he'd let the shot off before he even had time to register it. The heavy slug escaped into parts unknown, kicking Oliver nearly off his feet with the recoil. He stumbled and brought his rifle to bear on the object approaching him.

It was a clickrat. Moving slower now, it tottered forward on its six legs, maw opening and closing in random rhythm. The noise had been far too loud and slow to be from a clickrat, and that left one plausible alternative.

He'd hoped to catch up with Bailey's crew before the hounds found him. It should not have been difficult to spot seven lamplights in absolute dark. Most of the buildings of Old Whitechapel had long since decayed into lumps of sodden debris, so the terrain was mostly clear, but multiple trips to the tops of said mounds had garnered him nothing but more black all around.

And probably brought me to the attention of every whelp creature down here. Damned foolish.

The clickrat ticked a few steps closer. It sat back on its stubby tail and wailed a low buzzing sound, then tilted its head and regarded him in a pose resembling curiosity.

"Jeremy Longshore!" Oliver said. The clickrat bounced back to its legs and scuttled up next to his shoe.

Oliver smiled down at him. "You clever little bastard. You must mean Phin and Tom aren't too far. *Tom!*"

His voice echoed away into the dark. A growl like glass being ground down reverberated back to him.

Stupid. Oliver swung the express rifle back into position and began scanning the shadows as much as his fogged goggles would permit.

Jeremy Longshore hopped a foot forward and bobbed his nose in a direction to Oliver's left. Oliver swiveled to face the rifle that way, just as a black and silver shape broke the perimeter of the lamplight.

He put a bullet into its shoulder. The hound twitched, but did not back off.

Jeremy Longshore leapt forth and confronted the creature, balancing on tail and two rear legs and clicking into its face. Oliver shot the hound again, this time in the flank as it reared back to take stock of its second opponent. The impact jerked it to the side, but it barely seemed to notice, its attention fixed on Jeremy Longshore.

Oliver swept away the gun smoke with his left hand, keeping unsteady aim on the hound as it circled right, its sleek muzzle poking into the clickrat's striking range. Jeremy Longshore stood his ground, emitting an unceasing string of clicks in patternless rhythm. Oliver orbited the clickrat as well, keeping it between him and the hound.

The thing would eventually figure out that Jeremy was bluffing and crush him. Could Jeremy keep its attention if he bolted? Oliver had no delusions about outrunning it if it chased him.

The hound paused and dipped its head. From deep inside its silvery, steel-sheathed ribs, Oliver heard a ticking—like someone tapping a wooden spoon on a large pot. After a few moments of overlap, they began to tick one to the other, then the other to the one. Back and forth: a conversation.

Oliver squinted hard at the pair. For an instant, the hound seemed to have a human face, indistinct and blurred, like a botched daguerreotype. The face tilted and changed, shifting into and out of expressions that

Oliver could not quite identify. Jeremy, as well, took on an aspect far more human seeming. It was something in his bearing, in the gestures made with his front two legs.

The conversation ended, and for a long moment the two stared at each other. Then Jeremy dropped to all six legs again, and the hound turned and slunk out of the light. Jeremy Longshore ticked a few times and scuttled back over to settle beside Oliver's shoe.

Oliver remained perfectly still until the hound's receding footsteps passed into the distance. Then he lowered his rifle and breathed.

"You're a handy fellow," Oliver said. Jeremy clicked. "Remind me to stop thinking that Tom is crazy."

Oliver considered the mechanical animal winding around his feet. Tom hadn't had time to train the thing to do what it had just done. Jeremy himself was different from his kin.

"Can you lead me to Phin and Tom?" Oliver asked, thinking it was worth an attempt.

Jeremy clicked and buzzed, then started off at a fair clip into the darkness.

"Slow down!" Oliver called, and limped after.

The creature led him on a chase past tumbled beams, ruined buildings, and pits of dank slime. The rotted underworld passed through the arc of his lamp, fading into view from illuminated mist and seeping back into the absolute shadow of Shadwell Tower that flanked him and loomed always over his shoulder.

He scrambled along as best he could, hobbling on his ankle as the pain swelled with each step. He called out again and again for Jeremy to hold back, but the little creature tore ahead, hell-bent on whatever goal it had chosen. It escaped the range of his lamplight as they entered what might have once been a public square; the constant jumble of beams, debris, and upturned chunks of roadway gave way to an unbroken succession of tightly fitted bricks.

The pace wore on Oliver's lungs. Even through the mask, the air was coarse and heavy with particulates. The heat, unnatural even for Whitechapel, provoked an unending sweat that beaded and ran down his neck, slick and sticky in the oily air.

Panting, Oliver finally halted the mad dash. Holding his breath and his nose, he carefully lifted the mask and splashed some water in his mouth. It tasted of ash, but calmed for a moment the tickle in his throat and the rampant thirst drying out his lips and tongue.

Out in the dark, the skittering of clickrat legs faded. *No use trying to follow now.*

He set himself and his rifle gingerly down on the brick and rubbed at his ankle. He scanned his surroundings and made out nothing beyond the flickering lamplight but for a far-off glow. It might have been a hint of the bright lights of Aldgate.

If so, then that way was northwest, where Bailey's crew would be heading. *And since I couldn't possibly trace my way back to the stair . . .*

Oliver wiped his goggles, chewed a piece of jerked beef, and put some more oil in his lantern. After a few minutes' rest, he struggled back to his feet and began walking. For twenty or so steps the bricks rolled beneath his feet, unchanging. Then he came to a low wall of concrete, topped with a twisted and rusted wrought-iron fence: too tall and too uneven to climb. He unhooked the lantern from his belt and lifted it up. The light cast dancing doppelgangers of the fence on the wall beyond. Something twisted and fled as the light struck it.

I hope that was Jeremy, Oliver thought, knowing it wasn't.

Oliver tilted the light farther back, revealing the façade of a building reaching high above the fence's top. Mortar had worn away between the blocks used to build it, leaving deep black slashes on its pale surface.

A sudden scuffing sounded from behind the fence. Oliver hefted his rifle to face forward in one hand, then leaned into the fence and panned his lamp back and forth. The gap between the wall and the building seemed devoid of anything, including debris. A sparkle caught his eye at the far right of the lantern's light.

Red? He took a few strides down the wall to the right.

Red and yellow and purple and blue, a jumble of colours glowing in the flickering light. It resolved itself into the shape of a stained-glass window.

It's a church, he realised, then smirked. *A white chapel.*

He panned his lantern upwards, revealing an arched top to the window, a peaked roof, and hints of a steeple at the light's farthest edge. This was not a church as he knew them, as little decrepit buildings constructed from scrap and tolerated by the cloaks so long as they stayed that way. No, this church was a magnificent structure, designed to stand out from the city around it, bold and proud. It was a piece of that London spirit that Hews and Bailey always went on about. Oliver felt a welling of uncomfortable emotion: some mixture of pride, longing, shame. What was he supposed to feel at this sight? London wasn't his city. England wasn't his home.

Maybe it could be.

When the clacks sounded behind him he knew it was already too late to run. He hooked his lantern to his belt again and wrapped both hands around the express rifle. He took a deep breath, held it, let it go. Then he turned.

Faces: brass eyes, steel teeth, iron bones, and long snouts. Shapes: canine and simian, some hunched parodies of human, even sporting a few last remnants of flesh and hair. Not a sound from any of them, nor breath disturbing the air.

Oliver's own breath and heartbeat suddenly became thunderous.

The circle was tight against the wall on either side. He counted seven hounds, maybe two dozen clickrats of varying composition, a legion of Frankensteins behind that had once been men, fading shadow over shadow to the edge of the light. None of the clickrats sported the silver colour of Jeremy Longshore.

He fitted his bandaged hand around the stock and curled one finger on the trigger. The barrel shook wildly. *Hold together. You've been in worse spots than this— remember the battle in Marlow Square?*

Only that had been Boiler Men, and Boiler Men were slow. One might run away.

Oliver risked a glance over his shoulder. The fence might be scalable, if he abandoned his pack and his rifle.

The dogs could leap it, or might simply bite through. No good.

Oliver skipped his eyes back to his grim audience. There had to be a route of escape. He noted two gaps wide enough to run through, assuming the hounds held still. He could maybe hold them off with the rifle . . .

All of them? With the clickrats and . . . those ghastly things?

His breath began coming in staccato pulses. There had to be something else. Could he toss them some meat maybe? Or . . .

One bloody stick of dynamite.

With numbing slowness he shouldered out of his pack and slipped it to the ground. He knelt and reached inside. The dynamite slipped into his hand as if it had been waiting for him. The matchbox he clasped between two fingertips.

His eyes never left the horde around him. The snouts and muzzles and bared skull teeth began to shift, taking on more human features. They became rounder and softer, a shifting image of translucent flesh over the metal beneath, like a trick of the smoke, a trick of the light, the unhinging of a tired mind. A chill touched the air.

Hold together, he thought, repeating it like a manta.

Oliver set the butt of the rifle on the ground and leaned the barrel against his leg. With his left hand, he slid the matchbox open, then plucked a match out with his right.

One toss. How many could he catch in the blast?

The metallic heads continued their stares unbroken. The phantom images dipped as one, as if in prayer. The air grew cold.

Oliver laid the match head against the edge of the box.

A wind cut across the square. Yellow-green mist

began collecting in the empty space between Oliver and
the hounds. It lapped at the stones and the feet of the
creatures, seeping into cracks and between toes and
claws. Oliver stayed the match, retreating back against
the fence. The yellow mist, blackening as it swept the
brick, began a steady undulating pulse. propelling itself
along the stones like an inchworm.

The ground began to boil.

Oliver stuffed the dynamite in his pocket and leapt
for the fence. His injured hand landed on a rough-edged
slat of iron that tore into the bandages. He wrapped his
other arm into a tangle of bent crossbars and held himself up by the sheer strength of fright. His legs kicked
for purchase, scuffing the edge of the low wall.

Below, the square suddenly became a seething lake of
black-yellow pus. Bubbles churned to its surface and burst,
spraying up into the air. Tendrils of yellow mist snaked up
beside Oliver's face, then swept over him with a rank
odour of decay. They got in his nose, his throat, his ears.

And something crashed through into his mind.

Not this time, by God! Oliver released one hand and
grabbed for the dynamite, and at once the world evaporated.

He was hanging above an endless sea of filth: blood
mixed with oils, ashes, white and yellow ichors, and pus.
Above loomed a sky of towering grey fingers, their steel
ends lancing into the ocean. Bodies swam the seas,
drowning, choking, flailing, bloated and pustulant.

Oliver hung from nothing, having lost all perception
of his body. He clawed with no hands at the iron fence
he knew to be there.

A figure came walking across the ocean, stumbling
over the roiling bubbles. He wore an oversized long coat,
speckled with additional pockets, which the spurting filth
did not seem to touch. He fixed Oliver with startling
blue eyes.

"You're Oliver Sumner," he said.

Oliver clung to the invisible fence, still trying to secure
his feet.

Who's asking?

"My name is Aaron," he said. "Aaron Bolden."

Could I trouble you for some assistance?

His slight smile flattened. "I'm not sure how."

Perfect. Oliver gave up on his fingers and tried to will himself to stay above the frothing liquid. *You're the Aaron, aren't you? You know, Hews and Bailey speak very highly of you.*

"For watching, perhaps; for intelligence. I haven't had much luck with action, I'm afraid."

Hews mentioned that you had certain faculties of sight.

"And so I do."

What do you see?

"Do I see you hanging off a fence, you mean? Yes, you're there."

With a mental sigh, Oliver concentrated on loosening his grip.

"No, no. Don't drop down," Aaron said hastily. "It isn't real, but it may still harm you."

How do you know that?

"I . . ." A sudden jolt of pain stole across the man's face. "Grandfather Clock . . . hurt me. The noise wasn't real, not in the auditory sense, but it was still . . . I remember my bones breaking."

Oliver looked up and down the man's limbs. Aaron followed his gaze.

"It's strange, I know, that they're intact now. Though I'm not quite dead and may thus retain a bit of myself."

Bailey said they'd hooked you to the Chimney.

Aaron's hands began to tremble.

"I . . . true . . . though I . . ." He inhaled, still shaking. "I should not be alive. A thousand times I should not be alive."

You seem quite alive to me.

The small smile returned.

"A conclusion drawn from observation. I suppose I can accept that."

Oliver looked around, seeing no visible means of escape. He realised with some relief that his sense of smell did not appear to be working, nor could he feel fatigue in his clinging arm, nor nausea in his gut from the vile sights. The sloshing and moaning of the ocean's prisoners echoed undiminished by distance.

Where are we, Aaron?

"We are inside his mind."

Whose mind?

"The third one," he said. "Not the Lord, not the Lady.
Someone else."

I would hope I heard you wrongly.

"Except that you heard perfectly."

Aaron began to pace beneath Oliver.

"I have gathered through my limited observation of
him that he is an exile of sorts. He hates the Lord and
Lady so powerfully . . ." Aaron's eyes flickered almost
closed. He tilted his head as if craning to hear a sound
Oliver couldn't hear. "They've done something to him,
I think, to hurt him, to cause him pain. That's what all
this is." He swept his arm to indicate the sea. "His
pain."

And those? Oliver said, casting his glance at the moaning souls slipping between the waves.

"They are those of us who have been claimed by the
downstreets, and the machine disease."

You know that?

"He . . . showed me."

Has he claimed you as well, then?

The man's face fell. "I don't know."

Oliver thought for a moment as Aaron stood caught
in his melancholy.

Would he help us, do you think, Aaron?

"Help us? This is not some Titan that can be bribed."

*You said he hates the Lord and Lady. Well, if Bailey
does his job, we will have what we need to kill Grandfather Clock, but we may need help with Mama Engine.
We haven't even begun to look at how to deal with her.*

Aaron hunched his shoulders and glanced out across
the ocean. "He hates *us* too, Oliver."

Then we'll have to deal with him as well, won't we?

Aaron sucked in a breath. "He could very well have
heard that."

*Talk to him. Offer him an . . . an agreement. Between
him and myself. Let him know we have common enemies.*

"Are you certain about that?"

*No. It may turn out to be the most fool thing I've ever
attempted, but it's prudent to keep your doors open.*

The cries of the damned hammered on Oliver's ears.
He struggled to keep his concentration amidst rising
panic.

At last, Aaron nodded; then his eyelids began to
flicker again. Oliver hung for an endless few minutes as
his impromptu companion performed whatever inward
gyrations the contact required. Doubt worried at him—
What are you thinking, allying with this horror?—but he
quashed it with logic: one of these unholy creatures was
easier to deal with than three. That made sense, didn't
it?

Aaron jerked and came back to himself.

So? What's the word?

Aaron shook his head. "I can't tell. I know he understood." Aaron took a deep breath, rubbed his abdomen
absently with one palm. "But this doesn't feel right.
What if he turns on us after . . ."

And suddenly Oliver was hanging from a fence, with
his left arm cramping and a stick of dynamite in his
right hand.

The ground rushed up to meet him. He landed
squarely on the already-injured ankle, toppled forward,
and slammed cheek first into the brick. His stomach
clenched and he barely had time to tear the mask off
his face before yellow and white vomit surged up and
out. After that, the scalding air rushed in and he hacked
up more vileness. Vomit be damned, he slapped the
mask back over his mouth and took long breaths until
his lungs settled back from convulsions to mere searing
discomfort.

Bugger.

He pushed himself up and leaned heavily on the wall.
His pack and rifle lay where he'd left them. The lamplight guttered out, disturbed by its rough treatment. A
few minutes of exhausting struggle found a match struck
and the flame reluctantly wiggling back to life.

A silver, eyeless snout regarded him from just past
his shoes.

"Jeremy?" Oliver said.

The rat shook its head.

"Aaron?"

Jeremy ducked his head and clicked backwards and sideways without turning. Oliver lifted his gaze slightly and found the glinting brass eyes of his choir staring back. They'd stepped off to the sides. A clear path spread in front of him, out into the dark.

Jeremy backed some more and ticked three times.

"Jesus. Give me a minute."

Oliver took a pull from his rapidly emptying water flask and fixed his mask. Then, with aching joints and muscles, he collected his gear and his rifle and pushed himself to his feet. He kept the dynamite and the matches in his pocket.

Jeremy turned and scuttled away. Oliver followed at a slow limp. When he'd gone twenty feet he heard noise and turned.

Ticker hounds and clickrats and half-human Frankensteins gathered behind him. He stepped forward and they followed. He started again at a steady pace, and they trailed behind him like a herd of cattle . . . or a pack of wolves.

Guess we know his answer, eh, Aaron?

Albright had fallen with a bullet in his throat.

Kinney had died screaming with a hound tearing into his belly.

Sims had crawled nearly thirty yards with a severed arm before the Boiler Men cooked him like a pig with their copper rods.

Phineas had just vanished, and he'd last seen Thomas Moore assaulting a Boiler Man with his bare hands.

And who had run away and hid himself in the shadows of old Mile End Road?

Bailey crouched behind a piece of rotted and soggy wall, once the façade of a building, and clutched his rifle to his chest. It was an old Enfield from his days in the army, made in '41, and it had seen him through worse snags than this.

Worse than metal beasts impervious to bullets at war with metal men equally impervious?

He silenced his own thoughts to better hear the movements of the enemy.

The Boiler Men had been waiting right at the base of the rusted stair. Phineas Macrae had been the first to spot them. They might have been waiting for hours, not needing air or rest or water. Luck was with the queen's agents, however, as the Ironboys were some ways off and facing away from the stair, as if waiting for someone to return to it. Bailey had ordered retreat, hoping to slip away and circle around outside their field of vision.

Then the dogs had come at them, tearing out of old shop doors and from beneath the uneven flagstones of the street. Nothing Bailey's crew had thrown at them had done anything to slow them down. Then the Boiler Men had caught them, charging impassively into the fray and killing everything in sight with Atlas rifles firing as fast as Maxim guns and copper lightning rods lancing through the perpetual night. At some point Bailey had ordered retreat and fled.

There had been noise, then silence. Now there was only the thudding footfalls of the baron's soldiers patrolling the perimeter of the street, and the shuffle of their guns poking into cracks and beneath rubble.

Bailey held one lapel of his vest over his mouth and sucked a breath. His mask had vanished in the fighting, along with his lantern and half his ammunition. He squatted, sweating, and fiercely willed himself not to cough.

He wished for a moment he was back in India, where the heat was not so oppressive and the enemy died like men aught to. But Boiler Men did nothing like normal men. Even their movements were strange, executed with the confident, measured precision of creatures who knew themselves to be invincible.

A foot fell on the other side of the wall. Time to move on.

Bailey sucked one last burning lungful of air, blinked the soot from his eyes, and crept backwards from his place of concealment. The old shop's floor had rotted and fallen through, and had formed a shallow crater into which Bailey retreated. He slipped silently into a viscous pool at the bottom, cursing the lack of light.

The Boiler Men seemed to have no need for illumination, and thus hid their movements. Worse, Bailey could not see far enough through the smoke to determine how visible he might be. Did the sides of this hole provide any cover at all?

He exhaled his held breath quietly and drew another through his lapel. The Boiler Men could not be stopped with a single Enfield rifle. It would be at least another two or three hours trekking though these depths to reach the base of Aldgate Tower. Bailey had no mask, no eye protection, no water, no food, and thirty rounds of ammunition that were useless against such adversaries anyway.

But the tape had to be retrieved. No matter the cost, those horrid godlings of Whitechapel had to be dealt with.

"Praise to England," he muttered to himself. "God save the queen."

The oily liquid moved.

Tentacles shot out of the pool at the base of the hole, entangling his legs with terrible speed. In an instant the faithful Enfield was readied and a shot plunged into the opaque waters. Whatever lay beneath spasmed with the impact. The tentacles contracted, shredding though Bailey's trousers with serrated metal edges. The sting of sliced skin shot up through his spine, followed by the blazing fire of slime in the wounds. A second shot shattered the water's surface, sending up bits of metal and gore. The tentacles shuddered and fell limp back into the pool. Bailey staggered from the water, collapsing on the bank of the hole.

A ness. Damn it—how could he have been so careless? He tested one leg to see if there was any tendon damage. *Flesh, mostly. Good. First order is to get out of this blasted hole.*

He planted the butt of his rifle in the muck and pushed himself up.

A shot rang out, and a portion of Bailey's arm exploded.

Another, and a force like a charging elephant bore him to the ground, smothering his face in the clinging mud. White pain flared in his back and abdomen.

His gasp drew in the unfiltered razor smoke of the downstreets. Choking, he clawed at the slick, cold earth and cursed every machine built since the dawn of history.

The ground shook with the approach of iron boots.

Chapter 11

How many worlds They have consumed, I cannot fathom. How many small creatures They have leashed to serve Them—I cannot count them all. How many ghosts have been thrown screaming into Their bellies, I dare not guess.

What I do know is that They will continue in Their way until the end of the universe, for They are machines, and machines do only one thing, over and over.

—II. xvii

Pennyedge had to be killed.

In the short time since retrieving Scared's precious tape, Bergen had discovered he could not bring himself to take it back to its creator. He knew he couldn't stomach serving that troll one instant longer. The horrid things he'd done to maintain his cover mounted on his conscience with each step, freed to haunt him by the act of mercy just performed. He had to escape. He had to bring the tape into Bailey's hands and rejoin his true comrades in arms.

His cover might have been blown anyway. Scared

would not have sent his child-killer along if he didn't at least suspect.

And so Penny had to be killed. Mulls as well, as an inescapable consequence. That saddened Bergen a bit, for Mulls, if he had escaped Scared's trap and been raised by decent folk, might have become a decent man. Penny was a monster and Bergen spared not a scrap of remorse for him.

The question was *how* to do it. Penny was sharp, and as silent as a snake in the ferns, and was at every opportunity manoeuvring for a killing stab on Bergen. He probably wouldn't strike until Bergen led them to within sight of the rusted stair, which gave him perhaps two hours of time.

He passed up several opportunities to take his shot—times when Penny was beyond the range of a good lunge and scanning the dark after some suspicious sound—because Bergen was unsure of what to do with Mulls. How many shots would it take? Would the bullets even hurt him through all those mechanical growths? Mulls might have to be down long enough for Bergen to hit him with the steam rifle, and that was a long space of time indeed.

They passed a mound of sodden and collapsed debris on their right. Bergen heard the click of metal tines on stone. He drew his sidearm with his left hand, and aimed it into the dark. Penny spun the wheel on his flasher, then dropped into a crouch and spread his arms, knife in one hand and striking rod in the other. Mulls, after a moment's delay, brought his rifle up to his shoulder, though he apparently did not see anything to aim at yet.

A clickrat scuttled into the radius of their electric lights. Mulls let off a rough chuckle.

"Ha. Just a littl'un."

"Quiet!" Bergen hissed. The clickrat stopped and began to make buzzing and ticking sounds. Bergen tuned it out and listened to the other sounds of the dark around them. He let his ears guide his weapon, until its aim rested at the top of the mound.

"Come out where we can see you," Bergen ordered.

Mulls started and locked his rifle onto the same location. Penny did not move.

The voice came back. "We have you surrounded. Throw your weapons on the ground."

"There is only one of you," Bergen said. "And there are three of us. Can you shoot us all, do you think, before we kill you?"

The enemy fell silent, considering, Bergen supposed, what to do now that his bluff had failed. It was an opportunity.

"Boy, rush him," Bergen whispered. "Mulls and I will pin him down."

Penny turned his head just enough to examine Bergen in his peripheral vision, and did not move.

"What are you waiting for, boy?"

Penny's fingers flexed on the handle of his knife.

He knows. It must be now.

He reaimed his weapon and fired at Penny's back, but simultaneously, the youth darted to the left, ducking under the swing of Bergen's arm and dodging entirely the arc of fire. A clean miss.

Mulls, perhaps misinterpreting the action, fired his rifle at the hidden man on the mound.

Penny had spun about, quick on his feet like a dancer, and had already covered one of the two strides necessary to slip his blade into Bergen's throat. Bergen flicked his arm into position and discharged directly into Penny's chest. A spark exploded there, and the bent remains of the flasher's striking rod flew smoking from Penny's hand as he closed the final step.

Quick.

Bergen slammed the butt of his pistol onto Penny's stabbing arm as it swung in. The strike cracked soundly on bone, but an instant later Bergen's flank split with the passing of the boy's blade. Numbing shock spread like lightning into his left leg and arm. His follow-up swing went wildly askew as Penny darted past.

Another shot rang out and Mulls tumbled to the street in a spray of blood and oil. Penny pivoted on the ball of one foot and plunged the knife towards Bergen's belly.

Bergen locked the fingers of his right hand around the

boy's wrist, keeping the knife still. Penny yanked away but was held prisoner of the older man's greater strength. With a kind of calm and deliberation, Bergen planted his revolver against Penny's chest and blew a hole in him.

The youth spasmed and fell, releasing the knife. Penny writhed and sputtered across the flagstones, gurgling and choking—the first genuine sounds Bergen had ever heard him make. Bergen raised his weapon and sighted on Penny's head.

"Don't move!" came the command from atop the mound. The hairs on Bergen's neck tingled.

"Lower your weapon," Bergen shouted. "In a moment we will talk face-to-face, but these two must be eliminated first."

"No one else dies without my say" came the reply. "Throw that pistol on the street and we'll converse like civilised human beings."

Penny gasped in a shuddering lungful of air. He began to look around and take stock of his situation; his right hand fished into the pocket of his ragged trousers while his left clutched at blood streaming from the bullet hole.

Bergen held his aim steady. "I am an ally," he yelled. "A comrade of Sir Winfred Bailey Howe. I am not your enemy."

Unsteady footsteps approached from behind, twitching at Bergen's instinct to spin and face the danger. The unseen man did not sound experienced in combat; Bergen could probably cut him down before the man got a shot off, but he dared not take his eyes from Pennyedge. At his left, Mulls began to stir.

"What you are," the voice said, closer now, "is a man who just gunned down one of his own."

"Weren't you listening? I am a comrade of Winfred Bailey—"

"Don't think that tossing that name about gives you any clout with me," the unseen man snapped. "Place your firearm on the street. The boy isn't going anywhere."

"You are a damned fool," Bergen growled. He sank slowly to his knees and planted the barrel of his pistol against the street. Slowly, eyes on Pennyedge, he un-wrapped his fingers from the grip one by one.

Something of the predator slipped back into Penny's expression. Bergen locked gazes with him, trying to read into Penny's eyes. The boy's gaze broke for a moment and flicked to their captor, now only a few paces behind Bergen.

I am the only danger to you in the next few seconds, boy. Attacking him will only gain me the time to kill you. You must attack me.

Penny's right arm tensed. Bergen's fingers tightened back around the pistol's grip.

Penny's throw was awkward and slow. Bergen had his weapon up and aimed by the time the small knife departed Penny's hand. His finger yanked back on the trigger.

A blast splintered Bergen's left ear. White muzzle flash blinded him. Chips of stone and concrete exploded up from the street and Bergen's shot went wildly right.

Cursing, he blinked the sparks from his eyes and fired blindly after the blurred shape fleeing into the dark. An instant later, the gun smoke cleared and the only available targets were a red stain on the street and a cast-off electric lamp rolling to a tired stop.

With a burning fury Bergen stood, whirled, and cracked his captor across the face. The man clattered to the street, a heavy express rifle spinning from his grip. Bergen straddled him as he fell and jammed the pistol against the man's nose.

He was tall, over six feet, and thin. A flat-topped ash hat, slightly askew, barely hid his tangle of unkempt hair. Goggles and a mask mostly obscured his features, but he appeared to be smiling.

"You seem to have me at a disadvantage," he said.

Something yanked at Bergen's heel. The other man slapped Bergen's pistol aside and scooted from beneath him with surprising speed. Bergen ignored him for an instant and kicked away the clickrat gnawing on his boot.

He swung his weapon back towards the other man before even turning his head.

"He's developing a taste for shoe leather," the tall man said.

Bergen squinted at the man's firearm.

"My two shots to your one," the man said, with almost a shrug. He held a two-shot derringer in his right hand—a hand bandaged and obviously injured.

"You've been counting," Bergen said. "Do you honestly mean to hold me hostage? It is a long way back to the Shadwell stair."

"It's only until we decide what to do with you. Do you have a name?"

"I am Bergen Keuper, originally of Stuttgart, recently of Egypt and Sudan. And yours?"

The man considered a moment. "John Bull."

"That was impolite," Bergen said. "I spoke truthfully."

"We're spies, my friend. None of us are generally truthful." He gestured with his weapon. "Don't pretend ignorance when I ask this: do you have the ticker-paper?"

"Yes, I have it."

"Lay it on the ground."

"*Herr* Bull, you seem to be under the impression that you have an advantage over me. Allow me to elucidate our situation. Your derringer, while sufficient to wound me at this range, is no match for my Gasser. You must also realise that, as I am losing blood, I will be forced to end our standoff in short order. If you will not step down I must kill you."

"And you, Mr. Keuper," the man said with a twitch of the eyebrow, "seem to be under the impression that I am here alone. As I said, *we* have you surrounded."

"Do not try to bluff me, *Herr* Bull. If there were other men in your party, I would have heard them."

"I don't doubt it—*if* they were men."

Bergen squinted at the man. *He's bluffing, surely. I'd have heard . . .*

He let his senses expand, let the focus of his hearing drift and the primeval jungle awareness of ancient man predominate. Silence—but not empty silence. The silence of a tiger watching its prey. The silence of an unseen snake curled to strike. Dozens of watchers, all around.

"Jeremy," Bull called. "Bring a few up closer, if you'd be so kind."

A sudden string of ticks; the skittering crawl of a clickrat; heavier steps following. Into the light lumbered two monstrous hounds, a full hand taller than any that they'd fought earlier, with exposed gears churning along their shoulders and back. Soundlessly, they opened their enormous jaws and let oil-saliva slide out between savage teeth. The silver clickrat scuttled forth.

"Thank you, Jeremy," said Bull, then to Bergen: "There are quite a few more."

"Yes, I know." Reluctantly, Bergen lowered, then holstered, his firearm. "How?"

"Not your concern, Mr. Keuper," said Bull, also lowering his weapon. He popped the derringer into his coat pocket. "The tape, if you'd be so kind."

Bergen kneeled and began to shrug off his pack and the steam rifle. "I must know who you work for."

Bull considered a minute, then nodded. "I work for Bailey. Against my better judgement sometimes, I admit. I assume you work for John Scared."

Bergen snorted. "No longer."

"You were the inside man, then."

"I was."

"That settles that, I suppose," Bull said. "Since you can imagine what would happen to you were you to turn on me, I suppose I can trust you at least that far, eh?"

Bergen grunted. He reached into his pack to retrieve the tape. His first impulse was to unravel the steam rifle and try to make a fight of it, but he stifled that. "I have told you the truth. You have not even told me your name."

A muffled crack sounded from the right. Bergen and his captor spun to see Mulls, silhouetted by his own lamp, firing his air rifle into the dark.

Bull was the first to react. "Stop! They won't hurt you if you don't . . ."

Bergen turned his eyes away and said nothing.

A half-dozen scraping growls went up, followed by a

crash. Then Mulls' lamp sparked and died, and Mulls' screams began.

"Jeremy!" Bull cried. "Stop them! Get them off him."

The silver clickrat sat still and did nothing.

He had to die, Bergen reminded himself. *If only the bullet had done its work.*

Bull stepped closer to retrieve his rifle. Bergen clamped it to the brick with one powerful hand.

"What are you doing?"

Bergen set his face and eyes grim. "He is loyal to Scared. This cannot be avoided."

What's one more atrocity, after all the murder I have done for that man? Bergen thought. He stared into the younger man's eyes, wide and quivering behind the goggles, until the screams stopped and the tearing and crunching began.

"He could have been taken prisoner," Bull said quietly, venomously.

"He would have realised that bullets do not kill him and then turned on us."

Bull faced the horror perpetrated upon the dead man's corpse, though the dark hid it. With the breaking of that gaze Bergen felt something die inside him. He quashed the sting of it, and refused to mourn. *I sacrificed my soul to this work long ago.*

They sat in reverence until the feast ended and the silence rose once more.

Bergen released his grip on the man's express rifle. Bull held out his hand.

"The tape."

Bergen handed it over. Bull slipped it into a pocket, then snatched up his weapon and his pack.

"Gather your property and let's go."

"I know the way back."

"Then you lead."

Bergen hefted the steam rifle and his supplies back onto his shoulders and pulled the straps tight across his chest. They secured their burdens in silence. The younger man oozed regret and anger. Bergen steeled himself against his own sense of shame and said what needed to be said.

"I apologise in advance for asking this, but I must know."

Bull nodded for him to continue.

"Your hounds—did they get the boy?"

Bull's stare was granite. "We'd have heard it, don't you think?"

"Easy, Tom. Sit on up."

"Ollie? Ollie! Jesus, I can't see."

"You're breathing. That's a start."

"They got me! They got me with their damnable flashers and . . . Lord Almighty, it was like being burned alive and . . . They're guarding the stair, Ollie—the Boiler Men! They were waiting and we . . ."

"Calm down, man."

"Bailey's dead, Ollie. I saw it happen. And Phin's gone, and the other chaps, too. They're guarding the stair. We won't make it back to . . ."

"Don't worry about the Boiler Men, Tommy. Jeremy's new friends can handle them."

"Jeremy?"

"We ran into each other."

"I'm glad. But . . . Ollie, I can't see. I can't feel anything. I . . . I'm frightened."

"You'll be all right. Let's see if you can't walk and we'll get you back to Sherwood."

"Thanks, Ollie. Knew I could count on you. Always looking out for us, you are."

"Always."

Oliver had never seen a dead Boiler Man before.

This one lay sprawled across a decayed mound that might once have been a wooden cart. In his hands, he still clutched a spear-length, copper-tipped flasher hooked to a machine on his back by a length of rubber hose. His eyes had cracked, and his black armour was marred by deep, gleaming slashes and dents. His chest plate splayed out in ribbons where Bergen's rifle had cracked him like a walnut. Oliver leaned over the hole. The scent of dry dust and spent gunpowder crinkled his nose.

Ten feet onward, the road dissolved into a jumble of bricks mired in mud, afterward stretching into an uneven field of forgotten trinkets and stinking human refuse. There was some light here, shed by seepage through the domino hole above. It illuminated a thousand half-buried items cast off from the city above: pots, hats, empty matchboxes, bags and boxes of all description, wagons—whole or in pieces—and the occasional corpse. What a strange disconnection of the mind it was to think that the things one tossed from the towers were instantly gone forever.

Across that small plain, the soldiers of Jeremy's army wandered, stepping over the broken bodies of both their comrades and their enemies without so much as a glance. Oliver could hardly believe that twenty minutes ago these horrid gargoyles had been swarming the Boiler Men like a legion of hellish rats. The first wave had been shattered by the Ironboys' Atlas rifles. The second as well. But there were more, so many more, that the rifles simply ran dry of ammunition. And as they fell silent, the horde of screeching, buzzing, clawing, biting inhuman doom poured over hastily constructed defences and bore the baron's soldiers to the ground.

Even then it hadn't been over. Possessed of an unnatural strength, the Boiler Men had, one by one, tossed off their harassers and regained their footing. And then Bergen had blown them to pieces with his shoulder cannon.

Oliver shuddered to recall the look on the man's face: like a statue, eyes colder than those of the half-human wretches the downstreets had claimed.

He navigated between the remains of six or seven hounds, a good dozen of the Frankensteins, and two more Ironboys, eventually finding a clear path, and worked his way back to Tom. The big man sat leaning back against the oxidised remains of a copper boiler, arms piled in his lap, head lolling to the side.

The light danced over Tommy's features and Oliver felt his heart clench up. Tom's clothes had been burned through by flasher strikes to his belly and shoulders.

Wormlike scorch marks had been seared into his one real hand and the skin on his neck and face; some had cracked and were leaking runny brown grease.

Oliver had seen Tom injured before, had seen him with wounds much graver than these. It was Tom's posture that alarmed him: he sat with hunched shoulders and raised knees, shaking like a beaten child. To see this happy soul so lost and afraid brought tears to Oliver's eyes. He blinked them back, swallowed hard against the quivering in his gut, and knelt by Tom's side.

The big man started. His eyes flew open, panicked. "Ollie?"

Oliver laid a heavy hand on his friend's shoulder.

"Easy, chum. It's me."

Tom shakily exhaled. He reached up and clasped Oliver forearm with his real hand. "Jesus. Gave me a start, there. It was so quiet, I'd wondered . . ."

As Oliver looked on Tommy's face he felt the tears welling again. Tom's entire left eye had been burned away from the inside, leaving only an oozing scab over most of that side of his face. The right eye moved around with random jerks, squirting oil with each movement.

Oliver gave the shoulder a squeeze.

"The battle's won, Tommy. You should see it— Ironboys rusting in the mud. It's positively the most beautiful sight I've seen in years."

Tom's face fell. "I'd rather have fought."

"Buck up, man," Oliver said. The encouraging tone came automatically, quite in spite of any rational evaluation of Tom's condition. "Hews knows a doctor. I'll post him a telegram when we get back to Sherwood and we'll have you fixed up in less time than it takes to down a pint."

It was a weak lie weakly presented, but it seemed enough for Tom, who managed a smile.

"If you say it, Chief, then I'm game."

"There's my lad," Oliver said. He clapped Tommy on the back. "Now, let's get you on your feet. You still owe me that round."

Tommy's face crumpled in concentration. "How do you figure that?"

"I beat you to the ground, Tommy. And a gentleman like yourself'll surely keep to our bargain, eh?"

"Codswallop. You probably tiptoed like a ballerina down the whole route. There is no earthly way you could have beat me to the ground."

"Perhaps. But seeing as there is no apparent way for us to compare our arrival times, the round still goes to me."

Tommy frowned, adjusted his hat. "Again: how do you bloody figure that?"

"Simple: I now have to haul your not-inconsiderable bulk up that whole blasted stairway."

Tommy cracked a smile at that. He threw off Oliver's hand and lifted himself up to perch on unstable knees.

"A round says you'll have to do nothing of the kind."

"Double or nothing, then?"

"A deal, Chief."

Oliver held his hands ready to provide additional stability to his friend as Tom tested the motion of his legs. His joints shrieked terribly.

Tom chuckled. "Like a banshee. Hee, hee."

Oliver looked up at the sound of approaching footsteps.

"Twelve of them dead," Bergen said, in the manner of a soldier giving a report. "That is their full number. A lucky thing, since I am nearly out of ammunition."

Bergen's eyes had not changed. They were stone, lifeless, emotionless. The rest of his body kept perfectly still like a compressed spring, as if the man was still expecting battle.

The man was a killer; that was the long and short of it. There could be no guarantee of controlling him, no matter with whom he claimed to lay his allegiances. And if Bailey really had met his end, Oliver might not be able to pawn the fellow off on another crew. *No good will come of this partnership, and that's the truth.*

But that was something to leave to Providence and a later day.

Bergen tilted his head. "We should return to the city."

"Let's get ourselves to the base of the stair," Oliver said. "We'll wait there."

"Why would we wait?"

"So that Phineas Macrae can find us. Let's get on."

He urged Tommy into a slow shuffle by gentle pressure on his back. Bergen scowled, but fell into step.

"Do you truly still hold out hope that any of your party survived?" the German asked. "If the Boiler Men did not kill all of them, surely your rat's army finished the work."

Tommy swallowed hard before adding his comment. The pain of the admission contorted his face: "I hate to say it, Ollie, but . . . I haven't seen him. He'd have found me, I think, if he was still . . ."

Tommy choked off the last few words, and Oliver gave him a sympathetic pat on the shoulder.

"He isn't dead, Tommy. I wouldn't be terribly surprised if he was already waiting for us at the stair."

The German grunted—a half laugh. "If he's truly so resourceful as to have escaped his fate, he would be quite capable of rescuing himself without our aid."

The mockery in that tone raised Oliver's hackles. He ground his teeth a moment before making a reply. "You're quite correct, Mr. Keuper. He does not need our help. But getting Thomas all the way back to the Underbelly in his present condition is going to require more than one man."

"We have more than one man."

"Keuper, ever since you first laid eyes on my friend's state, you've been thinking that he is an unnecessary burden. You've been scheming ways to rid our expedition of him so that we can make better time."

Tommy gasped, looking towards Oliver for confirmation. Oliver's eyes tracked the rolling mud battleground ahead. He did not look at either of them. "And so I have decided not to trust you with my friend's safety."

His mood improved slightly as Bergen fell into a sullen silence.

"Fair?"

Oliver took the further silence as affirmation.

They found Phineas at the base of the stair, perched on the edge of an overturned rail car, one so out of style it might have predated the baron's takeover of Whitechapel. He stubbed his cigar out in the mud and left it there as they approached.

Oliver resisted the urge to rub his satisfaction in Bergen's face.

Phin greeted them with a tip of his impacted hat.

"If you blokes walked any slower I'd rent a cab for you. Hellfire, I'd *build* a cab for you and rope a couple of those dogs to pull it. And what in God's name is wrong with Thomas?"

Tom smiled through his grimace. "War wounds, you piss-yellow dodger. I assume you've none of your own."

"He took a few prods from those flashers of theirs," Oliver explained.

Phineas scowled. "I know that. I was *there,* or hasn't gear-guts told you? I mean that bloody noise."

Oliver helped Tommy to seat himself on a bent train wheel. The big man groaned with the effort. Oliver handed him a canteen—the last remnants of his water supply. "What noise, Phin?"

Phineas gestured at Tommy with a vague sense of disgust. "The . . . the *noise,* man. He's always been a damned factory all to himself but . . . Oy, bolt-britches, you hear that grinding?"

"I can't hear hardly any, you . . . you . . ." He sighed. "They burned me something terrible. Yeah, I can hear it."

Phin shared a look with Oliver, which even through Phineas' perpetual squint Oliver knew as a warning.

And now Mr. Keuper is thinking that Tommy is a danger, as well as a hindrance.

Bergen remained stony silent, bending a little now under the weight of his enormous weapon and several hours' long hike. He kept Phineas under a watchful eye. *Doesn't trust any of us. Perhaps Missy can crack him.* Missy would dive right into the man the instant she saw him: smile at him, charm him, melt him, rub him down under her heel.

Phineas was giving Tommy a pat on the shoulder and

muttering some encouraging, if vulgar, words. Oliver motioned him over. For Bergen's benefit, he announced ten minutes' rest.

The German nodded.

Oliver drew Phineas aside, to the edge of the rail car.

"What's this grinding, Phineas?"

"Something in his belly, I'm thinkin'," Phin whispered. "Wasn't there last I saw him. Like a clickrat crawlin' in mud."

"Any ideas on its identity?"

"Not a one, Cap'n. Ne'er heard it comin' from inside a man before."

Oliver sighed and glanced back at Tom, who had fallen into still, regular breathing. Bergen was unabashedly observing their conversation, though he was probably too far off to eavesdrop. Oliver turned back to Phineas.

"How did this happen, Phin? Didn't you warn them?"

"Wasn't any warning to give, Cap'n. Not firstly, anyways. The Ironboys, they don't make any noise."

"Codswallop. They shake the bloody ground."

"When they's movin', sure, but when they's still, they's silent as the bloody grave. No breathin', no gears grindin' or heart pumpin'. We didn't even know they were there until we's thirty feet away."

"But the dogs, man."

Phin crushed his hat farther down his head, until the dropping brim almost hid his eyes.

"I heard the damnable mutts ages before we got to 'em. Mr. Knight ordered us ahead anyway."

Oliver nodded. *Can't say I blame him. Hounds or Boiler Men? I'd have chosen the same.* "And the fight?"

Phineas spat into the mud. "What's I supposed to do against the Tin Soldiers, Ollie? I lit out. Not my fault that copper-balls goes berserk. He didn't even use his rifle, for Christ's sake."

Phineas ground his teeth

"I hid in the dirt, Ollie," Phin said through gnashing teeth. "'S what they all should've done. Blasted stupid, just like the Uprising."

"You gave them your warning, man. Everything else is on Bailey's head."

Phin smoothed out his impossibly wrinkled coat. "Bailey's dead, Ollie. He took two or three shots. I heard him crying those eloquent curses of his. The Ironboys, they charged him and stomped him down."

Oliver nodded. It was what Bailey had wanted—to die in service of his beloved queen. Oliver felt a curious hole in his stomach, like a coal burning there. *It's what I wanted, too: to be free of that man. To be free of his rules and his damn distrust*—Oliver felt guilty just thinking it—*and now I am.*

So, what now? With what the cloaks knew, would Joyce still be alive, to build this weapon on Scared's tape? Would any of Bailey's other nameless compatriots still be alive? Would . . . Hews?

"What do you think, Ollie? We's a bit buggered, eh?"

Oliver looked up. Phin stood expectantly, fiddling with his pockets.

"Let's get climbing."

They turned and walked back to the base of the stair. Jeremy Longshore had returned, and sat looking contented with his head poking out of Tommy's pocket. Tommy stroked the silver ridges of the thing's back, murmuring silent nothings to it. Bergen crouched like an ape, watching wordlessly.

"Stalwart like an ox, Chief," Tommy announced, proudly hoisting Jeremy into the air. "What did I tell you?"

"He's more than proved himself to me, Tommy," Oliver said. "Let's make him an official member of the crew, shall we?"

"The king bowing to another master? Never!" Tommy said, chuckling. Phineas helped him up, all four or five hundred scraping, squealing pounds. Oliver pointed to Bergen.

"You're our lead climber, Keuper."

Bergen rose. "So that you can keep a watch on me?"

Oliver held his mouth shut.

"So, tell me, since you have styled yourself our governor," Bergen said as he approached the first rickety, rusted and bent step of the stair, which at its base turned out to be more like its namesake. "What shall we do, now that Bailey Howe truly is dead?"

Oliver felt acute stares from Tom and Phineas. Once again they looked to him to take up that mantle he'd watched burn five years past, and lead them all to their deaths in some heroic folly. They wouldn't let him off, not again, not when he'd been hiding from the responsibility all this time.

You wanted this, chap. Deep down, you always wanted it.

A second chance. A second Uprising.

Tom rocked foot to foot. "Ollie?"

"We return to Sherwood," Oliver said. "We gather the crew and call in Hews and Sims and Joyce and whoever's left."

He stared at Bergen, matching the man's intensity.

"And then . . . we proceed, *my* way."

"I know who you are."

That was all Baron Hume had said.

The lift locked into place with a shower of sparks and the two Boiler Men jerked Bailey forward. His captors' titan strength had long ago crushed the bones in both arms, and Bailey was beyond the sensation of pain. He was aware only of the endless layered thrashing sounds of machinery to rival hell itself, and the smell of cooked meat drifting up into his nose. The Boiler Men had welded a metal plate to his skin using their lightning rods, to steal his death away.

Bailey had looked into Hume's impenetrable brass eyes and seen nothing—not anger, not satisfaction, only the cool detachment of logic. Bailey was not a defeated enemy made to kneel; he was a faulty part being corrected, so that the machine would run smoothly once more.

We are as nothing to them. Empty, lifeless soldiers that moved and killed and could not die, weapons that threw lightning and steam and bullets faster than a man could tap his fingers—*Lord, what were we thinking? What arro-*

gance to assume we could topple these creatures. These . . . gods.

His legs lost all power, and he fell forward. The Boiler Men dragged him by his shattered arms without breaking stride. Bailey's tears splattered on the walkway. His twisted feet smeared them as they passed.

They were deep inside the Stack by now, past the visitor ledges on the outer rings, down past the workrooms and storerooms and the holy places of the gold and black cloaks. Down here Mama Engine's furnace burned eternal with a heat to rival the sun, and the eldest of the black cloaks, their humanity stripped away by layers of iron limbs, tempered the foundations of the Great Work.

The endless gyrations of the machines faded, and a hum rose in their place. The sound boomed and echoed around the cavernous space into which they now passed, ringing like the song of a thousand angels, or the hissing of a thousand devils.

Good Lord, if I have ever been good to you, take me now . . .

The chamber stretched a hundred or more yards across, lined on all the outside surfaces with clocks of senseless and maddening design. The walkway extended into it, held up by gossamer golden cords, to the room's central feature.

Bailey could not look. He knew what he would see: row upon endless row of broken, drained, mutilated men and women and children; golden wires piercing their skin; muscle and flesh rotting off their bones; and yet none of them dead—none permitted to die, so long as the Great Machine had need of them.

The Boiler Men dragged him to a halt in front of a creature constructed of tangled strips of brass. Porcelain eyes assessed him, a single finger indicated the place of his fate. Bailey watched the creature as it turned away to its duties, and knew instinctively that it had once been human.

His shoulder came loose as his captors renewed their march. His bowels gave as they slammed him roughly into an empty brass chair. His last breath escaped as they forced steel bolts through his hips and chest to pin him there. His vision darkened.

Please, Lord.

A wire broke the skin of his neck and began digging into him, burning like an electric worm. A second punctured his rib cage, a third, his lower back.

Not this, he screamed. *Death I have always welcomed, but not this.*

The Boiler Men marched away, and the ticking began. It grew, instant by instant, pummelling his perceptions with its insane repetition, until it deafened his very thoughts. It stripped away everything he knew, everything he had ever thought, every hope and every plan. The weight of Grandfather Clock crushed him down, hammered him, shaped him. He became a perfect component of a larger whole, losing all that he had been before.

And all was harmony in the Great Machine.

The Second Day

*It must be dull and lonely to live in a new city,
while to live in an old city like London is to enjoy
the society of a very noble army of ghosts.*

—Sidney Dark

The Second Day

Chapter 12

His chosen will call themselves the Brothers of Order. They will be the expression of His Function, and the makers of His Harmony, and they will call me Master.

—IV. i

It was like a veritable sewer of the filthiest dregs of humanity, all coated in their own foulness, all gathered together in a drainpipe so clogged that no amount of rain would ever wash it clean.

Yes, that's it.

And those churls at the Stack had sent him knee-deep into it without so much as a clothespin to protect his nose. Yes, he'd botched the capture. Yes, he'd let the British sons of bitches shoot him to death. It hadn't been *his* fault. They'd been hiding in a tool cabinet, for goodness sakes; a bloody, bleeding, *fucking* tool cabinet. How could he have known? Yet his superiors had blamed him harshly and shipped him off to Shadwell to wallow in his shame.

Except that Marcus James Westerton did not feel shame, as it didn't do one a damned lick of practical good. What he felt was anger; anger at those queen-worshiping zealots and whatever inborn human stupidity drove such people to rebel against their betters.

Anger, you see, was *useful*. Anger made people do as you wanted.

"Look sharp, you," he growled, without warning or provocation.

The young lad who was the target of the growling shrunk back like he'd been actually struck. The Stack had given Westerton two fresh recruits as underlings and he had to go about breaking them in. The sooner they kowtowed to his every whim and cruelty, the faster they could become an adequate fighting unit. This one lad— Eugene?—Westerton had ordered to stay by his side as a bodyguard. The other marched some twenty feet ahead, in the company of the intolerable street urchin leading them to their prise.

And what a prise, what a prise.

"You, boy!" Westerton called. "How much farther is it?"

The little cretin turned a gap-toothed grin back at the question. "No' long, sir. Few mo' turns, i' is."

"It had better be soon, or I daresay you'll get no shilling. And if I'm in a mood I'll have you hauled off to the Chimney."

"No worries, suh. Few mo', likes I said."

His growl seemed to have little effect on the human rodent. *I might have him hauled off anyway, on account of his irksome presence.*

Despite himself, Westerton felt his foul demeanour slipping. Whether this creature was lying or not, the day would be a good one. Either he would send that animal to the Chimney, or he would have satisfaction on one of the men who'd shot him. He'd almost had him once, but the villain had eluded Westerton with the help of that damned bookseller Fickin. A traitor and rotten to the core, that one. Why didn't the Good Lady simply burn him up?

Because the Lady is as inconstant and as fickle as any woman. Not like the Lord. Ah, his is the beauty of structure and logic. Unassailable. He deserves to be worshipped.

"Here, sirs," the boy said. "Just here."

They had arrived at an alley, which, like all the alleys of this God-cursed tower, was dark and stank of mould and general hideousness. Westerton checked the street to either side. He recognised none of the tenements nor the guttering lamps or the stray dogs probing the stairways and doors looking for food.

"Where are we, Brother?" he demanded.

Eugene swallowed hard and shook his head. "I . . . don't rightly know, sir." He cringed at Westerton's gaze and mumbled an apology.

The street boy stood expectantly at the alley mouth.

"Presumptuous child," Westerton said. "You think I'll pay you before the job is done? For all I know you've led us to a whorehouse and will run off with my shilling."

The child shook his head. "Led you true, I did, suh. The door's at the end, in there."

"It had better be." Westerton motioned Eugene to move up beside his brother-in-gold. Westerton himself drew out his 1.20-calibre breech-loading sidearm, which he had ordered custom built at great expense. It was always a fine day when he got to fire the thing.

"You stay here," he said to the boy. "We'll be back presently."

The boy sat patiently on the curb and stared at his shoes.

"Forward."

The alley's shadows swallowed his two underlings after a single step. Cursing under his breath, Westerton followed. The dark that closed over him was nearly total, revealing only hints of the walls and the vague outlines of forms in front of him. He'd never been able to see properly in the dark since his initiation, when Grandfather Clock had blessed his heart and replaced much of his nerves with copper wiring. Westerton trusted that the Good Lord had a reason for this particular debility, though he sometimes found it irritating. *Not that I'm ungrateful, noble Grandfather. Not at all.*

Two shots filled the alley. Something wet splattered on his face and frock an instant later.

"To the sides, my brothers! Give me space." Without waiting, Westerton discharged his weapon directly down the alley's length. He thrilled to it: percussive force sufficient to shatter nearby windows and enough recoil to tear the arm off a mere human being. His enthusiasm dulled somewhat as the impressions the muzzle flash had burned onto his eyes resolved themselves into two bodies crumpled on the street in front of him wearing gold vests.

His heart-clock began to fall out of rhythm. "Brothers?" he said. "Answer me, you disobedient libertines."

At a whirring and grinding from behind, Westerton grabbed for another shell from his pocket and scrambled to reload.

That's it. Get closer, Englishman. Get up where I can see you.

Rapid, plodding footsteps accompanied the noise. At the last moment Westerton whirled and discharged the weapon into the centre of the massive shadow closing in on him. The shadow jerked and halted.

Westerton laughed aloud. "Take that, traitor. A taste of the Good Lord's justice."

The shadow swiped out a hand and ripped the gun from Westerton's fingers.

"What do you know?" it said, pointing to its belly. "Got me a matching pair now, Chief."

"Wh-what?" Westerton stammered. "You're a cloak! You're a bloody crow, that's what you are! Fickin put you up to this, the no good bastard."

Then a voice from behind: "It occurred to me that you probably don't see very well in the dark, Mr. Westerton."

That made his heart-clock twinge painfully. He was out of balance, his perfect order disturbed. He felt an infirmity creep into his knees, and spun around to find two figures, one hunched as if aiming a rifle, the other tall and thin. He pointed accusingly at the taller one.

"You! You're under arrest."

"I'm very busy right now, Westerton," said the man, "and I can't have you or yours prowling about the Underbelly looking for me."

At that Westerton cackled. "Do your worst, villain. Kill me again if you like. I'll simply come back for you tomorrow, and I'll have more men next time, now that I know where you're hiding."

"Ah, yes, that. Well, surely you don't think I hired that young lad to show you to my real hideout."

"It doesn't matter. I know your face. That is all I need to find you again."

"Be that as it may, I'll need a few days more. I'm going to have my associate shoot you and then we'll be tossing you off the tower."

"You wouldn't dare!"

"Listen closely, Canary. I'm going to give you your gun back before we drop you. Use it only to defend yourself. The hounds shouldn't bother you unless you become hostile."

"You . . . *savage*."

He'd intended something more eloquent, some scathing words to put these renegades in their places. Well, perhaps a sterling display of violence would suffice. One second was all he needed; a quick squeeze or a quick jerk and the battle was won even if they shot him down. A single tick of the clock.

The Ticking Lord had long ago taken away his pain, and then his fear of death. He hesitated only an instant, then lunged.

The third man shot him in the throat. The big man dragged him back by his collar, while the others closed in. He took seven rounds in the stomach and chest before his assailants were done. In each flash Westerton absorbed the grim-faced glare of his adversary, memorising its creases and features until he knew them as well as his own.

Body forced out of harmony, he slumped to the ground and found he could not move.

It doesn't matter. The Lord protects me. The Lord will bring me back to harmony so that I can strip the eyes out of that fucking creature and break his skull with my fingers.

His senses went dark, and he was alone with the ticking of his own heart.

The Ninth Prophecy was delivered to me as follows:

Whether this year I see will be a time for mourning or celebration I do not know, for so much will be lost and in a single stroke so much gained. How can She contemplate such an act, and how can I, knowingly, consent in its execution? I do not understand this strange path Providence seems to have laid out for me, to be a vessel for two warring minds and to aid in the slaying of one by the other.

For She will kill her mate, of this I am certain. Since the vision has come to me they have both consented to its propriety. Even He, the Great Machine, knows it is fated to occur, and though He cannot give the act His blessing, for such sentiment was long ago banished from His mind, His very incapability of considering another outcome admits his tacit consent.

This is madness, and yet She is not mad. She, after all, existed before She took Him as Her lover. Was He man or machine before that horrid affair? I cannot say. The answer is there in this terrifying new mind of mine, if I dare to ask for it. But I dare not. I haven't the courage.

Another is coming . . . I see . . .

I will name this my Tenth Prophecy, and it was delivered to me thus:

She will take a mortal lover, a new consort to fill the place of Her murdered spouse. Who this will be I cannot yet see, but he will be a creature of logic, as the Great Machine was in the beginning. She has been angry for so very long, and this poor man will bear the penalty for Her suffering. My mind trembles when I dare to dwell upon it.

This man is to be moulded as one moulds clay or stone. What She desires of him is Her secret to keep, though She would tell me, if only I was not such a coward.

Almighty God, why did they pick me? Of all the whelps wandering London's streets, why am I to be

*so cursed? For I know, too, what I am to suffer,
what terrible deeds I am to perform at the behest of
these creatures from Beyond.*

*I call these things my Eleventh Prophecy, and will
speak on them no more.*

—IX. ix–xi

Candlelight gave poor illumination at farther than
reading distance, and she hadn't made any sound. She
just had a way of being noticed.

Oliver closed the *Summa Machina* and set it on the
short wicker table.

"Miss Plantaget," he said. He rose, approached her,
then swept up and kissed her gloved hand. Her hair was
down and fell about her shoulders. The soft light seemed
to glow beneath her skin as her lips spread in a smile.
Realising he'd been staring, Oliver cleared his throat.
"To what do I owe the pleasure?"

She cocked her head and blinked lazily at him. "I
suppose you're aware that there are perfectly good reading chairs out in the lounge, not to mention better light."

"Solitary contemplation can be good for one," Oliver
said. "Phin says the Hindus and the Japanese do it all
the time."

She fixed him with a stare he found unreadable.

"I don't doubt that Phineas says it," she said. "He also
says he once owned a pet sea serpent he called Lila."

Oliver chuckled to hide his growing unease. Why was
she looking at him so intensely?

"I haven't heard that one before." Oliver straightened
his vest, then the suspenders beneath it. "What is it?"

"Thomas is awake again. I thought you would like
to know."

"Thank you." He made to push past her. When she
didn't move aside, he waited.

"Is there something else?" he asked.

Her eyes searched his.

"Michelle?"

"Oliver," she began. Several expressions passed over
her face in rapid succession. "It's the German."

Oliver sighed. "He's a sullen bravo, I know. I'd stick him with a different crew if I thought any of the others survived."

"You got word, then?"

Oliver nodded. "Joyce's address was hit by the Boiler Men early this morning. The cloaks assaulted half a dozen other places at the same time. I can't say there's much hope."

"I'm sorry."

Missy's face readjusted into the subtlest expression of sympathy, and suddenly all the sadness he hadn't wanted to feel flushed over him in one wave. No Joyce, no Sims, none of the other crews. Oliver knew how it would have happened: echoing footsteps coming up the street, a blast of steam through the door, another through a window, leaving the men to choose between fleeing into the street and being shot or hiding inside and being broiled alive.

During the Uprising he'd seen it happen to a neighbourhood family, and he'd run to his secret tunnel and hid. They'd chosen to stay inside, and he'd listened to the mother scream for more than an hour before the Boiler Men got around to executing her. That memory had always been caught on the question of whether she was screaming for her children or screaming from her own pain. Silly thing to wonder about, all these years later.

A warm finger poked into his arm.

"Come back, Oliver," Missy said, a soft, petite smile on her red lips.

Oliver cleared his throat. "Sorry, I was just—"

She held her finger up to interrupt. "I don't care to know where you were just then, Mr. Sumner. The past is really not something one should worry over. Don't you think?"

She lowered the finger. Her eyes awaited agreement.

"Right," Oliver said finally. "That's a sensible piece of advice."

"I'm glad you agree." She drew her finger through the air as if following the path of a fly, eventually landing it on an unseen piece of furniture. "Getting back to my original question . . ."

"The German. Right." *She* is *a distraction.* "I know he's abrasive and I don't want to make excuses for him . . ."

"Then don't." Missy's look became harder.

". . . but right now he'll do us more good than otherwise. You should have seen his shooting, Michelle."

"It might be better that I didn't," she said. "He's an evil man, Oliver. That's as clear as day to me."

"I wouldn't have chosen him, for certain."

"Then kick him out. Let Heckler use that ghastly steam gun of his. He can't be trusted; surely you can see?"

Missy looked to be in genuine earnest—no, in panic. He watched Missy's jaw and lips tighten.

"He can't be *controlled.*"

It's the same expression as the last mission, he realised. *She wore the same one just after she'd stabbed . . . Oh my.*

"I think he can be," Oliver said, trying to reassure her without exaggerating his chances. "I'm keeping an eye on him and I've got Hews doing the same. I think we can keep him in line. Besides, he wouldn't give up his cannon willingly, I don't think."

Missy scowled. Her fingers fidgeted on her handbag. "There are other ways to get it away from him, you know."

Oliver's eyebrows shot up. "What did that mean?"

A small gasp, and then Missy was all smiles and fluttering eyelashes. "Just a suggestion, Mr. Sumner, an attempt to be helpful. You were once a thief, were you not?"

Oliver smiled back, allowing himself to be led from the subject. "I know many people would have considered me one. This may be a different situation."

"Well, there you are." Missy gathered arms close to her stomach and tipped her head to him. "Just a suggestion, then. Well, please just . . . Well, watch him, would you?"

"I said we would keep him in line."

"Then, my gratitude, Mr. Sumner."

"Anything for a pretty face, Miss Plantaget." *A very pretty face indeed.*

She smiled at him, then strode into the foyer as if she had somewhere very important to be.

Dismissing Missy's strangenesses for the time being, Oliver stowed the *Summa Machina* on his bedside table. The language made perfect sense to him even though he had never so much as looked at it before. This oddity had been accompanied by a burning in the back of his skull, identical to when he had sighted the ghosts on the rusted stair.

He hurried down the hall to one of the unused chambers that Dr. Chestle had converted into a sickroom.

Oliver swung the door open and flinched at the smell of alcohol and the greasy odour of Tom's sweat. Thomas lay shirtless atop the covers of the room's single bed. The doctor sat on a short oak stool to the right, sewing shut the new gaping hole in Tom's stomach. Jeremy Longshore lay curled in one corner like a dog.

" 'Hoy there, Chief," Tom said with a wave.

Dr. Chestle calmly pressed Tom's arm back to the bed. "Please try not to move, Mr. Moore."

"Ah, the doc's a bit grumpy this morning, Ollie. Seems he's a bit miffed about me being shot. Imagine!"

Oliver walked up to the bed and inspected the wound. "Bigger than the last one, Tommy," he said.

"Three inches side to side," Tom said. "You could drop a shilling through me."

Oliver laughed automatically, trying not to betray his trepidation. Black veins lanced across Tommy's chest beneath the skin. They radiated from the flasher burns on his ribs and shoulder, like the tunnels of burrowing worms. Dark grey patches discoloured large portions of his arms and stomach. His chest was a patchwork of scars, notably the group of them over his heart.

"I am a right mess, aren't I?" Tom said.

"No uglier than usual, chum," Oliver said. Tommy's face was a wreck as well. Chestle had patched some of the wounds closed with stitches and bandages, but the left eye was still nothing more than burned, burst flesh.

The right watered constantly, but he seemed to be able to see from it, and that was a start.

"Bet my arm doesn't seem so strange now, eh?" Tom lifted his mechanical arm to show the point where iron bones pierced out of malformed human muscle.

Chestle again pushed the arm down.

"Kindly lie still, Mr. Moore." The doctor was sweating almost as much as his patient. Oliver detected the faintest tremble in the man's hands.

"Best follow his directions, Tom," Oliver said, "or I might have to shoot you again."

The poor doctor's eyes flared wide.

"The man is quite the disciplinarian, Doctor," Tom said. "Of course, I would have shot him as well if my aim wasn't so lousy."

The doctor paused. "That's appalling. That's no kind of talk for civilised men to engage in."

Oliver laid a pitying hand on his shoulder. "There's not a word of it untrue, Doctor. Surely Hews warned you about us."

The doctor cleared his throat and admitted, "He did not praise your good sense."

Oliver rubbed his own jaw, where the stubble had progressed to the soft beginnings of a beard. " 'Good sense' is a relative term, I'm afraid."

The doctor finished the final stitch and cut away the excess string with a penknife. "Good sense is good sense, Mr. Sumner. I'm advising that Mr. Moore stay confined to bed for now. He may have whatever food bolsters him but should refrain from imbibing for the time being."

"I've always wanted to try teetotalling," Tom said.

"I would see you outside, Mr. Sumner," said the doctor.

"I'll be there presently," Oliver replied.

Dr. Chestle packed up his equipment and left to wash his hands.

As soon as the door shut, a groan tore out of Tom and he curled his hands over his belly.

"Easy, Tommy, easy." Oliver fetched a cloth and dabbed at the big man's leaking eye.

"Bloody, I'm all right. Just feels like a rat eating my liver, is all."

Oliver's guts had long since knotted irretrievably. He tried to speak and found his mouth dry.

Tom scowled at him.

"Now don't you dare go and tell me you're sorry for dragging me out on business last night. I had to be there in case things went sour, and we both agree it's a better thing that I got shot than someone else."

"Ah, Tom . . ." Oliver felt tears coming to his eyes and blinked them back.

"I'll go out again, Ollie. Often as you need." Tom gestured after Chestle. "I'm a walking dead man, and the cutter knows it. I'd rather spend my last days pounding on cloaks than lying in bed like a grandma."

Oliver clasped him on the shoulder, trying to smile. "That's my lad." Oliver jabbed his thumb at the doctor's bag. "Don't think he'd mind."

Oliver left the room as Thomas stole himself some brandy.

He found Dr. Chestle in the bathroom, drying his hands with a frayed towel that had been in the building since Oliver purchased it. Grey and red wisps swirled in the large bowl that stood in for a proper sink. The tub was half full, it being the crew's only way of storing water; plumbing was reserved for Aldgate and Cathedral Towers.

The doctor looked half dead himself: pale skin, unkempt moustache and hair, eyes sunk deep into the head. Oil and blood stains marred his white shirt and vest.

"Tommy seems to be under the impression that he hasn't long to live," Oliver said.

Chestle's sigh was like the gurgle of air escaping a punctured lung.

"I'm unable to tell you how much time he has, Mr. Sumner." The doctor finished with the towel and hung it over a bent iron drying rack nearby. "I had one patient die on me in a matter of days. Some are still holding on despite all sense. Once the disease turns, there's no way to know." The doctor began absently rubbing his left hand where brass nibs poked through the skin.

Oliver crossed his arms. "Don't figure there's a cure."

The doctor spent a minute smoothing his moustache. "I've spent most of my career studying this ailment, Mr. Sumner. So have my colleagues. We've yet to determine a viable cause, much less a cure."

Oliver knew the cause—not that a man of science would believe it. Oliver offered his hand and the doctor took it.

"Thank you for your help, Doctor. The Underbelly could use a man of your talents."

Chestle smiled at that, but shook his head. "I have patients in Bishop's Gate and Fenchurch who need me, Mr. Sumner, but your offer is appreciated."

"Then how about the offer of a few hours' rest? We've an empty room if you'd like to make use of it."

"Your offer is very kind. I may."

Oliver escorted him back to the sickroom and left before the doctor realised his brandy was missing.

He detoured to Heckler's room briefly to check his progress.

The young American looked up from the tiny desk they'd acquired for the work of translating the tape. He set his fountain pen aside and mopped his brow with a well-used kerchief.

"What can I do for you, suh?"

"How's it coming along?"

"Jus' about done, suh." He shifted uncomfortably. "But Ah got some bad news."

"I'd say I'm getting a taste for it," Oliver said, then gestured for him to continue.

"Well, suh"—Heckler showed a few of his translated pages, coated in scribbled notes and freehand diagrams—"Ah'm almost done with the translation, but there ain't no way Ah can build this here contraption."

"Why not?"

"Ah don't have the tools it's gonna need, suh. I don't have the materials. And . . ." He placed the papers neatly back on the table. "Ah just wouldn't know how, suh. This ain't no gun and ain't no trap neither."

Oliver sighed. "Finish it anyway. At least that much will be done."

Heckler nodded and slipped the pages back into their

proper place in the manual, then bent to work without another word.

The poor young man had been slaving on that one task for six hours now, though Oliver knew he was desperate to be part of the planning. Heckler was the only one among them who had any kind of mechanical aptitude. Except for Bergen, perhaps, but Oliver wasn't about to let him lay hands on the tape.

"Suh?"

"Yes?"

"Is that really Bergen Keuper upstairs?"

Oliver looked at his young crewmate curiously. "I have no reason to doubt it."

Heckler fiddled with his pen. "Ain't that something else, eh, suh? Even back in Williamsburg, Ah'd heard of him. Is it true he took a lion through the eye at three hundred yards?"

"I have no reason to doubt that, either."

"Hot damn—beggin' pardon, suh. Do you think he would teach me if Ah asked?"

"I wouldn't know," said Oliver. "But let's just wait until after the ruckus dies down to ask him, eh?"

"Oh. Of course. Sure thing, suh."

Oliver left him to his work and climbed the curly staircase about Sherwood's trunk towards the lounge. He found Hews standing at the top, hand slipped into the pocket of his plaid vest, pipe smoking from between his teeth. His hair was roughly combed, his muttonchops ragged, his face downcast and sullen.

"Damnable shame," he said. "I served with Bailey in Afghanistan. There's never been born such a natural soldier as he."

"You have my condolences," Oliver said.

"Don't pretend you're too choked up, lad. You've hated the man since you were fifteen."

Oliver sighed and joined Hews in silent contemplation of Sherwood's random support beams. "I never hated him, Hewey, but I won't pretend now that he treated me well."

"I can't fault you for your honesty, lad," Hews said. "But he was a great man, and I'll go to my grave saying nothing less. He took me for a collaborator at first, you know; couldn't get past the fact that I owned a factory."

Oliver smiled at memories. "You might have called it a poorhouse, or an orphanage."

Hews shrugged. "I did my bit. The cloaks never caught on that my efficiency came from feeding my workers more than gruel and oil. Well, until recently."

Oliver turned to search Hews' face. "What do you mean?"

"A cloak came by last week," Hews said. "Told me I'd have to join up and take my vows or step aside. I'd love to believe they'd let me take my retirement in the country, but we both know them better than that."

"Why didn't you tell me?"

The older man shrugged. "Nothing anyone can do about it. The canaries know me too well."

"But Bailey might have been able to sneak you out on the airships. And we could still hide you here."

Hews gave him a wise, fatherly smile. "After tonight it might not matter, eh?" He left the rail. "Shall we?"

They entered the parlour, finding Bergen brooding over the main table. Maps and lists carpeted the room, stealing spaces on chairs, end tables, and great expanses of floor, some pinned on the walls concealing the nameless portraits and their disapproving glares. The one on the main table was a detailed map of the Stack, specifically, the terraced rings of factories, train stations, and chapels that coated its outer skin.

Bergen acknowledged their presence with a nod. His midsection had been expertly repaired by the doctor. Bergen had hidden the bandages beneath a loose shirt and now affected perfect health.

Oliver greeted both of them, then planted his knuckles on the table and leaned over it.

"We found an entry, no doubt," Hews said. "The Stack is actually fairly accessible. We've five entrances via cable car, four via rail, and walkways from Aldgate and Commercial Towers."

"Your American says the device will work only from within the Chimney," Bergen said.

Oliver nodded. He'd feared as much.

The map was bewildering in its complexity, a twisting

maze of hallways, walkways, lift shafts, staircases, chambers, and rooms and massive engines, pistons, and constructions arranged in no sensible order. The Work Chamber dominated the Stack's centre, at the base of the monstrous shaft from which the Stack took its name. There, in that dark place, the crows toiled endlessly on Mama Engine's Great Work. The Chimney paralleled it on the south side, much smaller and fifteen storeys down from the Stack's surface.

"Do we have an ingress yet?"

Hews traced a route on the map as he spoke. "I can get us to the freight lift that runs down the southeast edge of the Work Chamber. Only thing is, there's a large gold chapel three storeys down, so we're likely to be spotted."

"We will go in disguise, then," Bergen said from behind crossed arms.

"Won't do us a mite of good," Oliver said. "We can dress up all we please, but the canaries know their own."

Hews sucked his pipe. "I'm still waiting on telegrams from a few of my acquaintances. I might be able to get us down a steam pipe on the north side. It's all ladders and we'd need masks, but there's not likely to be any golds, at least."

"A long march around to the Chimney, as well," Bergen said.

Oliver scowled, his patience already wearing. "I didn't think you would balk at a little hike, Keuper."

Bergen glowered. "You mock me."

"You're the one moaning about it. Stiff upper lip, as we say here." He looked to Hews. "How long, do you think?"

Hews shrugged. "No more than a few hours, one would hope."

"Smashing. Keuper, you'll go out and get us supplies."

The German's face flushed. "I am no one's errand boy."

Oliver straightened to his full height. "You're irritating me, Kraut. This will be difficult enough without your obstructing us at every step."

Bergen looked a bit surprised, as if he was realising for the first time that he was not the tallest man in the room. "You accuse me of hindering you."

"Yes, Keuper, I do," Oliver said. "I need the support

of all my men on this. If you have some problem being necessary, we can discuss that at a later date. Besides, of all the ones here, you've likely been through the most hostile of environments, and presumably know how to prepare."

Bergen was slow in his nod.

Oliver bent back to the map. "Good. Get some money from Heckler and return in a half hour."

"So soon?"

"I expect more cloaks will be coming after me, and I am not difficult to find if one asks the right people."

Bergen nodded again. He uncrossed his arms. "You're more prudent a man than I thought. I apologise for my behaviour."

"Thank you."

Bergen strode out.

Hews had watched the entire exchange without a word. He lowered his pipe. "You realise those were the same words Bailey said to you just yesterday."

Oliver lowered himself into a chair. Suddenly his bones and his brain ached. "They worked on me, didn't they?"

"I must say," Hews continued, "that I, myself, wouldn't have known how to handle that man."

Oliver shrugged. "He needed to know I was strong enough to be followed. That was all."

Hews turned to wander, idly examining maps and portraits.

"You're becoming more like the boy I knew, who was always brazenly stealing my wife's Bundt cake but never any of my money or valuables."

"She made a good Bundt cake, rest her soul."

"I'm just glad to see you coming back into your own."

"What do you mean by that?"

Hews smiled and waved the question away.

Oliver took a moment of silence to run down the mental list of things that needed to be done. "Hews," he said. "I need to know more about Aaron Bolden."

Hews scrutinised a portrait of a particularly sad-looking woman. "Doesn't seem to be much point now, eh?"

"I need to know what comprises these abilities of his. I need to know what he is capable of doing."

"Bad form," Hews said, "to speak of the dead as if they're still around."

Oliver couldn't quite bring himself to assert that Aaron was not, in fact, dead. The hesitation stretched long enough that Hews turned from the portrait and raised a fuzzy eyebrow.

"My, my" was all he said.

Another minute passed before Hews began speaking. He wandered the room's perimeter as he spoke.

"Aaron had a gift, lad, apparently since his younger days. He didn't tell too many people of it, you understand, because of accusations of Spiritism and so forth. He said he could see the inner essence of a thing, whether person, animal, building, or machine. I never think I quite wrapped my mind around it."

Oliver leaned forward. "What did he see of Whitechapel?"

"Patience, lad," Hews said. "Aaron was born in Manchester, but he'd always felt a draw towards London, he said. He came here at the age of twelve. That was in 1877, just after the Boiler Men put up the wall and drove out the last of the British Army loyalists. They'd been fighting for eight or nine years before that. You've never seen them use their lightning guns, have you? What they could do to a man—to a battalion even—with a single shot . . . Such things shouldn't be allowed."

"*Hewey . . .*"

Hews chuckled. "Right—Aaron. He described Whitechapel as one might a garden or a reef. He spoke of Mama Engine's breath coming in and out of the Stack and the beams and pipes and all the larger things as her garden. He thought of the towers, that is, the floors, buildings, cable cars, and so forth, as Grandfather Clock's domain." Hews puffed his pipe, and finding it empty, tapped the ashes out in the small bowl provided for that purpose. "He said they weren't territories, as a normal man might govern, but rather limbs and organs. He viewed Whitechapel as two immense systems of biology intertwined."

"Only two?" Oliver asked.

Another pause. "My boy, you *are* full of interesting intelligence this morning, aren't you?"

"Did he ever talk of the other one, the one that lives in the downstreets?"

Hews considered. "Not as I recall. He did seem to have an intimate fear of looking down off tall heights, though."

Oliver sighed. *He likely knows more about that one by now.* He considered pouring himself a drink, just to have something to do with his hands. *It's ten o'clock in the morning, chap. Tea might be more appropriate, don't you think?*

"Must I beg for clarification, lad?" Hews said. He'd returned to the table and seated himself while Oliver was distracted.

"By the bye, there's a third god in Whitechapel," he said.

"I gathered."

"I think we may be able to turn it against Mama Engine. I just need to talk to Aaron again to arrange it."

Hews grunted. "You might start with prayer, or a séance."

Mercy. How shall I begin to explain this? Oliver pushed his scraggly hair back from his forehead. "Well . . . I suppose if you were going to think I'm mad you'd have already come to that conclusion."

"Long ago."

"Aaron isn't dead, Hewey. Rather, I don't think he is. He's a prisoner or guest of the third god. He's connected to it in a way that at least allows him to speak to it, and he may have intelligence about these creatures that could be helpful. He said he would be gathering information."

Hews rubbed his muttonchops. "All right. That rapping and séance nonsense aside, I wonder how one speaks to the, shall we say, *nebulously* dead?"

A sound ticked at Oliver's ear. Not a noise, so much as a pregnant silence hovering at the door. He straightened and cocked his head. "*I* wonder who it is that's standing in the hall, listening to us."

Hews started. They both turned their heads.

Missy stepped into view, bashful and charming. "You'll pardon me, of course. I was passing by on the way to the kitchen and found your conversation irresistible."

Both men stood. Oliver offered her an empty chair. "If it wasn't impolite to say so, I'd have to call you a sneak, Miss Plantaget."

"'A woman of many talents,' will suffice, Mr. Sumner." Missy slipped herself onto the cushion with a cat's grace. "You know, I met a man once who was a Spiritist. He said the dead can speak through a special board with letters on it."

Hews chuckled. "I doubt that this one would, lass."

"All ideas are welcome at this point, I think," Oliver said.

Missy set her elbows delicately upon the tabletop. She had chosen gloves of a deep red this morning. Funny that Oliver hadn't noticed them before.

Missy drew a cigarette from her bag and held it out for Hews to light it. He did so, with an air of importance about the action. Missy then turned her dyed lips and huge, glittering eyes on Oliver. "Correct me if this is a woman's simplification of what is certainly an important and complex situation, but couldn't you return to the place you met this dead man the first time?"

You're playing me, girl. I wonder what you want.

Oliver mused a bit. "That would be a mite difficult. I'm not entirely certain I was anywhere at all." Again that brandy tempted him as the memories of those horrible vistas stirred. "I don't think they can *be* anywhere, as you or I define the term."

"Poppycock," Hews muttered. "A body has to be somewhere. We just need to find the route, is all."

"There isn't any way to walk to this place, Hewey."

A voice from the door: "There's a way."

They all looked up to find Phineas at the door, sunk in his ulster coat and hidden beneath his hat.

"Sorry f'r eavesdropping, Cap'n, like some fool housebreaker," he said. "But there's a way, aye."

"Tick, tick, tick."

Irregular footfalls echoed down the long hallway. Windows of red stained glass in unknowable geometric patterns measured the wall space between arches. Clocks of brass and chrome gazed down from the ceiling. The floor shook with the rumble of the Stack's constant eruptions. These things passed in and out of John Scared's senses as he walked to his death.

Someone had betrayed his location. It was the only explanation. Some dishonest underling had turned informant and led the baron to him. He wondered how much money the baron had offered him, or what religious claptrap.

The cloaks had shown up on his doorstep. It could not have been accidental, as he had made an entirely new residence—in addition to his usual hides—at the side of a theatre, down an alley, in the most crowded and confusing level of Commercial Street Tower. They'd walked right up and knocked.

"Baron Hume, the First Favoured, requests your presence, sir."

Of course, Scared had presented his most congenial smile and informed them that he was glad they'd come, and that he had intended to give a report to the baron in the near future, in any case.

"I have information I'm certain will be of great use to him."

A quick train and lift ride later they had deposited him at the entrance of the Long Hallway, as it was called. The two cloaks who had fetched him still stood guard just beyond the bronze entry doors. There was no need for them to provide an escort, as the hallway had only the one exit.

He took another step, leaning heavily on his cane.

What bothered him was that the baron must know his intentions by now. The British agent they had captured two nights previous could not have held back any information about the designer of the god-killing device. Scared had to assume he was being brought here as a prisoner; yet if the baron had wanted information, he would have had the Boiler Men haul him to the Chimney and there would be no need for any personal meeting.

Scared did not like unknown variables.

"Tick, tick."

Hmmm, perhaps it is a nervous habit after all, my dear.

But perhaps Baron Hume was ignorant of who had asked Scared to design the weapon and then given him the intuitive knowledge to do so. Such information might be used as a bargaining chip. All he needed was to barter passage out of this hallway. Once back inside the Stack, a thousand avenues for escape presented themselves.

The Long Hallway led from the Stack to Baron Hume's personal chapel. Both hall and church hung in the air without any apparent means of support. An escapee, breaking through the stained glass, would find not even a beam to shimmy down to freedom. And given the proximity to the Stack's burning maw, the air would likely kill him before he managed to descend anyway.

The hall ended at another set of bronze doors, smaller than the hall's entry but set with greater detail. Gears and springs of all shapes and sizes covered both doors, churning faintly away. Scared studied for an instant the pattern of their movement, tracking motion from gear to gear; one spring wound another, which unwound and coiled yet a third.

Above these doors a silver clock ticked its regular time. Of all the clocks in Whitechapel, this clock alone told only the proper time and nothing more.

The doors ceased their motion, and steam blew out of their hinges as they swung outward.

You'll see me through, won't you, lover? he thought. *Half of the man belongs to you, after all.*

The heated tickle at the top of his spine, so long an indicator of the Mother's attention, had faded all too rapidly over the past few days.

The doors fastened themselves to the walls. With an effort, Scared straightened and took one reverent step into the chapel. For all the times he'd been in it, he could not help but marvel. Seething red light illuminated the chapel floor, cast by the Stack and entering through the enormous plate window at the peak of the chapel's arched roof. Every inch of every wall, even up in the arched ceiling, was covered in clocks. The clocks were of all sizes and shapes, rendered in brass, iron, copper, tin, and glass, all showing strange and foreign calculations of time, and all ticking in their own rhythm. Thousands of ticks. So many they washed together in a sound not unlike the sea, or a forceful wind blasting in the ear.

The faces of Grandfather Clock.

The baron waited beneath the great quartz clock that hung like a cross at the far end of the room, silk top hat and cane tucked under one arm.

Scared removed his hat. "Sir."

Baron Hume lifted his head and gazed at the quartz clock with reverence. Any human features he may once have possessed had long since been subsumed: his skin had become strips of brass, and his only identifiable features were his expressionless eyes.

"Jonathan Augustus Scared," he said.

John Scared waited, reading into the baron's stance and movements. Hume was a difficult man to read, given what had been done to his physical body by the two intelligences that inhabited it. He seemed to have taken more and more of the Clock into his habits, such that his movements read like a gear turning, and yielded no useful information.

Today, however, Hume's shoulders were ever so mildly slumped.

The baron turned smartly on his polished wing tips.

"On the one hand there are limits, on the other creations. When one ends the other must outgrow itself to the point of stagnation. The ending of one is the ending of the other, but one wonders where that ending dwells."

Heh. He actually needs my help, darling. What a lark.

"What do you need me to find, sir?"

Brass eyes, tinged red by the light, studied him. The baron wore a tailcoat and impeccable slacks, a crisp and gleaming tuxedo shirt beneath. Strange how he always made a point of dressing like the man he'd been.

"The ending of order without the growth of chaos, sealed in the code of scratches upon the skin of trees. Where is that which is yours no longer?"

He knows then. As expected. "I have yet to locate it, sir. When I do I will notify you."

The baron's featureless black head tilted slightly. "The enders of prophecy are men who walk upon two legs. These creatures of great words and frail bodies saw at the stem of that which must come to be. Do they hide in their own skin and resist harmony?"

"The Britons are mostly wiped out, thanks to the golds," Scared said. "I have my boys looking after the rest. Not to worry. I have them well in hand."

"A hand on the saw moves. Is the saw vicious when at the neck, benign when at the trunk? Who can hate that which is moved by another hand?"

Scared's eyes narrowed. "Your point, sir?"

"You are a tool, Jonathan Augustus Scared. You are the saw that revels in the shedding of dust, thinking itself mighty."

Is that you speaking, pet? Heh. You really know nothing about me.

"I live to serve, sir. Truly."

"A dog who walks in front of his master still cannot swing a cane. In this one thing he can be proud, but no more."

I already know what place you'd pigeonhole me, my love.

The baron continued. "Creation without limits is chaos. A yard without a fence is a plain. A sea without a shore is a place where men drown."

A long pause followed, so long Scared almost turned to leave. Then Hume spoke again, in a voice softer and more human.

"Why?"

The question carried genuine pain. Was it the man speaking now, and not the double tongue of the gods?

"Can you be more specific, sir?"

Another long pause, like a machine with a stuck gear, grinding to break loose. When the words finally did come, they emerged in a clockwork rhythm with gaps and starts, like Hume was choking on them.

"Brother slays—brother a plant—despises the—sun why—does a harp fall—out of tune when—the music is—so beautiful?"

Scared actually laughed. He cackled, his voice ringing

off the hard surfaces, mingling with the ticking, playing with the light.

"You don't understand, do you, Hume?" he said. "You can't fathom it at all. Under all those gears and pistons, you're still that same simpleminded architect who could never get his buildings to stand."

The baron stared with the eyes of a statue.

"She *hates* him, Hume. She hates him because she loves him and she loves him because he doesn't care one whit about her. It's madness, all of it. Mania and melancholy all around. Your gods are *insane*, Baron."

The baron replaced his top hat. The white ribbon wrapped about it near the brim sparkled like sunlight on water.

Yes, I said it, my sweet. I said it directly to his face and to yours. And yet he won't kill me for it because it is the God's own truth.

There was something of a man in the way Hume turned away to contemplate his Church of Measured Time.

Scared took it as his cue to exit. He deliberately planted his cane out of synch with the cacophony around them.

Yes, Hume, see if you can find your answer in that ticking monstrosity.

Marvelous! The weak-willed man who'd written the *Summa Machina* was still buried in that mechanised body, and still remembered the failing days of his own sanity. Back then, the baron had realised the absurdity of the Lord and Lady: a match made in hell and consecrated with shit and shackles. Scared had simply reminded him of that.

Scared had read him. The man inside had stirred, and begun thinking and feeling again. So much the better if his doubts rendered him unable to act. That just left more of the city open to acquisition by one Jonathan Augustus Scared.

Oh, my sweet. Even your adopted son cannot save you.

The bronze doors hissed closed, and Scared practically skipped down the Long Hallway.

Chapter 13

*The second principle of the machine is Harmony.
This is the core of the wisdom of the machine:
that component parts cannot but work together
towards the accomplishment of the machine's
noble Purpose. In that Harmony facilitates the
completion of this Purpose, the machine will de-
vote its resources to the promotion of Harmony
and the excisement of those elements that would
draw it into chaos.*

IV. iii

Gisella had never laughed, so why did Missy hear laughter? It had been echoing in her mind all day; that, and
a gravelly voice that whispered to her from every reflected surface.

*"Bursting apart," I believe it translates. In a few sec-
onds you'll cease even to dream, my pet. You will live
only for my voice, and will do all I ask of you.*

Missy still wore a smile, brushed with beet juice to
redden the lips. She wore red gloves and a red scarf
tucked around her neck. Had she dressed herself that
morning? It was so difficult to remember.

"You are certainly invited to join us, Miss Plantaget."

Missy started. Hews was offering to help her out of her chair.

"Oh. Of course, I should be delighted."

She accepted the man's outstretched hand and stood. Hews smiled at her and moved to join Phineas and Oliver in the hall. The instant he turned his back, she shot her fingers to her temples and gave them a good massage to clear the fog from her head.

She followed them down Sherwood's staircase and then down the hall to Oliver's room.

"Shut the door, be so kind," Phineas said. Hews quietly closed the door once Missy had stepped through. Smells of dust and spent candles came to her, along with the faint scent of a man's body odour, unmasked by powders or perfumes.

"Your face is distressingly grave, Phineas," Missy said.

"Didn't say it was easy or safe, did I?" Phin pulled his hat brim down, dragging it even farther over his nose. The single oil lamp in the corner caught only the wrinkles on his chin and neck.

Phin reached deep inside his coat and withdrew a box of pale wood, carved with Oriental symbols and painted in patterns of red, no longer than his stunted index finger.

Her attention turned to Oliver, with a vague notion that she was supposed to be watching him.

Oliver held out his hand for the box and Phineas placed it in his palm. Phineas' hand shook as he released it, and he withdrew from it as from a coiled snake.

"What is it, Phin?" Oliver asked.

The old sailor shuddered as he inhaled to speak.

"Chinamen call it *mei kuan*. Means 'pleasing to the eye,' near as it was explained to me."

They all crowded around Oliver as he undid the clasp of scarlet string that held the box closed. Missy could swear she felt a heat coming off Oliver above and beyond ordinary body heat.

Do not be frightened of your own heat when it comes on you, said Gisella. *Encourage in your own mind the breath to quicken and the face to flush, as both will be most arousing to your client.*

Oliver opened the box with a single finger. Within, nestled in a crumple of unspun cotton, lay a vial of blue glass. A glass stopper, held in place with copper braids, kept it shut. It could not have held more than a thimbleful of liquid.

Hews cleared his throat. "How is this to take us anywhere, Phineas?"

Phineas had turned away, and now faced into the darkest corner of the room. "Doesn't take you anywhere. Frees up the spirit. Lets the breath out. You'll be lying on the bed, no breathing, no heartbeat, even." Phin looked back over his shoulder. The lamplight caught electric brilliance in his eye. "But the places a body can go, Cap'n! The things a body can see!"

Hews frowned then. "Hogwash. Opium addicts say the same, pitiable creatures."

Phin eyed him over the rim of his collar.

"This ain't opium, gentlemen," he said. A hideous smile crept onto his gargoyle face. "This is St. Peter's gate in a bottle. You'll be bigger than the world, Cap'n. They say it would turn a man into a god, if only it didn't kill him first."

They all stared at the bottle. Eventually, Missy spoke just to break the silence.

"Well I for one am intrigued. Shall we try it?"

Hews huffed and retreated to the door. "I'll have no part of this foolishness."

Oliver slipped the bottle free with two careful fingers. "None of you will. Hold the fort, Hews. Find me that entrance to the Stack and keep the German under control. We'll be done when we're done."

Hews set his jaw, nodded, and departed. The door snapped shut in his wake.

Oliver offered Phin the bottle. "How does it work?"

Phin jerked away from it. "Confound it! Keep it back! Don't . . . don't tempt me."

Oliver wrapped his fingers over the bottle. Phineas visibly relaxed as it vanished from sight.

The old sailor exhaled. "Just . . . there are terrible things to be seen, 's well as wondrous. I never learned properly how to protect myself. A body's got to be so careful." He rubbed shaking hands over a face that suddenly gleamed with sweat. "I did a favour for some Chinese—what, I won't say—when I was over there. They let me have a sniff, just a sniff. I swear I saw . . . I saw . . ."

Missy shivered at the old sailor's next word.

"God." Phineas swallowed hard and audibly. "Spent twenty years just sittin' in that room, workin' up the nerve to drink it. I don't take it anymore—can't—but I could never part with it either."

Phin choked up. He clenched his fists and jammed them into his pockets, apparently done talking.

Oliver turned the bottle over in his palm. The liquid caught the light with the rich sheen of liquor.

I'm supposed to watch Oliver, Missy remembered. *Someone told me to. A man . . .*

The fiendish grin and teeth flashed back into her memory.

"No. I don't . . ." escaped her lips.

The man's voice: *You will not remember any of this, little one. No, not a whit, until I command you to.*

Oliver and Phineas were staring at her.

She cleared her throat and affected a broad smile. "Please forgive me. I haven't been . . . Well, never mind me. Shall we?"

Oliver lay back on the bed and Missy perched beside him on a fragile wicker chair.

Phineas hovered at the exit, sunken in his crumpled clothing, with his calloused fingers twitching towards the door handle. "Miss, you take the bottle. You pop the cork and hold it under the cap'n's nose, right? Ollie, you take a sniff. Remember, only a sniff. Like a pinch of snuff." He shuddered. "And don't dare drink it! Not a drop."

"I'll be careful, Phineas. Just get back on post," Oliver said, passing the bottle to Missy.

"Not a bloody drop, hear?" Phin hesitated, wringing his hands. "One bloody drop—look what it's done to me."

Then he left, shutting the door behind him.

Oliver looked up at her with that concerned, welcom-

ing gaze that so frustrated her. She forestalled him before he could speak: "How inappropriate, the two of us
shut in a room alone."

Oliver took her hand. Though the touch was light, yet
still the warmth of it penetrated into Missy's body. Her
insides began to quiver.

*Your client may wish to court you as he would a proper
lady, or he may wish satisfaction immediately. He will
indicate this through his gestures and expressions. In time,
you will learn to read these cues as clearly as letters and
will know the correct course to follow.*

She could not withdraw her hand.

"If something's amiss, Michelle, just tell me," he said.
"No one will think the less of you for it."

"Ollie, I can't say. I *can't*. I'm not . . . Please, don't
ask me . . . Don't ever . . ." She choked off, and painted
her mask back on with a fury. "Well, enough of the
failings of womanly temperament, I say. Shall we get
on?" She lifted the bottle.

Oliver did not release her hand. "As much as I'm able
and you're willing, Michelle, I'll take care of you."

A pause. Then, "I appreciate the sentiment, I truly
do, Oliver. But we're not here to trade pleasantries,
are we?"

Her hand withdrew from his. The heat of that contact receded.

He settled back on the bed, eyeing her curiously,
and nodded.

She unstoppered the bottle and held it beneath his
nose. He sniffed quietly, and she quickly withdrew it and
closed it.

Oliver's eyes drifted closed.

Oliver, be careful, Missy thought.

"Oliver, be careful," said her voice.

He nodded, then fell still.

Missy stared at him some long minutes, then slipped
her fingers back around his. Nothing moved in the little room.

He slipped from waking to sleep, and then into something else.

He was eight years old. He'd run away from Hews' factory, where he'd been sleeping under the smelting pots that kept warm long into the night. He'd stowed on the lift down into the Underbelly, and chased himself through streets and alleys. The vagrants eyed him, the vendors hoarded their goods away from him, and ordinary folk kicked him out of the way with a curse.

Behind a bakery on the Eighth Row, he made his bed. He smelled the scent of the bread and imagined he was tasting it, and lay down on the edge of the Underbelly, nothing but air and smoke beneath him. He would butter the bread, he decided, and he would have raspberry jam besides, and a glass of milk from a real cow. And it would all squish together in his mouth and get stuck in the holes where his baby teeth had fallen out, and he would worm it out with his tongue and chew it again, until it dissolved into his saliva and slipped down his throat like syrup.

He must have fallen asleep. A boot to his shoulder blade roused him, then another to his hip rolled him over. Then gravity took him.

He plunged down, leaving his body behind. The wind whistled through his hair and across his face. Ash flicked across his eyelashes and tickled his neck and toes.

Sherwood was above. Sherwood was below.

Where did he stop, when the falling became stillness and the rushing air silence?

Oliver opened his eyes.

Below, above, all around stretched an endless vista of light and dark. The roiling shapes of massive chains snaked between sparkles and flares of furnace fire. Embers swarmed in the air like fireflies, chasing shapeless creatures of molten glass. His eyes adjusted slowly, as if coming from the light into the dark, and the sky became muted fire of crimson and orange.

The landscape was not without form. Out of the web of chains and fire rose towering, geometric buildings of copper-shaded glass, edged sharp as razors. Silk-fine strands of brass and silver linked one to the other. Gears and springs turned to no apparent purpose on their outer surfaces. Oliver recognised them: Shadwell, Stepneyside,

Cathedral, and others in the far reaches of perception.
Where the Stack should have been stood a tower of
intertwined mechanical arms pulsing with red light. Sul-
phurous fumes billowed out like curtains raised by the
wind, and everywhere, the clacking of machines and the
roaring of furnaces.

"This is how I always see it."

Aaron sat beside him, perched on a steel beam connected to nothing. He sat with his knees pulled up to
his chest, and his coat-of-many-pockets dangling down.
In the manner of dreams, his features seemed to shift as
if seen through water, the only constant his eyes, an
unnatural blue that tracked on Oliver's vision.

Where are we?

Aaron twiddled his fingers awhile. "There's another
side to things. This is where one finds the *idea* of a place,
as well as its ghosts and its dreams. Manchester is built
of wicker and wool, and cotton rains from the sky."

Whitechapel hasn't fared so well, I'd guess.

"All its dreams here are dead, surely as night and day
were killed off by the smoke," Aaron said. "Now there's
only the three of them, and the little parasites that live
in them." He indicated the globs of glass.

And us.

"We aren't really here like men aught to be. We've
no histories anymore and no idea about ourselves."

Oliver scowled at him. *Remind me to speak to you
whenever I'm lonely for gloom and pessimism.*

Aaron laughed. "I am dead, after all."

Not from where I'm sitting.

Oliver tried to settle down beside the strange dead
man but found himself without limbs to move or a rear
to seat himself on.

Aaron, I'm here because I need your help.

"What happened to Bailey? I heard you talking
about him."

He's dead. Sorry to break the bad news to you.

Aaron shook his head. "He's not dead."

The Boiler Men shot him, Aaron.

"And when have you known that to kill anyone in
Whitechapel?"

What do you mean?

"I heard the bells silence him. He cried out to God when Grandfather Clock subdued him."

You mean he's on the Chimney?

Aaron nodded. "I heard him. The sound carried into this place."

Oliver felt his real heart skip a beat, perceiving it like the echo of a far-off drum. The crew wasn't safe. Damn it all, Bailey *knew* where Sherwood was!

That limits my time here, Aaron. I'll need to get back as soon as possible. But I need to know a few things first.

Aaron nodded for him to continue.

Scared discovered a method to kill Grandfather Clock. How do we kill Mama Engine and the other one? He had no finger to point, but Aaron followed his gaze to the depths of the city. In the shadows of ash and smoke, glinting in the red light, a sea of pale sludge shifted restlessly.

He considered a moment. "My researches always seemed to point to the production of an event in the same medium as the gods. I was always stuck on discovering what medium they dwelt in. Certainly, they are nonphysical, but are they mental, or spectral, or aetheric? I could never tell."

Scared must have found out.

"Mama Engine told him where to look," Aaron said. "And Scared must have designed a delivery system to carry his poison into Grandfather Clock. If he has discovered the effect necessary, then we'd simply . . . But I would need to see . . ."

Aaron looked ashen. His face thinned visibly before Oliver's eyes, skin paling, eyes sinking deep. For an instant it looked as if he might withdraw right into himself and crumble to dust. Then he clamped his blue eyes shut, breathed, and hugged himself. When he came back he seemed healthy again.

Aaron?

"I will need a close look at Mama Engine."

'You' meaning 'Jeremy'?

Aaron nodded.

I have a way.

Aaron's fingers began fidgeting again. "Be careful how you use me, Oliver. The third god is part of me. I can always feel him in my mind. I . . . might have sold him my soul."

Oliver had no hands to clasp the man with, no smile to reassure him.

I need you to stay fast, man. You took the same oath I did when Bailey recruited you, I'm guessing. You hold to that.

It did cheer him a bit. "Till St. Peter's gates, I suppose. Queen and country, and all."

Good man. I'm happy to have you on my crew, Aaron.

Aaron laughed. "Demoted! I ran my own crew up until three days ago."

The crew! Oliver looked about. *Ah . . . chum . . . how do I get back?*

"Think up," he said.

Before Oliver could ask the meaning of that advice, he had followed it. The city dropped away below him at a fantastic rate, dispersing like wind-blown leaves. Only Mama Engine's tower of arms remained and for only an instant.

He breached the red sky and awoke behind the bakery to find a heel of bread sitting on the concrete beside his right hand, buttered.

He awoke again, into a jarring shake.

Phineas bellowing: "Don't—bloody—that don't fuckin' work, Yank."

Heckler's thin face and moustache coated in sweat: "Suh!"

Oliver tried to shove him off, but his strength faded and the arm flopped down. He tried to speak, and the words came out slurred and useless.

"Get him the tea, woman!"

Phin hauled Heckler back. Missy appeared at Oliver's side, tilted his head, and poured warm, bitter tea between his lips.

"What?" he managed, spitting tea onto his chin.

Heckler clenched and unclenched his fists.

"They're here, suh," he said. His eyes quavered in

their sockets. "The cloaks, suh. Dozens of them. And the neighbourhood folk all on their tails."

Phin spat onto the floor. "Cap'n, 1812 about to break out."

"Oh, not again" escaped Oliver's lips. Images of the Uprising flooded his brain: fire reaching to the upper concourse, bodies left in gutters and streets, gunfire, and the hot, close confines of those tunnels they'd built, where for endless hours Oliver and his men had sat and listened to friends and families and neighbours scream and weep and finally fall silent. *Not again. Not because of me.*

He met the eyes of the others, anxious, expectant eyes, waiting for him to give the word.

Missy's finger wiped a drop of tea that clung to his lips.

"They need you," she said.

He extended her an arm. "Help me up"

Westerton was not above taking pleasure in his work. Those well-to-do ninnies at headquarters seemed to frown on anything but grim-faced, joyless discipline. They said it was Grandfather Clock's way, efficiency over emotion. Westerton disagreed. Grandfather Clock's way was for all parts to work together according to a single Purpose. Each part had a Function, and no part—certainly not those stiff-nosed codgers at the Stack—could impose its Function on another.

When I'm in charge I'll drum them out and make them into fucking Catholics.

They'd told him his understanding would grow as his brass bones and copper nerves did. He'd told them that he was the way he was because the Lord wanted him that way. At least they'd had the intelligence to let him lead the attack—there was no better man for the job of vengeance than Marcus Westerton.

"There's no place to go, you scoundrels!" he cried. "I've denied you every exit. I've a man covering every window. Come out now or I'll have my men blast that door apart and execute every last one of you."

His voice rang satisfactorily in the cavern beneath the Shadwell Concourse. Now if only he'd had something spectacular to wear to the occasion. His two best suits had been ruined by these foul Britons, leaving him with an old tweed frock coat, moth-eaten at the cuffs, and slacks without a crease or proper hemming. They'd also soiled his hat with so much of his own blood it might never come clean.

Ah, there was the anger again. Good.

The man beside him—Westerton hadn't bothered to learn his name; he was a foul-aspected churl—gestured with his rifle to the upper floor.

"Som'un in the window."

Westerton followed his gaze.

"Well, bloody shoot him, then," Westerton ordered. "Show him we're in earnest."

The man locked his rifle to his shoulder and let fly an expert shot that caved the glass and tore aside the curtains.

"Ha-ha!" Westerton bellowed. "There's a dishing of the Lord's Justice!"

"Din' get 'im," the man said, lowering his rifle.

Westerton wheeled on him. "Simpleton! I'll do it next time." He drew his weapon. Those few hours in the noxious and corrosive air of the downstreets had marred its perfect finish.

By the Lord's name, what a horror. The downstreets were much worse than anything he'd ever heard of them: the air, the stench, the dark, and those loathsome mutant wretches that wandered the place. It had ruined his suit, pocket watch, and much of his skin during the fall. Only faith had kept him alive, and his prayer that the Lord would bring him back to Harmony. And so He had. Rage and devotion had fueled Westerton's rapid and tireless climb back to the Lord's realm.

Now revenge was only ten paces away.

"Come out, you bastards!" He discharged his weapon into the tenement's front door, punching a hole in it and nearly splitting it down the centre. "I'll crush your heads with my bare hands."

Was that not a rallying cry? Was that not a marvellous cue for his assemblage of brutes to cheer?

He turned to the churl at his side. "What is wrong with your men? Don't they enjoy working the Lord's will?"

The man ground his bestial jaw. "The folk, gots a queer look on 'em."

Westerton turned around and surveyed the vast crowd of Shadwell's wretches that had gathered to watch.

"What, these beggars?" Westerton said. "Pay them no mind."

"Sir, they's angry wit us. Some's armed theyselves."

Westerton squinted at them. *(Damn this infernal dark!)* There *was* something shifty about them, some gleam in their eyes like hungry dogs. Some indeed carried weapons—butcher's knives, crowbars, pipes. Not a one of them carried so much as a pistol.

"Pay them no mind, I said," Westerton ordered. "They think they can best us with little bits of steel. Let them try."

Westerton pivoted back to the tenement. "You have a ten count, rebels! Then we make sieves out of the lot of you."

"He's got a set of pipes, that one," Phineas grumbled.

Oliver leaned heavily on Missy's shoulder for support. The potion had drained nearly all strength from his muscles.

"Bergen, what do you see?" he called.

The German called down from the mezzanine. "Three dozen. All armed. Rough men. We won't be able to bargain."

"Not with that fop," Hews said. "Loud-mouthed braggart. How many times have we killed that man, now?"

Bergen's window exploded. The German flattened himself against the wall.

"Are you hit?" Hews called.

"Nein," Bergen said. "A magnificent shot, though."

"Bergen, are you well enough to fire that cannon of yours?"

A savage gleam came into the man's eye. He ran to fetch it.

"Heckler, take his post. Hews, the other window. And don't be seen."

The two men ran to their positions without question.

Phineas shrunk to the floor, quaking, his hands clamped over his ears.

And it will certainly get louder.

Oliver turned to find Missy staring at him with a fire in her gaze, her jaw set. Her eyes were a pearly, almost opalescent blue, and completely unafraid.

"Michelle," he said. "Get Phineas and the doctor down into the tunnels."

"Oh? So I'm to run off and leave the killing and the dying to the men, is that it?"

"For the love of God, woman, not now! I need *shooters,* Missy. No amount of smiles or sashaying will help us right now."

"You ungrateful swine!"

"This is not a debate," Oliver said. "Move your feet or we'll have words."

Missy snorted. "I quite think we're having words now."

The door exploded. An instant later, a piece of the staircase followed suit. One or both of them yelped and together they dove towards the side hall, landing in a heap of tangled limbs.

Oliver coughed as dust and wood chips cascaded through the air. "You're all right?" he asked.

"The picture of health," Missy snapped.

Tom and Dr. Chestle appeared in the hallway arch.

"Ho, ho!" Tom said, clutching his gut with one hand. "Hardly the place, now, birds."

Missy shoved herself away and stood.

"What's going on?" the doctor asked.

Without another word, Missy grabbed Phin's sleeve and then the doctor's and more or less dragged them into the hall.

Thomas, now dressed in his soiled shirt and oversized jacket and sporting a boy's cap on his head, bent down and hoisted Oliver to his feet with a one-handed jerk.

"How now, Chief?" he said. "You seem out of sorts."

Oliver tried unsuccessfully to stand under his own power, and fell back on Tommy's arm. "Hewey! What's the word?"

"Westerton's rallying the troops, I think. First line's coming up to fire."

"What about the crowd?"

A pause. "They're keeping back."

Good. But how long would that last? This had to end quickly, before the anger of those poor coves overwhelmed their good sense.

"Find some brick or steel for cover," Oliver ordered. "Don't return fire."

Heckler froze in the middle of cocking his Winchester. His expression spoke his opinion of that order.

Hews saw it as well. "Swallow it, lad," Hews told him. "Find cover."

"Us too, Tommy."

Tom pulled them both up against the thick arch of brick around the door.

The cloaks' first volley burst like firecrackers and pieces of plaster and glass rained down on the foyer and the stairs. Two more volleys rang out, the cloaks firing with precision timing.

In the silence following, Westerton boomed again.

"Inside, my Brothers! Glory to the Harmony! Glory to the Great Machine! Bring them to me, my Brothers."

Footsteps approached the front door.

"Tommy!" Oliver hissed.

The big man looked at him in confusion.

"The traps, Tom!"

Tom swallowed Oliver in a hug and dove into the corner.

The first cloak kicked in the front door. The bolt disconnected from the doorjamb, causing a copper latch to fall into its vacant place. The latch touched a copper plate, freeing electricity to run from a hidden chemical battery into the four sticks of dynamite embedded in the brick.

The ensuing thunder ate the four or five cloaks closest to the door. The whole of Sherwood shook with the blast. Portraits crashed to the floor upstairs; more plaster and glass toppled from above. Oliver felt heavy impacts on Thomas' back, but the big man, braced shoulder to the wall, held fast.

Oliver choked on a lungful of dust and Tommy's oily odour. He heard and felt the grinding in his friend's abdomen. He swallowed to moisten his throat.

"Ready!" he called.

Tom released him, stood, and turned. Oliver slumped against the wall, finding some strength in his legs, and fished out his derringer. He checked above: Hews had his Bulldog out, Heckler, his Winchester.

And Bergen stood atop the stairs like a Greek god.

Three cloaked ruffians streamed through the door. Hews and Heckler set upon them instantly, raining fire down from above on both sides. One cloak fell dead; the others simply reeled aside as more came through. Oliver added his derringer to the barrage; Tommy hurled a brick. Together they subdued this next group, but as the third one came through Oliver realised both he and Hews were out of ammunition, and Heckler would be soon.

Oliver scrambled to reload.

"I send you to your places in hell," Bergen growled. Oliver grabbed Tom by the suspenders and dragged him back.

The noise alone shattered all the windows at the front of the building. The round burst one cloak into strips of red and brass. A steam cloud streaked after the bullet, cracking with white electricity, which lanced through the whole crowd of canaries. As one, they spasmed and dropped, smoking and twitching, to the floor.

"Mother of Jesus!"

Oliver didn't know who'd said that.

In the blink of an eye twelve Brothers died. Just outside the door, steam rose from a hole large enough to fall through.

If the functionality still existed in his organs, Westerton might have pissed himself.

"What was that?" he cried. He snatched the churl's sleeve. "What was it?"

"I dunno," the other man muttered.

"Egads! What on the Lady's black Earth could do such a thing? How would rebels get ahold of it?"

Lord Grandfather, protect me.

The Brothers' eyes fixed on him, their faces all identical looks of astonishment.

"What? Do you need me to tell you what to do? Kill them, you simpletons!"

When the Brothers hesitated, the crowd on their fringe shifted uneasily. Some raised their weapons.

"Do you want a fight?" Westerton yelled at them. "Then come and get one. We'll butcher you all!"

At that instant shots rang out from the tenement and the crowd surged forward.

The Brothers, distracted by the shots of the rebels, did not gun down the crowd as Westerton had imagined. The outer line of Brothers fell beneath iron pots and crowbars, screaming and panicking.

More shots rang out from the tenement, felling two more Brothers close at hand.

"I refuse to let you win again, you villain," Westerton bellowed. He raised his revolver and blew one of the crowd to mist. Then he charged the headquarters of his nemesis. Bullets hammered through his vest and coat, lodging in the mechanisms of his body. His next two shots destroyed large stretches of wall.

"I will avenge you, Brothers!" Westerton screamed as he barrelled through the shattered arch. "In the Lord's name and the pursuit of Harmony!"

On the other side of the doorway was a staircase, winding tightly around a support beam. At the top of the staircase, clearly visible through a gap between smaller beams, stood the largest gun Westerton had ever seen.

"Fucking . . ." was all he had time to say.

An impact hammered his right shoulder and tore his arm from his body. His collarbone and ribs collapsed on that side. He spun wildly, careering off the archway.

Lord, protect me . . .

Blistering steam rushed over him, searing exposed skin and eyes. Cracking lightning followed and . . .

White.

Oh, by the Lord, the pain! He couldn't stand, couldn't feel . . .

White.

The floor struck him in the face. His whole body burned, inside and out. Oil flooded his mouth and heat seared his brain. In an instant, senses and thoughts burned away, leaving only agony and rage.

Huge hands clamped around his neck and began closing with the force of a dozen steam-powered lifting claws.

The fucking crow!

His remaining arm shrieked and bent as he lifted it, but it obeyed him. With a towering effort of will, he lashed out at his attacker. The brass bones in his fingers sank deep into slick flesh. He tore it back and struck again, this time latching on to thick bones. He squeezed and twisted these, yanking them from beneath the skin. The pressure on his neck released and he drew a halting breath.

Another body tackled him from the side, this one lighter, flimsier. Westerton glanced down. Even through the white streaks that marred his vision, he recognized the drawn face of his nemesis.

Nothing noble or eloquent came up Westerton's throat, then, just shrill, bell-like laughter.

He yanked his fingers free of the other brute's rib cage and shot them out at his adversary's throat. He squealed with glee as they found purchase around a soft, human windpipe.

One quick twist, one tick of the clock.

Massive hands hauled his fingers back, robbing him of his prise. He struck out with his other arm, forgetting it was lost.

Then the bullets came into him. Round after round, six, ten, twenty penetrated into the core of his body, denting bones, knocking gears apart, twisting springs. His body shuddered, and with a curse on his lips he passed out of harmony and fell still.

*   *   *

Thomas collapsed.

Oliver forgot his burning throat. He wheezed his friend's name and reached out to him over a stretch of floor impossibly long.

Thomas Moore: the latest victim of Oliver Sumner's ill-fated crusade.

Oliver's vision ran with black spots and then vertigo conquered him. Through reeling perceptions, he watched Heckler rush up to the fallen cloak and put three more shots into him. The young American then ran to the door, sidled up against the remaining brick, and began shooting outside.

Oliver concentrated through the ringing of gunfire and the dulled sounds of combat and strained to hear the only thing that mattered to him: Tommy's breathing.

It was the German's voice he heard. "You must get to safety." Bergen lifted Oliver by the collar and dragged him to the side of the room.

"Check him," Oliver whispered.

"If he lives, he lives," Bergen said. Bullets pinged off the beams above. Bergen deposited him just inside the hallway and left him there.

Oliver may have passed out, for the next things he saw were Missy's moist eyes as she bent over him.

"That's it, Oliver," she said. "It seems I'm to be the one taking care of you."

She held a canteen to his lips and he drank like a camel. When he was done she wiped the excess off his chin.

His first question: "Tommy?"

For a single instant, Missy's face betrayed her panic, and then she was as calm and as soft as could be. "The doctor is working on him now. They want to speak to you when you're ready."

"Who?"

"Everyone."

Whoever remains. "Help me up."

Missy hoisted him with surprising ease, given her small frame. With him leaning on her for balance, they hobbled into the foyer. Thomas lay in a corner, splattered in slick blood. Dr. Chestle knelt over him, covered to his elbows in gore, while Phin looked on. At Oliver's entrance, the sailor looked up, and shared a gaze that communicated the hopelessness of the situation.

"A saw," the doctor said. "I must have a hacksaw, or anything that will cut iron."

Phineas hastened to obey, a pronounced stoop in his step. Oliver's gaze fell back to Tom.

I can't help him, Oliver told himself. *If he lives, he lives.* Then, *I've seen him weather worse.* He hadn't, but it was a comforting lie.

Reluctantly, he pulled his eyes from his friend and allowed Missy to guide him to the front door. Outside, he found Hews supervising the disposal of the dead cloaks and the distribution of their firearms. The townsmen were carrying the bodies one by one and tossing them off the side of the Underbelly, not half a block away.

As soon as they saw Oliver, the pointing and the questions began.

"Were they after you, Oliver?"

"What in heaven's name've you got in there?"

"Are we going back to war?"

"What do you need us to do, Oliver?"

Oliver gestured to Hews, who mounted Sherwood's front steps and turned to the crowd. "Quiet! We can do nothing until we all settle down and hold civilised council like civilised men."

The shouting died off, though murmurs continued. Oliver looked out on the sea of faces, stained with soot, blood, oil, some with tears. It was a force all its own, the mob anger, something beyond reason and beyond control.

A man Oliver knew, a baker, stepped from the crowd, his ribbon-thin teenage son with him. He still wore his apron and working shirt, covered in flour and ash and with the sleeves rolled up. The prints of bloody fingers stained the corners of his apron.

"Oliver, we know you're up to something. The whole place's buzzing 'round it," He began. "We want in."

Oliver swallowed. "Fred . . ." he began.

"You killed them, didn't you?" said the baker, moustache twitching rapidly as he spoke. "Ain't no one who's done it before, but you did, and the whole town knows it. We heard the battle down there, and lo, no Ironboys climbing back up. Just you. A cove draws that like a chalk X."

"Fred . . ." Oliver tried again.

The baker blundered ahead. "And what with these canaries showing up on your doorstep, we know you've got something new. We're sick of it, Oliver. I've been mixing ash in my flour for weeks, and yesterday this crow comes a-knocking saying my boy's got to go to work in some factory starting his next birthday. We want in."

How do I say no? Wasn't this what he had longed for—the average man finally digging in his heels?

Hews leaned in close to him and whispered in his ear. "They're willing, lad. You can't deny a man his proper time."

For an instant Oliver was aware only of the hundred pairs of eyes on him.

They wanted to fight. Oliver had felt it for five long years—in their stares, in their none-so-casual greetings, in their body language. Since the Uprising's bloody end, it had been simmering in the back of the minds of every survivor. Oliver had ignored it, placated it, redirected it, but now, with some forty cloaks murdered in the street, they were going to have war no matter Oliver's fears.

It's a second chance. It's a chance to do it right.

He tapped Missy lightly on the shoulder and, with some hesitation, she withdrew her support. Oliver wobbled a little but stayed upright. He gave the baker a smile, clasped his shoulder, and stared over him at the crowd beyond.

"All right, listen, now," he called. "I need all of you to prepare, as the Boiler Men may be down here in a matter of hours. I need the tunnels reopened and stocked. I need a weapon placed in the hand of every able-bodied man, and I need everyone incapable of

fighting evacuated to the tunnels. I need any other
cloaks in the Underbelly dealt with, and I need barricades set up on the Parade outside the lift station."

Immediately, the fevered undercurrent stilled, and the
crowd buzzed with galvanized energy. A rush of excitement filled Oliver toes to crown, a sensation of confidence and competence and indestructibility, and for an
instant he forgot the Uprising, and remembered why
he'd led them.

"And I need every explosive that can be found placed
in the hands of this man." He pointed to Heckler. "I
need all this done in one hour, gentlemen. One single
hour."

They held still, waiting for more.

Hews leaned forward. "*Now,* you slack-jawed cock-
neys! Hop to it."

The men ran in all directions. The baker grabbed his
son by the shoulder. "Now we give 'em what's coming,"
he said, and they both bolted away.

Oliver watched them hustle, swollen with pride for the
few instants before he remembered how many of them
would likely be dead by midnight.

"Goodness," Missy breathed. "You have them trained
like hounds."

Hews chuckled. "One needn't train a hound to sniff,
lass, nor to chase a hare. All the same, you're a regular
John Bull, lad."

Oliver nodded, surprised to find a grin spreading over
his lips.

"So they say."

Chapter 14

Her chosen will call themselves the Brothers of Creation. They will be Her Intention, the legacy of human creativity bent to Her purposes, and weaned upon Her ancient Methods, and they, too, will call me Master.

—V. i

Scared left Tuppence crying. They always cried, at first. In a while he would send the boy up to Gisella's house of sin and her girls would feed him and dry his eyes.

He toddled his ancient frame up the twenty wooden steps leading from his bedchamber, avoiding, with great difficulty, those that concealed his various traps. Blast, he must take some of these out. Security did him little good if he slipped one day and found himself stuck on the point of a poison dart.

It was a shame about the other boy. He'd died of fright, perhaps, compounded with malnutrition and general filth. He'd left the poor thing's body where it had fallen, as it provided a perfect learning opportunity for the one still alive.

Such darling things, children. Such wonders of God's

world. When you call me husband and master, my sweet, what wonderful offspring we will fashion.

"Tick, tick, tock, my sweet. The watch stops at the end of the day."

His voice echoed back from the plaster walls. The heat that burned in the back of his head flickered in time with the lamps in their sconces.

And what do you want with this other man, my sweet? Well, soon I'll know that secret, too, and in time I will own every scrap of soul you try to hide.

He wandered the halls of his labyrinth awhile, alone with his thoughts. When he was a boy, he'd wandered in a similar fashion through Hyde Park, sometimes halting to climb the Gate, until some policeman or well-meaning citizen chased him off. It had been a distraction then. Now it was a necessary exercise to keep the mind calm and functioning.

The labyrinth was one of four hidden in various towers close to the Stack. This one was his least favourite, lacking a proper amount of madness in its design. It was functional, for certain, but hardly inspiring. Unfortunately, since his hides in Aldgate and Dunbridge had been compromised, he had to settle for this one. It sat below Gisella's den of sin, so there was some consolation there. Fine and stern old woman, she was, and she'd be chaste to her dying breath, bless her.

He walked through halls and staircases, past row after row of identical doors. His mind churned and refused to lie silent. He caught himself ticking several times and each time angrily clamped his teeth.

Why did he feel anxious? It was planned, all planned.

He stopped, halted his breath. His ears picked up the last distorted echo of a scuffing. An intruder? Moran didn't know of this place. Neither did the German, or Boxer or Hobbyhorse. And Gisella would never lower herself to walk these filthy halls.

Scared twisted his cane's head, releasing the knife from the tip. The click it emitted resonated down the halls. Scared's senses picked at that noise, dissecting, calculating.

He flattened himself against a shadowed corner and waited.

At length a figure stumbled around the corner at the hall's opposite end, stooped and limping. The intruder placed his hand on each door as he walked, as if counting them.

Scared had not fought with his cane for years. It had to be used like a bayonet to be formidable. For a brief moment he feared his arthritic knuckles would not be capable of it.

He could hear the intruder's laboured breathing, the moist sucking of the terminally ill. The figure shrugged through a pool of light.

"Oh, my boy!" Scared cried. He rushed from concealment even as the figure collapsed to the floor.

Scared knelt down and gathered the boy's head in his hands. "Oh, my darling. What have they done to you?"

Tears rolled down Penny's cheeks, from eyes that stared glazed at the ceiling. The boy's mouth opened, closed. A bullet had cracked through his sternum; his shirt was black with old blood and filth. The wound had been cauterised, probably by the broken flasher still hooked to the lad's belt. His skin was pale and sunken beneath the grime.

"Lie still, my boy. I'm here." Scared knew Penny was dying. Nothing could be done but to give him up to the cloaks, and that, Scared could never wish on one of his sons.

Penny's breathing grew more relaxed as Scared stroked his hair. Eventually, the boy fell into a light sleep.

No, my child, I cannot save you. But there is life in you yet, and you deserve more than an infected death in a lonely hallway.

"Don't weep, my darling," he whispered. "All is not lost. There are potions, my dear, secret mixtures that can sustain you for a few glorious, final days. I will make one of these mixtures for you, my sweet, and it will fill your veins with burning blood and bring strength into your legs once more."

Penny opened his eyes again.

"And we will get you knives, my darling, for I know how you adore knives. And for those few days, you will express that one act at which you were so blessed by Providence to excel."

Penny's tears dried up. Some of that stone came back into his eyes, that carefully crafted heartlessness Scared had slaved over for so many years.

He could not help but smile.

Ah, pride; how can they call it a sin, my love?

The little bell dinged. Oliver found the shelves in their places and the lamp buzzing overhead. His first step onto the floorboards sent up a creak, and then the skittering of retreating rats. He let the door slide shut behind him, and waited.

Outside, Bergen sat casually on the front step, puffing on a thin cigar.

Oliver heard the whispering of shifting cloth, and turned to face the bookseller as he floated into view.

"I thought I'd be seeing you again," the old man said.

"You seem to be closed for a while," said Oliver. "Let's have a chat."

If anything, the man's smile grew toothier.

"Of course. Shall we?" He indicated the rear of the store.

"Right here is fine, if you please," Oliver said. "I have questions for you."

"I'm sure you do." The man's hands clicked softly as he folded them together against his stomach. He settled back into a sitting position, as if buoyed on whatever lay beneath his skirt. "I'm happy to accommodate them, with the Lady's blessing."

Oliver opened his coat and drew the heavy book from within. Fickin's eyes followed it.

"This is not the *Summa Machina*," Oliver began. "Not the real one anyway."

"It's the real one."

Oliver breathed slowly. "I want no lies, Crow."

"I have none to tell, Mr. Bull. That is the original script as written down by Atlas Hume in 1834."

"Then can you explain to me why the canaries haven't gone to war with you yet?"

"Ah, yes, the prophecies." Fickin steepled his fingers. "The Brothers for Order cannot go to war, Mr. Bull. Their only reason for being is to bring things into harmony. What wars have you ever known to be harmonious?"

Oliver rubbed the raggedy stubble on his jaw.

"So they know?"

Fickin nodded.

"And they do nothing about it?"

"You must understand the mentality of the clock, Mr. Bull," Fickin said. "A clock is a machine. It repeats one task endlessly, unchanged. That is its role. Even for its own preservation, a machine cannot alter that role."

"What is Grandfather Clock's role, in your opinion?"

"Grandfather Clock exists to bring about harmony and precision. He controls the environment, to make it safe for the Mother to create. He makes it possible for the Great Work to be built."

A faint sound penetrated the windows: two taps of Bergen's foot. Entry had been accomplished.

Fickin straightened, agitation coming into his eyes. "But Grandfather Clock never stops with simple harmony. He wants everything to tick to his tune, so that nothing can ever be out of place. Once he is done with humanity he will turn his efforts against the Mother herself. He will suffocate her, as he has for their entire union. Gods, when I think of the aeons he's been doing this to her . . ."

A flicker of fire lit Fickin's eyes.

And there you are, my Lady. Oliver tapped his pocket. Inside, Jeremy stirred.

"Aeons?"

"You have no idea, Mr. Bull, how old they are. They've been on our small little world since the great beasts ruled it, hiding in their primitive brains and waiting for a race capable of birthing them. We are their chosen people now, the builders of their womb and the stewards of their kingdom."

"She didn't think to kill him sooner?"

The fire flashed deep in those sunken eyes. "She didn't know how, Mr. Bull. She doesn't understand him well enough. It is like asking a tree to understand a steamship. We were the first she found that were capable of fathoming him; that is why she adopted us as her children. She needed our help. The Lord simply wanted to dominate us."

Jeremy nudged his nose out of the pocket. Oliver

spread open the book and began leafing through pages, focussing his attention on the flashing brass, to draw Fickin's eyes there.

"She found someone, didn't she?" Oliver said. "She found a whole gaggle of people lining up to help her cause. Like Scared. And myself."

The fire dimmed. "I've always been a bit ashamed that she felt she needed to look outside the Brotherhood."

"So it really doesn't matter who gets their hands on this weapon of hers. As long as it's used, she'll be the one who benefits."

Fickin licked his lips. "She's waited so long for freedom from her tyrant consort. And now, through our help, through the help of this man Scared, it is within her reach."

The emotion welling up in the bookseller was Mama Engine's own.

"We are *her* salvation, Mr. Bull. Can you fathom that? We tiny creatures of flesh and blood. She loves us so fiercely for what we are willing to do for her." He eyed Oliver with a smile. "She will need to take another husband, you know."

Three taps of Bergen's foot: instrument delivered, awaiting the go-ahead.

"I think she will be disappointed," said Oliver. "She and her kind aren't welcome here."

Fickin perked up. The fire danced in his eyes, casting its glow over the rows of spines lined on the shelves.

"So you know about the child, then?" he said.

Oliver nodded.

"Mother Engine always wanted children of her own," Fickin said. The heat of his body touched Oliver's face. The air began to grow smokier. Illumination from no discernable source spread into the room. "She once tried, long ago, to conceive from the Lord's seed. What was born was an abomination to both of them, a creature of disharmony and decay. It has dogged at their heels from world to world, unable to be rid of them just as they are unable to be rid of it. But what else could come from a union of such hatred on the one hand and indifference on the other?"

Fickin became distracted with the passions washing

over him. Oliver took the opportunity to scan the room and take in the changing light, the sudden smokiness of the air. Right now, in the back of the store, those four furnaces were flaring higher as a fanfare for the goddess' arrival.

It was time to leave. Oliver took one quiet step back towards the door.

"She likes you, Mr. Bull," Fickin said. "You have qualities she fancies."

Another step back. Jeremy poked his head fully out of the pocket.

"Qualities."

"I don't presume to understand her," Fickin said. He floated closer as Oliver retreated, stretching out his hands in a kind of pleading gesture. "She has needs and desires far outside the boundaries of human experience, and she engages in many kinds of unions."

There's a vile image. Oliver snapped the *Summa Machina* closed and slipped it back into his pocket. "She knows my opinion of her, Fickin. I'll be going now."

Fickin snatched Oliver's sleeve. The voice that spoke next was no ancient bookkeeper's, but a rattling gasp like the last breath of a dying man. "She *needs* you. She cannot suffer this again. She must have a husband who will love her."

The lamp overhead exploded, raining sparks onto the shelves. Strips of Fickin's skin peeled off steel bones when Oliver tore his sleeve loose, and Oliver bolted for the door. Jeremy burst from his jacket in a flurry of ticks and buzzes as the shop exploded into orange light.

Oliver did not see what Aaron Bolden did next. For an instant time suspended, sound deepened, and space expanded past comprehension. The cracks and fissures in the walls began leaking yellow pus. A sickly green light flared up outside the windows.

Fickin's cry for deliverance gurgled away.

The pus fell to the floor, where it picked up a sudden speed and rushed past Oliver's feet. An instant later a blast of heat struck him from behind, followed by a wall of hissing steam, and a shriek of pain went up like the beams of a tower ripping itself apart.

This time without hesitation, Oliver tore the door open and plunged into the street.

The crack of the sidewalk against his cheek brought him back to clear reality.

Bergen made no move to help him up. The German drew his revolver and trained it on the bookshop.

Oliver lifted himself off the street, straightened collar and cuffs.

"Light it now, Phineas," he whispered, knowing the sailor would hear him.

The derringer leapt into Oliver's hand.

The bookstore stood dull and darkened. The door creaked shut. They waited.

Phineas appeared by Oliver's side.

"Got the block evacuated, sir," he said.

Oliver nodded, keeping his eyes trained on the door.

"Better cover your ears," Bergen grumbled, leaving his own unprotected. Phineas ran off, already bunching his collar around his head to dull his hearing.

Oliver's heart stung for him. *I'm sorry to have to do this to you, Phin.*

Steel fingers slick with blood moved the shop door aside. One spindly appendage, bending evenly at a hundred different joints and arching like a spider's leg, reached beyond the doorjamb. Oliver heard Fickin's voice from inside.

"Why do you do these things?" the bookseller rasped, his face a hint of teeth and bloodied scalp. "Why do you hate her so? All she wants is your love."

The voice held all the sadness and hurt of the unjustly wronged.

The German loosed a shot that took Fickin in the face and drove him back. An instant later the building exploded and they all crashed to the ground.

The concussion broke windows halfway down the street. A gout of fire threw the back of the shop's roof and its supports into the air and lit the Underbelly with more light than it had seen in twenty years.

The roof of the bookshop rained down in fragments for blocks around. Some of it had probably struck the underside of the upper Concourse. Bits of plaster and twisted steel clattered on the street around him as Oliver lay curled on the ground.

"Gott in Himmel," Bergen cursed beside him. "How much did you use?"

The last pieces of the bookshop crashed to the street all around, and Oliver slowly uncurled.

"Twenty-seven," he said. "A full third of Heckler's supply."

"Why so much?" the German asked.

They both got to their feet. Oliver removed his hat and shook it off, then ran a hand through greasy, knotted hair. "I had to be sure that abomination of his never gets loose in the Underbelly."

"I wouldn't lay odds on it now, English," Bergen said.

"I won't be satisfied until I see it in pieces, Keuper," Oliver shot back. "Now keep me covered."

Obediently, the German raised his pistol and aimed it into the ruin of the shop. Oliver caught the rare flicker of an actual expression on his face—amusement? *Bugger him.*

Amazingly, the door and much of the building's façade had stayed intact. Dying fire flickered through the shattered windows. Greater fires than these had already claimed the atmosphere of Whitechapel.

The door cracked off its hinges as Oliver swung it open. The bookshelves had toppled forward like dominoes, spilling their wares all about the floor. Some were burning; most were simply blasted into pieces and lay snapped and mangled in piles against the remaining walls.

Beneath one shelf lay a twisted heap of iron and steel. It twitched ceaselessly, respiring puffs of dry, dusty smoke. It had too many arms, too many legs, and not nearly enough skin left on it, but it lived.

One of the old man's arms grasped feebly at Oliver's shoe.

"I'll tell you why I hate her, Crow," Oliver said. "I hate her because all the women and children that slave in her factories or twitch and rot on her husband's Chimney aren't alive enough to hate her. I hate her for the air, and the dark, and for the disease that's eating my friend alive from the inside."

The shape screeched like a heavy door on unoiled hinges.

Oliver watched Fickin trying to crawl and had to blink back tears. "I hate her because she doesn't let her people die."

He raised his eyes and stared into the empty space were Mama Engine had once come for him.

"Please," he asked, "let this one go."

The twisted shape continued to squeal, continued to grasp at unseen things with steel fingers.

Oliver sighed, and stepped over the body. He walked over the downed shelves to the back of the shop. The dynamite had broken a hole clean through the Underbelly. No sign remained of Fickin's monster or the four furnaces used to craft it.

Bergen, from behind: "Are we finished here?"

"Yes, Keuper, we're finished," Oliver said. "Get Tom ready to be moved. We'll be going shortly."

The German retreated.

Oliver stood amongst the ruins of the shop and let his sadness have expression. After the Uprising, with the Underbelly burning, he'd sworn it in a silent pact with God: no more children shot in the streets for getting in someone's way, no more families broiled alive by steam guns for hiding in their cellars, no more homes or lives burned and torn down.

And here I am, destroyer of my own city.

But this was the hideout of an enemy. This was the stronghold of an invader who would have brought only more misery. That made a difference, didn't it?

And what of those who might have been hit by stray debris? What of those who will suffer at the hands of the cloaks when they come down on you for this?

Strange. That had sounded like the German.

The echo of Bergen's momentary smile flashed in his mind. The German had never laughed; Oliver imagined him laughing over this.

He dug the crushed body of Jeremy Longshore out of the rubble before departing.

Chapter 15

I have not asked Them whether I am fated to die when Their work is done. I am too frightened that They may answer me.

—II. xxix

Windows shattered and cables broke in the world of dreams.

Ten thousand arms grasped at yellow-brown ichor. Towers swayed; brass and copper and glass puddled in the air before raining into the rising sea of bile. The searing heat of the fire and the sticky cool of the swamp clashed and annihilated each other. Steam burst upwards and tore the red sky, opening rents into horrid other spaces, which screamed above the incessant booming of the clock.

Aaron fled for his life.

The diseased child-god had used him. Whatever the Lord and Lady had done to keep their malformed spawn from invading the city, Aaron had undone.

At first he had seen her clearly, as Mama Engine emerged into man's realm at the beckoning of her priest. The layers of her essence unfolded in sequence, revealing progressively deeper levels of her mind, from the simplest surface thoughts, to capricious desires and whims, to deep convictions of love and pain, to an exacting point of fire, hungry to consume and smelt and mould.

At one instant he had been safe, buoyed inside his silver body and anchored firmly on Adam's earth. The next, he felt a tug at his mind, then dull claws slashed into it and a howl of pain ripped through him. In that instant he became a thousand individuals writhing in pain on a thousand beds, cots, and street corners, every sliver of his body ground apart from within by teeth and gears, black oil spilling from every orifice. He'd looked up and seen the faces of friends and family, tormentors and cloaks, sometimes no face at all.

The diseased child-god burst from Aaron's soul like water through a breached dike. In moments, the thing's pus-body had attached itself to the towers and walkways of the dream world, and then began to oxidise them.

As the tower of hands bent and closed in, Aaron had torn himself free. Something of him was left behind, to singe and curl and turn to ash.

The void. Where is the void? He ran through the copper-plated streets, through glass arches and across chain bridges. Every turn brought him to a new corridor, identical to the last, or to a new chain bridge over choppy, black seas.

It must be somewhere. He reached into it to get me, so there must be an entrance.

He reached a ledge and halted. From there, he scanned the sky ahead. A chain ran from the ledge some two hundred yards to the prismatic saw creation that stood in for the Docks Tower. Beyond, black skies and London's army of ghosts waited and watched.

Words came to him from that echo of his mind that knew the unknowable: *They guard the ancient dreams of London from all invaders, even yourself.*

He spun and looked back. Cracks spiderwebbed across the sky. Long trails of smoke flew in all directions as the tower of arms lurched and bent and smashed against its foe. The air filled with the wailing of souls on both sides as the gods threw those captured wretches into the fray.

Grandfather Clock ticked in steady rhythm, and did nothing to help or hinder.

He'd run as far as he could. The tower and the chains shook, and he wondered what good any amount of distance would do him.

There is always a way out.

He closed his eyes and reached up with his mind. The rock-and-dirt world shunned him as he touched it. A brief impression of pressure, damage, and deformity flashed over him: his second body had been lost, and with it, his link to the city above.

The heat and the noise swelled. Aaron began to hear the screams of men and women echo in from the real world, and longed for the peace of the void, which hid from his reach.

There really was no way out.

Was he to be a mute witness to this, then? Was he to sit and watch and do nothing?

What else could he hope for? His body was gone, and escape into the void unlikely. He dared not place himself between the two entities clashing before him.

So there was no other course. Seeing was what he had always been best at: seeing, thinking, planning, advising, but never acting. He had acted once, and he had been killed.

So he seated himself upon the hot air, and watched.

On a crowded cable car, halfway between Cambridge-Heath and Dunbridge, Thomas started screaming.

The cries flew out into the vast spaces around, vanishing without echo. White eyes in black faces turned. Oliver's company froze as one for an instant, uncertain. The stunned silence dragged on, each passenger waiting to see if the sound was repeated.

"Ah, bugger the dog! Jesus!"

Oliver leapt up into the wagon and tore the concealing burlap blanket from Tom's face. A visage of agony greeted him. Oil and pus squirted from Tom's burned eye.

"Sorry, Ollie," Tom managed.

Oliver knocked him on the head. "You should be. I've

told you a thousand and one times you make too much noise, chum."

Tom chuckled through his grimace. "Like a banshee. Awooooo." The mirth dissolved into a fit of horrid coughing that produced brown bile.

Oliver skipped his gaze over his crew. Bergen was already reaching for his pistol with his left hand. Hews was likewise reaching for his. Oliver shook his head at them and they stayed their hands.

"I'm terribly sorry." It was Missy's voice. "Our friend is very sick with the clacks. We didn't mean to be a bother. We're taking him to see a doctor."

Half the crowd nodded and turned away. Conversations began all about the car, passing quickly from mouth to mouth; everyone knew someone with the clacks, and everyone had a story to tell. The men of Oliver's troupe communally exhaled a held breath. Missy slid smoothly into conversation with a woman close by. Thomas coughed and spat up, but by then the crowd's attention had been redirected.

"Got a good tongue," Hews said, from his position at the right front handle of the wagon. "I couldn't have made that half as convincing."

"It's why I hired her," Oliver said. He pulled a rag out of his pocket and started blotting the fluids spilling out of his friend.

Tom chuckled. "Certain there weren't other factors, eh, Chief?"

"You're supposed to be sick."

"Wouldn't you know it," Tom said. "A dozen knives to the heart and two shots to the belly and it's a bloody fist in my gut that gets me."

Oliver jostled his shoulder. "You're going out pounding cloaks, remember?"

Tommy coughed again. "Ah. Right-oh. Where would I be without you, Chief?"

Packing coal in Aldgate, healthy and in one piece, that's where. "I'm sure you'd be neck-deep in trouble by now even without my help."

"Ah! Stung! God's own truth, if I ever heard it. Where is the king?"

Oliver started. "Jeremy?"

"Yeah. The little bugger didn't run off on me, did he?"

"I . . . er . . . sent him on a mission."

Tom's one remaining eyebrow perked up. "Truly?"

Oliver tried very hard for a casual shrug. "I said I'd make him a member of the crew, right? Little guy has to pull his weight. Besides, he's shown he's capable."

Tom squinted through his good eye. After a moment, his expression changed and his face fell.

"Knew he was a good pick," he mumbled.

Oliver gestured to Hews. "Take over, would you?"

The older man ended his conversation with a fellow passenger and obediently mounted the wagon as Oliver climbed out. The wagon was of native Whitechapel variety, made of iron rods, tin, and aluminium. They'd loaded it with a pack of supplies, Bergen's steam rifle, Lawrence's manual, and the translation of Scared's tape—and then Tom's body, for when he'd come to, he'd been unable to walk and was far too heavy to carry.

Oliver walked round into Hews' place at the right handle and faced Bergen, who stood at the left. Phineas, Heckler, and the doctor, they'd left in the Underbelly: Oliver expected a strike on Shadwell to come within the hour. Phineas could give fair warning and had been through the last Uprising; Heckler was a capable lad, and a prodigy shooter; and Chestle . . . well, he'd be needed soon enough.

It would have been nice to leave Bergen and his cannon there as well, but . . .

"Where is this mechanic of yours?" Oliver asked.

Bergen regarded him coolly, as if evaluating whether he was trustworthy enough for such information. "John Scared has a hide at the top levels of the Dunbridge slope, and the mechanic keeps his workshop in it."

Oliver crossed his arms and leaned on the wagon. "So you'll be leading us right into Scared's headquarters."

The German glowered. "I dislike your tone, English. Had I wished your death, I could have effected it any number of times."

That much was true. The man had certainly made an effort, and yet something about him tickled at Oliver's attention and set his mind to doubting every time the two ended up in the same room: *Why would Bailey, with his God-save-the-queen bravado, go out and hire a German? Why not a fellow Briton, born and bred?*

"Will Scared be there?"

Bergen snorted. "Doubtful. He's likely evacuated to a different hide, as I know the site intimately. He has another in Aldgate, and he has told me there are several more. I suspect one in Shoreditch, though I could not say where."

Oliver noticed Missy glance their way. After a second she turned back to her conversations with the other passengers.

"Why would he evacuate, I wonder?"

"Barring any other report, he has to assume I've been captured, either by the cloaks or the English," Bergen said. "Although his spies have probably noted me with you. Scared is a prudent man."

"Why did he hire you?"

Bergen crossed his own arms, arms much thicker than Oliver's. "I am growing weary of your distrust, Sumner. Do you interrogate all of your men like this?"

Oliver felt his hackles rising again.

"Keuper, I have a rule that I never question after the history of my people. I don't believe a man has to carry his past with him like Marley's chains, and so I will not ask you about your past. I will, however, ask you about the work you've done for Bailey, and for Scared, because *that* could be necessary."

The cable car bumped as it passed over one of its junctions, where the cables hooked through the bent, wobbling beams of an infant tower, still too young to hold inhabitants. The wagon car clanked and rolled, and for a moment Bergen and Oliver halted to steady it with the handles.

"So, tell me," Bergen said, when the car had stabilised again, "how do you choose your men, without knowing anything about them? A man's past is his definition."

"I don't believe that," Oliver said. "I trust my sense of people is all. I consider myself a good judge of character."

Bergen barked a laugh. "Character? Your American is a criminal, Sumner. Your woman is a whore."

Oliver's fist flew out before he even felt the anger rising. His knuckles cracked the German across the jaw, forcing him back and down against the wagon's handle.

Good Lord, chap, what were you—

Bergen's fist hammered into his cheekbone and drove through to the back side of his head. His neck snapped in a wrong way and his whole body gave out.

He felt the German take a heavy footstep in his direction. Then Hews rang out like a bell: "That's enough!"

Oliver groaned and tried to right himself. In his blurred vision, he caught Bergen, hand on his weapon, and Hews, hand on his.

Missy appeared behind Bergen's shoulder, eyes dark. She slipped one hand into her handbag and drew an object halfway out. Even through tumbling perceptions Oliver recognised what it was. Missy's lips moved, muttering something for only Bergen's ears.

"You came out the top on that one," Hews said, still covering Keuper with his pistol. "Let it go."

The German straightened, retreating into the general blur.

"I will not tolerate that again," he said.

"Then don't . . . insult . . . my crew!" Oliver slammed his hands down onto the grate floor and shoved himself up.

"They bring it on themselves, Sumner," Bergen said. "You have no discipline; you keep no controls on your men. Africa would swallow you alive."

"This isn't Africa," Oliver said. He grabbed on to the wagon handle to steady himself, then rose to his feet. Feeling began to seep back into his cheek: an acute, throbbing pain. "But tell me: if it were, could you kill every lion and tiger and snake and whatever else all by your lonesome? Could your one gun kill all of them before they got you?" He jabbed his finger out. "It seems you're so stupid as to think you can fight this all on your own, and while I'd be happy to be rid of you, I frown on people getting themselves needlessly killed."

Bergen harrumphed. "Then you are a weak and stupid man."

Hews stuck his gun in Bergen's face, then in Oliver's. "Enough," he said. "I won't stand for any more of this lunacy. The next one to say anything gets a lump in the face."

Bergen and Oliver exchanged glares. They stood that way for a long time. On their right, the slope of Dunbridge faded into view through the smog. Their audience stared at them raptly, caught in their moment.

Bergen broke the gaze and spat on the floor between them. Then he turned and strode away. The other passengers parted around him, and watched as he walked to the far corner of the car and took a post staring pointedly out at nothing.

Oliver sighed, righted himself, and turned to face the crowd.

"Don't." Missy pressed him back against the wagon with a firm palm. "Right now it's gossip and that's all. There's no sense turning it into something bigger."

"You all right, lad?" Hews asked.

Oliver checked his jaw, his neck; nothing seemed permanently damaged. He nodded.

Only then did Hews stow his pistol. He swung his legs over the edge of the wagon and sat. For a moment he wrung his hands. "That was far from prudent, Oliver."

Oliver rubbed his cheek and said nothing.

Hews frowned. "The man's been trying to get your goat since he met you and you just up and handed it to him."

Missy's face suddenly compressed and she snapped at Hews through bared teeth. "Hogwash, Hewey. If this is the only way to put that man in his place then let's have more of it."

"Lass?" Hews said.

"That's a vile man we've hooked up with. I've said it before that he can't be controlled. Do you need more proof than *that*?" She indicated Oliver's face.

Oliver watched the tiny twitches of Missy's lips and eyelids.

Hews leaned down over his shoulder. "Lass, our boy, here, struck first."

"The German struck first," Missy said. She looked at Oliver. "Didn't he? Didn't he really?"

After a moment, Oliver nodded. "That's the truth of it."

"Codswallop," Hews said. "Your bloody temper's the truth of it. That was disgraceful."

"I've enough of a lashing for that already, Hewey," Oliver snapped. "And you've no right to speak to me like a child."

Hews flushed. "I've all the right in the world, boy. I raised you—"

"You let me sleep under your smelting pots, Hewey," Oliver said. "You let me carry coal and ore and paid me a pittance to do it. And sometimes, *sometimes*, you told the other coves not to kick me for the fun of it and then walked around puffing yourself that you were helping some charity orphan boy and what a good soul you were."

Hews trembled for a moment, cheeks puffing, eyes bulging. The words came out with slaver through the teeth: "We fed you, boy. We clothed you and kept the Chimney gangs—"

Oliver cut him off. "I *stole* most of what I ate, Hewey. You weren't about to share any of your wife's cakes, either, as I recall."

Hews looked fit to explode. The next words came out barely a whisper: "Ungrateful child."

Oliver returned the man's glare until Hews turned away. Then Oliver dropped his head and chewed the insides of his cheeks. Missy stood back, scowled, said nothing.

The maw of the Dunbridge station, edged in random growths of iron like crooked teeth, sucked the cable car inside. The omnipresent haze of Whitechapel vanished, to be replaced by glaring electrics and blasts of hot steam from a dozen unfathomable engines. Half-human crows scuttled to and fro, tinkering, tightening, massaging, and placating. The Boiler Men that had watched every station for the past twenty-four hours were conspicuously absent.

As the gates slid apart, Oliver and Hews each took up a wagon handle. Oliver felt every muscle popping as he strained to move the wagon that first few feet. The wheels screamed terribly and caught on their own axle every couple of inches.

The exertion pushed blood into his face, which made the pain worse. He must have a jolly bruise by now.

If that was the least damage you'd caused today, it would be a blessing.

Hews marched beside him, puffing and sweating, unused to such work, but no one was about to ask Bergen to join them again. Oliver stole a look over. Hews, weighted with exertion, walked with dragging heels—crestfallen, tired, and old. Fifty-seven years of life scraped together on Hews' face in divots, wrinkles, scars, and jowls, and Oliver felt a powerful sense of wrongness.

Hews should be sitting by his fireplace in a country estate by now, sipping port and talking about the upcoming birth of his first grandchild to any ill-fated cove he could con into listening to him. Instead he had set up shop in Whitechapel, spied for the queen, lost a wife to cancer of the lungs, employed a whole gaggle of men, and kept one little boy from falling into his own grave.

The sudden rage, wherever it had come from, boiled away, and Oliver's guts sank into his shoes.

The wheels of the wagon clattered and bounced as they tipped off the ramp and into the station. Missy's silence and Tom's fevered moans trumpeted their arrival in Dunbridge.

Oliver should have known better than this.

Missy mopped her forehead with a lace-lined white handkerchief. It came away yellowed and soiled.

It was Gisella's cardinal rule: don't ever be a mess. A lady should never sweat, never smell otherwise than with perfume, never have her clothing or her hair out of sorts. She'd discouraged it even at the height of . . . moments.

Gisella isn't here, bird.

That didn't matter. Missy still felt vile, soiled.

You were born in filth, little girl. That had been the repeating refrain of her inner voice the entire climb.

It had taken considerable coaching and cold water to rouse Thomas enough to get him on his feet. Even then, he wobbled terribly with each step, flopping his tremendous weight to and fro without pattern. It had taken all three men to keep him upright, and Missy had added her shoulder as well, knowing they needed her but would never ask. Missy had never really been to Dunbridge. She had stopped through it on her flight from the bordello, those eternal months ago, but she had merely stopped over at the station, never experiencing the through-the-looking-glass maze quality of its platforms and walkways, its staircases and ladders and dead ends.

She found her eyes leaping with fright to the shadows slinking out of the smog. Always, they resolved themselves into Chinese women carrying baskets, men backing slips of metal, and stunted, bleary-eyed children tromping after. They watched her with tiny eyes.

And no wonder: Thomas lurched like Shelley's monster, falling every twenty steps to dent or crack a stair or rail. Hews directed them with a few terse words at every crossing as they marched on. Bergen had returned, but the men spoke to each other only in the sparest, most necessary exchanges.

She'd caught the German looking at her several times. She couldn't read the look. It wasn't lust, not as she understood it, but neither was it suspicion nor anger. It was a rapt and undisturbed attention, detached and frigid.

When will Oliver listen to me and turf him?

Well, it seems you have two men here that cannot be controlled.

At long last, Hews announced that they had arrived, and they proceeded to wrestle Thomas through a door far too small for even a normal man, and more or less dump him onto a thin mattress and a few blankets in the corner. Each of the men threw the supply packs they carried against the wall. Then they collectively stood back for a rest.

Missy glanced around. All about the place lay filthy blankets draped over filthier men. The air stank like a sick house: sweat and piss, and some other acrid smell Missy didn't recognise. The occupants could have passed for corpses, for how still they lay.

Missy tugged on Oliver's sleeve. He turned, still panting. Her nose wrinkled at the rough smell of him.

"Why did you bring us to such an awful place?" Missy whispered.

Oliver smiled. "It's not so bad, compared to some. Besides, it's friendly territory."

"I would hardly call it that."

"We find our friends where we can."

A squat, plump Chinese lady waddled from behind a red curtain at the back of the room. She wore a decorative Oriental dress of the most garish green with dulled gold detailing. Hews removed his hat and stepped up to greet her.

"Mrs. Flower, I'm afraid we must once again impose on your hospitality," he said.

The lady inclined her head slightly, then turned and vanished into the back.

"We'll take a few minutes' rest," Oliver said. "Then Bergen and I will go visit this mechanic of his."

A twinge picked at Bergen's lower eyelid and he glowered darkly. Much to her horror, she realised she understood that expression.

Yes, it's the murderous one, isn't it, child? Never forget that you are a killer now, too. Born a dog, trained a whore, now you are in full blossom. Isn't that just proper?

"Shut up," she hissed. She slapped her hand over her mouth.

Only Oliver noticed. His eye flicked momentarily her way. Hews interrupted before anything could be said.

"I'll go," he said, hitching pants and fixing vest as he spoke.

Oliver knitted his eyebrows. "Hewey, I'm not . . ."

"I won't hear it, boy. When was the last time you slept?"

Oliver blinked back his surprise. "I don't . . ."

"If the answer isn't 'this morning,' then you're staying here. In any case, I'm the only one who knows the ins and outs of this tower."

Oliver stood a moment, considering.

Missy's eyes flicked to Bergen. She recognised that look: studying a man to see how he could be controlled.

It is your duty to control your client, to bring him to his pleasure by whatever means are most agreeable to him. For each man, a unique set of actions, phrases, and gestures will be his reins. You will learn to pick these out through observation and intuition. Now, please, drink your tea, lay on your cots, and the training will begin.

Oliver could be controlled by treating him like a child.

I won't do it.

Of course you will, my dear. It is what you were trained for. The German lacks the flexibility to conquer him, but you, my child—you are as fluid as rain. You can be whatever he needs you to be.

It was a new voice, rougher than she was used to. Chills ran up her spine.

At last, Oliver sighed.

"Fine. Just be back quick as you can."

Hews screwed his bowler hat onto his head. The Chinese woman reemerged from the back, carrying a tray with a brass kettle and four porcelain cups. Hews took his hat off again and bowed towards her. He jabbed Oliver with an elbow and Oliver removed his hat as well, spilling unkempt brown hair to his shoulders.

"Regrettably, we must go, Mrs. Flower," Hews said. "By God's graces, we shall be back before the pot is cooled."

Mrs. Flower did not appear to acknowledge the sentiment. She merely placed the tray on the floor by Hews' feet and retreated through the room, checking on her various semiconscious patrons.

Hews replaced his hat. Bergen dropped his steam cannon into the corner and stood it against the wall. He'd climbed the whole way with it lashed to his back and barely looked out of breath.

He's going to murder Hews and then he's going to come back and murder you. But you'll stop him long before that, will you not? You and your little handbag.

Missy found herself piqued.

He would deserve it.

There's my little dog.

Bergen ducked out into the dark of midafternoon. Hews made to follow. Oliver stopped him with an arm on the shoulder.

Hews shook his head. "No time now, Oliver."

Oliver let him go. The door shut. Missy had never seen a man so alone in a room full of people.

Now would be the moment to do it: just step outside the door and put a bullet through the German's back.

"Come on, then," she heard her mouth saying. "Let's have a sit."

Oliver wandered in her direction, then swerved and flopped to the floor beside Thomas. He used his hands to draw his knees up to a cross-legged position, then shrugged out of his coat. Missy gathered the tray and sat beside him.

She poured the tea and tried not to let her hands shake when it came out red. Gisella's tea was always red—that awful soporific that conjured up the hobgoblin man.

Heh. I see you remember me.

The teapot rang as it bounced off the tray and regurgitated its contents onto the floor.

"Oh, God . . ." Missy breathed.

Oliver reached across and righted the teapot. "No one will notice."

That wasn't what she meant.

The hobgoblin man is real. He came to visit me.

She felt the phantom sensation of his ghastly fingers against her face, and she forgot.

She returned to herself to see the profile of Oliver's scruffy face. He stared at Thomas, who gurgled as he breathed, and simultaneously stared at nothing. Tea soaked into the leg of his trousers. His skin had turned several shades towards yellow. The lamplight reflected flickering flames into his eyes.

Something wasn't right. Oliver's mussed hair fell forward over his brow, shadowing his eyes, so that it could not possibly be reflected light.

She shivered. He reacted to the motion, and turned those subtly burning eyes on her own.

"What so you see?" he asked.

She told him.

His eyes drifted closed. "It's getting worse," he said. "It feels like a hot iron up under my skull."

She felt a chill rake through the moist air, and dared not ask what he meant.

He continued anyway. "It gets hotter the closer we get to the Stack. Mama Engine has taken up residence in my head. It seems she fancies me as a consort."

Missy sat very still, her skin crawling.

"The other one is in my guts. I'm not entirely sure what he wants from me." He grabbed and gripped Tommy's flesh-and-bone hand. "This can't be for nothing."

There's the opening. Take him in your lap, coddle him, sing to him, tell him everything will be all right and make him yours.

Missy began reaching for Oliver's hand.

I don't want to.

Yes, you do.

She stopped, stripped off her filthy red glove, and took his fingers, skin to skin, in hers.

"You never asked me," Missy said, "where I came from, Oliver."

His fingers were calloused and scarred, and rough against her skin. They lay immobile in her hand, but a slight flush crept up Oliver's neck.

"Who you were isn't my business," he said.

Missy swallowed. "Oliver, I won't . . . I can't . . . tell you, but just . . ." She breathed. "Just understand that the place I came from was a terrible place. She made us . . . I was dying there all the time."

He was staring at her, and the dancing fire did not seem so threatening now.

"Never think that it was for nothing, Oliver."

God, the *look* he gave her. She felt a heat in her chest, a lightness of limbs. He was beautiful, his lips in a small smile potent with such warmth that she . . .

She shot to her feet.

"Well, I'd best let you rest, I'd imagine," said her mouth. "Weighty mission tonight, if all goes well."

Still staring at her with that smile—that damnable alluring smile—he said, "I suppose that would be best."

"Indeed. Well, I quite think I'll step out for a moment, perhaps buy us some biscuits or whatever they sell here."

"That would be delightful, Miss Plantaget."

"And you needn't worry for my safety. I'm quite capable of caring for myself."

"That is something I would never doubt."

"Good. Well . . . I shall be back soon."

She fled to the door.

You forgot!

The handbag! She turned, snatched it, didn't look at
Oliver, returned to the door, and all but bolted into the
street. The grey of Whitechapel afternoon closed over
her. Dunbridge, not having any classifiable streets, had
neglected to install streetlights, and thus the day was
only slightly brighter than the depths of night.

The bag settled over her shoulder like an old friend.
Just the presence of it kept her safe.

Couldn't he keep you safe?

I'd rather have the gun.

The heat and the weightlessness ended with that
thought, and she screamed in her mind to take it back.

*Well, child. Is it not yet clear to you that your fate is
one of villainy? With such thoughts as that, it is a wonder
you even affect a liking for him.*

He would take care of me.

That was always my promise, as well.

She walked on, to move, to flee fitfully from the voice
that haunted her. She told herself over and over that
she would indeed go back to him, and that she would
bring something to eat. Something small, and perhaps
he would smile at her again, in that way.

Six turns, two flights of stairs, a pair of Chinamen
babbling in their disturbed language, and she was lost.
Hopelessly. The only landmark visible was the Stack, its
top crowned by a fierce, incessant red glow.

There were no proper stores to be found, only an endless succession of tenements, growing one into the other
with the vagaries of the tower's supports. No alleys or fa-
çades broke the endless stretch of doors unmarked and
without signs, even in Chinese. At last, she stopped in an
open plaza and stomped her foot. "Prick on a stick," she
said.

"Now, now. What would the good matron think if she
heard you using such language?"

The hobgoblin man shuffled from the dark.

Reflections boiled in her memory: his words, his

laughs, the too-sweet smell of his breath, the horrid prodding of his goblin nails, the commands that sunk down to stimulate the baseness of the animal, words inscribed on the mechanisms of thought.

He trained you. I fed you the tea; then he came to you to implant deeply the lessons I rendered. He primed you for this obedience, and you cannot cross him.

"With me, if you would," he said.

Her feet followed his. He led her down a thin walkway to a dead-end circle stacked with garbage. Rats—flesh ones—chittered and ran at their approach.

He's real. Why didn't I remember it?

"Come, my dear. Time is short," he said. "It wasn't unexpected, your lot coming here. The cloaks know about this den of yours, too. But not to worry. I've put them off."

He halted in the centre of the little circular end to the alley and pivoted, hunched over his cane. "What *was* unexpected was my German being with you. I assumed my boy had done his duty, though he was left a mess. Though his days upon the earth are limited, your Continental friend could still be of use to me."

Missy strained, breathed, whispered: "What do you want?"

The man perked. He adjusted his top hat and regarded her quizzically. "Tick, tick. Did you just speak under your own volition, my dear?"

Her head moved.

"Heh." The man reached one knobby hand into his pocket. "Either you are exceptionally strong-willed or you are simply a remarkable freak in nature's panoply. This will be quite dangerous, indeed, but I suppose there's no avoiding it."

He slipped from his coat a stoppered bottle of red fluid. Her chest tightened up at the sight of it. "I trust you remember this, my dear. Gisella's preference is to dilute it with hot water." The man opened the bottle with two rough fingernails, then upended it and allowed a single drop to fall onto his fingertip. It stayed there, quivering, like a blot of honey.

"Open your mouth, my dear."

Her head shook slowly, back and forth.

"That won't do, girl," the man said. "I have other affairs that need tending. Open."

Her mouth opened.

The man approached. "Stick out that tongue of yours, girl."

The tongue obeyed.

The hobgoblin man smeared the drop from his fingertip along the length of her tongue. He tasted like sweat and granulated sugar.

The gun, the gun, the gun, the gun . . . Words echoed in her mind. The fingers twitched. The handbag opened. Inside: deliverance, power, revenge.

And suddenly a prison of ice closed on her, a glacial field too vast to cross, and canyon walls too high to climb. It froze away the awareness of her body, the perception of walls and street and air. She dreamed cold dreams. She dreamed of the hobgoblin man.

"Always a new experience," he said. "I enjoy pure tastes myself time to time. It is a jaunt to heaven or hell, as you please."

Fingers rubbed her forehead, temples, cheeks, neck, prodded in armpits, ribs, hip bones, thighs, ankles, arches.

Her shoes were off. Did he take them off? Did she?

"Speak to me of Oliver Sumner, my dear."

Missy's mouth opened, and she dictated Oliver's every motion and word over the past day, up to his frightening and cryptic remarks in the den.

Fingers over the eyes. The hobgoblin man was whispering under his breath, into himself.

"Why did you choose him over me, my love? Was he to be your champion and liberator?"

Fingers bearing down, penetrating, shearing into the brain.

"I am wounded, my love. I am betrayed."

Fingers shaping, pulling.

"Heh, heh. But my, it is strange, my love, how things fall into place. Perhaps it is you intended to put our weapon into his hands, to stay mine." A gruesome smile. "But now my German is alive and he will carry our torch into your husband's depths instead."

The fingers withdrew, wisps of thought and intention clinging.

"And so now I will do as rivals are meant."

Missy floated up, buoyed on frigid winds ripped from the juices of foreign plants and the chemicals of the brain. The hobgoblin man wrapped his horrid hand about her chin and cradled her skull.

"Little one, listen now. And as always, forget after you have heard, and be as you always were."

Missy nodded.

"Heh. Or be as I made you, should I say? No matter."

Fingers from the other hand, snaking along the jaw, scratching, soiling.

"Here is what I wish of you, girl. Go to Oliver Sumner, on whatever pretence suits the moment. Then dispatch him by the most expedient means available."

The head nodded.

"Obey me," the man said. "But remember nothing until you next lay eyes on me. Now get on your feet, dress, and go about your business. This should be done with all haste."

Her shoes were back on.

"Off you go, now."

The moment crumbled and the memory fell with it. She found herself at the edge of a dim, unremarkable junction of several walkways.

"Prick on a stick."

Where was she going? What was she doing?

You went to fetch food, you scatterbrained child.

Yes, of course. Something to eat. Something to make Oliver smile at me.

A flash of inspiration hit her and she knew exactly what he needed.

What does our dog-turned-whore-turned-murderess have on her corrupted little mind, I wonder.

Shut your trap, you old bat.

Missy strode into the dark.

Chapter 16

The third principle of the forge is Pride. One may call it love, one may call it scrutiny, but it remains a necessary act to review and regard one's work, and to smash it or exalt it as it deserves. In this, how is the creator of the smallest thing unlike God? Judgement is the domain of the creator; artifices like ourselves exist only as victims of Her whim.

V. iv

Bergen's abdomen pulsed like it was about to burst. It took all his willpower not to double over with every step. It felt as if an unseen bellows pumped more air into his body with every movement. On top of that, light-headedness had set in, a sure sign of continuing blood loss.

"You're certain you know the way?"

Bergen shook off his thoughts; it would not do to be distracted by pain. He turned to his companion, who always walked a half stride behind and with one hand in his pocket.

"I am certain."

Hews simply nodded and gestured forward. "Lead on, then."

Bergen set off around the corner. The doors had begun blurring together the moment he'd entered the hide. The design of the hallways held a devilish sort of madness that kept the visitor doubting his faculties no matter how many times he had walked them.

"Here," he said. He reached for a doorknob. Either a set of well-lit stairs or a swift and ingenious death awaited him on the other side.

He gripped the knob, turned, pulled. The promised staircase stretched downward.

"How far down are we now?" Hews asked.

"The hide is built around one of the tower's support columns," Bergen said. "It goes much farther down than the streets do."

"Hmm." The Englishman pondered and rubbed his fat fingers into his facial hair a moment. "How does this mechanic get his supplies, all the way down here?"

Bergen spun on him. "Must you all assume I mean you harm? There is no trap here."

Hews smiled broadly. He did not remove his right hand from his pocket. "No offence was meant. I was merely curious."

Quickly, Bergen turned away and descended the stairs. Years ago he had convinced himself not to feel pain as other men do, but while that effort functioned it was detrimental to the temperament. He needed to maintain control over himself. Von Herder would have Scared's device together in a matter of hours, and then the real business would begin.

Bergen descended with stiff and heavy footfalls. By the time he entered the workshop, spots swam on his vision.

The old mechanic sat hunched over the sleek and beautiful form of a steam rifle. One of his boy assistants held a plate in place while von Herder secured it. Bergen's clomping drew his attention.

"Eh? Who's that?"

"Herr Keuper, sir," Bergen said.

"Herr Keuper!" The old man grinned toothily. "A pleasure as always. Who is that with you?"

Bergen was about to make some vague reference to "a comrade" or "another soldier" when Hews stepped forward. His right hand came out of the pocket.

"Herbert Lewis, sir. Very pleased to make your acquaintance."

Von Herder flashed open his pale, cataract-scarred eyes and reached out in the space across the table, searching for the expected hand. Of course, the old man did not see Hews' reaction to his blindness.

"Ferdinand von Herder," the mechanic said, at last finding Hews' hand and shaking firmly. "You are a servant of our mutual patron?"

Hews recovered. "Ah, no. I'm a companion of Mr. Keuper's. A business partner, as it were."

"Of course. I'll pry no more." Von Herder released Hews' hand and bent back over the rifle. The boy hadn't moved an inch during the conversation. His jaw clenched in the effort of holding the heavy boiler casing in place.

Hews' glance at Bergen communicated much of his confusion.

That's right, Englishman. He's blind.

Von Herder placed a rivet along the casing's edge, feeling around its edges with deft fingers. "So what brings you back to my little abode, Herr Keuper? From the quiet of your footsteps I assume you are not returning my steam rifle to me?"

"No, sir," Bergen said. He stepped up to the table and leaned heavily on one arm. The stitching that doctor had given him was little better than field dressing. "Though I will require more ammunition for it."

"Olaf has poured a new batch. Two dozen, by the wall." He gestured vaguely. "This one is nearly finished. Just the casing and a few modifications to the breech and handles and it will be ready for its work."

"Might we perhaps borrow it when it's finished?" Hews asked. "Might come in handy, if the other one's any indication."

Von Herder cast his eyes in Hews' direction, then back towards Bergen. "Herr Scared has approved this, yes?"

"The mission is his design," Bergen said, trying not to speak the lie as he felt it. "A second rifle would be invaluable."

Von Herder sighed deeply. "Well, what is an artist supposed to say to the enjoyment of his work? Unfortunately, this rifle is called to duty in other matters. It is to go with another of Herr Scared's teams later tonight."

The pressure in his stomach continued to increase, and Bergen found himself gritting his teeth against it; sweat had broken out all over his body.

"There is another reason we've come to you, Herr von Herder," Bergen said.

Hews stepped up and produced the American's translated pages from an inner vest pocket. He froze, indecisive for a moment, then passed the papers to the boy.

"What is it, Andrew?" the mechanic asked.

The boy set the boiler casing down on the table and scanned the papers. "Uh . . . plans, sir."

"Well, read them, boy."

Andrew spent the next few minutes fumbling through letters and instructions he obviously could not properly read. The lad's speech halted so often Bergen experienced a growing impulse to rip the papers from his hands and take over.

Von Herder nodded at each step. The paper contained physical theory and mechanical instruction of such arcane complexity that Bergen could not follow. Andrew explained the diagrams, which von Herder clarified by way of a hundred different questions.

When the boy finally reached the end of the last page, von Herder stood very still a long time. Bergen turned to the lad.

"A glass of water, boy."

Andrew looked first to his master. Seeing the old mechanic deep in thought and unable to approve the action, the lad set the papers down and ran to the back. He returned with a pewter stein. Bergen drained it in one pull, grimacing at the metallic warmth of the water.

Another few minutes passed. Hews eventually broke the silence.

"Not to break the gentleman's train of thought," Hews said to von Herder, "but can you build it?"

Von Herder ignored the question, facing Bergen precisely.

"It is genius," he said, voice filled with breathy awe. "Undoubtedly Herr Scared's work. I find myself wishing I had a better command of pure mathematics." Then to Hews: "Of course I can build it, *Englisch*. Once the principles are understood, the design itself can be made from the most basic materials."

He leaned forward, across the table and into Bergen's space. "You know, of course, what it does?"

"Yes."

"You know it will only work in one place?"

"We know."

"Then I will build it for you, my friend." He tapped the steam rifle. "Once this is done."

"How long?"

"Return by midnight, and we will see."

Bergen pushed himself back to his full height. The water had helped, but not enough: his knees were weakening, and the belly pain grew minute by minute. "You have my thanks, as always, Herr von Herder."

"Think nothing of it." He and Andrew bent again over the rifle.

"We shall head back," Bergen said. Hews regarded him with detached coolness.

As Bergen mounted the first of the stairs, von Herder called him back.

"I have been thinking about our conversation yesterday, Herr Keuper," he said, not looking up from his adjustments. "And I have determined that you cannot possibly be from Stuttgart."

Bergen tensed. *Not in front of the Englishman, you old fool!*

"I spent a number of years there as a young man," von Herder said. "My first job with munitions, as I recall. The accent is quite distinct."

The statement demanded an answer.

"No disrespect, sir," Bergen said, "but you are wrong."

To that von Herder chortled, then bent back to his work with a smile on his lips. A few seconds' passage found him barking at his apprentice for letting the boiler casing slip.

Bergen climbed the stairway, each step an eternity of weakness and struggle. They reached the hallway above. Bergen stumbled forward into the dimness, and decided it was safe to place his hand on the wall for support. The door clicked quietly shut behind them.

"Now, though he's young," Hews began, "Oliver is an extraordinary judge of character. Line up identical twins and he'll tell you which is the sinner in each pair."

Bergen felt a shiver on his nape, and knew that Lewis had drawn his pistol.

"Oliver thinks that you have a secret," Hews continued. "So does your friend down there, and so do I. I will have that secret now."

"You are a fool," Bergen said. "Without me you would be dead at the first door you tried."

"I have only your word on that, remember," Hews said. "The alternative is for me to do this again once we're safely on the streets, and I'd sooner ask my question where there's a bit of privacy."

"I thought it was the boy's custom not to pry into the past."

"I don't hold to the same custom, sorry to say."

Bergen hesitated. His wound shifted and he felt warmth spread through the fingers he held over it. He drew his hand away. Blood stained his palm and the shirt over his bandaged wound.

"We can wait here all evening, if need be," Hews said.

Bergen growled, knowing he was caught. His first impulse was to lie, but the fog in his mind precluded any vestige of creative thought.

"Will you tell Sumner?"

"Only if he needs to know."

Vague, noncommittal. Practical. *I might have said the same.*

"Bergen Keuper is dead." Bergen breathed before continuing. "I shot him."

"Do you have a proper name, then?"

Bergen stared down the long hall, seeing mockery in the flickering lamps, feeling defeated. "I was born Nicholas Ellingsly."

"Ah, the explorer. I've read a number of your tales."

Bergen snorted. "They're all lies. I was little more than Keuper's translator. Keuper shot the tigers. Keuper fought the Zulus and Boers. He never deigned to learn English, and so I could tell the tales however I wanted."

"Why do you use his name?"

Bergen—Nicholas?—sighed deeply. He had not done so in a very long time, and something passed out of him with that long breath. Some edge or anger softened, some tension of the mind evaporated as water in the hot sun.

"You'll want to hear the tale, then?"

"We have time enough."

He slid down the wall to a tense squat. The words poured out of him like so much oozing blood.

"We were trekking through Zululand to Ulundi—Keuper, myself, and seven or so native porters. We came across a group of Boers camped in a little valley. We were shooting at one another within an hour."

The ghosts of gunfire echoed in the halls of Scared's hide.

"It wasn't as if I'd never been in combat before. I knew my way around a rifle, and I brought down several myself over the first few hours. By the time night fell our porters had died or fled, and their men were spread over the hills and the forest. Bergen and I stalked them like animals. It was in the night when I started to slow down. I froze at ordinary night sounds. My hands and knees shook. Keuper took a hit in the arm defending me just after moonrise. At that moment he finally decided I wasn't worth the trouble."

Nicholas shuddered as the memory came upon him of the German's cold, stone eyes in the light of that moon, with the dry trees closing around like the fingers of death on all sides, and the air prickling cold as the last heat of the day seeped from it.

"He valued a life only so far as its strength. I knew he was going to kill me."

In his mind the German raised that long-barrelled Gasser he cleaned but never polished. A dirty, ugly, remorseless weapon.

"I killed him first."

The German hadn't fallen. He'd stood with his neck a mess, glaring and cursing, as blood gushed onto his shirtfront. After an eternity, he'd fallen, but fallen forward, and in that memory Nicholas swore he saw Keuper take one step to reach out to his murderer.

"His blood got into my mouth and my eyes. I don't know what happened then; perhaps I fainted. When I came to myself it was morning, and his body was in the grass beside me."

The Gasser had been lying inches from his right hand.

"It was all wrong. It should have been the coward lying in the grass, not the hero." He pulled the sidearm reverently from its holster. It sat in his palm like a block of lead. "And so I made a choice: the hero lived, and the coward died."

Hews shifted his feet. "Killed by Zulus, as I recall."

"One more lie to the British public."

"Did Bailey know?"

Nicholas nodded.

"You should know he kept that secret to his grave," Hews said.

A pause. The Gasser found Bergen's hand, natural as rain into soil.

"And so will I."

"I wouldn't allow it any other way," Bergen said. He slipped the pistol back into its holster and pushed himself to his feet. When he turned at last to look at the older man, his eyes were hard as granite.

The Englishman examined him a moment without expression, then pocketed his British Bulldog and straightened his vest and coat.

"Well, I have the answers I need. We'd best get on so we can tend that wound of yours."

Bergen nodded and led the way up through the maze and into the fading light of evening. Then Hews, now the only man who knew his secret, took the lead through the incomprehensible ways of Dunbridge.

Much to Bergen's surprise, he didn't shoot the Englishman in the back.

He should sleep. He should eat. He should drink.

The red tea had cooled to match the temperature of the sticky air. The sots in the room lay insensible again, having woken one by one and gasped and pleaded for Mrs. Flower to bring them the pipe. She had obliged in her efficient and dignified way and relieved them of their coin in exchange for their demon. In the corner, beneath burlap blankets painted with Oriental writing, one poor wretch shrieked and gibbled in the grip of his nightmares.

Lucky bastard, Oliver thought.

It was not with his ears that he heard the war going on outside. Mama Engine's roars and Grandfather Clock's ticking rang inside his head. The sound of the god from below resembled a wet towel dragged rapidly across an uneven floor. When they clashed, Oliver felt the city shake, and a jolt in his body as if his heart had suddenly pumped hard in shock. The room around him remained static and gloomy.

The fire in the back of his neck had spread to his eyes and cheekbones. The nausea in his stomach had become a weakness in his legs and knees and cramps in his bowels.

Oliver gazed over at Tom, who lay beside him, still unconscious. *Is this what it's always felt like for you, chum?*

Tom lay as still as the addicts all around, lost in some private dream.

He'll either live through it or he won't. The thought was far from comforting, but it did provide a certain release from worry. It was in God's hands, after all, wasn't it? Hews' wife had always said such things.

He pulled his eyes away from his friend. He wiped them with the back of his bandaged hand, then quickly hid the hand from his peripheral vision. He was afraid of what colour his tears might be.

Mrs. Flower's den was busier tonight than the last time he'd been here. The floor was carpeted in twitching,

shivering men of the working class, not a one of them
Chinese. Oliver imagined it must smell, but couldn't tell
through the horrid sensations growing in his body.

Was he actually envious of these wretches?

"I was taught that all men possess a hidden desire that
they deny."

The lamp didn't get any brighter—he was sure of
that—but the room was suddenly clearer, warmer, the
wall hangings more beautiful.

"That desire, being denied, grows in magnitude until
the man either gives into it, or rejects it entirely and
goes mad."

Missy bent daintily down into his field of vision. Her
red lips twitched up at the corners.

"So in consequence: those who hold themselves in
check are mad, and those who release themselves are
only being natural. Polite society holds these two conditions reversed, which is why they are all buggers and
hypocrites, though they get on quite well, for, being mad,
they never quite realise it."

She knelt down.

"Michelle."

"Whomever did you expect, Mr. Sumner?" She adjusted her skirts and settled onto the blanket beside him.
From behind her back she produced a frayed, cheap basket filled halfway with lumps of bread that could not
completely be called biscuits and unidentifiable black
rolls that gleamed unhealthily. She plucked one of these
and offered it to him.

"The man I bought them from said they are made
from ginger and seaweed, that is, if I penetrated his atrocious accent properly. I'm ashamed to admit I've tasted
one already."

Oliver watched her eyelashes blink.

A peach, indeed. More than that: a warm fire, a full
belly, a sensation as satisfying as the best night's sleep.

Her hand swirled in a little gesture of impatience.
"Am I to sit with this sticking to my fingers all day?
They're really not so bad as one might think."

*And here I am a right mess inside and out, body and
mind.*

He accepted it, despairing at how his scarred, dirty fingers compared to hers. He brought the object to his mouth and his stomach curdled.

So the little god didn't want him to eat? Bugger him. He opened his mouth to bite down and nearly vomited. After one or two silent gags, he shoved the blackened thing between his teeth and bit down hard. Half of it came away, tearing like rubber, and plopped onto his tongue.

Even then he might not have been able to swallow it, but that Missy sat watching him, trying to feign that she didn't care if he liked it. Normally in a moment like this, Oliver would curse his talent for reading people. Now it gave him more strength than he would ever have guessed was needed.

A bite: the bitter tang of the seaweed engulfed his tongue. A chew: a potent, rash flavor took its place. A swallow: his throat constricted around it, his gullet fought it, but with a few contractions he forced it into his boiling stomach. He sat back and licked the flavour from the backs of his teeth.

"That's good," he said, by which he meant it was the most satisfying morsel he'd ever tasted; by which he meant that she bolstered him and energised him even in this most ruinous and dejected state.

He elaborated: "Very good."

"I'm glad." She fetched one herself and slipped it whole into her mouth. They sat in silence a moment, chewing, each trying not to look too long at the other. The moans of the afflicted and the echoing warfare of beasts greater than man seemed farther away for a time.

"A man I met once," Missy began, reaching this time for a biscuit. "I didn't know him very long, mind—told me a tale of the country outside London. He said there were fields that rolled on and on once one gets far enough out. He said there were places where one could look in all directions and see not a farmhouse, nor a road, nor any signs of human habitation." She chipped off a piece of the biscuit and spoke around it. "Can you imagine that? Just trees and grass and the sky."

"Hews tells the same kinds of stories." Oliver reached

for another of the black treats, nausea be damned. "Like how the Thames looks during sunset or the way the waves crash at Dover."

"Do you think we'll get to see it?"

Oliver had seen it every day in his daydreams, until the Uprising had wiped all that innocence away. He saw it again now, that childhood vision of Hews' ideal London. He saw the cattle markets and fishmongers. He saw stately cabs hauled by magnificent beasts of burden. He saw private courtyards and balconies and country homes away from the bustle, where one might read in quiet contemplation, or enjoy a cup of tea on clean china beneath naught but the sun. All of it flashed in brilliant, hopeful colour, the wishes of a child. Wishes that could come true, because one man said he had seen them and then made a little boy believe.

Oliver answered her.

They chatted as they ate. It had been a long time since Oliver had simply sat and enjoyed another's company. Fascinated and engaged by Missy's every gesture and turn of phrase, he felt himself coming slowly back to life. He could almost imagine them sitting in that field, gentle breeze and warm sun and all.

This is how life should be, he thought. *Everyone should have such moments.*

They talked about all those things neither of them had ever seen: about the Channel and France, about the great savannas of Africa, the palaces of India and Siam, the Swiss Alps, and even Heckler's America far off in the New World. Oliver laughed as each of these images entered his imagination. The world was so much bigger than Whitechapel alone, and its gods but one of a whole series of wonders scattered over the Earth. Oliver promised to take Missy to each of those places, and others not yet discovered, and he promised her a house in the country and a tea set of china, and sun all the year round.

He reached sadly for the last biscuit, knowing that when it was consumed, the moment would end. It turned out not to be a biscuit at all, but a leather drawstring pouch.

"Your hidden desire, Mr. Sumner," Missy said, "is to

be a spit-polished, well-dressed, member of proper society. You wish nothing more than to be clean-shaven, wear tailored suits, and sit about drinking cognac all evening, telling inflated tales of your adventures to other venerable gentlemen of advanced age."

Oliver turned the pouch over in his hand. "That's awfully specific."

"Furthermore, you have denied this desire entirely and rejected it in all its pretences. Therefore there are certain things you do only infrequently and with great reluctance."

He drew from the pouch a folded razor and laughed aloud. "My," he said. "I haven't shaved in days."

"And don't think a woman won't notice it. There's some soap in there for lather as well. Now stay put a moment and I'll prevail on our hostess for some hot water."

Missy whispered to her feet and stepped off. Oliver stared after her and shook his head. *I've got how many injuries and she thinks I need a shave?*

Well . . . he did.

By the time she returned with a wide-brimmed bowl of water, he had decided a shave would be a little moment of heaven on Earth.

Missy held aside the hanging curtain on one of the enclosed areas that looked to be deserted. One of Mrs. Flower's girls trailed after her, and set down a short table with a small hinged mirror on the back end. It was worn and dented, with paint and scrollwork hinting at lost beauty.

Missy set the bowl easily on the table and Mrs. Flower's girl retreated without a word. Oliver shuffled over to her and knelt before the mirror.

"Our hostess says we may proceed in here," she said. "I might have suspected there was no proper washbasin in this place." She slipped the razor away from him and replaced it with a yellow hand towel. "Wash and lather, now."

"Yes'm," he said.

The water was just on the edge of steaming, but against his skin seemed cool. He scrubbed every inch of his face and neck. He didn't recognise the man in the mirror. Sunken cheeks and wild hair greeted him. Blue-black circles rimmed his eyes. The bruise Bergen had given him was puffed and purple, while the rest of his skin was yellow, almost to the point of jaundice. Small, coherent flames burned deep inside his eyes, exactly as they had in the old bookseller's. He probably had machines growing in his guts already.

"You've missed several spots," Missy said, and proceeded to point them out with the razor's handle.

"Thank you, Miss Plantaget," Oliver said, then wiped where he was told.

In the mirror, he saw Missy watching him. Some sadness or darkness or fear passed over her face.

"That's quite sufficient, I think." She snatched the cloth out of his still-moving hand and laid it carefully on the tabletop.

Oliver took the soap and lathered his face. All the while, Missy watched him through the mirror, her expression oscillating between her familiar detached charm and that fear she tried to hide. His mental bell jingled quietly.

It would be polite not to pry, and with Missy, for some reason, he always wanted to be polite. But . . . something didn't *feel* right.

He held out his hand for the razor with an if-you-please. Missy smirked.

"With that hand? You'll leave yourself more of a mess than you are."

"Ah, yes." Oliver had completely forgotten about his hand, what with all else that was going on in his body.

Missy knelt behind him and slipped one hand beneath his jaw. There was something sacrilegious about those smooth fingers grating on his wiry beard. Oliver watched in the mirror as Missy deftly flipped open the razor and lowered it to the base of his left cheek. He decided to ask before he had to keep his face still.

"What's troubling you?"

She looked at him coyly through the mirror. "It's not polite to pry, Oliver. A woman's musings are her own."

She held him still with surprising strength and dragged the razor slowly down his cheek.

Well, he'd tried, at least. *She likes her mysteries.*

On the second pass, she spoke. "Will you go out to-night, if the machine is ready?"

"The Underbelly is unlikely to hold out longer than that," he answered.

She passed the razor over his bruise so gently he barely felt it.

"I suppose, in the proud tradition of male leadership, that you'll be ordering me to stay behind?"

He didn't want to admit that he hadn't thought that far ahead. "Hews is handling the details." He fiddled uncomfortably with his bandages. "I would as soon not take you into the Stack itself." Oliver mentally braced himself for a flood of loud indignation.

"Maybe that would be best."

"Sorry?"

"You *do* expect me to be difficult all the time, don't you?"

He cleared his throat. "Well, I . . ."

"Pish. Yes, you do." She started on his left cheek. "I think it would be a good idea; let you men handle the important things. I'll stay behind like a little trophy for you when you get back."

The words were sarcastic. The tone was genuine.

The bell rang loud in his brain.

"Michelle?"

She swallowed. "I just don't think it would be a good idea to take me along, is all. I . . . I'm not safe to be near."

She scraped gently across his upper lip, then his chin. *This isn't right.*

On impulse, he began to turn to her, but her fingers on his jaw held him in place.

"Why do you say that, Michelle?"

She placed the razor on his neck. "I don't know, Oliver. I can't remember . . . There was a man, but . . . I'll just finish the shave. I'll finish the shave."

"Missy?"

Her fingers clamped on to him. The tips of her nails dug into his skin. "I'm almost done. I'm just about . . ."

In the mirror, he saw sweat glistening all over her

face. He saw tears bead in the corners of her eyes.
"Missy . . ."

Her fingers locked around his jaw and pulled his
chin upwards.

"Stay still! There was a man. He told me . . . He
trained me to . . ."

The razor finished its last upward stroke. The shave
was done.

"I'm sorry."

A sting in his neck. His hands shot up to her arm.

A pull, cold inside the skin. Yellow and black spraying
on the mirror. Fingers around her arm, clutching, pulling, without enough strength.

The razor bit in, slid, parted skin and flesh and windpipe. A gurgle as his lungs emptied. A warm splash
down his shirt. His hands left her arm, wrapped around
his own throat. Close it up. Stop it from spilling out.

A woman screamed. He felt a sudden burning flash
behind his eyes and a sudden chill flood from his toes
up through his gut. His gasp brought fire into his lungs.

I had so much left to do.

He fell forward and spilled his life onto the blankets.

Chapter 17

I have scribbled these pages in desperation, as a warning to those who would follow or as a vain grasping for absolution or for a thousand other reasons. I want others to know my truth, and to hear these alien thoughts that encroach upon my mind. I want the world to hear my confession, to know my crime and hate me for it, and condemn me to a right and proper hell.

I am Faust. So I name myself, and so will I inherit his doom.

—I. vii

John Scared was in such a good mood that he poured himself some wine.

It was a fine rice wine of the Orient, flavoured with peach and aged several decades, though the Siamese who'd sold it to him had been unable to give an exact date. Scared had never intended to drink it, but had brought it back in case it might be useful in wooing an informant. Men of power, after all, appreciated fine things. He'd won Moran over with a bottle of Scottish brandy from '54.

Well, perhaps it had been the six thousand pounds, but the brandy had oiled the wheels, certainly.

He poured the wine into a shimmering crystal goblet of French design and settled into his chair. The familiar curves and upholstery nestled against him. He looked once around his bedroom, bidding adieu to the sanctum that had served him so many years. The traps at the door had been set. If anyone ventured down to find his body, they and any with them would suffer a dozen painful deaths.

He let the bouquet tickle his nose.

You'll never know the pleasure of earthly senses, my dear. A terrible pity.

Scared had always placed little value in ritual. The repetition of things not only made one vulnerable to prediction, but also dulled the mind into ignoring recurrences in the environment.

Nothing repeats endlessly, my love. You expect your new husband to be the same as the last. Oh my dearest, I pity you your ignorance.

But he could not help feeling that *some* observance was in order. The ending of things needed to be acknowledged, and the beginnings of other things celebrated.

He sipped the wine, letting the delicate flavour swirl like vapour atop his tongue before opening his throat and letting gravity draw the liquid down. *Heavenly. Would that it could be the last thing I taste.*

Of course, the last would be the *mei kuan*. He eyed the clear bottle where it sat exposed on his closet shelf. Four drops of it, and no more, to swell his consciousness larger than the forces he faced, without killing him outright. He'd calculated it all precisely while in trance that morning.

The fire in the back of his mind flared and whirled, stinging his old thoughts with its agitation.

Patience, my love. All was ready: Gisella's little girl would rid him of his rival; Moran would rid him of the city's master; his German would release his bride from her vows, and then Penny would do his duty. With a palpable regret, he set the wine aside and took up the liquid gates of heaven.

Scared uncorked the bottle. Keeping it far from his nose, he dipped an eyedropper inside and filled it to the black mark he had made earlier. Mama Engine's fire skipped and jolted.

Ah, the city will shake and crumble to our nuptials, my darling.

He opened his mouth and squeezed the dropper. Clear liquid splashed over his tongue as the vapours shot into his nose. The world dissolved into a string of equations and fled to the four winds.

Scared's body slumped in his chair, and did not breathe.

Now, it seems to me that while I made you into a whore . . .

Missy looked down at the gun hanging limp in her fingers: shining, dull, beautiful, terrifying, ugly.

. . . you became a murderess all on your own.

"It was the hobgoblin man," she whispered. The words vanished into the smoke around her. The wind blew down from the Stack, stinging her eyes and burning her lungs and she could not care. She had run for hours, blindly, through the Dunbridge maze, to arrive here, at the edge of the tower, with the abyss beneath her and the twinkling lights of Shoreditch taunting her from afar.

Oh? Then I suppose you went after that handsome German fellow at his beck as well? And what about that perfectly respectable accountant?

Gisella's stern face in the haze: her sharp nose and bladed cheeks shimmers of bone white in the shifting ashfall.

Do you remember how you would wish a man dead when you led him through the bedroom door? Do you remember that silent prayer to God to strike him down?

Missy looked off the edge of Dunbridge at the factories on the slopes of the Stack. Lights winked out, one by one, at the approach of night.

Do you remember when you wondered how it would feel to commit the deed yourself?

Oliver's face in the mirror: eyes wide, hands grasping, before his spraying blood obscured it all.

How did it feel, dirty little dog?

"It was the hobgoblin man," she said again.

Was it any hand but yours upon the blade, my child?

She couldn't feel this. Couldn't feel . . .

She heard a clattering, and looked down to see her hands shaking, to see the gun bouncing back and forth in her grip. The threat of pure realisation pressed against the cushioning wall of shock. In an instant she would feel it all, and it would destroy her.

The gun stopped shaking, and rose. Gisella gasped and fixed her with a reproachful scowl.

What impropriety. Wipe the thought from your mind, child. I'll have no lady of mine contemplating such nonsense.

"But . . . I can put it to an end."

You are an arrogant and presumptuous child, to think such a thing.

The gun retreated and hung loose from her fingers.

Did running away help, child? Did defying my lessons? Did wishing men dead?

She could run to the end of the Earth and Gisella's voice would always be with her. That, and the memory of whom she'd just killed.

This was your fault she raged, *always talking to me inside my head. You drove me to all of this by never giving me a moment's peace.*

Preposterous. There is only one person in your head, my dear.

Silence, and Gisella's face was just a pattern in the ash.

The memory pressed in, the vast, crushing horror of what she had done. It loomed like a phantasm in the smog, whispering to her.

She lifted the gun again and drew strength from the steel, until she was hard, cold, unfeeling.

A dog, then a whore, then a villain.

Fine.

Yes, she'd murdered Oliver. She'd cut his throat open like a pig on Sunday. And she'd murdered that other man, stuck him through the chest like a slab of beef. She *was* a killer. The proof was drying under her finger- nails at that moment.

Then I'll do as killers do, she thought.

Because there was someone who needed to be killed.

And after her, someone else.

"He will not let you go."

It's my time.

"They've robbed us of that time, Oliver. The child- god keeps your body for you. He's not done with either of us."

I'm done.

"You've nowhere to go, Oliver. Like me, they deny you your rest."

It's too late.

"You came to me once, when I thought it was too late. When I was lost, and didn't know what to do . . . Do you remember the oath we both took?"

"Until we meet at St. Peter's gates, or we drive them from the face of God's green Earth." Bailey's melodra- matic drivel. I never really believed in Bailey or this Brit- ish Empire of his.

"But you still took the oath."

I took the oath so I could join Bailey's crew, to get access to his funding and resources. I don't care for En- gland. I don't care for her queen.

"You didn't take the oath for England, Oliver, but you took it with sincerity. I can see that love and loyalty whenever I look at you. Why did you take it?"

. . . I took it for Whitechapel.

"And we're not at St. Peter's gates yet, are we?"

Why are you doing this to me, Aaron? Let me rest.

"Because I've found a way, Oliver. All three of them in one stroke."

I don't believe you.

"It is you, Oliver. You and only you can bring them low. They've each of them sunk their hooks into you and tried to claim you for their own. They're in *you*, now. They're *vulnerable*."

. . . Are you trying to cheer me up?

"Am I succeeding?"
Bastard.

The instant the door swung open, Bergen's jungle senses flared and the Gasser leapt into his hands.

"What is it?" Hews asked from behind.

Bergen motioned him silent and slunk into the opium den. The first sign that something was wrong was that the den was empty. Every last opium sot had vanished, leaving behind stained blankets, coats, hats, and the foul reek of their presence.

The second sign was Moore. He sat slumped against the wall, a dark, shivering lump. The Chinese woman stood beside him, arms crossed, ringed fingers flexing. She turned her slanted eyes on Hews as he blundered through the door.

"My lady," Hews began in his most congenial tone. The words shrivelled up in the palpable fear of the room. The Chinese woman snapped a few syllables at him in her native tongue.

Bergen crept up to Thomas. The big man had his knees drawn up to his chest and his face buried in them.

"What did she say, English?"

"She's upset at us."

"That much is beyond debate."

The Chinese woman yammered some more. Bergen knelt in front of Thomas Moore, pistol ready.

"She says . . ." Hews said, the struggle to understand rattling his voice, "that we've brought a *jiangshi* into her house."

"What does that mean, Lewis?"

Bergen tapped Thomas lightly on the shoulder. The man's block head lifted just enough for him to stare at Bergen with the torn eye, white, drooling fluids.

"It shouldn't have been him," he said.

One of the partitioned areas at the back of the room moved. Bergen's eyes snapped up.

Hews called again over the assault of that woman's words: "I'm afraid I can't make out everything she's . . ."

Bergen blocked him out and crept up to the partitioned area. Clear sounds of life slipped past the hanging blanket: a gurgling and wheezing, as of someone drowning in pneumonia. As he pressed up close, the rank stench of vomit struck him.

Bergen grasped the blanket and flung it aside, jabbing the pistol into the space. A sudden wave of heat forced him back.

What turned from the mirror to regard him was barely human. Its skin was putrid yellow with green blotches. Its right hand hung pulsing and swollen and leaking pus. A bubbling, crusted wound bisected the neck side to side. The watery red glow of its eyes regarded him.

The voice had the frailty of a dying man's and all the ferocity of a demon's: "About bloody time you got back. We have work to do."

The Final Night

I hold it to be the inalienable right of anybody to go to hell in his own way.

—Robert Frost

Chapter 18

My people will call me a great man, will call me a High Priest and revere me above all others. They will not call me coward. They will not call me failure. They will not even whisper against me in secret. To them, I will always be First Among the Chosen.

I. xvii

The clocks had ticked for ages beyond counting. They had ticked in the aether between worlds. They had ticked in the minds of the dull and pedant creatures of the primeval swamps. They had ticked in the tortured brain of a young architect, crippled by drink and shame and guilt. And finally he had built them of wood and metal and they ticked for the hearing of all men.

Atlas Hume stood in the Church of Measured Time and listened to the last hours of Grandfather Clock's life.

The rhythm had already begun to break. Five of a thousand coordinated sounds had fallen a fraction of a second behind. Pendulums swung out of phase, their arcs getting farther and farther apart. It was harmony seeping away from the Great Machine, as it turned its attention to the assault of its accursed child.

He spoke, to the clocks or to his lost soul: "The wind blows on the flowers at their edges, and they bow to its beck and smile no more at the sun."

Perhaps he should have been afraid, but like those souls he'd condemned to the empty iron suits of the Boiler Men, he had been carved hollow. He, like those others, was denied the serenity of eternal repose, and likewise the restless clamouring of the unruly ghost. There was nothing in him—not heat or cold, not silence or noise, not motion or stillness. He was a great void infinite in measure and bounded only by the iron strips of his own skull.

Yet in that void, tears fell.

The British were coming. Beyond the walls, the English army loaded their guns, having seen the trembling sky above Whitechapel, and felt the change in the wind. And inside the walls, the servants of the crown approached, bearing death for the immortal.

The tears were for Grandfather Clock. The tears were for himself.

"God creates only the day, and the grasses wither in the heat, and the beasts never know rest. God creates only the night, and the grasses never grow, and the beasts stumble about in blindness."

He'd known it would be his decision, when he had agreed to take them into his mind. It was his price for the gift of void they had given him. They had carved his pain and sorrows away and left nothing behind. And now no true man remained to choose between life and death.

Yet a decision must be made.

Scared had spoken the only truth he could now believe: *it was all madness.*

With measured movements, he opened a leather folder that lay on the featureless marble altar. He ran his white gloves over well-used loose sheets, with strange symbols scrawled in a messy and desperate hand. These were his words, a record of the nightmare visions suffered by a lone man sixty-six years ago.

It was a man he had once been, but had chosen not to be.

Since that day he had been a vessel for forces beyond

his ken, acting as an extension of two conflicting wills. He had been a tool since that long-ago day, and had never had to choose.

He chose now.

The call went out through the void. His soundless thoughts traveled to all those other empty spaces that touched his own emptiness, stirring them to life. Metal feet thundered as they stepped down from their pedestals, row upon endless row. Iron fingers grasped rifles, flashers, and steam guns, readying and loading in perfect unison. Those thousands of feet began to march—left, right, left, right—up secret stairs no human eye had ever seen, rising from where the supports of the Stack ground into foundations of the Earth.

His soldiers, giving their allegiance to the only creature emptier than themselves.

Atlas Hume closed the folder. He decided he must be a man again.

Oliver's body didn't hurt anymore; the pair of gods that inhabited him had made certain of that. But it didn't mean he wasn't in pain.

He played that last vision over and over, scrutinizing Missy's expression. The memory was frantic, and difficult to look at, but he recalled her terror as strongly as his own. Was it hope distorting truth? Did he remember it that way because he couldn't bear to think she could actually . . .

"Sumner. Stay with us."

The German.

"I'm fine," Oliver said. His throat stretched as he pushed air through it. Moments after the cut, white ichor had rushed into the wound from some unknown part of his body. It had saved his life, but had congealed in thick welts that restricted his throat and windpipe. His voice echoed in his own ears as if off metal plates.

"We're returning with you to Shadwell. Chestle will treat you."

Oliver shook his head.

Hews, standing over the German's shoulder: "None of that, lad. You need attention."

"We can't go back," Oliver said. "Heckler destroyed the lift."

Bergen and Hews both gaped.

"It was my order; to slow the Boiler Men down."

Hews rubbed his muttonchops. "You weren't planning on going back, then?"

"I reasoned," Oliver said, "that either we would finish what we came to do and could take our time returning, or we wouldn't return."

Hews nodded sagely. So did Bergen.

Really, I thought we might all die.

The memory of a stinging line crossing his throat burned into him, blotting out his senses.

Maybe one of us did.

Missy smiling, Missy chewing, the razor, the shave. He'd been a fool. He'd felt it coming, and he hadn't trusted himself to act on that feeling. He'd known Missy wasn't *right* at that moment. Maybe it wasn't her doing.

Or maybe she played me just as well as she played everyone else.

"Sumner!"

Oliver snapped back—the den, the crew, the mission.

"Sorry," he said. He tried to rise from the bed of blankets, but strength had left him. "What about your mechanic?"

"He will build Scared's invention," the German said. "In three hours we will be returning to his workshop to retrieve it."

Oliver nodded. He concentrated on breathing for a few seconds, since it was becoming more difficult. The gods still fought and shrieked in his mind's ear, and the den shook with blows only he could feel.

He noticed a slip of yellow cloth in Hews' hand. Hews saw him looking and held it up for him to see. It was a long strip with Chinese characters written along its length.

"Mrs. Flower," Hews said, with some discomfort, "gave me this. It's a ritual of some kind. A spell, to send you back to the afterlife."

Oliver couldn't help but laugh. "If only it were that simple." He laughed more, until it became a screeching, grating sound, emanating from vibrations deep in his chest. He choked and stopped.

"Sorry."

"I'm certain both of us have heard worse," said Bergen.

Oliver looked him over. He was the same steel-eyed, tight-jawed soldier he'd always been, and yet something had changed. Something had softened, so that Oliver no longer felt that irrational anger the man had inspired. And was that *concern* in his expression?

"So have I," Oliver said.

Hews looked grim. "Who did this to you, lad?"

Oliver could not keep the tears from his eyes. He looked away. "I didn't see."

Hews moved his lips for a moment, gloom written on his face. "In any case, the question now becomes—Do we proceed or do we hole up here until you've recovered?"

Oliver looked down at his hands. The burned one had swollen, unraveling the bandages. *There's no recovery from this.* "Where's Tommy?"

Both men shifted uncomfortably. Hews cleared his throat. "He's outside. He isn't handling all this well."

Bergen scowled. "He's handling it like a child of five, but that he has no skirts to cling to."

Oliver struggled again to rise. "I'll see him."

Hews and Bergen helped him onto numb legs.

Bergen seemed about to say something. Hews quieted him with a subtle shake of his head. Oliver opened the door and, gripping the doorjamb for support, hobbled out.

The Stack burst and sputtered at its peak like a volcano, lighting the whole of Dunbridge in the colour of fire. A chill wind raced through the streets, carrying with it the scent of rot and decay. He was not surprised when the acrid air passed through his throat without so much as a tickle.

No one was about. A lone, apelike hump crouched on a step leading down from the platform's far edge.

Oliver struggled over and seated himself on the stair next to his friend.

Tommy's shoulders hunched farther down. He gazed without focus down the stairs to where they vanished between two walls of plaster.

"I'm sorry I shot you," said Oliver.

No reply. Only his breathing indicated that Tom wasn't a statue.

They sat in silence for some minutes. In intermittent mental flashes, Oliver saw the tower of arms and the sea of illness jockeying in the sky. He shut his eyes against it, but that only made it more clear.

Tommy swallowed hard. "Was it Missy?"

Oliver choked on the answer.

The big man wiped his bad eye with the back of his hand.

"I don't understand it, Ollie. Why did she do it? I mean, I thought she was one of us, right? She played poker with us, Ollie. She sat down and drank and played cards and did she have one hell of a poker face—" He cut himself off.

"I know, Tom."

"Did she play us, Ollie? We're not all fools like that, are we?"

Oliver gripped his knees to keep them from shaking. He had no answer.

Tom sniffled. "I liked her. She seemed a good soul."

"We all liked her."

"I was awake when she ran out," Tom said. "I heard it happen. And I crawled over and there you were. I messed up, Ollie. There I was lying on some comfortable mat with you getting murdered in the corner."

"They're not that comfortable."

"And *then*," Tommy continued. "Then you *weren't* dead and that was so much worse."

"It isn't your fault, chum," Oliver said, hoping some of his sincerity came through his tortured voice.

"But I was *there*, Chief."

"So was I. Don't take this all on yourself. We were hoodwinked." Oliver clasped him on the shoulder. "But we're alive to tell the tale."

"Are we?" Tom sighed, still not looking over. "I died when I was sixteen, Ollie. Someone didn't tie a knot right and I had a crate of shingles fall on me. So I don't care if you shoot me and I don't care what the cloaks or the clacks do to me. But I didn't want this to happen to anyone else. I saw enough working the docks, those poor coves with gears growing out of their chests. They should've died—some of them even asked for it."

Oliver remembered a time after the Uprising, when he'd gone into a steam-blasted house to look for survivors. He'd found only one young woman, skin boiled off, flesh poached, who sat and twitched and mouthed words he could not understand. The gears in her heart and brain churned away endlessly, holding her in this world.

"I could never blame them for that."

"It's a funny state," Tom said. "Men fighting for the privilege of dying. Who'd've thought it?"

"We're fighting for dignity, so we can be human beings again."

Tom chuckled.

"What?"

"You sound like Hewey. All 'dignity' and 'civility' and 'neighbourliness.' "

"Go jump in a hole."

"That sounded like a roar," Tom said. "Is the lion back?"

"Is the ape?"

They chuckled once or twice. Then the mirth drained away into the night and melancholy settled in again. Oliver felt the churning and vibrating in his gullet, and the motion of some viscous fluid inside the injured neck. His heart sank, but he spoke anyway, because something had to be said.

"We're neither of us dead, Tommy."

The words vanished into the smoke. Tom looked at his big hands and said nothing.

"But we have to consider that once they're not around anymore to keep us going, we might just up and die," said Oliver. "So might every other cove who's got a pump for a heart or wire for a spine."

Tom twiddled his thumbs. "Some wouldn't mind, really."

"Would you?"

Tom looked at him for the first time in their conversation. It was a long, troubled look, like he'd never considered the question. Eventually he shrugged, and stared forward again. " 'S bigger than me, Chief."

So it's the Uprising coming 'round again—coves who thought their lives didn't matter when compared to the cause. Oliver buried his face in his hands. It had cost hundreds of good, innocent lives the last time he'd tried to rebel. Would it cost thousands this time?

I'm a walking, talking dead man. Should I really be worrying about my conscience?

Good one, chap. Reason *your guilt away.*

Quiet as a mouse, Tom started to weep.

Oliver reached out and clasped him on the near shoulder.

"When I saw you, Ollie," Tom began. "When I saw you lying, I couldn't believe it. It wasn't right, it happening to you. That's what *I'm* there for—to get hurt—because what does it matter that it's me?" He rubbed his eyes with his knuckles. "I thought for certain *you* would make it out to see Chelsea and meet the queen and all that other stuff."

"We'll see it together, Tom."

"Codswallop. I've got two holes in me and I can feel that thing growing in my guts again. My life was over at sixteen, but I thought I could take that same blow for you, and maybe your life wouldn't be cut so short. And then, there I am lying on the floor while you're being cut a second smile."

He hammered the stair with his metal hand. It cracked and splinters flew up. "I thought if you made it, maybe my death wouldn't be so damned worthless."

Oliver inhaled through his teeth. Tom sat very still, breathing hard.

"You're not dead," Oliver said. "Neither am I. We've had our lumps, we've got our diseases, but we're still walking and talking, and if a crate fell on you and you're still around that's a damned *good* thing."

Tom's face scrunched up in a pained expression.

Oliver shook him. "If you just sit here and wallow,

your death *will* be meaningless, *when* it comes. We still have cloaks to pound. We still have gods to bring low. Do you think I hauled your sorry, *heavy* person all the way up here to have you quit?"

Tom's bleary eyes fell. Oliver stopped himself.

"Tom," he began again, voice calmer. "You once told me you would be with me to the bitter end."

"Of course, Chief,"

"Well, this isn't it. That was a blow—that was a bad blow—but that was all. We've taken knocks before, and this is the same."

"If you say so, Chief."

"I do say so."

Tommy grumbled some assent.

Oliver finally allowed himself a smile. "Then on your feet. We can't leave Keuper thinking he has the run of the place."

Tom rose reluctantly, and Oliver led him back to Mrs. Flower's.

Hews and Bergen greeted them as they stepped inside.

"Have you decided?" Hews asked.

"We're going ahead as soon as we have Scared's device," Oliver said.

"It will not be ready for some hours," Bergen said.

"Well, then," Oliver began. "On the advice of a good friend, I have decided on our next course of action."

They waited to hear it.

Oliver lay back down on the blankets and closed his eyes. He heard chuckles from Hews and Thomas, and then the rest settled onto mats of their own.

Oliver tossed and turned at sounds and memories and wondered if he would ever sleep again.

John Scared rocketed into the red sky as the Whitechapel of dream stretched beneath him. The *mei kuan* rushed through him, rolling his consciousness out to far horizons and inflating him to cosmic size with the pressure of its vapours. From every point, he watched himself looking back, felt himself channel a universal rhythm, felt his thoughts flit through the very atoms of reality.

Now I am ready, my love. Yield to me.

He reached out an infinite array of hands that clasped, one by one, on to her own. He felt her struggle, felt the cries inside her mind, felt the ripeness of her furnace-womb. His fingers crawled through her veins, scuttling forward like spiders, deep inside her. There, they turned valves and bent pipes and redirected her fires, bending the engine to a different function.

She cursed at him in her tongue-without-language. At the same time she shivered secretly with pleasure.

A man to love, a man to hate. A man to use you, my love. You have never found one such as I, in all your long days.

He twisted and she cried out.

You will beg for me, my love, until the end of time.

She melted, blazed, writhed at his urging. Whitechapel shook from its roots. Scared watched the towers crack and tilt. Some came apart. The vapourous ghosts of humanity tumbled and fell.

Something rushed up to catch them.

What is this, my love? Who has been hiding in your skirts?

The putrid sea was on him before he could react. It burnt and corroded his fingers. A wash of violent, diseased energy rushed through him, and far away, his body gasped.

He pulled his fingers from Mama Engine and retreated back against the red dome of the city sky. This new entity of disease lashed at him once more, then fell upon the Mother with equal ferocity.

You are that broken castoff from Grandfather Clock's impure seed. Poor, downtrodden boy. I would have taken you in, if only you had spoken to me nicely.

Alas.

He reached out once more, and made the child scream.

Aaron fell to the ground as the dream of Whitechapel jolted and came apart. For one terrifying instant, he was everywhere and nowhere, lost beyond the red sky and beyond the stable dreams of men and women, caught in a nightmare realm of horrors his mind could not fathom. Then the phantom city cracked across its length like a pane of glass shot through, with the coming of the new arrival.

Aaron dug his nails into the brass grate of the walkway. He craned his neck to see, through his thrumming vision, what had just manifested.

He beheld a towering skeleton form, a chain of a thousand skulls larger than steam ships, which faded in and out of view as if passing through fog. From the base of that shifting pile grew bony fingers as tall as the towers themselves. Some had flesh and nails still on them; others were but wisps of smoke.

Aaron saw through it to the laughing man at its core. *John Scared.*

The diseased child's pus-body shuddered as those long skeleton fingers penetrated it. Aaron felt the tremors of that contact ripple through whatever connection he still shared with the creature. The giant fingers tore long gashes through the surface of the putrid sea. Ribbons of pus flew into the air and evaporated, and the child struggled away.

Aaron rose and moved, stepping with a few paces through a hundred corridors, up a dozen lifts and out onto the roof of Cathedral Tower. The structure shone like sunlit platinum, unsullied by oil, by fire or chains.

He took advantage of the rhythmic tolling of the Great Machine, which echoed from the building up through his feet, using it to steady himself. Looming a hundred storeys above him, Scared's snake of skulls tore its fingers into Mama Engine and her child, prying them apart. Both gods struggled and fought to no avail.

Aaron looked into Scared and let his perceptions carry him deeper and deeper through levels of demeanour and desire. He dove through memories of the rolling mountains of the Far East, back through acts of violence and depravity that would chill the blood of any hardened criminal, past a dozen changes of name and identity, past dull days of medical school, ungrateful patients, and uppity colleagues. Finally, as had been his gift since the day of his birth, he saw into the essence of the man.

He found two souls: the one, respectable and timid, a tangle of worries and insecurities hiding from the world inside a thin veil of education and status; the other, a monster of suppressed desires given life and form, a deviant creature who drew sustenance from subjugation, and who, when first loosed, had dominated and imprisoned the good man who'd spawned him.

Now I know who you are. And I know what you're trying to do.

Now there were four gods, and one of them was a flesh-and-blood man. The poison would not work on him, just as it would not work on any living man or woman. Aaron had worked that much out himself, when he'd been after the same weapon in a different lifetime.

And he had no way to warn Oliver.

Chapter 19

*The third principle of the machine is Function.
Each component is given a task that does not
vary. Diversity or commonality is the prerogative
of the machine itself, and who are mortal men to
argue when their destiny is regulated upon them?*

Then who am I to protest such a thing?

IV. iv

"That's all?"

Oliver gaped at the little bauble the mechanic held
out to him.

The old man wrinkled his nose. "What did you expect, exactly?"

No bigger than a pocket watch, the device was a little
oval of gold with curved copper wires sticking out of the
rim, five or six ounces in weight.

"Not this."

The German mechanic harrumphed. "It is the mechanism inside that is important. If you desire, I can build
it to be as ungainly as you like."

Hews lifted the device reverently from Oliver's open
palm.

"Of course, we're grateful to you, sir," he said. "The

lad's having a bit of trouble believing it will work, I think—a condition I must admit that I share."

Von Herder hobbled to one of the large cabinets on the wall. "Grandfather Clock has as many bodies as there are gears in all the clocks in Whitechapel. It is as if he has no body at all. What instrument would *you* make to destroy such a creature?"

Hews rubbed his cheeks. Oliver stole the device back and turned it over and over.

Von Herder removed a faded, moth-bitten frock, about forty years out of style, from the cabinet and shrugged into it. "I have had long debates with Herr Scared over the nature of these beasts. It is always a satisfying way to spend an evening. His hypothesis is that the creatures consist of some manifestation of thought. As to whether the medium involved is energy or matter, or whether just patterns in the aether, both he and I are undecided."

He reached up and pulled a cord. The lightbulb in the rear half of the workshop died, leaving only the glimmer of lingering furnace coals.

"Herr Scared seemed to think that no transmission of thought could ever affect the gods. He instead proposed an electrical method. The problem with that was that the gods were not electrical."

"Grandfather Clock is," said Bergen, from his post at the base of the staircase with both steam rifles and a bag of ammunition at his feet.

Von Herder shook his head. "Not as such, but there is an exchange of an electrical nature between himself and those attached to the Chimney. Those people are used as part of the Grandfather's mind, and so present a direct route for the energies of that device."

Oliver ran the fingers of his good hand over it, finding it cold. It resembled a large insect, tipped onto its back.

"Aaron described it as poison."

"Accurate enough."

It seemed good practice to ask what that poison did to its "direct route," but if what Aaron had said was true, that wouldn't much matter.

Hews was not through asking questions. "We'll be

using one of those poor buggers on the Chimney as our target, then."

Von Herder answered in the affirmative. Oliver did not contradict him.

You're the key, Oliver, Aaron had said. *You alone out of all these souls have a connection to both the child and the mother. There's only one more, and he's only too willing to have you connected if you irk him. There we have three minds in one body.*

If the poison got into his body, it would leech into those three minds. What did it matter what became of his own?

He nodded as if listening. Let Hews think what he would, and let Thomas, who was waiting for them on the street above, do the same. Hews might still go ahead if he knew the outcome, but he'd lose Tom.

"The tines must puncture the skin," Von Herder was saying. "Once a circuit is made, the device will activate automatically."

Oliver slipped the device into a pocket, tines pointing outward.

"We're in your debt, sir," Oliver said, trying to sound confident and grateful.

The old mechanic smiled. "Considerably." He reached to a second cord and pulled it. The bulb in the front half of the workshop died as well, leaving them all in pitch darkness.

Bergen grumbled from the stair: "I suppose you find that terribly funny, Herr von Herder."

"Terribly, Herr Keuper. I'll see myself out. The hour is late and I've a want to soothe my throat with your grotesque English brew."

Somewhere off to his left, Hews stiffly thanked the man. Oliver pictured him bowing and tipping his hat.

Slow steps, then a sliver of amber light as the door at the stair's top opened, spilling over Bergen's tight jaw.

"I hope you two have a plan for accessing the Chimney," Bergen said. "It is not a place most men return from."

"You've been to a few such places, if your tales have been any indication," Hews said.

"And in any case, you're not coming with us," said Oliver.

The German's glare was that of a statue in some ancient, vine-tangled ruin.

"I do not think I heard you properly, Sumner."

"Don't fight me on this one, Bergen," Oliver said. "What use is that cannon of yours when one shot will bring the entire Stack down on our heads?"

"There are many noises in the Stack to cover such things."

"I need you in Shadwell."

There in the bottom levels of the hide, the noises of the city seemed distant, as did the safety they provided.

"You are trying to rid yourself of me again, Sumner. Why, after all I've done for you, do you still expect treachery from me?"

"Why do you expect me to expect it? Shadwell won't hold out, even with the lift gone. The crows may build another lift. The golds may just climb down. Heckler's a good lad, and Hanley as well, and all of them, but they aren't soldiers."

The expression on the German's face was clear: he was deciding whether Oliver's leadership was worth the trouble.

"Bergen, there are hundreds of people in the Underbelly. The canaries have just been waiting for an excuse to revenge the Uprising, and they won't spare a quarter. I need your gun there, Bergen. I need you to lead them."

Some distant vibration hummed the air in the long silence before Bergen spoke. "You care for these people."

"Yes, I do. And I trust you to honour that."

Bergen's words became very quiet then, whispered without a hint of an accent. "Maybe he was wrong." The German turned and silently ascended. His shadow fell across the stairs and then they were in light again.

The room felt suddenly empty, as with the release of some pressure.

Hews' hand fell on Oliver's shoulder, gave a squeeze, and then he, too, mounted the stairs.

Oliver stood alone in the dark a moment, then followed.

Half an hour later they walked into the most dangerous place on Earth.

Oliver's first step onto the platform at the Stack's station sent shudders through his bones. The metal vibrated with a subsonic tone, feeling slippery and loose, as if it moved beneath the feet. The beams of soot-coated iron rose up in their thousands and bent inward towards their Lady. Steam shot into the skies like escaping dragons, and on the higher slopes where no human being could go, gears the size of cities churned relentlessly. Oliver could not help but despair at the inhuman mass of the structure. It was one thing to witness it from afar; quite another to have it surrounding him, touching him at every point like a thousand-fingered claw twitching slowly closed.

The Stack had grown up like the towers, irregardless of tiny human concerns. In places, the walkways had to skirt monstrous boilers and furnaces, sometimes vast stretches of slope where mechanical arms bent and shaped metals to their Mother's purposes. It was a living expression of the iron goddess, surging mindlessly into the sky, and crushing those weak creatures fool enough to interfere.

The fire blazed in the back of Oliver's mind, hotter than lightning, and his eyes burned like magnesium. He wore his hat low over his face. He'd wrapped a veil of cloth around his eyes to dull the light, but it was thin enough that he could still see.

Hews went first, as he knew the Stack and had been there many times.

"Like stepping from church directly onto the lake of fire," he'd said of it. Hews wore a thick, wet handkerchief tied over his mouth and nose against the air. Oliver had found that, like Tom, his lungs were not bothered by it.

Gold cloaks watched them dismount with the rest of the small crowd. Their eyes tracked in jumps, in perfect rhythm with the station's giant clock. These ones showed clearer signs of Grandfather Clock's influence: their bone structure was more rounded, their faces more angular, with stretches and sometimes splits in their skin to accommodate growths beneath. The platform emptied into a thin corridor between shapeless steel monoliths where Boiler Men stood like statues, row on row, guns to their shoulders, glass eyes staring into some unseen void. Oliver felt a chill as he passed in front of each, a hint of some emptiness that seeped into his mind from their gazes.

Two more cloaks scrutinised them with luminescent electric eyes as they reached the grand arch that exited the station. They betrayed no hint of recognition.

You don't even recognise yourself, chum.

They cringed and drew back as the light of Oliver's eyes fell on them.

The arch emerged onto one of a hundred concourses that ringed the Stack at different altitudes. Sparks lanced along naked copper wires hung between the beams above. Heat pummelled them from all quarters, carried through the building's supports, walls, and floors. The sounds of the machines were like the cries of giants locked beneath the Earth.

They walked the empty streets in silence, not daring to think, and frightened sometimes to breathe. Those men they did pass, labourers kept at the machines long hours, moved like hollow ghosts, only the red light of the Stack's angry fire to define them.

The rumble of the titans' struggles beat on Oliver's inner ears, and their blows shook his knees. Oliver found himself leaning on Tom more and more for support as they worked their way in. He did not miss the glances Tom and Hews exchanged.

They walked one of the many broad avenues that connected the rings with the Stack's central tower. On either side, endless rows of closed doors led to the factories. Now and all night, those unfortunates confined within would run the machines to Mama Engine's unknowable purpose, under the direction of their semihuman masters.

From the avenue, Hews led them along catwalks

toward the Stack's inner walls, over huge smelting pits and lonely arenas populated with twitching mechanical creatures. They passed lightless wells hundreds of feet deep, cranes and engines and monstrous glass spheres with dark fire burning deep inside. There was not a single clock to be seen, and their march became timeless, eternal.

Oliver felt nausea welling up, and shut his eyes awhile as he walked. The gods savaged each other somewhere above. Grandfather Clock's tick was omnipresent. And there—something else. Laughter?

"This is the place," Hews said. The words stilled the atmosphere like curses spoken in church. "It has a steam lock, and my contact was unable to obtain a key."

Oliver stepped forward. The door was pitted like pig iron, and sealed across by four bolts. The lock was a small hole in the casing, no wider than two fingers.

Oliver knelt before it and produced from his pocket a copper tube that split into six pipes at the far end, each pipe capped with a rubber cup. Oliver felt around the inside of the lock, noting the shape of the interior. He bent the six pipes to match.

In a moment he rose and gestured to Tommy. The big man knelt down, drew in an enormous lungful of air, and blew into the pipe with all his strength. Some colour came back into his cheeks and a click sounded. There followed the hiss of escaping steam and the bolts withdrew. Tom drew the heavy door back to reveal an abyss on the other side.

"You're certain your chap wouldn't lead us wrong?" he asked.

Hews stepped past and into the door. "They're all like this." The darkness swallowed him whole.

Tom shifted uncomfortably behind.

"Abandon all hope, ye who enter here?" he said. His chuckle died in infancy and he cleared his throat. "After you, Chief."

Oliver stepped through. The light of the street vanished and new light replaced it. Oliver walked on a net of woven chains above a bed of white coals. Glass creatures of indefinite form wriggled between the links.

"What can you see, Hews?" Oliver asked.

"As much as a bat in the daylight."

"I thought as much."

Heat withered him, blasting up from below, pressing in from the sides. He focused on his shoes, fearing to look up and have the vision of Mama Engine's true self drive him mad.

He heard Hews fumbling with an electric torch. With a hiss, it brought light into the hall—beautiful, mundane light. The vision faded into a barely illuminated pipe hallway, ending in a malformed ladder leading down.

Tom stepped in and closed the door. "Cloaks outside," he said. "A pack of golds, and they might have seen me."

"The baron knows we're coming," Oliver said. He had no torch, electrics being difficult to find in Whitechapel, but the radiance of his eyes seemed to work just as well.

"Lad, when were you going to tell us that?"

Oliver looked over at Hews. The older man's face was cut with two sets of shadows.

"Truth be told, I wasn't, but this is all pressing my mind and I let it slip."

"You weren't going to tell us at all?"

"It didn't seem relevant," Oliver said with a shrug.

"Not relevant?" Hews said. "We'll be caught for certain, lad. He'll have guards at every entrance."

"We will walk in a straight path all the way into the Chimney," Oliver said. "The baron won't stop us. The crows won't stop us. All we need to worry about are the canaries."

Creases formed around Hews' eyes. "Explain yourself, lad."

"We have divine favour on our side, Hewey."

"Tell me you did not deal with these creatures."

"Perhaps I did. Or perhaps this is all just fortunate happenstance. If you're looking for an explanation, I will have to disappoint you."

Oliver grimaced as a wave of nausea hit him. He must have swayed, for an instant later Tom's big hands were on his shoulders, steadying him.

"We trust you, Chief," he said. "Always have, always will."

He must have been sharing a look with Hews, for the older man ground his jaw a moment, then turned away.

Oliver removed his blindfold. "Let's get on."

The ladder led them to more tunnels, which they navigated by way of a map hastily scribbled during the evacuation of Sherwood. More than once, Oliver looked at the map with the flickering light of his eyes, and knew, beyond doubt, that it was incorrect. Then he led them rightly in spite of Hews suspicions and Tom's worry. It was the same as it had been with the *Summa Machina*: the knowing sprung from Mama Engine's fire in the back edge of his mind.

Why didn't he tell them? Wouldn't they be able to understand and accept what had happened?

They jumped when the black cloak came crawling from the dark and he had his answer.

This is bigger than them.

Only the last vestiges of a human face remained: skin hung in tatters from metal cheekbones. Scraps of black cloth hung from the rest of the body. It came at them crawling on the ceiling, bracing itself with a dozen limbs, clicking and scraping and pushing a wall of heat before it.

Thomas immediately jumped in the way. Hews drew his pistol and took a firing position at the tunnel's edge.

Oliver pushed Tom aside with a gentle hand.

The cloak angled its neck to stare at him with glass eyes. Oliver stared back with his. Some ripple of kinship, barely felt, passed between them, stirring the fires in Oliver's head. It swivelled its head back to the fore and crept off down a side tunnel.

"We are all the children of God."

Mrs. Lewis had said it once, in the distant past when she was still alive and trying to mould him into a good Christian boy.

Oliver started off down the next tunnel without waiting for the others.

The sounds of machinery rang all around, and the corridors stank of rot and rust and mildew. Each step became an eternity; each movement an exercise in navigating not only the Mother's physical innards, but the flashes of terror and desire that for moments blanked out his own thoughts with those of the goddess.

And then he heard laughter in the halls—horrid, human, distorted by echo.

"What do you hear?" he asked.

"Damnable machines," Hews said. "Why do you ask, lad?"

"Tom?"

"Same ol', Chief, and the, uh . . . I got a buzzing in my guts, Ollie."

Oliver nodded.

They kept walking, coming up on what the map described as a machining room. Oliver's intuition pinged, so he stopped them again.

"Chief?"

Oliver motioned for silence. The laughter was still there, louder now, closer.

It could be nothing.

"Put out the light, Hewey."

Hews reached down and struggled until the electric went dark.

"Sit tight a bit."

Oliver opened his eyes wide, spraying white light onto the corridor. Then he squinted, focussing through the metal. The tunnel fell away. The heat became red fire, the structure became chains and glass. Beneath the chains, a stream of embers floated through the air.

It might destroy him to look, but he couldn't ignore his intuition again.

"Fellows," he said, hoping his voice would echo in the solid world. "Keep a watch."

He lifted his head. His eyes passed over the field of chains and glass creatures and ashen corpses. The vista stretched endlessly, folding back on itself in his perception and blotting out the city that lay beyond. The corpses twitched and spasmed, grinning with blackened teeth. He lifted his eyes farther, to where more corpses hung on lines of flaming coals. Hundreds of them swung there, illuminated from above by orange light, all limbs rocked with the arc of their motion, shedding ash into the world below.

The laughter persisted, still higher.

More corpses greeted him as he leaned back, condensing in their thousands and tens of thousands towards a single point. They overlapped and mingled, sharing the same spaces with their fellows, tricking the eye into seeing them all at once. As he drew his eyes up, the corpses became less and less human. He saw creatures as tiny as spiders and as large as towers, of blasphemous and alien proportions. He looked through these, around them, his vision passing unimpeded through them though they blocked its line.

Powerful desires and impulses washed through his mind—nameless drives and consuming hungers. At each of these he felt his body jerk as it reacted. He found his own voice screaming them.

I want to be alone! I want to be loved! I love my children! I must be controlled!

His eyes came to a point on which they could not focus, where his perception slid about as if distorted through a thousand shaped lenses. Around this one point the fire raged and whirled, streaks of orange and red biting at the corpses, then dragging them into it. Urges tore through him, burning into his brain, shredding any of his own thoughts that dared take root in action. He couldn't move, couldn't think, could not *be*.

The laughter called him on. As it echoed once again through Mama Engine's thoughts and bones, that single point of madness shuddered and shrank, and its orbiting fires stilled. Oliver escaped its pull, and looked up one final time.

Suddenly the heat vanished, to be replaced by a bitter cold. Snakes of impassive logic reached down from above, ringed and coated in scuttling creatures whose images formed in his mind as nonvisual flashes of knowing. His reality fell to pieces in so many disconnected memories: a boy shamed, a chemical burning, an escape—murders, tears, midnight masturbations, and things done to little boys. How he loved the boys, how he wanted his own . . . and then came the disgusting touch of woman.

He saw a skull laughing, empty within and bare without, shadowed faces in each socket.

Yes, my love! I will lash you in chains of your own pleasure. Moan for me, my love. Moan and ripen!

A figure ran towards the skull's teeth, his feet scuffing on the air. It wore a coat of many pockets.

"Aaron!" Oliver cried.

Aaron ran straight into the skull's maw.

Glass creatures leapt upon Oliver's arms and sank their teeth into him.

"Light!" Oliver screamed. The creatures rolled over his body, searing through his clothing and gnawing through his skin. "Hewey, for God's sake, the light!"

A click. Dark fell like a theatre curtain. The glare of a single bulb brought him back. Tom was holding him, shaking him, calling his name.

Oliver cried out as the fresh burns on his arms and chest scraped against the cotton of his shirt. His clothes were still whole; his body was not.

"Don't touch. Don't . . ."

Obediently, Tommy dropped him against the tunnel wall, where he writhed against the burning.

"What happened?" Hews boomed. "What did you just do, lad?"

Aaron will take care of it. Just keep to the mission.

Oliver regained his footing as the burns dulled into a mute throb.

"I'm all right," he said.

"Boy, you are going to tell me what is going on *right this minute*," Hews thundered.

Oliver stared down at the short, fat man. "No, Hewey, I'm not. I haven't the strength or the time for it." He started down the next corridor at a pitiful hobble. "Are you coming?"

It was four lengths of tunnel and several turns before Oliver was certain they were following. The electric light cast a shadow ahead of him that vanished as they reached the exit.

Oliver drew in breath at the sight of the next chamber.

A thousand glass eyes, smoldering red in furnace light from below. Hanging from chains, dozens of malformed iron monsters, in the same pattern as the one Fickin had built, stared blankly ahead. Their tentacles and arms twitched and flicked. Amongst and upon them black cloaks lay in crumpled heaps, twitching and moaning with sounds both human and machine.

Oliver waited for Hews to come forward with the light, then started onto the long catwalk that led across the chamber, one of many crisscrossing it without geometric logic.

"Ollie," Tom whispered. "What are they?"

They're the end of the world. They're the death of every man, woman, and child on Earth.

"Shit trouble."

Laughter echoed down from the arches above. Oliver ignored it, and focused on putting one foot in front of the other.

"What the hell was that?" Hews said. He flashed his torch about the room.

"What?"

The laughter sounded again. Different this time, omnipresent, multitoned.

"Can you hear that, Hewey?"

Oliver jumped his eyes over the unconscious cloaks. They shuddered, their mouths opened. The next bout of laughter exploded from all those throats, in perfect unison, ringing from the walls and ceiling until it became a battery of noise. The metal creatures bounced in their restraints to that rhythm.

A tentacle moved. A cloak's eyes opened. The whole room came alive.

Chapter 20

*Oh, how I wish I were mad and this were all
some phantom of my mind. But I look around
my quarters and see my pipe cool and cleaned,
see the bottle of brandy stoppered and full, and
know that I am no longer dreaming.*

I. xviii

The wind tried to pull Bergen to his death with arctic
fingers.

The chain ladder had been where Hews had said it
was. Bergen had discovered it in the back closet of
Hews' wire factory, having to navigate through a mob
of workers waiting for the plant to be opened, then
through the factory to Hews' personal office. A trapdoor
beneath the desk opened a hole right through the foun-
dation of the building, through which the chain could
be lowered.

Bergen was no stranger to climbing. Not that any
amount of experience would have made the task easier:
with one heavy weapon hanging from his shoulder, an
arm still bruised from the previous night's fighting, and
a stomach wound that the sway of his body constantly

reopened, it was a wonder he hadn't fallen already. Nicholas Ellingsly certainly would have.

And in addition, he was being followed.

He'd first become aware of it on the cable car ride from Dunbridge to Cambridge-Heath. He'd inspected each of the passengers as best he could without being too conspicuous, and had found nothing. It was no ordinary cloak or turncoat tracking him, then, but a predator. He could have deduced that from his senses alone.

He stopped to rest a moment, pulling his body upright and close to the rope to lessen the pull of the rifle. He kept his muscles taut, knowing that to relax them was to invite the fatigue so anxiously waiting to enter.

Another ten minutes of climbing brought him to the street, where he immediately dumped the rifle and the ammunition and squatted, panting and rubbing his palms.

He had come down into a circle of men with guns, whom he ignored until he had recovered his breath.

"I come at the request of Oliver Sumner," Bergen said, not getting up. "I bear weaponry. I need to see the American."

"Oi," said one of the men. "That's the cove what blew up them cloaks at Sherwood."

"Heckler's up by the lift, mate," said another. "I'll take you."

"Good." Bergen rose, finally, willing his legs and arms not to feel their overuse. He turned to two of the men, middle-aged labourers who nonetheless looked confident holding their weapons.

"Shortly, a man will come down this rope after me," Bergen said. "He must be killed."

The men nodded.

"He is not to set foot in the Underbelly. Do you understand?"

"Relax, Gov, we got it."

"Good. Lead me to the American."

Heckler had indeed destroyed the lift. The Beggar's Parade ended in torn beams and swaying cables. A

boarding platform of wide, textured steel led to a hole
where the lift itself had once rested. Of the machinery
that had powered the lift, only fragments remained, the
rest having fallen into the downstreets. The braces and
the frame of the chute up which the lift traveled still
stood, being far too thick to yield to any mere explosive.
Fastened firmly to this by chains and bolts, high above
the street, the monstrous clock ticked away, immune to
the angry glares from below.

Bergen took stock of the defences as his guide led
him to Heckler's post. The lift chute stood at the very
end of the Beggar's Parade, with no buildings or other
streets on any side of it. A succession of two-storey
buildings began some fifty yards away from it along the
Parade, the two closest bearing the unmistakable wounds
of gunfire. Heckler and his men had set up a crude barricade of tin wagons, crossing the street between these
two buildings, having tipped them on their sides and
layered them to provide cover without blocking access
to the street beyond. Several dozen motley defenders
crouched behind them, swapping port and cigarettes and
fidgeting with their weapons.

That street and the boarding platform were littered
with gold-clad corpses.

Sumner should have given them more credit.

As he approached, someone called from the left building: "Got one movin'."

A shot rang out.

The old sailor, Phineas, poked his head from the
shadow of a wagon.

"Stow that fucking iron, you rat-faced caw. I'm trying
to listen."

" 'e was moving, 'e was," the shooter came back.

Bergen and his guide reached the barricade. Bergen
kept low, accounting for the steep angle at which the
cloaks could fire on them from the clock above. Half of
these men were totally exposed and didn't even realise
it.

What else can one expect from bakers and stiffs?

Bergen stepped over and around the crouched men.
They muttered as they saw him, and something of a

spark came back into their bearing. They, like their comrades, recognised him and his weapon.

These men were happy to see him. It was an unfamiliar experience and the German—the Englishman?—found he didn't much care for it.

Bergen crept up to the huge iron four-wheeler that served as Heckler's command post and heard what no soldier ever wants to hear his first five minutes on the battlefield.

"We canna hold here, Yankee. We canna even lift our heads to shoot at 'em next time—no' with them bastards up there."

"We ain't got the men to hold a wider line. We fall back and they get into the buildings and into the streets we'll never beat 'em back."

Bergen crouched behind the American as another of the four men with him spat his dissatisfaction. This one was obviously a baker, owing to the flour still caught in his cuticles.

"Heckler, boy, we can't stay. We haven't the ammunition for it, nor the will. I mean, look at us!"

Bergen watched quietly as Heckler's resolve weakened. The lad's finger picked at his mustache, his hair, his ears. "What can we do, then? We can't retreat. For God's own sake, these are *your* families."

Sumner was right. The boy is not fit to lead, and these four are swelled-headed fops who will do something rash if left unchecked.

His guide deposited the steam rifle at Heckler's side. He fixed all five men with a withering scowl and spoke. "Discipline problems, Yankee?"

"Bergen?" the lad's eyes spread wide in reverence. "Is Oliver with you?"

"Sumner sent me to take over," Bergen said. "The men are low on ammunition?"

Heckler nodded. "We've got maybe a dozen shots apiece. And we keep wasting 'em because them ones we already killed won't stay dead."

The other four men opened their mouths at once to add their voices. Bergen silenced them all with a gesture.

"We will hold at all costs," he said to these men.

"There can be no retreat or they will indeed get into the city, and after that the defence will be too messy for us to maintain it." He unbuckled the harness on his steam rifle.

"But we've no bullets!" said one of them.

"Then we will get more."

Bergen pulled the weapon out and watched the mens' eyes widen as they beheld their new ally.

Five minutes later Bergen gave the signal, and a dozen men began raining fire on the clock. Bergen lifted the steam rifle, backed six paces from the barricade, and shot three rounds through the face of the clock while all the other men ran onto the killing fields. Four cloaks fell dead and sparking from behind their shelter. Bergen let loose three more shots, sending two more cloaks into a long fall. Bergen retreated back to the barricade as the men returned with rifles, pistols, and pockets full of extra bullets.

Bergen reloaded his rifle, then checked the boiler—three-quarters full—and the battery connections—still hot.

Heckler's smile as he showed Bergen handfuls of shells warmed him within in a way he did not find uncomfortable.

"Ammunition," Bergen said.

"You son of a whore!" It was the sailor, grimacing from the third wagon down, hands pressed hard over his ears. "You've bloody deafened me!"

"It had to be done, Macrae," Bergen said.

"I heard footsteps, Kraut," the sailor snapped. "Bloody hundreds of them. And now I can't track them until my ears level out."

"Hundreds?" said Heckler.

Phineas nodded.

They both looked to Bergen, who only smiled.

"We will greet them with open arms. Do you have any explosives left, young man?"

They were running the instant the first crow gained its feet.

Oliver shouted some orders, which even he could not. make out over the sudden din of crashing metal, and the three lone human beings broke for the opposite end of the rail.

Hews ran in front, Tommy behind. Oliver pulled his derringer.

Why do I even bother carrying this thing?

Cloaks rose up on the other walkways, howling and cackling. They leapt inhuman lengths and grappled onto the room's chains like monkeys or spiders. Their black eyes glittered like far-off stars and their tattered garments trailed after them as they moved.

A multilimbed cloak dropped into their path. Hews shot it down and seconds later Oliver found himself leaping over it even as its arms twittered back to life. Thomas stomped it an instant later.

The laughter degenerated into cries of pain and desire. A cloak clambered up the railing beside Oliver and he discharged one of his shots into its face.

Hews drew up short and Oliver bumped into him from behind, cursing. An instant later a cloak crashed with enormous force against the walkway's edge. The impact bent cloak and railing into accordion folds. Oliver looked up sideways and saw one of Mama Engine's monsters mounting its own chains, swatting the crows that clawed and chewed at it.

"They've all gone mad," Hews breathed.

The monster fixed one of its limbs onto a cloak's head and twisted it clean off.

"Go, Hewey!" Oliver ordered, and shoved him.

"Blast!" Hews dove against the railing and clung to it. Something struck the walkway from below, bending it up into a low ramp and shaking Oliver off his feet. He slid back into Tommy's boots.

"Got you, Chief," Tommy shouted. Oliver looked up and watched the big man reel back his fist and hammer a cloak leaping for the rail.

The walkway shook again and split at the point of impact, about twenty feet past their position. Shapeless limbs reached from below and began slicing the metal like soft cheese.

Oliver pointed towards another walkway, ten feet below and fifteen away. "There?"

Tom looked. "I can make it."

Oliver leapt back to his feet and grabbed Hewey by the shoulder to haul him back. Hews fired his last three shots at the monster breaking through the walkway.

Tommy wrapped huge, sweaty arms around both of them. Oliver gagged as the force expelled the air from his lungs. Black spots danced in his vision, and his mind, deprived of vital oxygen, shrunk back and rang with the roar of fires and the tang of alien laughter.

Thomas crouched, shuffled, launched.

The room shifted and fell back, spreading in Oliver's perspective until the full battle presented itself: cloaks tearing one another apart, beasts scraping at the walls and the chains. Some dropped into the red furnace fires with the vacant stare of the suicide.

Tommy's feet bent the steel as they landed. His friend released him and acrid air rushed into his chest.

"There!" Oliver said, and ran for the tunnel at the walkway's far end, an arch rimmed in brass, with a many-limbed abomination crawling down the wall to block it.

"Are you mad?" he heard Hews shout, but did not slow.

That's the way we must go, Oliver thought. He leveled his weapon at the monstrosity above.

Move aside. He reached into the flickering fire in his mind, and through it, to the creature. The visions of Mama Engine's dream self surged into the periphery of his sight. *The Mother wants you to stand aside.*

A ram of emotion toppled him: fear and anger, confusion. It was wrong, so utterly wrong, that a clear purpose could be so subverted. The creature unloaded all its anguish into him, and Oliver's body convulsed. His gun went off.

Strong fingers snatched up his collar on the first bounce, and Tommy dragged him bodily towards escape. The monster Oliver had connected with slowed and eventually fell, careering off the edge of the walkway and bending the last ten feet into a dangerous slope. Tom slid to a stop and almost fell. Oliver found his feet and watched the creature fall, feeling a deep, deep sadness through the fire in his mind.

Hews emptied his revolver and began thumbing new shells into place. Oliver did the same.

"Holy yellow dog piss, Ollie," Tommy said. "What kind of shells are you plugging in there?"

"Lucky ones." Oliver clicked the derringer closed.

Across the room, two of the monsters, upper limbs tangled in the architecture above, grappled with each other in as fierce and as noisy a conflict as the gods above. Then a new sound undercut the cacophony: a low, vibrating growl. Oliver knew it at once; they all did.

An Atlas rifle. The Boiler Men were coming.

Hews' prayers faded into choking, then coughs. Oliver slapped him hard on the back and let him finish.

"I shouldn't have come, lad," Hews muttered. "I'm bloody old."

"You've still got your hat on," Oliver said. "Get at the railing."

One by one they crossed the slanted section by sidestepping across its highest point, white-knuckled grips on the rail, then fled into the dark beyond, with only Oliver's eyes to light their way.

They ran through Gothic halls, past steam-seeping constructions that might have been statues and might have been machines. The empty spaces echoed with shrill laughter and the repeating rhythm of iron-clad boots. Oliver guided them at each turn by Mama Engine's silent direction.

They met black cloaks at every bend and archway, more than Oliver had ever thought existed. The cloaks yowled in their madness, running amok and clawing at walls and floor and one another, oblivious to intruders. Every once in a while, the deep rumbling of Atlas rifles smothered all sound.

As they descended, the architecture became cleaner, straighter, composed more of brass and copper and shining metals. The ambient light faded from red to white, the halls ceased their twisting, and the beating of footsteps dimmed.

Oliver signalled them to a halt before a brass wheel two storeys in height, rotating slowly through the actions of a hundred chattering gears.

Oliver placed his hand on the wheel. "This is a canary chapel. There's a lift inside that leads down to the Chimney. They won't have weapons while they're in prayer, but we can still expect a fight."

Tom pounded his fist into an open palm. "Right and ready, Chief."

"Hewey?"

The old man let off a sigh that rattled with all of his fifty-seven years. "There won't be another time to say this, Oliver."

Oliver had the impulse to stop him, to tell him there would be plenty of time, though he knew there wouldn't. His guts felt sick for reasons unrelated to infection.

Hews breathed once and removed his bowler. "You were always bigger than me, lad."

"Hewey, don't . . ."

Hews pressed on. "I couldn't supply you a life that you would accept. I used to lay awake and wonder what I was doing wrong that forced you back out the door every few weeks."

Oliver squeezed the man's shoulder. This was too much. "Hewey, you don't need to—"

"I do, lad!" Hews snapped. "You would have been a dullard backer if you'd listened to me! Oliver, I never meant to—"

"Stop it." Oliver stared Hews straight in the eyes, heedless of the stinging light that caused Hews to wince back. "Whatever happened, it doesn't matter. All right? *It doesn't matter.*"

"But—"

"No," Oliver said. "I won't have it. Anything you think you've done, anything I've said you've done, it's all passed now. I need you *here*. I need you with me. Now."

Hews sniffed back something, swallowed whatever he was going to say.

"Right," he said.

"Right," said Oliver.

And Hews chuckled, grief and weight lifting from his

shoulders as if they'd been a joke the whole time. "For queen and country, eh? Bloody patriotism—kill us all."

Oliver let out a held breath.

"Not on my watch."

They shook hands and Hews nodded with satisfaction. He replaced his hat and led them in a quiet, genuine prayer.

Oliver reached into the door and turned a key that could not have been found with a dozen hours of visual inspection. Steam hissed out from the rim, gears ground and reversed course. The brass wheel rolled aside into the interior of the wall.

And Oliver felt sick again.

Beyond stood the upper end of the Chimney, ringed around and around by a curtain of human beings strapped to chairs, twitching, rotting, unable to die. Hundreds were visible with thousands more held where the structure extended below the floor. The chapel was a concourse around the Chimney, bare and plated in gold. Clocks covered every inch of wall, locked together at their rims and rotating in one coordinated motion.

A sea of gold cloaks rose from prayer and turned to face them. There were hundreds—hundreds—of glowing eyes, hundreds of metal hands, hundreds of heart-clocks ticking in rhythm with the room.

Thomas bellowed like a bear and charged. Hews and Oliver ran in after him, drawing their weapons. The cloaks closed from all sides.

Tommy hit the first line and sent three into the air with a sweep of his arm. Another he knocked in the face with his good hand. Flesh sheared off it to reveal the same iron bones beneath. Oliver and Hews held the sides, Hews cracking finely placed shots into every face he saw, Oliver holding them back through only the threat of his weapon and the Mother's fire-glow in his eyes. They reeled back under that gaze, unable to approach.

Tommy grabbed two cloaks in his hands and flung then twenty feet in the air. He put his shoulder into the next line and knocked them sprawling. Oliver jumped his gaze from cloak to cloak. It was a few seconds before the fire drove them back, and when he released one another would run in from the side. He used his two shots and fell back to lashing out with the pistol's handle.

Hews dropped into Thomas' wake to reload; Oliver did the same. They shuffled backwards, as fast as they could manage, while Tom cleared them a path.

There were so many; so many flashes of cloth of gold, so many brass limbs and blue lapis eyes and all of them surging together at the same instant. Oliver took to sweeping his gaze across the crowd, causing them to hesitate, but it did not slow them long.

How much father. A dozen yards? A hundred?

Thomas roared in pain and stumbled back into them. Hews ducked close to Tommy's back as the cloaks reached for him. Oliver stepped in front of those hands and drove them back with his gaze.

A creature of brass strips and wire landed against Tommy's chest, sinking long, savage fingers into his shoulders. Cloaks leapt onto Tommy's arms, holding them down with sheer weight as the inhuman creature tensed its limbs, closed its claws and leaned back.

A sound like a cable snapping and Tom's iron bones burst out of his skin. The creature dragged ribs and collarbone clear of Tommy's body. Skin and flesh fell loose, oil and blood cascaded over the crowd.

Oliver cried out his friend's name as powerful hands closed over his arms and his face.

Tommy screamed. The cloaks dragged him down and tore him apart.

Oliver's eyes burned with rage and tears. He wrenched his head down and unleashed Mama Engine's fire on his closest assailant. The man fell back screaming, but it wasn't enough. Every passing second more hands closed on him, binding him, crushing his muscles and tearing his skin and clothing. A steel-hard arm closed around his neck and hauled his head back. The wound on his neck split with an audible tear.

The cloaks yanked one arm out of its socket and crushed his hip bone on the left side, and he knew it was over. He wished only that the gods would let him go when the cloaks were done.

A hand crushed his windpipe. His vision began to swim, portions vanishing in swirls of black and red. Somewhere in the press of bodies, Hews cried out.

And abruptly, the pressure released and Oliver fell hard to the floor, splattering blood and pus. The sea of arms and faces and feet retreated, and he heard the approach of light, crisp footfalls. Dull, brass eyes found his, and stared into him with mute emptiness.

Then a voice like the last judgement: "I know who you are."

Chapter 21

But it is not only the Lord and the Lady who will craft the chaff of humanity to their whims. I, too, am fated to do this thing, and my Chosen will be as lost as I, and as immune to human sentiment.

—XI. v

"Seven more," Phineas reported.

"Makes . . ." Heckler tried and failed to seem that he wasn't counting on his fingers. "Forty-eight?"

Bergen nodded. The clock was large enough to hide that many and more. By the old sailor's count, that left some fifty in reserve in the streets above.

If they are smart, they will come at us all at once, sending their most indestructible first, to absorb our bullets.

But gold cloaks were known for their efficiency, not their wits. Being children of the Machine, they would likely not stray far from their original tactics.

Bergen peeked over the wagon's edge, making a quick sweep of the field. The distance between the barricade and the lift's boarding platform measured a scant forty yards. It was an ideal killing field: well lit by electrics above the platform, free of obstacles and cover. It would be something of a shame when it was gone.

"Nine more," Phineas said. He crouched like a gargoyle in the wagon's shadow. "Wait . . . ten."

Bergen could hear the faint sounds of the cloaks climbing down to their roost behind the clock.

Heckler held his Winchester in a calm and steady grip, looking up and listening. The man was confident with a firearm, if with nothing else.

Bergen ducked back down and checked the steam rifle for the fourth time.

It is Ellingsly who checks his weapons, he remembered. *Bergen never has need to. He simply trusts.*

With deliberation, he set the weapon aside.

Then the air changed. Bergen knew it immediately: that anticipation, the silence and stillness that boomed louder than any noise. He knocked thrice on the wagon's interior, and all the urchins-turned-militia readied their guns.

Heckler peeked up at the clock again. "Are they climbing, Phin?"

The sailor hunched farther in concentration, eyes shut tight. "I can't tell, boy."

Bergen slipped his Gasser free. "Try harder, Macrae."

"Drown and rot, Kraut. I'm doing what I can here."

"Do more."

Bergen felt it even as the sailor said it: "They're loading!"

"In cover," Bergen ordered, and the men at the barricades stepped close into the wagons, gaining the protection of the wheels and side paneling.

The shots began, distant and empty pops of sound, and bullets began striking the wagons. It was like a light, intermittent rain. Perhaps five or six shooting, which meant the rest were climbing down, right into the sights of the men in the buildings.

Bergen felt his heart begin to pump harder. It was Ellingsly's heart, the heart of a man who, despite all pretences, was in truth ruled by fear. Bergen felt vulnerable, felt sick, but he stilled himself with the German's long-practiced calm and waited for the battle to begin.

It began with a crash that shook the road beneath their feet.

"Phineas!" Bergen said.

The old sailor shook his head slowly, mouth hanging open.

Bergen risked a peek over the wagon. A dozen cloaks all shot at him the instant they saw his head. Sparks flashed as he plunged back down.

"They're down."

Heckler's eyes went wide. "How?"

Bergen ignored the question. He yelled a command to the front lines, and all two dozen men unhesitatingly stood and opened fire.

The first line of cloaks reeled under the barrage, but did not fall. The next volley drove them back into a second line of cloaks. Behind these, more filled the field that instants before had been empty.

Bergen loosed the Gasser's thunder until it clicked empty and then ducked back.

In the corner of his vision, one of his men dropped to the ground with a shattered face. He shoved more bullets into the chambers and glanced up at the clock in time to see eight more cloaks clamber onto its top.

He clicked his weapon closed, and waited.

The cloaks spread their arms. Not a hint of hesitation or fear showed in any face as they leapt from the clock's edge.

He shot three before they hit the ground. One crisp thump and three disorganised crunches sounded from behind the wagons seconds later. By then more were mounting the clock and preparing themselves.

He stood and emptied his weapon into a bearded face with a brass cheek and lapis eyes.

The next wave landed, two of them shattering their own legs upon impacting the pavement. The ones already on the ground had divided into a firing line perched on the boarding platform and an assault party braving the withering fire of the men of the Underbelly. They had indeed selected the most indestructible on their first wave; Grandfather Clock's children had crossed half the field already.

On the right of the line, another of his men fell. He ducked to reload, fighting a shivering in his limbs that he had not experienced in a long time. Ellingsly's personal sickness: all-consuming cowardice.

Damn that man and damn the day he was born.

He needed Bergen. He needed the German's confidence. He needed to shoot and act without thinking, without fearing the consequences—just knowing where to aim, how to shoot, when to retreat.

He closed his eyes and did not move. For three long seconds he turned inward, away from the crack of gunfire, and beat that shade of Ellingsly that made to rise in him. He beat it until it cowed and cried and fled back where he had banished it.

He was Bergen Keuper once more, and he knew what to do.

"Heckler," he yelled over the din. The American emptied his Winchester before dropping closer. Bergen said nothing further; he gestured to the dark corner of the wagon. Heckler nodded, slung his rifle on his shoulder, and pulled a matchbox from his pocket. Bergen holstered his revolver and lifted the steam rifle.

"Retreat!"

The men broke immediately and fled. The men in the buildings turned their attention exclusively on the shooters hiding in and behind the clock.

Bergen ran low, the weight of his weapon straining at his back. With Heckler on his heels, he fled twenty yards back to where a lone steel wagon lay on its side. The men fled along the sidewalks, taking station in alcoves, doors, and alleys. Bergen rounded the wagon's edge and stopped.

Heckler darted in behind him just as the explosives went off.

It was not a large enough explosion to hurt their enemies. Even with the best of luck it would slow them down only a few seconds.

Which is all I will need.

Bergen lifted the steam rifle and sighted along it. Its boiler rumbled. Its wires buzzed. His finger hauled back on the trigger and he felt the rush of steam filling the chamber while magnets powerful enough to distort steel held the bullet in place.

A perfect shot. The bullet sliced through the chain holding up the clock's right side. A second shot parted the chain on the left. Bergen lowered his rifle and watched the clock groan and bow.

I have brought down larger monsters than you, devil.

The clock wailed and screamed as its moorings tore free. Gears and springs burst from its back as the face cracked across and the whole edifice began to fold. Men in gold vests, gold jackets, gold hats tumbled out like leaves off a shaken tree.

The clock broke free with a tear that sent vibrations through all the beams of Shadwell. Then it pitched forward in silence, the motion of so massive an object seeming to dull all other events, and plunged down.

Bergen waited.

The crash came an instant later. Behind the curtain of smoke, cloaks died by the score. The Beggar's Parade, cracked and weakened by Heckler's explosives, gave in and crumbled. The clock passed through it, dragging the children of the Machine down into darkness, and into the embrace of the creatures who waited there.

The booms continued for long minutes: echoes of bodies, wagons, and concrete striking beams on their way down. A gap of thirty yards now separated the Underbelly from the lift platform.

The cheer that went up from the men poured through Bergen like sparkling wine. He exulted and cheered with them. He clasped shoulders and shook hands and felt more alive than he had since that deep night near Ulundi eight years ago. Men gathered around him with congratulations and Bergen did not hear their words for their overwhelming gratitude.

Bergen wished it could have lasted. He spotted Heckler making his way up the street with his weapon in his hand and fright in his eye.

"Excuse me," Bergen told the circle that had gathered around him. He pushed out and met Heckler a good distance from them.

"What is it, boy?"

"A runner just came from Valley Lane," he said. "Five men there, guarding your rope. They're all dead."

"How?"

"Throats cut, suh."

Bergen swallowed back what he felt, what he thought. *I should have made sure. I should have tracked him like a gazelle and shredded his heart with a bullet.*

"Gather everyone who is still alive and bring them here," he said. "Take two men. No one is to go off alone."

"Yes, sir," said Heckler. He grabbed two of the celebrating gentlemen and ran down the Parade into town.

Bergen turned to the men. Some had gathered around the lone wagon left in the street, others at the edge of the hole, spitting over or yelling down.

"All of you!" he yelled. "This does not mean the danger is over. Gather the wounded and move them here"—he indicated the two buildings closest to the hole—"and here."

The men, grumbling, moved to obey. He drew breath to whip them into it, when Phineas materialised before him. The sailor had shrunk even farther into his clothing, now nothing but a set of hands and a scarred nose compressed under a hat.

"What is it, Macrae?"

"There are more of them," he said.

"I have not forgotten."

"Well, neither have I, Kraut." He poked a finger at the Concourse above. "Because I can hear them."

"I never intended to get them all," Bergen said. "How many?"

"Two dozen."

"An annoyance, nothing more."

"Boiler Men. Two dozen Boiler Men."

Bergen stopped and listened outside the local pocket of warmth in a cold world.

Above: heavy marching; perfect unison.

One cannot fight the Boiler Men.

Aaron Bolden had said it. Bailey Howe had believed

it. Every servant of Scared had lived by it. Every man and child in Whitechapel whispered it in private places, like the transmission of some dangerous truth.

We shall see how truthful it is.

He retrieved the steam rifle and ordered his preparations.

Missy curtsied automatically when the door opened. "Matron."

Gisella did not spend a second moment looking at her, but turned and strode back into the hall. "I shall punish you for your impudence, young lady," she said. "Come along and shut the door behind you. The air is dreadfully thick tonight."

Missy did as she was told, obeisance taking a quick hold of her.

She followed Gisella's lace-trimmed skirts down the long entry hall, past paintings of country scenes and royalty. She walked with her head bowed, her feet clicking softly on the tile, her skirts whispering, the handbag clutched tight in her fingers, and a smile upon her lips.

The matron had her hair tied in a tight bun, held in place by a net two hundred years out of fashion. She walked with steps that, for all their rapidity, planted into the floor with enough force to echo in the hall. The expected sounds came down from the upper floor.

Gisella led her into the ladies' parlour, furnished with lavish drapes in red and purple, soft couches, and a grand piano shining like the day it was made. Half the girls were there as well as some new ones, all dressed in their evening finery. This is where they always sat to practice their polite conversation while awaiting the suitors of the evening.

This ritual had been a part of Missy's life for nearly seven years, since Gisella had deemed her old enough and when her training was well along. Sometimes the gentlemen picked her, sometimes they did not, but they all had hungry eyes for her. Always, she was the first that they inspected upon entry.

Her eyes had floated to a young girl she did not recognise, a pale-faced child with too much rouge and a green dress that did not yet fit her. She was only a year or two into womanhood, younger than Gisella used to allow.

"Ladies, your errant sister has returned," Gisella said, addressing the room. "Emily, please help her out of those rags she is wearing and into something appealing."

"Yes, Matron," one of the youngest girls murmured. She rose from her seat and scuttled to Missy's side, then took her hand and began to lead her to a small door at the back of the parlour.

Yes, I must freshen up, Missy thought. *I'm frightful. I haven't changed my skirts or blouse since this morning. I must be ready for the clients when they show; not hair nor hem out of place. Granted it is a terrible night, but one may yet find the mood upon him and I must be prepared.*

She stopped so suddenly, the girl's hand slipped out of hers.

Conversation had resumed, lighthearted chatting about current events and society pages—some real and some fabricated for the right tone. The girls beamed with pleasant smiles and polite nods and kept their hands folded in their laps. The room vibrated with tension, but no one spared a glance at the prodigal daughter.

"Come along," said the girl—Emily?—at her side. "You need to get presentable."

Missy looked down at this creature not yet even a young woman. The girl's eyes stared wide and placid up at her without a hint of nervousness or haste. Her modest smile was fixed on her face and did not flutter even with the act of speech.

"Come along," she said again. "We don't want to keep the men waiting."

She had the twiddling pixie brogue of an underclass child, but the words were Gisella's own. The girl could not have been there longer than three months. Could Gisella truly do this to them so quickly?

"No," she said, gently as she could manage, though her voice was shaking. She moved Emily aside and turned to face the hard, indifferent eyes of the woman who had raised her.

Gisella held her face in a familiar expression of disdain, features chiseled as if from stone, skin stretched tight over thin bones. Missy had never before looked the matron in the eyes for more than an instant—none of the girls had. The moment that disinterested, superior gaze hit her, Missy felt her resolve wither and flake away. Her throat and neck tightened, and her breath came short.

Obey! screamed her mind. *Duck your head, do your chores, and look presentable and be a good little girl and be safe!*

She had kept out of trouble so many years by listening to that voice. It had guaranteed food, shelter, family, and woe to those who disobeyed.

Gisella looked her over as if evaluating a dress halfway finished.

"It seems obvious you are not ready to assume your duties and earn your keep. Nevertheless, I will be charitable. Emily, take her to the sleep room and lie her down. I will be there presently with some tea."

This time the girl managed to lead her from the parlour into the dreary and unfinished hall that led to the kitchen and the room that held hammocks for the girls. Gisella strode in after, filling the hallway with her presence. She was a looming shadow in the light of the parlour, impossibly large, powerful, immovable.

I am going to the locked room where you were never allowed to go. I am going to mix my tea and make you drink it. I will rid you of the killer you are and make you a whore again.

They passed the nondescript door of the locked room, where all of the matron's poisons were stored.

Killer or whore, then. What shall it be?

Missy stopped again. Emily again slipped forward of her and turned back, an affronted look in her eyes and the smallest mist of confusion.

"Gisella," Missy said.

"It is improper for you to speak to me in that tone, young lady." Missy heard the jingle of keys in the matron's hand. "Off to the room. You shall be deservingly punished at a time of my convenience."

Missy swallowed, moved her fingers, undid the clasp on her handbag.

What is she but a sack of meat waiting for a bullet?

An endless pivot, heels of her shoes grinding on dirt beneath them. "No, Gisella."

The matron did not bat an eyelash at this comment. She simply returned her stone gaze to Missy. "It was not a request, nor an option, young lady. Obedience is required of a proper girl. Mr. Worthingen of Cathedral has made an offer for you, and I do not intend to disappoint a client."

Missy looked into the eyes—flat, hazel eyes, stern and implacable. But also shot through with veins, lines across the irises like cracks in china, black spots here and there.

" 'What has a lady, if not her reputation?' Is that it?"

"It pleases me to see you have been paying attention," said the matron. "You are a black mark on my otherwise flawless professional record, young lady. I'll have no more of your willfulness. Tonight I will move you on to the *beng lie* in its pure form and we will have not another disobedient word from you the rest of your days."

The handbag opened. Bare fingers slithered in and coiled around something cold. That cold spread into her.

You are a killer now. You are a hawk, dear bird. You are a snake.

And suddenly Oliver's death made sense. Oliver had died to show her what she was capable of. If she could murder him, how could she balk at this?

She drew out the gun.

Emily yelped and sprinted into the sleep room.

Gisella gasped. Her brows bunched together and she began shaking her crone finger. "You ungrateful shrew! How dare you, after all I've done for you!"

"Shut up, you witch," Missy said.

Gisella's eyes flared. "I took you in when you were a mongrel child and prey on the streets. You were headed straight to the Chimney, mark my words, and then you have the audacity to run off, and now *this*? I should have left you where I found you."

"Yes, you should have," Missy said, jamming the gun

into Gisella's face, right at the end of her pointed nose. "Now *shut up!* I have a question to ask you and you are going to answer it."

Gisella huffed and folded her arms across her stomach. "Such presumption. You are a no-good devil child."

Missy poked the gun forward another inch. "Where is the hobgoblin man?"

"And insane as well," Gisella said. "He is nothing more than a figment of your disturbed mind."

"Where is he?" Missy slapped the matron across her wrinkled nose with the pistol's barrel. Gisella reeled back, yelping, grasping at the blood that began to trickle out.

"Put down that ugly thing this instant," she ordered.

Missy clawed Gisella's shoulder with her free hand and dragged the old lady's face against the barrel. "Do you think I won't, Gisella?" Missy said. "Do you think me too weak? Or do you think it isn't loaded?"

Missy fired a shot into the ceiling, inches from Gisella's ear. The old woman shrieked and clutched at the side of her head. Missy rammed the barrel back against her cheek. Something inside her grinned as Gisella jerked back from the heat.

"Tell me," Missy yelled.

"Unhand me this minute," the matron cried.

Missy bit down with her free hand, digging fingernails into withered muscle and sinew. She forced Gisella's head backwards and placed the gun against her forehead.

"Tell me!"

Gisella screamed and Missy struck her on the chin. Her old crone's teeth clacked together and a chip broke from one. Gisella gasped and sputtered.

You'll never be anything, you rotten child. Born wicked.

"Shut up!"

Something cracked this time. The old woman cried and begged.

It does not matter what you do to me, young lady. To your dying day you will be a whore, and men will have you whenever they please by dropping notes upon your doorstep, and you will always remember that it was I who trained you for it.

"Shut up!"

She broke the woman's nose.

I have already conquered you, child. You are a dog in truth, chewing on her master's ankle—a rabid bitch not fit for feeding or breeding, merely for getting kicked.

"Shut up!"

She twisted the woman's arm backwards until it popped.

"Tell me where he is!" The words tore out of Missy's throat, raw and painful and exhilarating.

Gisella whined and cried and gasped out words.

You are mine, you useless tart. Now and forever.

A crack like that of a whip. The sharp scent of gun smoke. A thump and thud, with the swish of skirts.

And the girls' eyes: staring bright and glassy and so very wide from the parlour, and Emily's from the kitchen, with not a word spoken by any of these ones in their perfect dresses.

"I had to," Missy cried. "It's all I have left. You heard her, didn't you? I'm nothing to her. I'm nothing at all." She shook the gun. "This is all I have. Can't you understand? She took everything else away from me."

The eyes stared, painted statues. A young girl began to cry.

"Damn you all. It had to be done. Liz—" She reached out to the sharp-nosed blonde she knew so well. "You remember, don't you? We used to talk about this. We used to lay awake and say how someone should do this to her, and to all the men. Don't you remember?"

Elizabeth swallowed, dropped her eyes, her hands shaking. She backed and hid behind another girl.

"No, Liz, please." Missy's hands burst into shaking; tears rolled down her cheeks. "You all wanted it, didn't you? Didn't you want to be free of her? Why isn't anyone saying anything?"

She cradled the gun against her chest and sobbed.

You had your chance. You had peace and bliss and freedom, and you ended it all with a single cut. Your life has always been pain and you chose to come back to it.

She lowered the gun, watching the barrel and cylinder move past her and glisten with blood.

"The hobgoblin man is real," she said. "I need to know where he's hiding."

Some of the younger girls started to cry.

"Shut up, all of you! It's very important that you tell me."

The older girls turned to the younger to comfort them, led them away and vanished one by one from the arch of the parlour's door.

"Liz? Annie? Ethel? Don't go. It's not done yet. *I'm* not done yet"

My life can't end like this. I have one more thing to do.

"Doesn't anyone know?"

"I knows."

She turned. A small boy, no older than seven and dressed in stained tweed shorts and a crumpled cap, stepped forward from the sleep room.

"I knows where 'e is," the boy said. " 'E took me there once."

Missy reached out a trembling hand, drained of colour.

"Take me," she said. Sobs choked the rest of her words, of sorrow and relief and gratitude.

The little boy stepped past Emily, who was near tears but trying not to show it, brave thing.

"I won't hurt you," Missy said. "Don't be afraid."

"I ain't afraid. The girls was always nice to me."

His little hand slipped into hers.

"But 'e wasn't nice. Not at all."

The thing that had been John Scared cackled and howled into the red sky.

Moan for me, my love.

He twisted and Mama Engine writhed. He grasped her and her desires ran amok, flashing hatred and lust and fear into his mind, which he drank like syrup. Her machines and her crows swarmed about the city like mad ants, devouring one another in their pleasures.

I know you, my love. I know you to your last secret. I know every beam and organ and whim you have ever had.

The *mei kuan* pulsed through him like his native blood. The calculations came automatically, showing him the far-reaching probabilities of each motion he made. He read his bride now instant by instant with a knowledge as complete as God's.

He held the diseased child under one set of his thousand claws and paid him little attention.

It is a shame we cannot be alone on our wedding night, my love. He ground the child down. *But I have done worse things in front of children.*

With the tendrils of his inflated intellect, he wound down deeper into her body, into her burning furnace-womb hotter than a star, hidden beneath a mountain of metal. He tore her wide, bathing in the heat, then filled her with a glacial seed.

Ecstasy rushed through him, vibrating his every limb, shuddering to his core. He gasped and squirmed and blazed to new proportions as he finally tasted woman. Far away, his flesh body reacted in kind.

Look to your husband, Lady. Even as I ravish you he sits like a dullard. I will never ignore you like that, my sweet, for you are mine and I claim you forever.

He had her over and over, until her screams and his tore the red sky into strips of black, through which dripped the seeping fluid of other places. All sensation warped into his pleasure and for an instant he knew himself to be Almighty.

He did not notice a lone soul cross his boundaries and enter him.

Oliver took stock: broken hip, couldn't walk; broken shoulder, couldn't lift his arm. His neck wound had sealed again and he was running a fever of about one hundred ten degrees. He actually thanked those gods that had ravished him for the gift of their anaesthesia.

Hews wasn't so fortunate. The Boiler Men dumped him on the floor without ceremony. He had been badly beaten. He breathed short, thin breaths and lay unmoving where they dropped him.

He was willing. He knew the risks better than I did.

The thought brought him no comfort, only a deep

loathing and sadness that anyone—anyone at all—had
to die for this revolution. How could all these people be
so willing and eager to give up their lives? He'd never
understood it, this fever that men took into battle. When
he'd organised the Uprising, he'd honestly believed
that it could be done without loss. He'd believed that
will and cunning and, well, *rightness* could carry them
through. He'd never considered sacrifice. He'd never
accepted it.

Afterwards, he'd kept his crew quiet and safe for five
years, fighting by night through theft, sabotage, espio-
nage, always out of sight and away from confrontation.
He'd kept them alive against all odds.

And then he'd led them to their ends.

Oliver squinted against the tears and tried to believe
that Tommy had gone out as he wanted to, and that he
was at the Gates with a smile on his broad face and not
lying in pieces under the cloaks' boots.

"The allergic man always listens for the buzz of an
awakening bee."

Oliver looked up. He knew exactly where he was. He
knew the identity of the tuxedo-clad man standing across
a marble floor beneath a hundred clocks.

The baron of Whitechapel stood facing his altar.

"A stone rolling down a hill is arrested by the presence of a tuft of grass. When that grass withers, the
stone will move again; such is the inevitability of
gravity."

He turned then, facing Oliver's bright eyes with his
dull ones. The tuxedo was crisp and clean, as was the
white shirt beneath, the whole a ghostly vision lit only
in the sizzling flares of Oliver's eyes. Upon an altar behind him sat a black top hat and cane. Through the
skylight windows on the ceiling, Oliver could see only
blackness. Where was the light of the Stack?

Baron Hume approached with stately and measured
steps. His wing tips clicked on the floor, and Oliver suddenly realised that none of the clocks were ticking.

"Could a rain choose which plants to nourish? Could
a fire choose which houses to burn and which to let be?"

The baron halted and stared down at the two of them, hands clasped behind his back. "I choose to be a man."

Oliver didn't know if he was supposed to reply. When he had been silent for some time, the baron continued.

"The skin of trees has passed beneath your nails. It has grown to a galvanic jewel and clings now to your flesh like the teeth of a remora."

Oliver realised what he was talking about and fought the urge to check his pocket and see if the device was still there.

"I don't have it," Oliver said.

The baron inclined his head forward in what could be mistaken for a knowing expression.

"As hidden as the stars near the moon, you bear the fate of the soundless wall, at the behest of the colours swirling in water."

Had they searched him? Had they taken it away?

Oliver stalled: "I don't work for her."

The baron stood straight again.

"You clean the crocodile's teeth, and the beast does not eat you. It is simple." He glanced upwards. "Day passes the world to night's gentle hands, night returns it to day. Thus there is time and turning."

Night and day? He and I?

Oliver said nothing, feeling the situation out. Baron Hume folded his hands together in front of him. "You are knives shredding the pages of a troubled mind. You are the death of the words written by a shaking hand and a dying soul."

Oliver blurted it out: "Your prophecies?"

The baron nodded. Oliver gasped as his memory hit him over the head with the obvious. This was the same man who had written the verses of the *Summa Machina* who had cried and railed against his own weakness even as the Lord and Lady consumed him.

He's not an enemy, Oliver thought. *He's just another of their victims.*

His mind started churning.

"What are you asking?" Oliver said. "Do you want the same as we do?"

"A hare shivering in his hole also profits from the ceasing of the thunderstorm."

Instantly, all of his fatigue was forgotten. Oliver tried to stand and remembered that his leg would not work.

"I need to get to the Chimney," he said. He at last patted his pocket and found a comforting lump within. "It's the only place it will work. Can you help me get past the cloaks and the Boiler Men?"

The baron's gaze drifted slowly to the pocket where Scared's device lay hidden. Oliver's heart jumped into his throat, as he realised he might have just betrayed himself.

Hume only looked aside a moment, as if considering, then spoke. "Raindrops will wash away once loosed from the cloud. The ticking little scrubs and the burning ones are so many ashes, and the wind will carry them over the hills." He looked back. "But the lost souls listen only to the whispers in their own darkness."

Oliver tumbled that in his mind a few minutes. "*Your* darkness?"

The baron nodded. "What use has a gardener of a hole that cannot be filled? Only the echoes call it home."

Hume turned once again to face the altar, and walked in measured strides to just below the quartz clock, then halted, lowered his head, and stilled.

Oliver settled back and wondered how far Providence would string him along before crushing him down.

Beside him, Hews stirred and burbled some words past the blood on his lips. Oliver leaned towards him, tried to reach out with his broken arm and found he couldn't.

"Hewey," he said. "Are you all right?"

"Don't ask stupid questions, lad," he grumbled. His eyes fluttered open, revealing themselves to be bloodshot and watery. "I didn't quite catch the end of it. What did he say?"

"He . . . well, I *think* he promised that he would help us to the Chimney," Oliver said carefully.

"He always was difficult to understand. I assume he hasn't gotten any clearer." Hews made no effort to rise. "Where is he now?"

Oliver glanced at the mechanical man. He stood in the same pose, still and unreacting. "He's just over at the altar. I think he's communing with his gods, or perhaps with the Boiler Men."

"Do you trust him, lad?"

Oliver watched that still form and reread the passages of the *Summa Machina* in his mind. "Yes. I do."

"Good enough for me." Hews reached into his pocket. "I appear to have lost my gun. Shame on me."

"You can have my knife."

Hews chuckled. "I wouldn't be caught dead with just a knife, lad. I hesitate to ask . . ."

Oliver shook his head.

"Ah. He was a good lad. I wish I'd gotten to know him better." Hews found Oliver's eyes. "Don't regret, my boy. We all came into this with our eyes open and we'll leave it with our consciences clear."

Oliver nodded.

"Consciences *clear*, right? And don't mourn me."

Oliver felt a new knot twisting his innards. "How bad is it, Hewey?"

"I can't feel my legs," Hews said. "Nor my right arm. I don't think I'll be moving again."

"Christ, Hewey . . ."

"Don't mourn, lad," Hews said. "Barbara's waiting for me. I'll be in good hands." He took a long, calm breath. "You've never asked about your mother, lad."

The knot grew tighter. "I never wanted to know."

"Well, I've been waiting twenty-odd years for you to ask me, lad."

"I still don't want to know."

"Well, since I'm the one who's dying *I* will set the topic of conversation." Hews took another slow breath. "Do you remember her?"

Oliver sighed. "A little. I remember I used to go out looking for her."

"We couldn't keep you in the house, lad. Even at that age you would disappear for a few nights and then we'd find you sleeping on the factory floor." Hews chuckled and his eyes glazed over with remembrance. After a few sharp coughs, he went on. "I woke up one night because

I heard someone breaking a window into the factory. Barbara shoved me out there with a lantern and my pistol wearing nothing but a dressing gown."

Oliver didn't need to hear this. Maybe Hews needed to tell it, and he was right: of the two of them, he was closer to dying. *Damn you and your courtesies, old man.*

"Shadwell was crawling with ruffians in those days, just after the wall went up. I came in all fire and brimstone and to my surprise, the intruder was a woman. She saw me and bolted, jumped right through a back window and left you behind."

Hews grew serious a moment. "Her eyes glowed, lad."

Oliver sunk into his shoulders. "She was a crow."

"Aye. I thought you should know."

Oliver considered the implications, rejected them. "Thanks, Hewey."

Baron Hume stirred. With a scraping noise much like a yawn he lifted his head, then turned and approached.

"Herbert Francis Lewis," he said.

Hews tried feebly to tip the crushed hat still sticking to his head. "Mr. Hume."

The baron looked at both of them, and at neither. "A Roman road is clear and leads to the palaces of gold and marble."

"Thank you kindly," said Hews. "One of your men will need to escort young Oliver there. I'm afraid I'm not fit to move."

"Wait," said Oliver. "What about the Underbelly? Would you please withdraw the Boiler Men from attacking the Shadwell Underbelly?"

The baron's head tilted in his thoughtful pose. "A sparrow chirps for its flock, but a rooster crows to herald his own magnificence."

Oliver glanced at Hews. "What did that mean?"

"He's asking you why you're making the request."

"Ah." Oliver turned back to Hume. "They're no threat to you or to the Boiler Men. They're simply trying to survive."

The baron nodded. "The sun setting . . ."

An explosion. Copper gears and springs sprayed out to clatter on the marble floors. Steam rushed into the room. All three turned to see that one of the two copper doors to the chapel had been bent inward, and sported a monstrous hole in the centre.

A second explosion broke through the other door, bending it from its outer edge and knocking its delicate mechanisms loose. Steam rushed in through the hole, followed by white electric arcs.

It could only be one weapon.

"Get back," Oliver said, searching for and finding the tiny derringer in his pocket. He fumbled some bullets out with his crippled arm and tried to load.

A string of masculine grunts sounded in the hall, then the damaged doors caved under the weight of a steel battering ram.

"Who is it?" Hews asked.

Oliver slipped the second bullet in and clicked his weapon shut. "Scared."

The doors burst at the second hit and eight men stormed in, clad in workers' soot-laden clothing. They dropped the ram and began winding flashers that hung on their belts.

Hume turned to face them. Oliver watched in horror as all eight men suddenly clutched at their eyes, toppled on their faces, and slid to a stop on the marble floor. There had been no impact, no arcs of fire or projectiles leaping from the baron to these men, and yet pools of blood had already begun to seep out from under their bodies.

Then a third shot, and Baron Hume's head parted into ribbons of iron. Steam rushed along the path of the bullet, carrying deadly lightning that lanced into the baron's chest, scorching the white shirt and tailcoat. The empty husk fell to the ground with a clang.

Oliver leveled his gun at the door and stayed silent.

A man strode through, barrel-chested and built like an ox, with a broom moustache of brown wires that nearly covered his face. On his shoulder rode the brass-hued weapon Oliver had last seen in von Herder's workshop.

"That's far enough, thank you," Oliver called.

Faster than lightning, the man drew his army revolver and shot Oliver twice in the chest. Oliver found the impacts no more jarring than swift jabs with a broom handle. He returned fire.

The steam rifle fell to the floor and cracked the marble. The man faded to his knees, eyes wide with surprise, then keeled forward and ceased to breathe.

The derringer fell between Oliver's feet. He coughed and choked, as sharp convulsions distorted his chest and fluid rushed into the two bullet holes. Oliver gasped as the bullets spat out onto the floor, splatters of white paste following.

"We're alive," he said, to Hews or to himself or to the dead people littering the room. "Isn't that just a lark?"

The space swallowed his words. Not even breath disturbed the settling air, aside from his own.

Hews had expired sometime during the fight.

"Did I ever thank you, Hewey?" Oliver asked. "If I didn't, I meant to. I'm a proud bugger, but I guess you knew that."

He wished his new vision would allow him to see Hews one last time before he went off to heaven.

It isn't right, you dying like this after all you've done for me and for your homeland.

He wiped tears from his eyes. The pus and grime transferred from his hands simply made them water more. "I hope to see you at the Gates, Hewey."

And it isn't right, me still being alive.

Nothing could be right in Whitechapel until the day was done.

With agonising slowness of the joints, Oliver tipped forward until he landed on his belly, then crawled. It took him perhaps ten minutes to drag himself to the altar. There, he stood, using the marble block for support, and grasped the baron's cane.

It was mahogany wood, polished darkly and oiled. The handle and foot were sheathed in silver, both completely without style or scrollwork. Oliver examined Hume's top hat a moment, then set it back down.

A good hat for a good man, right, Hewey?

He tested the cane, finding he had to hunch like an old man to make use of it, but it let him hobble. The white fluid that ran now like blood in his body had already begun healing his bones and straightening his muscles.

He started walking, past Hume's inert body, past the remains of assailants and friends. He hobbled out into the Long Hall, and there, stopped to look from the windows.

He did not know which tower he saw far away to his right, but it was in flames. He saw the antlike shadows of people running, and the occasional flash of gunfire. No doubt the cloaks had gone mad all over the city, and perhaps the Boiler Men as well, deprived of their director. Without the constant light of the Stack illuminating the underside of the clouds, nothing more of Whitechapel could be seen. He watched a burning tenement break from its supports and plunge into the downstreets.

At the other end of the hallway, he found another set of broken doors, these ones not shattered but scored by flasher hits—a crude but fast way to open certain types of locks. Beyond, a lift shaft plunged far down into the heart of the Stack. Oliver stared down it and saw the lift itself clacking its way up out of the dark. It reached the level and halted, spitting steam from mechanisms beneath it.

Metal fingers an inch and a half in diameter hauled the gate aside. Two Boiler Men waited for him to board. Oliver stepped between them and turned to face the door.

He looked out one of the hall's windows until one of the Boiler Men shut the gate, knowing he might never see Whitechapel again.

The mechanisms beneath the lift churned, and his descent began.

The echoes of gunfire faded from the vast space between the Underbelly and the Shadwell Concourse. Bergen waited, Gasser in hand, steam rifle close by. It had been the fire of Atlas rifles—unmistakable.

He turned to the sailor.

Phineas's eyes gleamed glassy and bloodshot from the

small gap between his collar and hat brim. "I can't hear
the cloaks anymore," he said. The sailor's trembling
flapped the folds of his ulster coat.

"It is quiet," Bergen said. Even the ordinary bustle of
the Concourse, usually all too audible from beneath, had
softened to an ambient hum. "What do you hear in the
Underbelly, Macrae?"

The old man withdrew further. "Women talking. Ba-
bies crying. All your men fiddling with their guns."

Bergen held still a moment, listening for that subtle
absence of sound—like the stilling of birds and insects
and leaves—that signaled the presence of a predator.

"Where is Heckler?" Bergen asked.

Phineas answered without hesitation. "Moving up the
Parade with two men."

Bergen nodded. "There is someone else afoot in the
city, sailor. He is a young man who walks without sound,
but he would be badly wounded, perhaps breathing
heavily, and he will be carrying a knife."

Bergen surveyed the street. Bergen and Phineas sat in
the shadow of the last wagon, now pulled from the centre of the Parade and lodged against the wall of one of
the two buildings closest to the lift. From that point,
Bergen commanded a good view of the Parade, except
where it dipped beneath itself and wound around the
thick beams that cut the Underbelly to hold up Shadwell
Tower. Nothing moved.

"Find me this man."

They sat in silence a few minutes.

"I can't hear shit," said Phineas.

Bergen had made certain the street was empty. The
men had been crowded into the single building to the
lift's left, along with the wounded and that fussy but
capable doctor that Oliver had fished up. A concentrated
resistance would deter the prudent predator, but one
man, alone and without support, was an inviting target.

So where are you, boy?

Phineas' presence was an unfortunate necessity. Bergen told himself he had no intention of protecting the
old man if Penny showed.

"The Ironboys are moving," Phineas said. "They're gathering somewhere near the old square."

"Where is that?" Bergen asked.

"About above the Parade three or four streets up from Coll's," said the sailor.

"What are they doing?"

Phineas snorted. "Damned if I know, Kraut. It's not like they bloody talk to each other, is it?"

Bergen stilled the impulse to chastise the man for his tone. He knew too well that bluster was a coward's only courage.

Heckler and his two escorts appeared from an alley mouth three streets down. An easy shot from this range, if Penny followed them. But no, he would never be so careless.

Heckler approached, white-faced and drawn. His moustache had thinned pitifully as sweat stuck the hairs together. He and the two men with him stank of fear.

Bergen kept his eyes roving: alleys, rooftops, lift, bends of the Parade.

"What have you found?" he asked.

Heckler squatted behind the wagon and swallowed before speaking.

"It's the Wordsworths, suh. The mister's got his throat cut and the missus's been stabbed."

"He is trying to draw me away." Bergen looked at the young man with narrowed eyes. "Have the tunnels been breached?"

"No, suh," Heckler said. "The Bemets hid in their cellar. Someone broke off the lock and kicked through the trapdoor."

"Why were they not in the tunnels?"

Heckler shrugged, looked away. "Some folk wouldn't go, didn't want to leave their homes. It ain't like we can force 'em to."

"You can. You should have. This is not a time to have the city spotted with stray civilians. Why didn't you tell me about this attack, Macrae?"

"Because I didn't bloody hear it, Kraut. The noise from those God-cursed guns almost broke my skull."

Bergen grunted in response, and let his eyes wander again, let his instincts guide them, point to point, shadow to shadow.

After a few minutes of silence, with Heckler and his men shifting like admonished schoolboys, the American spoke. "Suh, should we be here? What Ah mean is, shouldn't we be guarding the tunnel doors?"

Bergen tolerated the question. "If we gather there, the attack will come there. We gather here because this location is of no value to us, and will yield no power to our enemies should they take it."

"But with that killer out in the streets . . ."

"He has not the strength to break the tunnel doors, nor the voice to convince the women to open them. And in any case, they are not his quarry."

Without warning, Phineas jumped in place and slammed his palms over his ears.

Bergen shot to his feet, followed instants later by Heckler, already shouldering his Winchester. The two nameless militiamen struggled to their feet with more trepidation than haste.

Thunder broke out in the vast space.

Bergen localised the sound, pinpointing it to the upper Concourse, a spot some six blocks away. As he watched, bits of concrete from the roads above chipped off and fell. Larger pieces followed them, crashing onto the tenements below, and then an entire segment some twenty feet across tore away, braces and supports and all, and crushed the building beneath it.

"Gather the men," Bergen ordered, not turning away to see who obeyed.

Soft gaslight shone through the hole in the upper concourse onto the rising cloud of dust. Then the light grew dark, and exactly two dozen shapes dropped through the hole in perfect unison, shapes too tall and round to be men. Bergen watched them smash through the roof of their landing spot, and watched the whole building come down in a splash of debris.

They would have to extricate themselves. Perhaps two or three minutes.

He turned to his army, his ragtag group of labourers,

bakers, wheel menders, and plebeians—old, feeble, bowed with years of work or with rickets.

"Do as I say and you may live," Bergen said. "Run from them. Shoot them from windows and dark alleys. Lead them astray from the tunnels. If you are swift they will not catch you. Any man who stands his ground deserves his death."

He holstered his pistol, reached down, and hauled the steam rifle onto his shoulder.

"I will do the hunting."

He rapidly divided them into teams. Some he assigned to run, others to shoot from rooftops and windows and keep out of sight as much as possible.

"Do not stay in one location," Bergen said. "Spread them out as much as you can and if caught in a motion, always retreat. If you get a shot from safety, aim for their weapons and their mechanisms." He pointed to three teams and told them to run past the bystreet and closer to the Blink. He ordered three more to run into the tenements on the east side, where the streets curved and connected without any order. The rest dispersed as they saw fit, with one team remaining to guard the wounded.

"Heckler, you are with me."

The American nodded and stepped up. Bergen was not surprised to find that Phineas had vanished.

As the men ran off down the Parade, Bergen looked Heckler over. The lad stood ready and expectant, capable and confident. He was how Ellingsly should have been.

"Your task is to cover me, boy," Bergen said. "With this weapon I am not mobile, and you may need to draw fire away from me."

Heckler nodded without hesitation. "Yes, suh."

"Good."

The rumble of Atlas rifles drew their attention. Bergen simultaneously felt fear building in his gut and a smile growing on his face.

"This time Bergen Keuper will *win* the day," he said aloud.

They began the hunt.

* * *

Scared's mind manifested as a field of ice, bordered on each horizon with savage, unscalable crags, and torn across by a savage wind. The sky was dark and without stars, though strings of sparkling fluid crisscrossed it. Aaron struggled for each step, casting about with his unique vision for Scared's trapped other self.

Beneath his feet lay images frozen in the ice. These were the memories and nightmares of the creature that called itself Scared, locked away where they could not hamper him. Aaron glanced at them only a moment, for he found he couldn't stand to watch the atrocities that played themselves out over and over under the surface: things done to women, to children, done with chemicals and knives and bare hands. They were monstrous. Still, Aaron could not help but marvel at the mental discipline required to erect such a place, and at the strength of the personality that had done so.

The images told him a story, a story of a once-good man, corrupted by sinful thoughts, by guilt and shame and lusts he could not control. The man had done terrible things. Though he longed to be caught and imprisoned, the police did not connect him to any of his crimes; he was a respectable man, beyond suspicion. Finally, unable to bear the weight of his shame, he had withdrawn deep within, and abandoned his life to the monster that called itself John Scared.

"You are not him."

Aaron looked down to find himself walking across a face that looked much like Scared's own might have, in days of youth and health.

"No, I'm not."

"You are not a nightmare," said the man, whose lips stayed still and frozen, and whose voice came on the wind. "You are a living man."

Aaron nodded gently. "Yes."

"I do not understand."

Aaron knelt above the man. "I am here to free you."

"I do not understand."

"It's all right." Aaron stroked the ice above the man's face. "You're the man he was, before his twisted passions took him. You're the part of him that doubted and was ashamed."

"I had terrible thoughts," said the man. "Thoughts I could not live with. They tortured me every night and every waking hour, until I gave them away to him. I don't want them back."

Aaron nodded. "I know," he said. "It will be hard, but there will be peace afterwards. I promise."

He reached into his pockets, and withdrew the tools he needed. In this dream realm, anything he wished met his hand within the fabric. He tried a saw, an electric arcing device, a quantity of pitch and fire, and finally a hammer and chisel. The ice would not yield.

Aaron let his mind think on it.

"How did he do this?" he asked the face. "How did he build this prison?"

"Do you see the river?" said the face. "The heavenly river."

Aaron glanced at the streams of fluid above. "This liquid?" He reached up and touched some. Its white glow lingered on his fingers and skin.

"It is divinity in a bottle," said the face. "That is what he said. It is heaven or hell as he pleases. And hell pleases him. How it pleases him."

Aaron looked into the glimmering fluid with his vision, seeing the yellow flower that grew in the deepest South Asian jungles, seeing the decrepit, starved monks who would rather smell it than eat or sleep, seeing the tendrils of its scent spin in the human body and mind, until both burned up with wonder. It was the infinite power of a mind unfettered.

He breathed it in, letting it flow about his astral form until he glowed as bright as a night star.

I need be a watcher no longer, he thought.

The ice began to melt around him, and the nightmares growled as they emerged.

The brass wheel had been jammed open, its metal twisted and locked together by impacts. Oliver stumbled over the threshold and into the temple.

The Stack was a war zone. Mad crows and machines

danced and cackled and cannibalised one another while canaries ran about trying to restore order through reasoning, commanding, destroying. And the Boiler Men marched through the halls, murdering everything that moved.

Oliver felt it as much as he heard it. Mama Engine's perpetual fire in his mind had gone cold, as had the sickening pulse in his stomach and bowels that belonged to her diseased child. The open spaces and grand halls had fallen victim to a chill wind. The machines built into the walls stuttered and stalled, pressurised steam leaked from conduits, and the copper wiring strung against the ceiling sparked erratically.

The black cloaks that he and his guard passed had died in terror, their last expressions frozen on their faces.

Only twice did they meet resistance. On the first occasion, a pack of gold cloaks blocked their path as their leader demanded that the baron put a stop to the disorder. The Boiler Men had taken two steps in front of Oliver and gunned the cloaks down with cold efficiency.

The second encounter had been with a crow gnawing a steam pipe, oblivious to the heat scorching the skin from her face. The Boiler Men had dispatched her with the same precision.

The Boiler Men had obviously been into the temple already. The hundred cloaks that had brought down Tommy lay about the mirrored floor literally blown to pieces. Not a single one moved.

Oliver's bodyguards led him across the floor to the edge of the Chimney. The promised lift waited there, a plate of gold and steel mounted on tracks. This vantage brought him close enough to see the individual people in Grandfather Clock's thrall. The lift started up with a hum and a crackle of electricity, and began to roll sideways down a descending track that spiralled the outside of the chamber, always facing the Chimney.

The sound of hidden machines was deafening, the stench of ozone overpowering. Oliver forced himself to watch the endless rotating gallery of faces, wondering how many he had known, how many no one had known. So many of them were the child victims of the Chimney gangs, and some had been here long enough that their bodies had rotted away, leaving dry, cracked organs and nerves clinging to bone—yet still they were unable to die.

You will rest tonight, he told them.

Electricity arced between the Chimney and the copper threads extending out to the far walls. The lift circled the chamber over and over, descending two or three storeys with each loop. As they approached the bottom, Oliver estimated that they must be a quarter mile underground.

The lift reached its destination, locking into place with powerful magnets. The Boiler Men escorted him along a walkway that extended out into the room to a ring at the base of the Chimney. At the edge of that ring, they found a creature built of bent strips of brass and copper wiring. Oliver looked into its porcelain eyes as it assessed him and realised this was the one that had brought Tommy down.

It looked inquisitively at the Boiler Men, who did not speak or react, then reached out to a bundle of copper wires wound about a railing. Arcs leapt from its fingers and ran along the wires, jumping between different coils until they vanished into the Chimney. The Chimney reacted with an electric hum and the lowest two rows began to turn. The chairs carrying the Machine's victims shifted, some sliding up, others down, bringing an empty spot onto the bottom row, then rotating it towards them. In the gaps revealed during these movements, Oliver caught a glimpse of the Chimney's interior: a spider's web of interlaced copper balls and wires, alive with wiggling electric worms.

The bottom row slid to a halt. The creature pointed a single wire finger at the tarnished chair settling in front of them.

Oliver reached into his pocket and palmed the golden device. The Boiler Men closed ranks behind him, blocking any route of escape. Oliver allowed himself one deep breath, then hung the baron's cane over the railing and climbed awkwardly into the chair.

The Boiler Men remained where they stood, blocking

Oliver from the other creature's line of sight. Oliver drew Scared's device up to his chest, tines pointed inward. He gazed into the eyes of the Boiler Men, looking for answers to the questions he should have asked hours earlier: when was he supposed to activate it? How deep did the tines have to sink? The Boiler Men gave no answer, not in voice or gesture.

He should wait until he was connected. How would he know when that happened? What if Grandfather Clock stopped him from moving?

He felt a dull sting as something penetrated his back. He felt acutely the tearing muscle and flesh as the wire curled back on itself and looped between two of his vertebrae. Another punctured his right arm at the shoulder, two more, the base of his neck. He felt these wiggle about as well, finding purchase on bones and nerves that began sparking with pain. Oliver watched his legs and fingers jolt and jerk.

I can't wait any longer.

He drove the device into his chest. The tines poked through his shirt like sewing needles, pricking and penetrating his bruised skin and slipping expertly between ribs.

A ticking spread to his inner ear, beginning bright and quiet and growing louder and more expansive with each repetition. Images flickered over his eyes: thousands of intersecting gears, beams, and bells tolling, thoughts like rays of light shooting back and forth in an intricate lattice beautiful beyond words.

He felt a hum and crackle about his chest, and smiled. *This is from all us lowly coves, you bastard.*

Awareness began to fade from his physical body as the Great Machine gobbled up more and more of his mind. Oliver succumbed without struggle, though the relentless pounding wounded him in ways he did not know he could be damaged. The ticking tempered his soul, shaped it into modes of thinking that fell in harmony with Grandfather Clock's rhythm. It beat him down and moulded him, and Oliver smiled all the while.

Then a sickening rush filled his chest. White fluid pushing the tines out, healing the punctures. Oliver couldn't feel his arm, couldn't see, couldn't hold the device in him as the child-god's pus rejected it.

"It has to stay in!" he cried. Any perception of the chamber vanished, and the words echoed into Grandfather Clock, crushed and tempered and put to use by the machine even as it did the same to Oliver's own mind. Oliver's thoughts ended. His mental space became home to the calculations of the machine.

For an instant, all was in harmony.

Then, a black shape appeared to mar the infinite perfection. The ticks and tolls beat against it, but it refused to be made compliant. The shape rushed out, slipping into the empty spaces between Grandfather Clock's thoughts, and began to devour everything it touched.

Oliver's awareness flew back to him. He opened his eyes and saw the chamber around the Chimney blended into the mental realms of the three gods that claimed him. Fires burned everywhere, bells tolled, and electricity crackled, a putrid sea lapped at his soles. In this maddening vision only one thing stayed constant: a Boiler Man, holding the device firmly into his chest while the creature of brass ripped it apart plate by plate from behind.

Grandfather Clock fell out of rhythm. His million sounds phased away from one another, changing pitch and timbre. The Great Machine collapsed from within as Oliver laughed.

The poison turned. It suddenly rushed back into him, cutting through his brain and lancing outward through Mama Engine's connection in his head and her child's in his gut. Nothingness enveloped him and his laughter turned to screams.

Chapter 22

These writings are Holy. They are Divine. And yet they are the words of but a frightened young man, whose life has ended before his appointed time. Read them and despair, for if you have deciphered my scrawl, I fear it is already too late for you.

—XII. xi

"No doubt about it, suh," Heckler reported. "They're heading for the old entrance to the main tunnel. They must not know the cloaks welded it shut."

"They know," said Bergen. "The seal will not be an obstacle for them."

"They're heading for the women and children," said one of the half dozen militiamen sheltering with them. He was unshaven and emaciated, and Bergen had never bothered to ask his name.

Bergen turned to this man. "I told you to lead them away."

The man yelled his response. "They don't care about us. They just ignore us unless we shoot at 'em, and then they bleedin' kill us."

"Then you are not running fast enough."

Bergen leaned back against the pillar that gave them cover. It was one of the beams that held the upper concourse in place, being full seven long strides end to end. It was the only one on the block, and the only thing Atlas rifles could not shoot through.

Bergen knew he had to rest soon. He had fired the steam rifle seventeen times in a half hour and it was beginning to get too hot to hold near his body. The electrical discharges were also starting to make him lose focus. His balance felt off, his vision ticked if he moved his eyes too rapidly.

But they were women and children.

Bergen had never cared for such weak creatures. Ellingsly, being weak himself, had loved them.

Blast.

"Take your men to a different tunnel entrance and free them," Bergen ordered the men. "Lead them back to the lift and stay with the wounded. Under no circumstances leave them unguarded. Do you understand?"

The unseemly militiaman nodded, desperation replaced with equally desperate energy. At least it got the man to run off. The rest followed, leaving only himself and the American.

"You are my eyes, boy," Bergen said.

Heckler nodded and dashed from cover. He bolted across the street and took shelter behind a brick stair leading into a shop across the street. Atlas guns would tear right through it, but there was no other viable vantage point.

Heckler watched the Boiler Men. Bergen watched Heckler. Heckler held up three fingers, then motioned right to left. Bergen nodded and brought his weapon back up to his eyes.

Heckler aimed his Winchester. Bergen stepped out around the corner, having to step far from cover to keep his line of fire clear of the support beam, lest the electricity lance back through it.

Three Boiler Men marched from a street on the right into the line of fire. Bergen thumbed the trigger and thrilled at the rumble of the boiler. He had yet to miss a shot; neither was he disappointed with this one. As his target fell, the other two turned and opened fire with exacting precision. Bullets as large as a man's index finger tore the street to shreds where Bergen had stood an instant before. The beam thundered as bullets clattered against it from behind, a sound that might reverberate all through the tower. The fire spilled over into the building closest, sending up clouds of plaster dust.

Ellingsly exulted. Bergen shut him up and signaled Heckler to fire. The lad complied without hesitation, cracking off a single shot and then diving onto his belly behind the flimsy cover he'd chosen. Altas fire ripped up the stair and the wall behind it, shattering the shop window and wooden door frame. Bergen stepped from cover again and loosed his second shot—perfect—then leapt back as the bullets came his way.

Only three targets remained for six rounds. Bergen could hear their footsteps clearly now. He peeked from cover to see the two stragglers join with their only remaining comrade and begin their inexorable march up the nameless street.

He checked Heckler. The lad rose covered in dust and rubble, his cover gone and another volley impossible to evade. The Boiler Men did not fire. As before, they ignored the threat as soon as it ceased to actively harm them.

Bergen let the rifle cool a minute while Heckler dashed back to the beam.

"They're walking away," he said, then tapped the support beam lightly. "There ain't too many of these between here and the tunnel."

"I will not need them," Bergen said. He placed the weapon's thick barrel on the street and leaned it on the beam. He stretched and flexed his shoulder. "This weapon can fell them at any range."

Three more shots to be a hero in truth, as well as in words.

He reached down for the weapon, and spotted black and glistening fluid pooling at its base. With a sinking heart he crouched and turned it to see the top. A bullet had struck it just behind the barrel, peeling away part of the casing, mangling one of the magnetic coils and penetrating into the interior. Bergen could only surmise that the fluids drizzling out were the chemicals from the battery.

"It's useless," he said. His lip trembled. "Fuck." He rose and gave the weapon a savage kick. "It's bleeding useless." He stomped on it, then kicked it again.

"Bergen," Heckler said. "What are you doing?"

"We're lost," Bergen said. "I can't save them now." He stomped the rifle once more, then turned and swung his knuckles into the support beam.

Heckler caught his arm before he could strike a second time. "We can't give up, suh."

"No?" Bergen snapped. He threw off Heckler's hand and whirled on him. "We have no explosives left, boy. We have no weapons that can hurt them."

Heckler drew back, confusion on his face. "But . . . we have to try."

"By all means, go and die, then," Bergen said.

"You're not coming?"

"Drill this through your skull, boy," Bergen said, jabbing a finger at his own. "I've failed. I'm useless now. If you want to martyr yourself, that's your business."

Heckler stood dumbfounded. Bergen turned and pounded the beam again, welcoming the pain. A failure. A coward. His face flushed with rage and shame. His insides shook with the pressure of emotion. He'd failed these people who might have accepted him. He'd failed this young lad, who, for a scant hour, had trusted him, even admired him.

He pulled his Gasser free and spun on the vacant buildings across the street, arms wide. "I'm tired of jumping at shadows, boy! Let's have this out."

He heard Heckler sprint up the street after the Boiler Men and did not care that he had left.

The shadows moved in an arch where a door hung broken on its hinges. The door swung inward with a squeak.

"I'm a sporting man," Bergen called. "I won't start shooting until you hit the street."

Pennyedge shot out of the arch immediately, running low, a wide-bladed knife in his right hand. Bergen's first shot went wide as Penny dodged right. His second caught the boy in the shoulder and spun him. Penny cracked into the pavement like a sack of bricks, but rolled and was up on all fours before Bergen could finish him. His third shot ricocheted off the street.

Penny moved like a monkey, bouncing and scrambling to gain ground. Bergen held still, all concentration in his aim.

His fourth shot cut a chunk out of Penny's left thigh. The boy stumbled to a tight crouch and Bergen sighted on his face.

The boy sprang, powering himself entirely with his right leg, causing Bergen's fifth shot to take him through the stomach. Bergen had a flash of bloodshot eyes and fever-red skin before Penny landed on him.

Bergen managed to knock the knife arm aside but lost track of it when Penny's fingers clawed his face, plunging into one eye and the soft spot beneath his jaw. Bergen brought the Gasser's heavy butt down on the side of Penny's neck. Penny choked and whirled aside. Bergen shot him a final time as his hands released, though he did not see where.

They parted. Penny spun and took a low stance just out of arm's reach. His injured leg hung delicate and curved like a dancer, his other tensed and bent like a cat. The knife floated in front of his eyes, and his left hand hung loose at his side, injured but not useless. His shirt was in a tatter. Bergen could still see the hole where he had shot the boy during their first confrontation; it quivered with a red jelly. The fresher wounds, however, leaked copiously.

Bergen tossed the Gasser away.

"Now there is only me," he said. "Come and see what stuff I'm made of, boy."

They shared the intense, calculating stares of equal opponents. Bergen stared hungrily into Penny's eyes, red veins around dilated pupils, and waited for the moment of synchronicity to come, when they both charged and the lesser man met his fate on the asphalt.

Penny sprang. Bergen rushed in low. The knife whistled past his ear and Bergen brought his fist into Penny's gut. Blood splattered out as red as his satisfaction. Then Penny's left clapped him open palm on the ear. The blow was weak, but Bergen's head still exploded in spots and pain.

A line of fire flared on his back as Penny's knife sliced back—it hadn't been a miss, but a feint. Bergen clamped his left hand on to Penny's elbow and shoved it away. The left hand hit him again, a clumsy strike across the face. Bergen ignored it and clamped his right hand around Penny's throat, digging his thumb into the boy's windpipe. Bergen growled and pressed in.

Penny's teeth opened in a silent, slavering roar. His left came in unseen and hammered Bergen on the wound in his stomach. Bergen choked as weakness and nausea flooded him. His left arm and legs buckled. Penny plunged the knife into Bergen's body between his collarbone and back, and drove him to his knees. Bergen snarled and leaned in, and Penny's windpipe cracked inward like a dry reed.

The boy did not react. He leaned his weight onto the knife. Bergen pushed his left hand into Penny's elbow, but the slashed muscles could not drive the knife out. Penny's left struck another haphazard cuff on Bergen's cheek. Bergen released the boy's neck, drew back, and pounded him squarely in the teeth.

Penny's head snapped back and he fell. Bergen fell as well, crashing hard onto his back and winding himself. The instant the spots cleared he drew the knife out, heedless of the sting or the damage. Absently, he pressed his right palm over the wound while he rolled to look at the boy.

Penny lay on his back, his chest convulsing, his hands mechanically groping at his throat. He must have heard Bergen's chuckle, because his eyes drifted sideways.

Bergen watched Penny's face turn purple, then blue. He watched Penny's eyes water and shiver. He watched Penny twitch and lie still.

Sterner stuff than you, boy.

He used the knife to cut his sleeve off and jammed it

down over the wound, holding it by pressure since he had nothing to bind it. He chuckled to himself all the while—a mad, exhilarant act.

He left the corpse behind, shambling up the street in pursuit of Heckler and the Boiler Men. After just a block he faded from weakness and collapsed in the middle of the road. He dragged himself upright against a nearby abandoned cart, and waited there, slipping in and out of consciousness until Heckler found him.

"Bergen! They're all right," the lad said as he ran up. "The Boiler Men were after cloaks. There were two crows in the crowd. That's all they wanted and now they're just standing there like they've been shut off or some such."

Bergen smiled. "Good."

Heckler's cheer wavered. "You all right, suh?"

Bergen could only nod. Heckler bent and gently moved Bergen's hand aside, cursing when he saw beneath.

"Ah'll get the doctor. You just hold on, Bergen."

Bergen looked up at this brave lad and saw something that brought up tears. "Don't," he said.

"Suh?"

"Don't call me that."

"Uh . . . All right." The lad hesitated, puzzled.

"Get the damn doctor, boy."

"Right."

He fled.

It was all wrong. Missy knew that. Though her hands shook and her knees felt watery and her stomach sat heavy with fear and sickness, she could not help but see it through.

The child brought her to two polished oak doors.

" 'E's there," the boy said. They had halted at the far end of the hall, at the top of a flight of stairs. The boy pointed to the doors and did not descend the staircase. " 'E said not to step on the third stair or the fifth. And 'e said to open the door by twistin' the handle. Two turns left, one turn right, 'e said. Was real perticaler about it."

Missy felt the boy's fingers tighten around hers. She knelt next to him and smiled. He looked at his shoes.

"Thank you for showing me," she said, as soft as she could manage. "Run upstairs, now, and the girls will give you something to eat."

The boy nodded slowly.

"Run along." She gave him a gentle shove back the way they'd come. The boy shuffled off a few paces, then ran, leaving Missy alone with nothing but her task.

The doors loomed before her. Doors to hell. Doors to heaven. Doors to nothingness.

God is always just, said Gisella. *A wicked and low death for a wicked and low animal.*

The doors were her whole world.

Who are you to defy fate, bird? That is your end. Every woman has her time.

She could not go back. Without the boy's direction she would be either lost or slain in the maze.

She could see Gisella staring down her nose. *And every woman has her duty.*

You're dead.

And you are not. It was not I that made this decision, young lady. I am not the one with the diseased mind.

She rose.

It won't matter. You'll never leave me.

Quite correct.

Then I will leave you.

Gisella laughed. *Two bullets for him and one for yourself, is it? You are quite foolish, to think you can escape me in such a manner.*

Missy took a step down.

But you are still going to try, and that is both lovely and insane.

She marched heavy and slow, walking her last towards the gallows. Tears ravaged her cheeks until they stung. Her whole body sagged with exhaustion. She lurched with each step, the gun swaying in her hand, the doors in her vision.

Quiet lay beyond those doors. Eternal and deep and pure.

How many more will you take, bird, after this one fails

to rid you of me? Will you go on killing to silence me? Perhaps Emily, perhaps Elizabeth, perhaps strangers you have yet to meet? Will you prefer men or women, I wonder? Will you develop habits or favourite methods? How many more bullets, I wonder?

Missy placed her cold fingers on the iron doorknob.

"One, if it rids me of you," she said. "Two if it doesn't."

She turned as the boy told her and drew the doors wide. The air blew out down the hall, carrying the stench of human sweat and urine, overtones of acrid and fruit smells, and an invigorating chemical tang. A single lamp lit the room, placed on a side table beside a beaten, ancient armchair.

On the left sat a bed, heavy velvet curtains scorched and torn. On the bed lay an unmoving figure who could not have been taller than three feet. On the right, a closet gaped wide, showing rows of tubes and bottles, a collection to put Gisella's to shame.

In the chair lay the hobgoblin man. His skin was flushed a deep red, his fingers curled into palsied knots. Drool ran down from his mouth, and an empty glass bottle lay on his lap. His menace had fled, leaving him a shrunken old man.

She'd wanted to find him like this, so he could not turn those black eyes on her.

This will not end it, bird.

"It will."

She raised the gun.

Ah, my love. Look to your husband! Watch him shrivel and die, and do nothing to win you back.

Scared's spectral grin spread wider as he watched the infinite copper lattice of the Great Machine collapsing from within. Black tendrils raced over it, strand by strand, stifling the sparks of calculation, corroding the wires, and tarnishing the brass. He'd known it would work, of course, but to actually see the fruits of his lover's inspiration and his own intellect . . . it staggered him. He had brought down a god.

I never thought it would be so beautiful, my love. Won't you watch?

Mama Engine lashed with molten fury against the claws Scared had driven through her. The child struggled as well, though its toils were weak and barely noticeable.

Mama Engine cried out, loosing streaks of fire across the city that burned and scorched the towers.

He was your protection from the wicked world, I know, Scared said to her. *And protection from yourself, as well, wasn't he?*

He leaned closer to her, dripping a thousand tongues of obedience from his skull-jaws, lashing them to the wounds in her psyche and ensnaring the desires that ruled her.

Well, you will soon be a queen of that wicked world, beloved. And I will keep you in the cage you so long for.

The Great Machine came apart. The enormous sheets of glass fell from the towers around. Sparks leapt into the air and burned away. The golden metals in the Stack and the towers rusted, flaked, and broke apart in an unfelt phantom wind. Scared laughed to see them flutter away.

Does it not excite you, my love? You and I in eternal . . .

A shadow fell over Mama Engine's fires.

You and I . . .

Her fires went cold. Her furnaces closed and dimmed. Scared gasped and drew back.

What is happening?

The tower of arms arched back and fell still. The sun-heat of his bride's womb faded.

No! He clutched his bride to him, drawing her close as she slipped through his claws like ashes. *How did this happen? We were careful. We were in control.*

Mama Engine whined for him, as her chains cooled and her glass parasites solidified. She cried as her mechanisms jammed, and she slid out of his reach.

The *mei kuan* burned in him. He lashed out with his hundred fingers, raking the sludge and shattering the towers, tearing holes in Whitechapel's dream and filling them with his tears.

It wasn't possible. It wasn't fair.

If he could not rule it, it would die. All of it. This accursed city would crumble to rust. Then he would eat the dreams of the world, of all these frail humans that had failed him and the Englishmen who had fought against him.

He ripped down a tower, shattering its lifeless beams and supports and scattering them into the putrid sea below. He pushed over another. In the other world, rivets snapped and beams bent, and the real towers began to fall. The souls of the dying burst into the dream with screams on their lips. Scared ground them between his teeth.

He would have them all. He would—

Missy pulled the trigger three times.

—What was that?

The *mei kuan* evaporated into nothing and his equations splintered. Scared swung his skull-eyes inward to see the last wisps of power leave him, sucked into a black point that had appeared at his roots. Even without the calculations to aid him, Scared recognised it and shuddered with a primal fear. He had anticipated at least a few days to consolidate himself as a god, and to bind himself to his bride. This was too soon, far too soon.

The city rumbled, and he glanced up to see thousands of spectral forms crossing the Wall, free now from whatever force had kept them at bay. They were the ghosts of old London, angry at the affront to their pride and their city. Scared looked at his skeletal fingers, his thousand tongues, and realized he could not face them without the Chinese drug. Then he shrieked as his nightmares broke through from beneath his skin and leapt for his face.

He made to flee, slashing his own body. His mortal death eagerly consumed his roots and tendrils while he turned his upper body towards the cusp of the red sky. He could escape into the dark rents, ride them anywhere in the world, find a safe place, and there, heal and plot. He snagged his fingers on the edge of one, when sparkling blue eyes filled his vision. Tendrils of the *mei kuan's* influence curled around them.

What is this? Get out of my way.

"I've come to know you, John," said the other, "and I'm sorry."

The blue eyes beheld him sadly, and their force stayed his motion. The ghosts swarmed up his flanks, tiny creatures dressed in the fineries of all the city's lost eras, right back to knights and legionnaires. His nightmares tore open his carefully disciplined mental defences, and led the ghosts within.

They'll kill me.

"You are already dead, John. Perhaps you were never really alive."

The ghosts dove into him and ran amok, shattering his carefully constructed ice caverns and freeing the nightmares he had so long kept hidden. They closed on him from all sides, faces of forgotten children and memories of hurt.

He screamed. The ghosts grabbed him as one and hauled him down into the black well of his death. He and his nightmares fell into the void and vanished.

Oliver's eyes flew open. His vision blurred. His body jerked.

Brass claws entered him through the chest. A rush of pus greeted them and a flash of fever brought Oliver's eyes into focus, to watch the creature of brass tearing at him. It ripped Scared's weapon out and crushed it.

Oliver broke into a grin and a cackle. His neck tendons tightened to steel cords, and his back bent inward. *You're too late.*

Images in his mind: prophecies, whispers. *An end,* they promised. *Preserve us. Build us a home-body-kingdom. Give birth to us and we will make all your pain end.*

The poison coiled in his vision, whirling, spreading.

The brass creature staggered, rusting and weakening as the poison fed on his patron god.

Blackness, circling lights, devouring, lessening, shrinking.

The brass creature with hands around his throat,

crushing down. Fluid rushing into his neck, then into his joints and limbs, hardening them, filling gaps and repairing damage.

Oliver ripped his hands free of the chair, grabbed the creature's arms, pulled them away.

Fluid in veins, pulsing like blood. Hands oozing pus, fingernails bursting with it.

Gods screaming. Lights flickering and fading. Sparks showering from above.

Porcelain eyes cracking. Brass limbs breaking.

The world jolted. The Stack shook.

His assailant came apart and clattered to the ground in pieces.

Oliver rested his head against the high back of his chair and let air trickle out of his lungs.

The gods cried out to him in their alien tongue, and he understood every word and inflection. Mama Engine and her child screamed their terror as the darkness took them. Grandfather Clock faded away without a sound.

The last spark of electricity fizzled out. The omnipresent churn of machinery turned to grinding, then scrapes, then clatters and clangs, finally halting altogether.

The light of his eyes faded, until the chamber was a glimmer of afterimages in pitch darkness. Oliver removed his hat and set it on the arm of his chair. He smoothed his hair back and folded his hands in his lap.

He stayed awake a long time, listening to a silence more perfect and profound than any he had ever experienced. Then he closed his eyes, and gave himself to dreams.

Epilogue

He who dies a thousand deaths meets the final hour with the calmness of one who approaches a well remembered door.

—Heywood Brown

Missy closed her eyes and tilted her head back, listening to the play of the wind on the fields. Her hair fluttered across her face and she pushed it back. Her skin was already red from the sun today, and her nose was peeling from an earlier sunburn, but she couldn't resist it.

She set her heavy basket of clothing down beside her and sat in the soft grasses. Some bowed and moved under her, others cut her with their edges, but her hands had grown callous working in the laundry, and she barely felt it.

She rolled down her back until she came to rest on the ground. The movement was still fresh for her, as she had spent so much time wearing corset and cage and had since forsaken both. The grasses cushioned her, and immediately made her sleepy. She smiled and blinked herself back to wakefulness. The head housekeeper would be cross if she lingered much longer. Too much time spent getting lost, she would say.

Missy wished the moment would last, knowing it wouldn't, knowing it would come again. Eventually, she forced herself to her feet, gathered her basket, and turned to return to the mansion. It was a summer home for the lord and lady who owned it, with grounds as large as a whole level of Shoreditch Tower and acres of fields besides. The servants lived and worked in the lower levels. They were officially not allowed out onto the grounds, but Missy had found that if her tasks were attended to and she didn't disturb the guests, the owners paid it no mind. Missy found her small, sparse room comforting, and the work forgetful.

She walked back a ways and spotted a man standing in the shade of the tall willow that stood alone at the edge of the lawn, just past the low brick wall encircling the grounds. He was tall and dressed in a smart blue vest and black coat, sporting a top hat and leaning on a cane.

One of the guests. Well, I hope he doesn't tattle on me.

She strode purposefully towards him, with a mind to pass him by with a polite greeting and then through the gate and into the laundry by the side door. He watched her as she approached, holding a small wicker basket over his right arm, obviously laden as he seemed to have difficulty holding it up.

"How do you do, sir?" she said.

"As well as can be expected, Miss Plantaget."

She hesitated. "Do you know me, sir?"

"Try as one might, you're not an easy one to forget," said the man. He held out his basket. "If you'd be so kind."

Missy wedged her own basket against her hip and freed a hand to take his. It was indeed full. The smell of fresh bread drifted up from it.

"Thank you," he said. "I've developed some kind of damned weakness from the whole affair and it's taking ages to go away." He reached up and removed his hat, revealing long and shaggy hair, and his face, his eyes.

The laundry scattered over the grasses and its basket rolled down the hill into the fields. Missy shrank back against the wall.

Hat tucked under his arm, he smiled at her, so understanding and aware. Her legs shook. Her hands trembled on the handle of the picnic basket.

"Oliver?"

"Alive, if not well," he said, absently rubbing the stretched white scar that crossed his neck, just above the collar line. "I'm glad to see you."

She couldn't say anything. Glad to see her?

He waited a minute, then went on. "I've spent a long time thinking it over, Michelle," he said. "I don't pretend to understand the least bit of what happened, but I don't feel that it was your fault."

She stammered a few nonsense syllables, looked away, looked back, looked at the basket. Fresh biscuits, a silver knife and butter dish, two plates of white china.

"You can't be here," she said.

"I'm trespassing, this is true," he said with a shrug. "Dress correctly and act correctly and people simply assume what they will. That I learned from you."

"That isn't what I meant."

"I know. The last favour of a god, perhaps? I hesitate to try to explain it." He gestured to the basket. "Besides, I'm here for the picnic."

Tears on her cheeks, dripping onto the buns.

"Oliver, you can't be here. Why would you even think of finding me? You must hate me."

When she looked up he was a step closer, half out of the shade, tears on his own cheeks.

"Quite the opposite, really," he mumbled, then cleared his throat. "Michelle, it's not my custom to hold people's pasts against them. I've always known who you are. I don't much care who you were. I have a gift that way. And, well . . . since we're being truthful today . . . I just wanted to see you again."

Missy wiped her eyes.

"Oliver, I thought you were . . . that I was . . ."

He caught her as she collapsed. She buried herself in the soft cotton jacket, and cried into his shoulder for a very long time. He gathered her up in one arm and stroked her hair, saying nothing, and held her while her every nameless shame bloomed to life and passed out of her and shrivelled to nothing.

When she was done, his shoulder and lapel were a mess of tears and snot. He discreetly passed her a handkerchief, and cursing audibly, she wiped her nose and cheeks clean. She parted from him and breathed, and for an instant the wind felt cold, the sun distant. She made automatic apologies and snits at herself and handed his kerchief back to him at full arm's length.

He took it and absently mopped his shoulder.

"I found Phin's old ship, still crewed by the same captain. In a week or so he'll be sailing down the African coast and around to India. He has a passenger cabin, and he's willing to take us along." Hesitation in his eyes. A little boy. A caring man. "But I suppose we can talk about that later."

Missy shook head to toe, hopes and daydreams and possibilities crowding her imagination. She didn't speak, couldn't move, not daring to break the moment and risk the fragile hope it brought.

"First, a picnic." Oliver offered her his hand. "Will you do me the honour, my lady?"

Her eyes lingered on the waiting palm.

She reached out and took it.